Georgina Wroe has written for *GQ*, *Esquire*, *Marie Claire*, *The Times* and the *Mail on Sunday* among others. She lived and worked as a journalist in Moscow for six years and now lives in Suffolk. Her first novel, *Slaphead*, won WH Smith's Fresh Talent Award.

Also by Georgina Wroe

Slaphead

Fleeced

White Meat and Traffic Lights

MILKING IT

Georgina Wroe

review

First published in paperback in 2003 by REVIEW
An imprint of Headline Book Publishing

10 9 8 7 6 5 4 3 2 1

ISBN 0 7472 6518 6

Typeset by Palimpsest Book Production Limited,
Polmont, Stirlingshire

Printed and bound in Great Britain by
Clays Ltd, St Ives plc

HEADLINE BOOK PUBLISHING
A division of the Hodder Headline Group
338 Euston Road
London NW1 3BH

www.reviewbooks.co.uk
www.hodderheadline.com

To my agent James Hale,
with love and thanks

My sincerest thanks to Paul Gardener who rescued my book when my computer died.

Prologue

Honey Dew Reveals All . . . Only in the *Pump*

Busty contestant Honey Dew, who bounced out of the *Big Sister* house last night holding the winner's cheque for a hundred thousand pounds, is to strip for *Pump* readers. The twenty-nine-year-old redhead, who stunned viewers by refusing to split the money, reneging on her deal with fellow contestant twenty-six-year-old Sandy West, will reveal all in a saucy *Pump* countdown.

'It's a dog-eat-dog world in there,' said the curvy winner. 'At the end of the day, I'm a survivor and I didn't think twice about shafting her. I had to go for it.'

Honey Dew, whose chest was voted the 'must-see' of the series, tantalised randy viewers by refusing – despite tasks including mud wrestling – to bare all. Now the *Daily Pump* can reveal Honey Dew will strip exclusively for our readers in a ten-day countdown.

She said, 'Readers should stick around. No one will want to miss what I've got to show.'

In the game, twelve female contestants completed tasks voted on by viewers. The losers were asked questions emailed by viewers, and were allowed one chance to 'call on a housemate' if they couldn't answer. The housemate chosen negotiated a percentage of the overall winnings if they answered correctly. If they answer wrongly, both women are asked to leave the house. Producers said there was nothing in the show's rules that prevented the winner from keeping the money, even if a pact had previously been made either on or off screen. Full story plus pics pages 2, 3, 5, 8 and 10.

Chapter One

I

At 3.17 p.m., two minutes before storming the editor's office, Gaye Butterworth printed out the email in case the whole thing went legal. Standing opposite the editor, she held it at arm's length and said, 'Well, I think it's fair to say I have never been so insulted in my entire professional career.'

Tony Miles found that statement difficult to believe, but before he could question it, Gaye Butterworth called him an arse lick.

Despite himself, Tony said, 'Pardon?'

'You heard me, arse lick.'

Gaye Butterworth, deputy features editor and columnist, specialised in what she thought were American insults, believing they made her come across as more hard-edged. Or, as she might have termed it, more hard-boiled.

'Gaye, I'm only asking you to hand over your column until the day before Honey Dew reveals all – keep the *Big Sister* interest going on two fronts, so to speak.' Tony ripped a page from the calendar on his desk. It put him a day ahead but showed control combined with exasperation. At the same time he nudged his 'managing editor' place name, a gift from his wife, towards Gaye. He said, 'It happens all the time, even on the up-market tabloids – especially on the up-market tabloids. Just look on it as an opportunity to concentrate on something else. I, for one, never thought your piece on sexism in the workplace ever got the show it deserved.'

Gaye edged her bottom on to the editor's desk. The weight of her left buttock dislodged the pile of expenses Tony had spent the afternoon going through.

She said, 'But can this tramp write?' She crossed her left thigh over her right and swivelled to face him, narrowing her eyes. 'I mean really write?'

Gaye Butterworth's own career in journalism had started with a twice-monthly cookery slot on the women's page. It was hand-written in between serving customers at a shop specialising in antique-looking gas appliances. Four months later, her recipes went weekly and, when the agony aunt retired into sheltered accommodation, Gaye was offered her own column chronicling an offbeat look at modern family life. Her real break on the *Daily Pump* came when her marriage failed and she started 'The Gaye Divorcee', a contemporary look at being suddenly single.

'My point –' said Tony – 'actually, *our* point – is, we've already got the winner taking her kit off, so this Sandy woman would make it a bit more cerebral. In touch with our readers; a bit more happening. This is a chance for the *Pump* to compete with the big boys. Make it more urban while at the same time embracing our suburban readership. More –' he shrugged – 'more now.'

He didn't need to spell it out. Twice in the last year, offers had been made to turn the *Pump*'s three-storey office block, half a mile in from the South Circular, into a Texan theme bar and a tenpin-bowling alley. The rumour gaining currency was that the proprietor was close to selling up unless circulation and revenue increased. The classified and display advertising departments, on the second and third floors, blamed the poor editorial content. Editorial was on the ground floor. It didn't signify a pecking order, said the editor, just that most of their interviewees couldn't make the stairs. The Honey Dew coup was the paper's chance for the big time.

Gaye bit her cuticles.

Tony went on, 'I need hardly add that you'll be editing all her copy. Your job, in this respect, will be key.' He paused while she took it in. Her skirt was too tight and had ridden up her thighs. Tony eyed the expense accounts and tried to sound upbeat. 'Now, whaddya say?'

'This email says she's coming in today.'

'Four thirty,' said Tony. 'We've got to act fast. No one's going to remember the contestants of that show in a couple of weeks. She lives somewhere in the boondocks. Four thirty is the only time she could make. One of her nail clients cancelled.'

'Oh, great.'

'Actually, Gaye, I'd really appreciate you sitting in on the brainstorm.' Tony thought of his brain. 'In fact, I'd really love the two of you to sit down on your own, throw a few concepts around, see what you come up with.'

'You've made out,' she jabbed the email at him, 'that the whole thing is wrapped up. A diary piece of Sandy West's London visit, you said.'

'Thus far, Gaye, thus far.' Tony Miles had not been a runner-up in the Press Agency's Editor of the Year in 1982 by being an ideas man. He was a hack. 'I'm leaving the brief very much in your court, Gaye. I mean, just think what you've done for "The Gaye Divorcee" over the years. All those letters.'

'True,' said Gaye. The fact was, she couldn't keep Bernard, the separated father of two she'd met at salsa classes, quiet for much longer. By March she was looking to take her column back to the world of washing machines and head lice. The interlude might give her the break she needed. 'OK, then,' she said, standing. 'I'll see her.'

'That's my girl,' said Tony, stopping when he remembered Gaye's four-page exposé on sexism in the workplace. 'I mean to say, that's my co-worker.'

* * *

Sandy West was smaller than Gaye had been expecting. She was no taller than five two, and, against the Impressionist prints in the newsroom reception, looked malleable. Gaye had the larger woman's dislike of the compact and bendy, so early on in their encounter she resolved to tell her to keep her feet on the floor, if she started twisting them underneath her bottom the way small women did.

'Gaye Butterworth.' Gaye put out her right hand. 'You've had your hair coloured.'

'It's supposed to stop people recognising me,' Sandy said, rubbing her nose. 'I'm never what they expect.' She adjusted her shoulder bag. 'I'm Sandy, by the way. I've read your column,' she added. 'I like it.'

'We'll have to use an old pic for the by-line,' said Gaye, refusing to be charmed. 'I mean, there's no point in a celebrity column if nobody recognises you.' She started to walk. 'Let's find somewhere quieter.' She pointed to a room humming like a fridge. 'In the computer room. I've had a bitch of a day and I'm gasping for a ciggie.' They walked past the newsdesk, a bank of back-to-back terminals operated mostly by subs. Fluorescent lights bounced off the windows, reflecting the two women as they walked. Next to Sandy, Gaye felt like an ogress.

Gaye said, 'Tony said you're not from round here?' She had read the double-page spread in Sunday's *Bugle*, but didn't want to let Sandy know that.

'Near Norwich,' said Sandy, two steps to Gaye's stride, 'a little village on the coast.'

'What did they pay?'

'Who?'

'The *Bugle*.' She closed the computer room door and sat down, crossing one leg over the other, pulling out a packet of Kool menthol cigarettes from her bag. 'How much? Personally, I find that lot a load of cocksuckers.' She made no apologies. The sooner Sandy West got used to the hard-bitten world of journalism the better.

'They were ever so sweet to me,' said Sandy. 'They gave me five hundred pounds and a free classified.'

'Bully for you,' said Gaye, inhaling. 'Smoke?'

'No, thanks.'

'So.' She exhaled, keeping the cigarette at eye level, leaning towards her. 'I guess Tony's told you what we're after.'

'Not really,' said Sandy, who sat on the edge of the plastic stackable chair. 'I thought it might be to do with the van.'

'The van?'

'I run my own mobile nail clinic.'

Gaye noticed Sandy was wearing a light trouser suit and when she sat down her thighs didn't meet. She kept a bag tight to her knees. Her boots were cheap but, taken as a whole, had what the women's editor might dub 'fashion potency'. Sandy said, 'I always mention it when I'm interviewed because it's free publicity.'

In the corridor outside, two of the sports writers, Ben Phillips and Martin Ringwood, were using the excuse of a trip to the drinks machine to gawp. In the interests of research, as a single gal, Gaye had snogged them both. Now they were eyeing up this little dolt. Gaye's new column, which she was loosely calling 'Glad to be Gaye', would expose the weakness of all men. Even Bernard.

'Well, much as I hate to shatter your illusions about a van,' she said, 'I'm afraid to tell you, it's a column.'

'What is?'

'What we want is a column. We want you to spend a few days in London attending celebrity functions and writing about them for us. We'd pay you –' she paused. She hadn't discussed money with Tony – 'two hundred pounds per piece plus expenses. Including somewhere to stay.' She stubbed her cigarette out in a foil ashtray, the sort you got at Christmas parties, in the centre of the table. 'And I dare say the fashion department would let you have a riffle through their racks before you go.'

'Why?'

'Because,' said Gaye tiredly, 'it's a fashion capital.'

'No, why me? Why a column?'

'Well, sweetheart, *Big Sister* has made your face one of the best known in the country. After, of course, the woman who won it. What's her name . . .'

'Honey Dew,' Sandy prompted.

'After her. And, more to the point, for our readers it'll be like they were actually going to these bashes. That's because you have girl-next-door appeal.'

'But I can't write.' Wisps of fine newly blonde hair fell on to her forehead, tweaked from a ponytail coming out of her scalp like a fountain.

Gaye tutted. 'Leave all that to me,' she said. 'I'm the professional. You just need to get the colour. I'll do the rest.'

'When would I start?'

'How about tomorrow? The *Pump* prides itself on being first with the news.'

'It's a bit soon.'

Gaye shrugged and looked at her watch. She was meeting Bernard at six. 'Oh, and there's absolutely no way we'll be able to spare a snapper, so you'll have to take your own camera.'

'But I can't take pictures,' said Sandy. 'I'm terrible. Everyone says so, even—'

'Let us worry about that. An amateurish feel is what we're after. A sort of impromptu post-party report.'

In the corridor, Angus McCreash, the chief sub, was making no effort to disguise his stare. He didn't even have the decency to stop at the Coke machine.

Gaye said, 'So? What do you say?'

'I don't know . . .'

Gaye took her deliberation as a sign she wanted more money. 'OK then, two hundred and fifty per piece. But I cannot, I will not, go higher than that.' At this rate Tony would be delighted to get her column back.

Sandy looked at her. 'I . . .' she paused. 'Um, when would I go? I mean, where would I stay?'

Gaye cracked a smile. 'Do I take it that is a yes?'

'I'm not sure.' Sandy jerked her head from side to side. 'I guess so—'

'Excellent,' said Gaye. 'As I said, don't worry about accommodation. The paper's got a place up there where us real hacks stay anytime there's a really big story about to break. We call it a safe house.'

Gaye stood up, smoothing out the tramline of creases from her skirt, then reaching for another Kool. 'Before you go,' she said, 'I must just ask one thing.' Sandy was still seated, staring ahead of her. 'Why did you go on that programme? Now I've met you, you just don't at all seem the type. I thought they were just attention seekers with no talent and nothing better to do. Don't take this the wrong way, but you seem so, I dunno, so wet.'

Sandy stood up. 'You should never be fooled by appearances.'

Gaye said, 'But you can't have ever thought you were going to win.'

'You're wrong,' said Sandy. 'I always knew I would win.'

'But you came second.' Gaye reached for her handbag, bored by the way the conversation had unexpectedly swerved away from her.

'Ah, but you see, it's not over yet,' said Sandy.

Gaye's broad back was already turned. She was worrying that calling her column 'Glad to be Gaye' might lend it an optimism that she simply couldn't maintain, especially living with Bernard and his trio of delinquent teenage sons. Which was how Gaye Butterworth missed the tabloid scoop of the decade.

As she left the newspaper office, scraping her boot heels on fake marble steps, Sandy West started thinking. It had stopped raining and the air would have been almost fresh but for the damped-down smell of exhaust fumes. Her first thought was, sod Gail Butterworth and her column. Then again she knew in order for her to get anywhere she was going to have to learn to control her anger. As she crossed the tussock of park towards the bus stop, her heels now sinking in the wet grass, she thought she would have to apply a lot of nail extensions to come up with money like the *Pump* were offering.

Her next thought – which she wanted more time to dwell on – was about Honey Dew and her treachery. This was the start of her revenge. So that by the time the 134 bus drew alongside to take her the short hop to the train station, she was smiling so hard she thought her lips might crack.

II

In the seventeenth hour of the third Monday of the month, Mickey took the bulb blowing as a sign that the superstitious stuff had to end. It was a light-after-dark sort of metaphor, or the end of an era. Maybe. What had his horoscope said? 'Your day will go with a bang.' Exactly right. Then it went on, 'But by the end of the week you will be in no doubt as to where your future lies. Be careful of strangers.' The second part had made him laugh. Sardonically.

'Aren't you going to clean that up?' Ray Mallone, Irish Karaoke King of 1981, pushed himself into the studio, jutting one shoulder then the other, as though he was walking underwater. Conjuring an attitude out of thin air, thought Mickey. But a lot of short men were like that. Swaggering on his four-inch Cuban heels, Ray reminded Mickey of a Dickensian figure who made a living scavenging on rubbish piles. Under the remaining bare bulb, under faded denim flares, his hairless legs were pale enough to shine.

'You do it,' said Mickey, eyes never leaving the reader's wife Polaroid. The format (three inch square, with a white border) if not the content reminded him of childhood Christmases. A picture of him under the tree, solitary as the fairy, waiting for the patriarch, Father Christmas. He blinked the image away, dragged his spatula back to the X-rated wax effigy, and said, 'Besides which, I'm not a cleaner.' He meant it as a dig, because in the four years he'd worked at Waxy Ladies there'd never been a cleaner. Jade flicked a duster around when it was quiet, but it was a long way from what you'd call hygienic.

'So,' Ray said, ignoring him, sucking on a cigarette and looking at the bench with medical concern, 'how's the lovely Miss Dew coming along?' He snatched the Polaroid of her reclining in bra and pants, legs separated, on a leopard-print beanbag.

For the first time Mickey realised Miss Dew sounded like 'missed you'. He wondered if it was deliberate. He only thought of Honey Dew, as in melons. The name was slick, economical even. Mickey considered whether there was more to her than a 42D cup and a talent for self-publicity.

'Yeah, good, thanks. Not too bad,' Mickey told him. 'She's a big girl.'

'You can say that again.'

'Aureoles you could set a tea cup on.'

Mickey was showing off because he had a familiarity with the female form due to an HND in technical drawing and fine art. Whereas Ray probably thought an aureole was a baseball player. Or a biscuit. Nevertheless, Ray lunged at them, dropping the photo, trying to cup them in both hands, jokily heavy breathing while Mickey tried to elbow him away. He was superstitious about people touching his models before they were finished. Close to, Ray smelt of stale alcohol and cigarettes.

Mickey told him to piss off and, in case he took offence, added, 'What do you want her to wear when she's finished?'

'That thing she was wearing when she won. Had her picture in all the papers,' said Ray. 'That time when she waddled down that platform and they almost bounced out, you know.' He blew into his hands and rubbed them; half cold, half lascivious. He picked the Polaroid off the floor.

'Yeah,' said Mickey, 'narrow the field. Her tits bounced about so much, wasn't she called the Barnes Wallis of *Big Sister*?'

'Yes.' Ray pointed his cigarette at him. 'But we never got to see the old zeppelins, did we? Good on her, I say, protecting the old assets like that.'

'Well, forgive me for having a life,' Mickey didn't look up. It was a lie but one he thought he could get away with, 'but I didn't stay in to watch the night when she won.'

'It was a pink see-through baby-doll thing on top of a furry bra-type whatsit and a G-string.'

'What recall,' said Mickey. 'And what's she say?'

'Happy to let us have them, Michael, old son. She's bringing them in later in the week and she wants to give the old waxwork the once over.' Ray shrugged. 'You know how vain some women are. I told her it'd be finished on Friday.' Mickey didn't reply. Ray went on, 'And I'm pretty sure I can get a few more from the show. Called the producer, got hold of the girl who almost won, the other one. Nice-looking girl-next-door type. Sandy something.'

'Excellent,' said Mickey without conviction.

Ray rubbed a cigarette butt into the concrete floor with the uppermost point of his crocodile-skin boot. He stopped grinding when he heard a voice from upstairs. 'Ray, come up here a minute, will you?' Jade called down. 'My ticker thing's gone again.'

'Christ,' said Ray. 'That bloody woman.' He kissed the photo before heading for the door. It was more than lust. Mickey knew what he was thinking. Reality TV had been a godsend to Waxy Ladies. Without it he'd be using his HND to sketch chalk versions of *The Birth of Venus* alongside a begging bowl on the Embankment. Then again, with it, he was dedicating his life to an art form a long way from Rodin. Sublimation of his true ambition, his mother called it. She would. Days like this reminded him of a morgue rather than an artist's studio. Or lab rats in restricted space just before they started gnawing their own limbs. Around him, two full body effigies, one a soap star who had recently done four pages naked for a men's magazine, and a Shakespearean actress who had turned up to a Golden Globe premiere in her bra and knickers; a couple of templates joined in a haphazard embrace on the lower shelf; piles of celebrity magazines tossed spread-eagle around the studio.

Five minutes later, Ray reappeared in the half-light, mumbling. When Ray's lips twitched on opposite sides of his nicotine-stained teeth, it meant he had something on his mind. Mickey didn't want to hang about to find out what, so when Ray suggested tea, he said, 'No thanks. I've got to be somewhere at six.'

'Suit yourself.'

Mickey touched the foot and then the head of the waxwork, for luck, pretending to Ray he was smoothing over the wax. Then, like a lover, he absently caressed the nipple one last time, draped a muslin over the waxwork and stooped to grab his coat from the bench's lower shelf. Over his head, he said, 'You ought to clean that glass up. It's a hazard. And that gas cylinder's running out,' as a farewell. The corridor at the back, cluttered with a tin bucket and mop, was so narrow only one could pass through it at a time. Mickey had got into the habit of using it when there was a queue of visitors to the gallery at the front. Then it occurred to him, at roughly the same time he remembered he hadn't touched the model's foot after he touched the breast, that it was a needless avoidance. There hadn't been a queue outside Waxy Ladies for some time. Ray was right. Reality TV or not, times in the wax pornography industry had never been so tough.

Outside, the soupy early evening was hardly darker than the basement. The streetlights' dim sulphur yellow showed up triangles of thin drizzle. Mickey wrapped his jacket tight across his chest like a strait-jacket. Out of the alley on the main road, he was surprised as he always was by the movement: couples meeting, afterwork drinkers. He heard his mother tell Nigel it was what the French called the lover's hour, showing off as usual. The hour of the day when his loneliness really hit home. Hit home, he said to himself. Ironically, home was OK – home was better. Millions of people were at home in the evenings. Work was OK, because everyone had to work. It was the transit parts he detested. The insecure passages where you couldn't avoid glimpsing other people's lives. He looked right then left, then right again, as his superstitious custom dictated, even though Brewer Street was one way. Then headed north towards Oxford Street. He bunched his arms close to his chest and barrelled past a group of office workers lingering on the pavement outside a bar, jostling to get the order right. Men first, to head to the bar, or should the ladies be ushered in out of the cold?

Mickey bent round to avoid them, moving into the road, causing a cab to honk and swerve around him. He looked behind as he jumped back on the pavement. Across the street, ten metres above head height, he saw a billboard lit up by the reflected neon from two bars. He did a double take and turned to face it. It was a giant photograph of the body he'd been working on all day. The backdrop was sky blue and Honey Dew was looking down at him, over her shoulder. She was wearing a pair of pink shorts that caved into the crease of her buttocks, but her body twisted so that you could make out the shape of her breasts. It was sponsored by the *Daily Pump* and, in their familiar eighties-style typesetting, read, 'Ten days and counting . . . The *Pump* . . . happy to bring you more of the action.' This was just a taster. The countdown was to begin tomorrow, apparently. No doubt Ray would be delighted at the hype Honey Dew was getting.

Next to the billboard was another poster of a woman in the doggy position advertising a popular brand of instant coffee. Mickey sighed, looked at his watch and hurried on. His appointment was at six.

III

There was no doubt in Mickey's mind that Edwin Adebayo was a doctor. And it wasn't even as if his qualification had come from some obscure university in remotest Africa – not that Mickey would have minded; his own claim to be a member of the professional classes had come from a Fenland teaching institution that hadn't made it to polytechnic status. No, Dr Adebayo's qualifications, a first from Cambridge and doctorate from UCL, were beyond reproach. Mickey just doubted whether he was a doctor of medicine. True, the off Harley Street address appeared to convince the smattering of patients Mickey bumped into on his weekly appointments. And Dr Adebayo's plum-blushed skin, silk tie and pastel-shirted elegance hinted at calming professionalism. But it was the small things – his collection of tribal art, letters stamped from the School for Oriental and African Studies – that spoke of ethnography.

Sometimes, when the doctor spoke of ritual and the Yanemami tribe, Mickey wondered if he wasn't studying the obsessions of the English middle classes in post-industrial Britain in the same way gentlemen anthropologists spied on his Nigerian ancestors. In the sleepless nights after especially frank outbursts, Mickey clenched his buttocks and rocked himself, wondering if his paranoia might end up as part of a slide presentation to the Social Science Department of the University of Lagos. How they would laugh at the paranoia of the white man.

'Do please take a seat.' Dr Adebayo snapped his mobile phone shut and levered himself gracefully out of his leather office chair. Mickey noticed the way his tailored pin-striped trousers clung to the hump of his groin; making him stare. His was the flawless body women, and men, wanted to see naked. Mickey flushed, not out of homoeroticism, but was the undertone racist? He dodged the handshake by hanging up his coat.

The doctor began, 'Long time since your—'

'Yeah, that's right,' said Mickey, not turning. 'Lot on. Work. Busy time of year.'

'You're a—'

'Wax sculptor,' Mickey told him, sitting down.

'That's right.' He sat back down, ramming his weight into the back of the chair. 'Effigies of the dead,' said Dr Adebayo, writing something down. 'Some might say votive representation.'

Mickey didn't know what 'votive' meant. 'Some might,' he ventured, trying to gauge if it was a joke. 'And the living, of course.' Apart from Marilyn Monroe, they were live celebrities.

'Fascinating.'

'Yeah, well, it's a job.'

Mickey tried to stop counting the number of books on the shelf behind the doctor as he asked, 'Do you concentrate on men or women. Or both?'

Mickey thought of the galleries, *A Streak Through Time*, *Beyond the Bikini Line* and *Hot Wax*. 'Women mostly,' he said.

'Ah,' said Dr Adebayo. 'The mother goddess, what a potent image she is—'

'Well, I wouldn't say goddess, exactly . . .' said Mickey.

'Fertile. You know, in many cultures the breast isn't even considered sexual, and in Britain in the first years of the twenty-first century it's become almost a secular religion. An object of worship.' He uncapped a green felt pen and made a sweeping movement over a sheet of foolscap. 'Is it a rounded buttock?'

'Some,' said Mickey, wriggling and looking at his watch. 'Actually, dimensionally speaking, mostly they're pretty small but Ray encourages us to make them bigger.'

'More feminine.'

'Well, Ray reckons models having small bums is a poofs' thing. Sorry, not poofs exactly, so much as fashion designers. You know what I mean.'

'Quite,' said Dr Adebayo. 'Sublimation of the feminine, in the face of the rising power of women.'

'Something like that,' said Mickey, even though it wasn't what he had meant. He wondered where he was going. 'Look, isn't this supposed to be more about, I don't know, me?'

The doctor stroked his chin. 'I like to put my clients in a socioeconomic framework. And I think your work could be the key to your complaint. Your ritualistic behaviour.'

Mickey has never heard it referred to as a complaint before. It scared him. Before now it was a habit, no more than that. No one could call it more than a quirk. Now, suddenly, it was ritualistic behaviour.

'Listen,' he said, through a half snigger, 'it's not as if I go around worshipping Satan or killing virgins.' He went to stand up. 'I just like things in a bit of order. I think it's because my mum was so anti tidiness. Actually, the more I think about it, the less I think I need some sort of counsellor.' He pushed himself out of the chair.

Dr Adebayo followed him up, paternally cupping his hand on Mickey's shoulder across the desk. 'I'm afraid,' he said, 'I really must apologise. I can get carried away with analogies.' His hand was heavy and warm, and Mickey felt comforted. They both sat down. 'In our last session we spoke of how your, for want of a better word,' the doctor smiled, 'ritualistic behaviour had started to impact on your life.'

'Well,' objected Mickey, squirming, 'I'd say "impact" was a bit strong. OK, fair shout, there are a few things I don't like doing . . .'

Dr Adebayo read from his notes. 'Crossing water, touching strangers, leaving the house before you have checked all the taps are turned off, turning mug handles to the left, not being able to stay in the bathroom while your bath runs, filling a kettle, water in general, looking in a mirror if you've forgotten something—'

Mickey felt the need to stop him. 'Stuff like that, yeah. But think about it. Everyone's superstitious. I bet you don't walk under ladders. And everyone, even Ray, reads their horoscope.'

'But that's not really why you're here, is it?'

'No, I guess not.'

'So why do you think you are?'

'What?' Mickey concentrated on the creases of material over his knee. 'Nutty?'

'No,' said Dr Adebayo. 'Here.'

Mickey felt tired. He wanted to rest his head on the doctor's hair to find out if it was spongy like foam or springy like moss. 'I guess I want to find out why I do these things. The doctor, my GP, Dr Perez, said I only had to worry when it got so bad that I was changing what I did. How I acted, my routine.' Mickey paused. 'So now it is. A bit. Water's the worst. I can't seem to abide the stuff. It's like I'm phobic.' He waited. 'Actually, you don't think it is rabies, do you?'

'No,' said Dr Adebayo. 'I don't think it's rabies.'

Mickey swallowed. 'Is it curable?'

'I believe so.' The doctor nodded. 'But I'm afraid we will need to do a fair bit of stripping away. Find out what's really going on in that noddle of yours.'

That's what Mickey meant. Would a medical man use the word 'noddle'? Mickey's head circled in a figure of eight, unsure of how to go on. He gave his best half-smile. 'Whatever you say, Doc.'

'What did you call me?'

'Doc. Short for doctor,' Mickey told him. 'It's a, you know, medical term.'

'I know that,' said the doctor.

IV

Sandy's footfall on the metal step, a gift from her Uncle Pete when they moved into the caravan, hardly made a sound. It was close to seven by the time she arrived at the train station, too tired to wait for a bus, calling a cab instead. Waiting inside the trailer you got a feel for callers. Her mother's weighty thud seconds before the clank of bottles on the metal wall while she fumbled for the key. Sandy never understood why she didn't keep it handier. She told her, it wasn't as if she didn't know she was going to need it. Anything could happen in the dark. There were no lights to speak of round the lots and hardly any bulbs in the coloured string along the prom. But then forward-planning had never really been her thing.

In the winter, when the convector heater was on, you knew the best way to get in was to open the door just wide enough to squeeze through, using your body to push back the escaping current of warm air. Tommy was the worst – he'd stand for minutes with the door open, just chatting to his mates with a football under his arm. Either his mother pushed him out with her outstretched palm between his shoulder blades, or hauled him in by his parka hood.

Today the caravan was tidy. It smelt familiarly sour of instant coffee and cigarette smoke.

'How did you get on, love?' Her mother was sitting at the far end of the caravan in the bay of the window. It was nearly eight. She was watching the tail end of a game show and painting her nails. Monica West, forty-one, former beauty queen, mother of three, all from different fathers. She used to say it herself when she met new people, by way of introduction. She thought it was funny or ironic, or at least she said it got the pity thing out of the way from the start.

She had the portable on for company. Even when she had a

visitor she turned down the sound but didn't switch it off. Cards from an abandoned game of patience swam into each other on the pull-down Formica table. She had a glass of still, transparent liquid next to her. Sandy did the calculation automatically. Definitely not water but wouldn't be neat, not at this time. Most likely the tonic was flat. Under the strip-light the drink shone pink at the edges. For a terrible second Sandy thought of meths.

Her mother told her, 'There's some corned beef in the fridge if you want a sandwich. Nothing hot, though. The meter's out again.'

She wasn't slurring but had that definiteness, overcompensating, she got when she was on her way.

'No, thanks,' said Sandy. 'I ate already.' She waited in the kitchen half. 'Where are the boys?'

'Jason is at a mate's.' She didn't look up from her nails. 'Christ knows about the other one.'

Sandy kept her coat on and sidled towards the TV, perching next to her mother, hoping she took it as a sign she wasn't staying. She noticed the answerphone she kept as a business line was flashing. She was too tired to check her messages.

'How did you get on at the paper?'

'OK,' said Sandy.

'Did they pay for the interview?'

Sandy said sullenly, 'No, I didn't expect them to.'

Monica took a gulp. Closer to, Sandy could smell the gin. 'And how much do you think that trollop charges for her interviews? How much do you think they're paying her to take her clothes off?'

'Shut up, Mum. That's different. She won.' On the TV, a couple of newlyweds threw their arms round each other, yelping with good fortune. 'Besides,' said Sandy, 'they're offering me a job.'

'How much?' There was a faint slur in Monica's voice now.

'You don't even know what it is yet.'

'What is it?' Monica West didn't look at her daughter. She looked at her scarlet nails, wet and glossy like drops of fresh blood, and then beyond them to the portable.

Sandy said, 'They want me to write a diary piece.'

'And what's that supposed to be, when it's at home?' Sandy wondered if she'd been out that day. She was wearing a gash of lipstick. But she was vain. She was most likely trying it out with the nail varnish.

Sandy told her, 'I'd go to parties and then write about them for the paper.'

Monica looked at her. 'And who'd be interested in what you do?' Rolling credits on the TV gave way to adverts. The noise in such a cramped space came in jagged stabs, like a badly tuned radio.

Sandy said, 'They seem to think people would.'

'And that's what they call work these days?' She picked up the drink.

A gust of air blown from the sea lifted the flimsy tartan curtain. A north wind – cold. She reached past her mother to tuck the curtain behind the foam cushion.

'Yes, Mum.'

They half watched the start of a soap opera. Then Monica said, 'Anyway, what parties? Who has a do round here?'

'No one,' said Sandy towards the TV. 'I mean, it wouldn't be round here. It's in London.'

'You can't go to London.'

'Why not?' said Sandy, unbuttoning her coat. 'That's where I was for the show.'

'But that was in a house for a fortnight. Besides, you didn't have any choice.'

'So what?' said Sandy. 'Millions of people live there.'

'What about Perfect Nails?'

'I'll tell my clients I'm going on holiday.'

'That's no way to run a business.'

'Yeah,' said Sandy, peeling a blackened banana out of a fruit bowl. 'Like you'd know.'

'What's that supposed to mean?'

'I'm going to bed.' The banana was mush, nearly liquid.

'I'd like to see you bring up three children on your own.'

Sandy had her back to her and threw the banana in the bin under the sink, already close to overflowing with an empty bottle of tonic. Maybe the drink had been neat after all. Mum's mood was like that when she didn't use a mixer. Sandy said, 'Yeah, well, some of us wouldn't get into that state in the first place.'

Sandy stripped as quickly as she could, folding her clothes and leaving them on the end of her bed for extra warmth. She didn't switch the light on. She'd wait until everyone had gone to bed if she needed to use the bathroom and her teeth could wait till morning. The polyester sheets were so cold they felt wet. She thought herself into another place using the same thought she'd had for the last five days. Ever since Honey Dew had cheated her out of her half of the money. Now she would find her and make her pay. After twenty minutes she heard her mum's low voice on the telephone. Then she heard her slip out, closing the flimsy caravan door behind her, leaving a slipstream of cold air on her way to meet her fancy man.

V

Mickey left the doctor's rooms at seven thirty after making an appointment with Carole, the middle-aged receptionist, to come back in a week. 'Or sooner, if you need it,' she'd added. Mickey wondered what she'd meant. Did he give the appearance of a man about to lose his mind? The doctor had told him to keep a diary of all the times he exhibited ritualistic behaviour. Again Mickey had to ask the doc to stop making him sound like a psycho.

'It's not like I'm making a shrine out of people's skulls,' he'd said.

'Define shrine,' the doc had told him.

Mickey needed a drink. Nothing sprang to mind. He had a feeling there was an Irish place nearby, but he wasn't in the mood for raucous. As he walked he forced his head up from the pavement where he was trying not to step on the cracks. 'Walk on a crack, break your back,' he was reciting to himself when he bumped into her. The woman yelped like a big cat.

'Can't you look where you're going?' With his head down he'd caught her with his elbow. Her voice sounded subcockney, as if she'd learnt English from soap operas. She spun on a heel and allowed herself to be buffeted towards the road.

'I'm sorry,' said Mickey.

Her ginger bob, the colour of the inside flesh of a cantaloupe melon, was tucked down the back of her coat. In the collision her handbag had slipped off her shoulder on to the pavement. It was unzipped. A sheaf of papers fanned out.

'For Christ's sake, why are you lurching about like that anyway? Are you pissed, or what?' She was smaller than most women Mickey had met, but solid, looking as if she wouldn't be washed away.

'Let me help you,' he said, stooping over. The fine drizzle continued.

'No, thanks, I can manage.'

'No, really,' said Mickey, bending over. 'I'm not drunk. I was just watching the pavement.'

'Why?' she said. 'What's it supposed to do?'

Mickey stood up, not sure if she was serious or not. One of the brochures was for hair removal – he caught a glimpse of a row of follicles, stubborn as soldiers. She snatched it back with a fierce parry. She wore black leather gloves and he saw her hands were doll-like compared to the rest of her. He said, 'Don't I know you?'

'No, you frigging don't. Now piss off.'

A couple of theatre-goers, he in black tie and she in a fur, overtook them in an exaggerated arc. Mickey watched the redhead totter behind them towards Oxford Street. He still felt the sting of her parting shot. In black and white films, chance encounters were how couples got together. He shrugged his hands in his pockets and went back to checking the cracks. Was it any wonder, he thought, he'd been single for nine and a half years in the last decade?

VI

Ray Mallone reached for the whisky bottle. Waxy Ladies had been closed for near on three hours. Experience taught him that as soon as the first strip joints flickered into action, very few punters were interested in wax. No matter how finely crafted. What chance had the discerning purveyor of pornography amid the heaving fleshpots of Soho? Ray Mallone was a man in need of a gimmick and he needed it fast. He poured a four-digit drink into a mug the advantage of which was he couldn't see how much he was drinking.

The techno thud from the topless joint next door taunted him. As much as Carlo told him that he was lucky because his girls didn't answer back and he didn't have to contend with the police, infectious diseases or the immigration department, or wages, he felt anxious.

One thing was for sure, there would be no more karaoke king for him. The future for a fifty-two-year-old club singer whose CV could only boast a failed attempt to revive northern soul on the south coast was bleak. He had no choice but to make a go of Waxy Ladies. Wasn't wax ideally suited to the here-today-gone-tomorrow nature of today's stars? He wouldn't give up on it now. He drank a long draught of Jack Daniel's.

The Teasmade in front of him, light aluminium with a pink

plastic front, had come from a hardware shop in Canton Street. The seventies revival, according to the boy in the shop, young enough to think of the seventies as an historical period, had made them very 'now'. For an extra tenner he'd even throw in a fondue set. Ray declined. He turned the Teasmade on its side and picked up his Swiss army penknife, to get to the heart of it. A few adjustments here and there, and operation Madonna would be underway.

Chapter Two

I

Out of character, Mickey had bought the *Pump*, from the mini mart on his way into work. Not for the horoscope – he preferred astrologer Mervyn Massive to predict his future – but to study the finer anatomical parts of Honey Dew, whose countdown to revealing all was now into its second day. She appeared on page three in a swimsuit cut so low it made him think she was wearing it back to front. Then on page eight the *Pump* warned him to keep in touch with natural elements. Ray pointed out it was his turn to change the gas canister, but Mickey felt something altogether more portentous in the air.

Which was why he waited until the third ring before he picked up.

It was a woman's voice. 'I can't talk for long, I'm in a call box.'

It was the first thing she said, like a disclaimer. It was far too early for Mickey to be put out. Picking up a Biro he answered, 'OK,' with an easy voice. 'What's the number? I'll call you back.'

'No, don't bother.' Her accent was hard to place. It sounded West Country. It was reedy. Like the noise that came from blowing into a small thin bottle – Orangina rather than a milk bottle. 'I need to fix up a time to see you. Someone left a message for me, on my machine. My mum said.'

Mickey nodded. 'Sure,' he said. 'No problemo. Who are you?'

'Sandy West.' She waited for a couple of beats and when Mickey didn't say anything, added. 'I was in that TV programme.'

Mickey had to think twice. He said, 'Sandy, great, yeah.' He wanted to sound professional and laid-back. 'Ray said you'd be calling. We're expecting you. In fact, looking forward to it. When can you make it?'

Then the line went dead as if she'd cut them off. He looked at the receiver, examining it like a bogey. From the radio in the kitchenette he heard raised male voices taking part in a talk show. The exasperated host was trying to move on by hushing a guest. Mickey thought, why ask them to call in if you're not interested in what they have to say? Then he wondered how come his caller had hung up? Could he have put her off so soon, just by speaking to her? Her name was Sandy. Sand was a natural element.

He replaced the receiver and immediately it rang again. He grabbed it on the third ring. He didn't have time to speak before he heard, 'It's me again.'

'Oh, hi.'

'My money ran out. I meant to ask, how much do you pay?'

'That's not really my department. You see,' Mickey told her, 'I'm the sculptor. Ray does all the negotiations.' He didn't want the line to go dead again. 'It's a lot, though, I'm pretty sure of that.' When he heard nothing, he added, 'Maybe a grand, or more. Actually, come to think of it, it's more. Definitely more.'

There was a ten-second silence during which he heard the clunk of traffic driving over a manhole.

She asked, 'Is it a one-off or for however long I'm in the exhibition?' It was clear she'd thought this through. Or someone had. She went on, 'If you think about it, really it should be how long I'm on display for.'

The talk show had given way to music, an early contender for the Christmas number one. Mickey inhaled deep into his lungs. 'Like a library book,' he said, exhaling. 'Yeah, maybe that's the way it works. That sounds fair. Look, how about you come in to discuss it?' Then he laughed, inappropriately.

'OK.'

'Cool,' said Mickey.

She didn't sound like most of the women he'd sculpted. Most acted as if taking their tops off was the greatest favour they could bestow. Sandy was more reticent. Now she said quickly, 'I have to come into the middle.' He could hear her tapping a pen on the receiver. 'What about this afternoon, at three?'

'No worries,' said Mickey.

She hung up before Mickey could give her any instructions. But he figured she must have already spoken to Ray. Maybe that's why she was acting so scared. Ray had his own brand of unctuous charm when he was reeling in what he called a 'live' one – a real celebrity who'd agreed to be modelled. Mickey had once seen him dribble into the receiver as he scudded up and down the studio in his cowboy boots. Mickey felt it was up to him to provide the charm – professional courtesy with an artist's inevitable hint of sexual menace. Not that it had landed him much in the last four years – one date with the teenage lover of a Channel Five weatherman and dinner with a footballer's girlfriend in return for three inches sliced off her hips. Mickey went to the back door to collect the bucket and mop.

There were few visitors to disrupt the bachelor feel of the studio. His mum said it was a teenager's dream in a land where mothers hadn't been invented. Like she would know. Mugs with bites taken out of them, self-sealed with a green skin of mould; ashtrays mopping up some of Ray's roll-ups, the rest stubbed on the floor, in sinks, mugs and tabletops; chisels and knives kicked under work surfaces. Lack of lighting disguised any more serious lack of cleanliness, like mould bubbling on the low ceiling or the plaster gaping from the walls. Mice droppings were so frequent, but somehow so hard and inoffensive, like crumbs, he barely registered them any more. But in the face of a live female visitor, he felt ashamed. A couple of porno mags were open on the bench. Ray bought them so Mickey could better study the female form, like Stubbs and a racehorse. He was being kind because he knew Mickey's knowledge was less than empirical.

'Tidying up, are you?' He hadn't heard Jade on the bare board steps. Then he saw why. She was wearing a pair of sheepskin slippers below a full-length blue duffel coat. On warmer winter days, or when it wasn't raining, Ray told her to go on to the street to lure punters. Coming to work in her bedroom slippers was her way of staying indoors.

'Girls stand in doorways in other places,' argued Ray. 'Is it really too much to ask you to do the same?'

'They're all drug addicts,' Jade told him.

'Shame you're not. Might stop you being so bloody cheeky.'

Mickey smiled. He liked Jade, a former arts student, who wanted knowledge of retail and had then stayed on, going up from volunteer to minimum wage before hitting the Waxy Ladies glass ceiling.

He said, 'Yeah, thought I better had. We've got someone coming in.'

'Yeah?' Jade's body slouched in the doorframe. 'Like who?' She had a Big Mac in her hand.

'Some woman from that programme. Ray's spoken to her and she's agreed.'

'Not the one with the tits?'

'They all had tits,' said Mickey, piling magazines to hide the porn. 'That was the point of the programme.'

'No, babes, I mean the really big ones.' She nibbled at the bun. 'Melons something.'

'Nah,' said Mickey, 'I'm already doing her. This is a different one.'

Jade nodded and walked towards the kitchenette. 'Fancy a cuppa?'

To add to her height, Jade had a six-inch Afro that bounced on the ceiling. She was skinny as a rake, her body not visible underneath her coat. Adding to the vegetable smell of the basement, she moved in a luxurious cloud of coconut oil.

She called, 'How's your mum doing? Ray tells me she's planning on a visit.'

'So she reckons,' said Mickey.

'Don't sound like you're too keen on the idea, babes. My mum and dad ever threaten a visit? I disconnect the phone for a month. My dad snores so bad one time I made a tape recording. Can you imagine?'

Mickey said nothing. He crossed the studio and shook dirt out of the brush into a bucket next to the back door. 'What happened?'

'It was weird, man. Never came out on the tape. Like he's some sort of snoring poltergeist. No way will that man ever stay in my house.'

'Wow.' Mickey backed into the studio, jabbing the broom towards a curl of dried orange peel, pock-marked with mould. It fell in the shape of an S. It could be a sign? he thought. But then, rationally, S was the natural curve of peel.

Jade clanked two mugs together. 'She thinking of staying long?'

'Depends on her job.'

'Bummer,' Jade whistled. 'Could be bad, man.'

Mickey felt a stab of guilt. His mother wasn't *that* bad. 'Was that the door?' he asked. 'You better get up there. Ray might be back soon.' He straightened up. 'Where is he, in any case?'

'Gone to Carlo's for some hair.'

Mickey nodded and felt his chin, wondering if he'd shaved that morning. He picked up the orange peel and felt its brittle contours. He leant on the broom. Orange peel cellulite, his models' biggest fear. But there was no sign of it on his sculptures. Like the picture editors he sliced and pared them to an unreal perfection. Why did people only want to remember the best bits? Why keep the picture of the smiling baby if most of the time it bawled? Lovers kissing, rather than moody and depressed; who were they trying to kid? If the best of you was one per cent, where did you hide the other ninety-nine? He tossed the peel into the bucket.

II

Sandy stared at the blank computer for ten seconds, mesmerised by the blackness, and then looked around the room. Her suitcase spewed clothes on the single divan a foot away from the one she'd slept on, chosen because, out of the two, it had the fainter traces of hair grease on the wall behind it. Even then the mattress was buckled midway down, forcing her to occupy either the top or the bottom half. Gaye Butterworth had already called three times that morning and it wasn't yet eleven o'clock. Sandy had tried to make out she'd been clubbing, by making her voice low and husky, but Gaye told her the conference was in an hour and she'd better have some copy filed by then or she could kiss her motherfucking cheque goodbye. When she said filed, Sandy thought of nails. Anything would be better than this. Extensions, French polish, even a pensioner's day pedicure special.

She'd been out once that morning in search of a phone before a promised mobile was sent by Gaye. Her room was one of three opening into each other at the end of a corridor. Cigarette smoke seeped from one and Indian music from another. There was a pay phone in an alcove next to the dining room, but she'd been put off by the heavy-hooded stares of men mopping up breakfast plates with bread and butter. Instead she followed the line of one-way traffic to the main road, spotting an old-fashioned red box outside a Jamaican greengrocer's. A man in a turban pushed past her while two children played on scooters. The first time she'd called, a few days ago, she'd got through to an Irishman. When she'd introduced herself as Sandy from the show, he'd asked her if she wanted to model for him. 'Tasteful wax works dedicated to the female form,' he said.

'You mean Madame Tussaud's?'

'Not exactly,' he replied. 'It's more for, you know, like your adult visitor than that.'

'What, you mean kinky?'

'Good heavens above, I assure you, my dear, nothing could be further from the truth.' He sounded like a man used to persuasion. 'Why don't you come up to talk about it? Meet our classically trained sculptor. We are very free with our hospitality. I'd pay your expenses whether you posed or not.'

It was the word 'posed' that had put her off. 'I'll think about it,' she'd told him.

Now that she'd got to London, for want of anything else to do, she'd called him back and got through to a different man, who'd said 'Cool'.

She stabbed at a couple of letters to chase the screen saver away. The truth was she didn't have a whole lot to report on since she'd arrived in London. Nothing to fit her 'West One' column. First off, according to her A–Z, she was two pages away from W1. The Malindi Sands Guest House turned out to be just off Acton High Street. When the cabbie who'd picked her up at Liverpool Street Station dropped her off, he told her she was right on the border of the Knowledge. That was how she felt.

'You be careful of those blasted minicabs, though,' he said. 'Crooks, the lot of them.' When she asked for a receipt, the driver, who signed his name as Jeff, told her she could have the whole pad for a fiver. Then he asked, 'Don't I know you?'

'Yeah, I'm on MTV,' she told him.

'Thought I recognised that smile. It's what they call star quality, innit?'

Her first night had been spent eating all three packets of free biscuits and dusting the crumbs from her bed, pulling the polyester cover above her head, revealing two cigarette burns like peep holes.

She flexed her fingers and set them over the keys.

Gaye had told her the key was to write as if to a friend, only an upmarket sort of friend, like Victoria Beckham. 'Use your imagination. Plenty of colour. Remember not all our readers have been to London. Write about the sights and sounds. The people, the stars, the luxury.' When she'd explained she wasn't on any sort of celebrity circuit Gaye had given her a handful of invitations sent to the women's desk. One was the launch of a new eye shadow range at a shop she'd never heard of. Another was to review a Greek restaurant off New Oxford Street.

When she exhaled she could see her breath. The window, looking out on to a parade of shops, was cracked from corner to corner, making the discoloured net curtain flutter in sharp bursts.

> Oh boy. I can hardly believe my luck. Here I am in my favourite capital city. Better than Paris and even Milan! Here I am in London. I wish you could see the penthouse suite I'm staying in. The porter told me just last week Michael Caine was here.

Sandy got off the bed and poured a glass of water from the bathroom tap. The water tasted chemically and warm so she brushed her teeth. Looking up, she dabbed water on her fringe, turned frizzy by the half-wash she'd given it over the sink earlier, or the complimentary sachet of cheap shampoo. She recognised the advert jingle from a morning show coming through the wall from next door. Downstairs the pay phone rang five times and was ignored.

Sandy had no idea about how to find Honey, but she knew she was in London. The idea gave her comfort, like the sound of the daytime talk show. And knowing revenge was at hand made things a whole lot sweeter.

She flicked the TV on. The reception was fuzzy but there was no mistaking the woman on the sofa, over-the-knee boots below a short tartan skirt and a baby-pink cardigan straining to keep done up. It was Honey Dew.

'Some might think I acted unfairly, but really I was given no other option,' she was saying. 'Of course, a lot of the money I made will be going to charity . . .'

Sandy thought about calling the TV station. But what had that cabbie told her? She was on the border of the knowledge. It would pay for her to wait awhile.

III

By the time Honey Dew left the studio on the South Bank she barely had time to stoke up on an Americano – which in her opinion was no more than a black coffee – and a low-fat blueberry muffin, before it was time to get to the shoot. It was an unseasonally hot day, too unexpected for even the Channel Five weatherman to have gone out on a limb. Honey was overdressed in man-made fibres and her red hair was brittle when she patted it. Either side of her nose sweated where her dark glasses touched her skin.

On top of everything else, as she struggled to find a cab to the *Pump*'s improbable address, batches of early Christmas shoppers spread out unevenly across the pavements, making walking unbearable. They dawdled hand in hand in smug little lines, forming impenetrable ribbons. So far the day had not gone well for Honey. Her shoot was booked for eleven. Taffy couldn't go with her because he had broken a tooth on a bowl of Fruit and Fibre at 8.23 a.m. and had an appointment for a crown.

'Lack of calcium,' Taffy told her, inviting sympathy.

So much for a bodyguard, Honey thought, but didn't say anything. It meant she had to lug her own outfits all the way from the cab and up the steps of the *Pump* office, three floors of an incongruous glass-fronted building in the middle of an industrial estate. A blast of hot air immediately she stepped inside the automatic double doors made Honey sweat even more. The receptionist was dressed in shapeless androgynous grey and maintained an unnerving eye contact when she told Honey 'third floor'. She was eyeing her, thought Honey, as if she was a piece of meat – not prime sirloin but an opened tin of Spam, out of date and only useful as a last resort. When she'd printed Honey's name on the security pass she put it between two snide inverted commas, as if she was no more than an invention.

'Well, at least I *have* breasts,' Honey said, staring straight at her. Then she noticed from the security guard behind her that everyone's name was printed in inverted commas. She didn't apologise.

The lift opened directly opposite a notice board fluttering with job applications.

'Thinking of applying for a job?' The man who eventually appeared to meet her was six foot six, exfoliated to the point of scrubbed, and model thin. His jeans sat on the bones of narrow hips perfectly but were held up by the gold G of a Gucci belt. Honey knew better than to waste a smile. The last heterosexual male journalist she'd met had been on the *Herts Advertiser*. He said, 'I'm joking, of course.' He had the slightest French accent. Honey smiled. The gusset of her tights was slipping. He went on, 'My name's Humphrey Harriman and I'm the fashion editor's assistant.' He smiled. 'Well, I'm one of them.' He looked her up and down. 'Obviously,' he said, 'you're not fashion, but there's a bug going round. We're having to double up.'

Honey took his hand. His fingers were fairytale thin and his handshake damp. She said, 'About bloody time too.' Second to attractive women, gay men were Honey's worst-case scenario. They tended to regard her chest with affectionate good humour rather than lust. She tried to straighten the wobble board of her Midlands accent by clipping her vowels.

'Like I said, it's a virus. You're lucky we didn't have to cancel.' He slid a security pass down one side of frosted double doors leading on to another reception desk made entirely of a mosaic of glass bricks.

'Afternoon, Humph,' said the blond man behind the desk, winking. He wore a tight white T-shirt and faded jeans.

'Hiya,' said Humph, returning the wink. 'Joshy, I'd like you to meet—'

'Miss Honey Dew,' yelped Joshy, clasping his hands across his chest. 'I can't tell you what a fan I am of yours.'

'Honey,' said Humphrey, 'I'd like you to meet our latest young recruit, Joshy. He comes from Jigsaw Youth. We were ever so lucky to get him, drag him all the way out here.' Both men giggled.

The youth had leapt to his feet. 'Honey, I just have to tell you how much I loved your outfits. I mean, those tassels.' He twirled imaginary nipples. 'I mean, really they were too much.'

'Thanks,' said Honey.

'Well, I'm ever so sorry to have to tell you this, Joshy,' said Humph. 'I can hardly bring myself to be the harbinger of unfortunate tidings, but there will be no tassels this time.'

Joshy's face fell and he put a hand to his cheek.

Humphrey went on, 'She's here for the final shoot.' They both screwed their faces up.

'You mean . . . ?' said Joshy.

''Fraid so,' said Humphrey. 'She's here to get her baps out.'

'Yuk,' said Joshy.

'Do you mind?' seethed Honey. 'How dare you marginalise me? I have never been so insulted.' Her tights gusset had slipped to her hemline. She said, 'Let me speak to the editor.' She rummaged in her bag and pulled out a scrap of paper with scrawled names and haphazard extension numbers.

'Soz,' said Joshy, 'Maxie boy is on a long weekend in Milano.'

'Not the fashion editor,' said Honey, hardly moving her lips, 'the editor. He is a personal friend of mine. I will not be marginalised.' Her shoulder bag slid from her shoulder; she patted her forehead.

'Come on, sweetie,' said Humphrey. 'We're all huge fans. Calm down. I tried to explain. It's a skeleton staff at the moment.'

'No one,' said Honey, 'has ever treated me like this before. Not even the dykiest dyke on the left-wing Sunday supplements.' Honey picked up her bag and spun on her heel. 'You can both expect to hear from my publicist.' She started to totter to the lift, but the momentum with which she swung her shoulder bag hit her off balance. Reaching out to stab the down button, she turned back, craning her neck so revealing an angry pulse.

The lift door opened and a grubby man in a white overcoat, cigarette in hand, stepped out. 'Honey Dew?' The air after him smelt of fungal infection.

'Yes,' she said.

'Bill Fothers, *Pump* snapper.' He had a canvas bag resting on his hip. 'You ready for this, then?'

Honey nodded and followed him, head high, glad to be basking in the warmth of a hot-blooded male. As she sauntered past Joshy and Humphrey she said, 'At least I have a vagina.'

Humphrey and Josh gaped after her, and then at each other.

'Sometimes, Joshy old boy,' said Humphrey, 'I really wonder if the entire female species hasn't had its day.'

'Couldn't agree more,' said Joshy, touching his chin. 'I think we may have somehow evolved past them.'

Humphrey said, 'Apart from Kylie.'

'And Lorraine Kelly.'

'*Oui*,' said Humphrey, '*naturellement*.'

IV

'I can't stay long,' said Sandy. She hadn't been expecting much from a wax museum dedicated to female celebrities as you've never seen them before, and what she saw met her expectations. Two entrances shared a doorway, at right angles to each other, the other a hair emporium specialising in thick sleek hanks of Asian hair. To its left, a shop front advertised cut-price designer trainers. At first glance, the fading Hollywood billboards in the window, every crevice a bluebottle graveyard, made Waxy Ladies look like some sort of film buffs' hang out. The door was on the latch.

'Pleased to meet you,' said an exotic-looking girl with an Afro, seated at a desk. 'My name is Jade and I'm glad to welcome you. Have you booked?' She left the question dangling along with her extended hand. Sandy didn't reply. Jade went on, 'Welcome, babes.'

Sandy stepped forward, her head slightly crooked. 'No, I've got an appointment. Someone said something about a model. Of me. I'm Sandy West. I'm supposed to pose for it.' The way she spoke made it sound as if she had no say over what happened to her.

'Sure, baby. I get ya,' said Jade.

Sandy looked down at a pile of car stickers that read 'Wax workers dip their wicks'.

'They're bumper stickers,' Jade said.

'I don't get it,' Sandy told her.

'No, babes, me neither.' Her laugh bubbled out of her chest.

Sandy felt that she'd passed some sort of test.

Without leaving her seat Jade twisted her head towards the stairs. 'Mickey,' she bellowed still looking at Sandy, 'there's a woman here for you.' She waited five seconds for a reply but when none came, she picked up a telephone on the desk and, delicately using a forefinger as though the varnish hadn't dried, stabbed in three numbers.

Sandy loitered by a glass case labelled 'Celebrity Hair'.

They heard the phone ring downstairs. Jade told her absently, 'Every tress is guaranteed to come from a star.' The phone picked up at the end of the third ring. She spoke quietly into the receiver and then said, 'You may go downstairs now. Our sculptor is waiting for you.'

V

Carlo Franchetti's salon was established in 1972 on the site of a medieval monks' brewery. According to one of his clients, a celebrity palmist with his own column in an upmarket Sunday, it was built on a Hogarthian ley line.

'Which means what, exactly?' Carlo had asked. Religious mumbo jumbo had made him leave Italy after the war, so he rarely gave any credence to what couldn't be proved.

'It's the site of Gin Lane,' said the celebrity palmist. 'Can't you still somehow *feel* the desperation of those poor souls?'

'Bollocks,' said Carlo. 'No one feels nothing in my salon, matey, but the back of my hand if they don't pay up.' Celebrity or not, the palmist's hair had gone straight in the bin.

'How's tricks?' Ray sat on the bench under the window with his back to the street and balanced a copy of *Hello!* in the crook of his knee.

'Crap.' Carlo twirled a pair of scissors in his left hand. They were dark silver, like gunmetal, with an elaborate thumb holder.

Ray and Carlo went back to August '91 when, in addition to the Soho salon, Carlo launched a clothes outlet devoted to fashions for the senior clubber. They met at a gig in Bournemouth when Ray was touring the south coast trying to revive northern soul, and agreed they could work to mutual benefit, plus any clothes sold in the foyer provided Ray with ten per cent commission. When the rave culture eclipsed them both, Carlo went back to being a full-time stylist and Ray pondered the uses of celebrity hair.

'They all come to Carlo,' he had told Ray in the early hours in a travel motel on the M3. They'd finished the mini bar in Ray's room and had moved to Carlo's. Carlo sat on the edge of his bed, knees wide, making sweeping movements with his empty hand. 'The Hollywood greats,' he said broadly. 'Jerry Hall, she big client. Plenty hair. Even Jackie Collins. What you think of that?' Ray thought of the mileage in hair. Hair that actually came from the follicles of the famous must be worth something. Had he read about a museum devoted to the cars of the rich and famous? Well, this was better. Hair grew out of the essence of celebrity. Some magical alchemy that turned the champagne and cocaine into hair, like the transubstantiation of fame. Eight months later, he opened Waxy Ladies, with the boast 'Real Ac-tresses'.

The sun bored its way through the Venetian blinds into the salon, heating the smell of ammonia and coffee. There was one man in the chair but none waiting. Carlo said, 'People these days don't want skill. They want a salon with the fancy funky drum-and-base music and skinny women showing their tummy buttons.'

'True enough.' Ray didn't look up; he'd noticed before that the heat made Carlo phlegmatic.

'And barbers that call themselves hair meisters. I am not competing with that.' He brushed hair from the neck of a man with glasses frames made of thin black rectangles. 'You know it makes me laugh, all the people here thinking Italians are cutting hair. Before I came I never picked up a pair of fucking scissors in my life and that's the truth. In the UK, though, everyone is saying Luigi is a haircutter. It's bollocks, really.'

'Maybe that's why your man is going to the hair meisters,' suggested Ray.

'Bollocks.' Carlo ripped the green poncho from his client. 'Pay at the desk.'

The client stood up, half bending, looking in the mirror as he pulled at a wallet from the curve of his buttock. He said out of the corner of his mouth, 'Cheers, mate. Good job.'

'Yeah, mate, cheers, good job,' Carlo echoed scowling; shoulders already hunched. He wore a plaid short-sleeved shirt made out of towelling material and moveable polyester brown trousers held up by a grey plastic belt straining on the last notch. He relit a cigar stump. 'Here, Andy, clean up this bloody lot.' He pointed the cigar at a teenager with sideburns slashed down his cheeks and then at the red lino around three chairs. 'It's a pigsty in here. Bloody sight worse than a whore's bedroom.'

'And you'd have seen a couple,' said Ray.

'Married a couple is more like it.' He sat beside Ray, the swell of his belly settling perfectly round above his belt.

'Anyone been in, then?' Ray threw the magazine on the table.

'We've been as quiet as a porno movie with the sound turned down.'

'Pretty quiet.' Ray nodded. 'What, no one at all?'

'Listen, I'm telling you, right?' said Carlo, pointing his cigar at Ray. 'Even that man from the radio, he go to major West End salon now. One that has its own products, I ask you. And he only read the frigging sport.'

Ray stretched his legs and picked up the same *Hello!* he had discarded. 'You know, you need a niche market.'

'Fucking aye,' said Carlo. 'You know something?' He swivelled to face Ray. 'One thing I ever wanted to do was play the drums. That's it. Not even in a band. Maybe a band but a small one. And that would be it, bang, bang, bang, all day long. Now tell me if that's too much to ask?'

Ray turned the page and sucked his cheeks in. 'So you're telling me you've had no one in this week?'

'No, I tell a lie,' said Carlo. 'Today, I have tasty morsel for you. Woman in our ladies' salon. Big girl. She underwear queen. Big titties. Three-inch trim, I have for you.'

He called out to the boy sweeping up, whose back was hunched, shoulders rounded around the broom, with a put-upon air. ''Ere, Andy, you bring Mr Ray that hair.' He smiled at Ray. 'For you, sir, that'll be thirty quid.'

'Make it twenty.'

'I tell you, it's three inches,' said Carlo. 'Twenty-five.'

'I'm not even sure,' said Ray, 'who it is.'

'Tittie woman. Does the bra thing that stops the cars. Makes men crash.'

'If it's a foreign bird,' said Ray, 'call it twenty.'

'Done.'

'Good.' Ray reached for his wallet and pulled out two notes. 'There you go,' he said. 'Stick it in your bongo fund.'

VI

Sandy presented herself to him like a child, standing too close and staring up at him as if he knew all the answers.

'Hello,' she said, hands by her side. Her thinness made her almost two-dimensional. 'I'm Sandy West.'

'Pleased to meet you,' said Mickey. 'I'm Mickey Defoe.'

She cocked her head to one side. 'Like the writer?' she said.

'That's it,' said Mickey, making a nervous laugh. 'But I'm a sculptor.'

'Where's the one I spoke to before?'

'Ray? He's out at the minute.' They were facing each other, still standing. Mickey crossed then uncrossed his arms. 'But I mean I'm in charge. I do the sculpting. It's me you need.' He backed away from her, embarrassed.

She nodded. 'But he does all the money stuff.'

Mickey told her yeah, but they could sort all that when he got back. Then he offered to take her coat. She refused. But then it was cold in the studio and Ray still hadn't replaced the gas cylinder.

'Have you ever posed before?'

'Once in art at school for two periods,' she said rubbing her nose. 'Charcoal.' She put her hand back in her pocket. 'But he told me I wouldn't have to pose. Bring a photo and my measurements. That's what he said.'

'Yes,' said Mickey, 'usually I can do it from a photo. It's just if you're here and you're amenable.'

'I wouldn't say that, exactly.'

'What?'

'Amenable.'

'You're here.'

'True.'

She locked herself firmly in her coat, binding the belt around her waist, and adjusting the top button. 'Can I have a glass of water, please?'

Close to, even in the semidark of the studio, Mickey could make out the pockmarks from teenage spots beneath a layer of powder. Her fringe must have been grown long to cover her forehead but probably made her skin worse. Other than the powder, she wore no make-up. She was attractive, there was no doubt, with dark almond eyes and an almost invisible nose, but she looked as if she was still at some pupa stage, and any morning could wake up a very ugly individual. Her movements were jagged, as if she knew she should be making the most of this transition period, but at the same time was resentful.

'How about milk?' he asked. 'Or tea?'

'I don't mind tap water,' Sandy said, 'if that's all there is.'

'I would,' he said. 'I'm afraid it's polluted.' Mickey shook his head. 'Terribly bad. In the olden days all the people in this part of London died of cholera, from pollution in the Thames. Did you know that cholera killed more people here than the plague?'

'I didn't know that,' said Sandy.

'Besides, milk is good for you.' He came back from the fridge and handed her a mug. She took a sip and thanked him. Her hands cupped the mug, ignoring the handle. She said, 'So, what happens now?'

'Could you take your coat off?' Mickey smiled nonthreateningly, and laughed. 'I just need to get a feel for your overall dimensions.'

Sandy set the mug on the table and pulled at her coat tie.

Mickey said, 'Actually, you looked smaller on the telly.'

'Really? You're the first person to say that.' Out of her coat she was slim enough to float easily, like a leaf, or could be carried in water, lightly, under an arm. 'I thought I looked big. But then, the others were bigger than me.' She smiled and at the same time rubbed her nose, hiding her mouth.

'What happened to your tooth?' When she spoke he saw her front teeth were chipped, as though a tiny triangle had been nibbled away.

'Long story.' She offered the coat with a frail left arm. He took it.

'What about your jumper, now?'

'I'll freeze.' Then she told him, 'Don't put it there. It'll get dirty. Hang it up.'

There was nowhere in particular to hang coats, so he used the hood to loop it over the kitchen door. The jamb would be even grimier than the bench but she didn't seem to think of that, just liked a sense of neatness. She said, 'I'm cold,' but took the arms out of her jumper and pushed it over her head. Her breasts were large, swollen and too heavy for her body.

'It's not for long.' He nodded encouragement, picking up his sketchbook and a pencil. Then added, 'You were saying about your tooth?'

'It's dumb really. I had a fight with a dog. An Alsatian.'

'Cool,' said Mickey. 'Woman bites dog.'

'Not exactly. We were fighting over a rubber toy.'

She was still standing in a way that suggested Mickey knew what was going on. Her body was almost limp, waiting to be manipulated. The pink T-shirt she was wearing had 'Hot Babe' glittering across the chest and, even though it looked as if it had come from the children's department, left a dark gap between her pale upper arm and its cap sleeves. The imprint of her jeans had left a scarlike crack round her middle as if she'd been sawn in half and reconstructed.

Mickey moved away from her and angled the sketchbook so she couldn't see it. He said, 'So how was it?'

'How was what?' She stared him full in the face when she spoke, tucking a strand of hair behind her ear.

'The show, the *Big Sister* thing.'

She folded her arms. 'It was OK.' In profile her nose was like a button mushroom. 'A bit weird but you got used to it.'

Mickey nodded. 'That's what the other one said.'

'What other one?'

'Whatshername,' Mickey looked up. 'Dew. The one who won it.'

Sandy narrowed her eyes and took a small step towards him, arms by her side. 'You've done a model of Honey?'

'Yeah,' said Mickey, smudging a line, 'Ray's trying to get the full set, all the women from the house. That's the thing about wax—'

'She came here?'

'Well, no, we did her from a picture,' said Mickey. 'And her measurements.' He frowned, wondering if Sandy hadn't seen enough of Honey Dew in the time they'd spent locked up together. He pointed his pencil at a model in the corner covered in a flannel sheet. 'She's there, if you want to have a look at her.'

'Do you know where I can find her?'

Mickey shrugged. 'I guess Ray'll have a number for her somewhere,' he said. 'Why?'

Sandy shook her head as if it had all been a big misunderstanding. 'No reason.' She reached behind her for her jumper. 'I was wondering,' she said. 'It's quite late and I have to be somewhere soon.' She smiled and her face seemed to change. Two pockets of flesh slid over her cheekbones and a small dimple pierced her chin. 'I thought you might like to come with me. It's nothing fancy, it's just something I have to do, like a work thing. Only I don't know many people here – in London, I mean. Only if you're free, of course.' She laughed out loud.

Mickey frowned, at odds with the loop his internal organs were making. 'I'll have to make a few calls,' he lied, 'but I guess I could be.'

'Good,' said Sandy, pulling her jumper on – like the pie man, thought Mickey, putting away his wares.

VII

'I'll be goddamn damned, who the hell would have thought it?' Gaye breathed the question to no one in particular on the news desk. When no one took any notice, she spoke louder. 'That skinny little motherfucker can write.' She held Sandy's printed-out copy in her left hand. 'I mean really write.' With her right she yanked a red pen from behind her ear. 'Of course, it needs tidying up.'

'What does?' Women's page features assistant Beverley Wilkinson drifted in holding a plastic bottle of shampoo.

'The stuff,' replied Gaye, 'that this *Big Sister* trollop has written.'

Beverley wasn't sure if females could be referred to as trollops, not on the women's page desk.

'Really?'

'I mean, bugger me if she hasn't captured what I was after.' Gaye was hunched over the copy, speaking as she wrote. 'Glamour but with a certain amount of country-girl innocence.' She looked over at Beverley, checking to see who else was about. Most of the desk was on a cigarette break. Lesley Ann James was making a fool of herself at the water cooler and McCreash was holding court near the coat rack. Suddenly Gaye was wondering about the security of her 'Gaye Divorcee' column. She drummed her fingers on the desk.

Beverley said, 'I love it when that happens.'

'What?' snapped Gaye.

'When someone exceeds their expectations,' Beverley paused. 'Especially a woman.'

'Oh yeah,' said Gaye. 'Me too. Isn't it just the best fucking feeling in the world?' There was more to the tramp than she'd thought. When she looked down she saw the nib of her red pen had broken.

VIII

'So tell me more about the fight with the dog.'

For a split second Sandy wasn't sure what he was talking about.

'The Alsatian,' urged Mickey. 'Your tooth?'

It had taken forty minutes to find the restaurant, tucked down an alley three streets away from Covent Garden. Sandy had suggested taking the Tube but Mickey had assured her it would be quicker to walk. Besides that, it would help her get her bearings. When they'd got lost, he'd refused to ask passers-by for directions. Sandy had told him not to be such a dope and asked a female policeman, walking straight up to her with such a limp and lost expression that the WPC had walked them there. Rhodes was the only light in a small terrace of three four-storey buildings. Inside, it was bright and noisy, as if diners knew it was up to them to battle off the encroaching darkness.

Mickey sat opposite Sandy, facing the wall. If she was doing a restaurant review, she'd told him, she had to be able to see what was going on. At the window a cardboard frieze of two reindeers held a banner reading 'Season's Greetings' between them. Red, yellow and green fairy lights edged the bar, looking more permanent than just a Christmas display.

Sandy picked up a soldier of pitta bread and dipped it in hummus. 'The dog belonged to a neighbour. I was seven and I just wanted the rubber ring,' she said.

'Didn't you have your own toys?' Mickey lined up his olive stones around his plate . . . tinker, tailor, soldier . . .

'I dunno,' said Sandy. 'Probably. I can't remember.'

A woman came over and took their wine order. Sandy didn't look up when Mickey asked for the house white. The waitress asked, 'Water?'

'Not for me,' said Mickey.

'Milk, please,' said Sandy. She looked over at Mickey. 'I think I've got a taste for it now. And it's good for me.'

'With wine?' asked Mickey.

'I don't drink,' Sandy replied. 'Except,' she frowned, 'when I feel I'm losing control of the situation.'

'You know,' said Mickey, trying to eat his way on to tinker again, which was the only one that could fit Sandy, 'adults are supposed to be allergic to milk. It's designed only for growing mammals.'

'That's what I must be, then,' said Sandy, picking up another piece of pitta and biting a pattern around its edge, 'a growing mammal.'

Halfway through the main course she ordered a vodka and tonic. 'Not slimline, the proper stuff,' she told the waitress. She had ordered moussaka made from chicken, and a salad. Mickey had leg of lamb in a thin gravy that he was being careful not to spill down his front. When Sandy told the waitress she was from a paper, they got a glass bowl of chips to share. It was still early. The pre-theatre crowd had been and gone and, other than a French couple in the corner, they were alone.

'Shouldn't you be taking notes?' asked Mickey.

'It's a bit more free-fall than that.'

'How do you mean?'

'Imaginative,' Sandy told him. 'You'll see.'

She finished her drink and asked for another. Already she'd told him about the caravan, her nail business and the way a newspaper had signed her up to write a column from London. Her mother was a former beauty queen who had made Sandy take part in pre-teen pageants, not even stopping when she chipped her tooth.

'Then, when I got spots when I was ten, I remember thinking, thank you, God. That's it. I'll never have to wear a leotard and parade up and down one of those stages in front of a bunch of perverts ever again. We never had a washing machine so I had to wash out my outfit by hand, in that poxy caravan sink. All of it, then try and dry it by the morning because some of them lasted two days. But I never could get it dry in the winter because the caravan was too cold. So the next day the tights would be damp and the leotard as cold and wet as hell. Can you imagine what that was like?'

Mickey said he couldn't and asked if she wanted another vodka and tonic. She agreed.

'Then when I needed a bra she wouldn't buy me one. I developed my chest early. Great big balloons. And she just would never get me one. I don't know if she resented them or was jealous, or just didn't even see them. I used to walk around department stores and nudge her into the bra section, hoping she'd make the connection, but she never.'

'Why didn't you just ask for one?'

Sandy shrugged. 'It wasn't that sort of relationship. I was embarrassed, most probably. Felt like I was letting her down.'

'You couldn't help having breasts,' said Mickey.

'Maybe not,' muttered Sandy, as if some doubt still lingered. She ate a forkful of salad, ignoring the feta. 'But you know what it's like.'

Then because he thought that was what it was all about,

Mickey told her about his childhood: how it had been just him and his mother; what a great job she'd made of bringing him up.

'We're the same, then,' said Sandy.

'How do you mean?'

'No dads.' She bit into her slice of lime. 'What happened to yours? Did he die or did he just piss off?'

Mickey was definite. 'No. I've got a dad, for sure. Only I don't know who he is. My mother was a single mum.'

'Yeah, same here. But you know who he is. Like, mine was a purser on the cross-Channel ferry,' she said. 'And yours is . . .' She left it hanging. 'You know who he is, right?'

Mickey said, 'Not exactly, I don't.'

'Aren't you interested to find out?'

'No,' said Mickey. 'I'm really not.'

She ate slowly, defiantly, and Mickey sensed the dinner table had been her battlefield, her only chance to get her own back on her mother. He recognised it because he's done it too – chewing like a ruminant to make his mother wait. The waitress came to clear plates. She was Greek with fine dark eyebrows plucked in the shape of a wingspan. She asked if, as a reviewer, Sandy wanted to speak to the chef. Sandy declined but told her she didn't expect a bill, it being a review and all.

Mickey said, 'That was pretty cool.'

'What? Not speaking to the cook?' she sniggered. 'What would I ask him?'

'No,' said Mickey. 'Telling her we weren't going to pay like that.'

'So what?' she said, reaching on the chair next to Mickey for her coat. 'It pays to be upfront. People prefer it. Besides that,' she wriggled out from behind the table, 'it gets me what I want.'

Mickey frowned, brain starting to unravel after a bottle of retsina. Was she pushy or the reverse, anti-pushy? He looked at his watch with a theatrical flourish and asked her, because it was still early, if she fancied going on for a drink somewhere.

'Why not?' she said, and took his arm.

He took her to a basement bar down an alley, around the corner from the restaurant. It was called The Cube and specialised in after-hours drinking for actors on their way home from performances. It was mainly fringe stuff, according to the reviews in frames around the bar, though Mickey spotted a signed black-and-white publicity shot of John Boy Walton, whom Mickey had never had down as much as a drinker.

Mickey sat with his back to the bar. They were both perched on large cubes covered in red felt. The wall behind Sandy was covered in leather.

'Cool,' said Mickey.

Sandy didn't reply but just bunched her coat round her. She sat with her head forward, her hair almost dangling in her glass. The restaurant had been intimate but this was more free-wheeling abandon. Most of the drinkers looked as though the happy hour had left them too sloshed to move on anywhere.

'Yeah, it's nice,' said Sandy. Above the bar was a slide show of black-and-white Charlie Chaplin stills, with subtitles.

'Bit noisy,' he said.

'Bit.'

'Maybe we should go somewhere quieter.'

'No,' said Sandy, taking a slurp of her drink. After the vodka, she'd asked for a White Russian. 'This is fine.'

Mickey waited until the song had finished. It was a remix of a country-and-western song that he recognised from his childhood and that had made a line of people at the bar whoop like cowboys.

'So tell me about the show,' he said. '*Big Sister*. What was it like? A laugh?'

'Not really.'

'Like what?'

'Like how can it be, being holed up for a fortnight with a load of strangers and having it broadcast on satellite TV?' Her mood seemed to have changed from euphoric to truculent.

'So why did you do it?' The music had gone softer and swaying, calming the bar in a stroke. Mickey used his legs to somehow hunch his pouf towards Sandy.

'Money,' said Sandy. 'Why else?'

'But you couldn't be sure you were going to win.'

'Oh yeah?' She pulled a sour face. 'Why not? Making people like you isn't difficult, you know.'

'But,' said Mickey, 'from what I remember, don't the viewers have to vote who stays in and who goes?'

'Yeah, and wasn't I the most popular one for ten days?' said Sandy as she leant towards him. 'Trust me, I can *do* popular.'

'So what happened?'

'You never watched it, then?'

'Not as much as I'd have liked to,' said Mickey.

She sucked on her drink. 'I made a pact with Honey that if I knew the answer to her question when she looked like being a loser one day I would let her stay in return for a cut of the winnings. Which I did.'

'And she won, right?' said Mickey.

Sandy didn't hear. 'Only when it came down to it and it was her turn to answer for me, she stuffed me up.' Sandy shook her head. 'There were the two of us left and I had to leave without so much as a penny.'

'Blimey,' said Mickey.

'Yeah,' said Sandy, 'something like that.' She drained her glass and looked to the bar. 'So now she's all penthouse suites and *Hello!* magazine and I'm living in a caravan doing a column for a fourth-rate tabloid.'

Mickey shrugged. 'Can't you complain somehow?'

'Like who to?'

'I dunno,' said Mickey. 'The producers.'

'They don't give a flying fuck,' said Sandy. 'Why should they?' She leant back on the leather wall. 'It made great telly.'

'What about telling your side of it in the papers?'

'Listen,' Sandy turned to face him. 'No one cares about a loser kicking up a fuss. It just looks like sour grapes.' She rubbed her nose. 'No,' she said, 'it's up to me to find Honey.' She put her glass to her lips.

'And then what?' asked Mickey, doing the same.

'Kill her.' She spoke into the barrel of her glass so that Mickey thought he'd misheard. It took three beats to register what he'd actually heard.

Then he said, 'Yeah, right.'

'No, I'm serious,' said Sandy. Her body, it seemed to him, had hardened. She was no longer rag-doll limp as she'd been at the studio, more rigid as a ramrod, as if her resolve was filling her up.

IX

The river oozed black and still in front of him, reflected by the string of lights along the Embankment. It was close to eleven and, from the vantage point of his stern, the pleasure boat captain still hadn't seen him cross the bridge. It was a cloudless sky and the deck of the *Lady J* was cold in the night air. True, he didn't spot him every night, but there was something about the youngster's frame, as he half ran over the water, that made him stand out. If the captain went below he could still keep an eye out for him from the stern window but he was reluctant to leave his post. Around him he felt the tide about to turn; the current was slackening and the water had that limpness, like the body of a woman about to surrender.

He felt the water beneath him when he thought of the tide; how the water sank, leaking out to the sea and surrounding the island like a foetal sac. On the south side of the Thames, his side, a couple swayed home arm in arm, propelled by alcohol, refuelled under every lamppost with a kiss.

The captain eased himself out of his chair and made his way around the stern, automatically checking the bowlines. He was about to turn off the lamp and admit he'd missed him, when he caught a glimpse of the unmistakable gait of the skeleton body propelled along under the dark jacket. Only when he was three-quarters of the way across, the captain saw that the man wasn't alone. The companion's head hardly showed above the parapet of Vauxhall Bridge, but he was definitely with someone. Not only that, it was a girl.

Chapter Three

I

That morning's *Pump* horoscope had warned Mickey that today would be harder than usual. Once again, it had been spot on. He'd had an erection since eleven that showed no sign of abating. He would be the first to admit there was something not quite right about feeling sexual attraction for a lump of wax, what Ray called the honer's boner, but since his encounter with Sandy he felt permanently aroused.

But now he had to work fast. A draught from the kitchenette turned the damp air clammy and his breath milky. As he worked, his tongue ran one way along his upper lip and then back again. Beneath him, the nipple hardened under his rotating forefinger. Making him think of Sandy. He pressed himself against the bench and moved his hands over her body, below her breasts and along a ribcage larger, leaner than he would have guessed. She was wearing a blue satin thong that covered a thin slice of her pubis.

'Oh aye, what's going on here, then?'

Mickey yanked away from the bench. Ray was in silhouette at the door. Ray's energy derived from the number of visitors. Summer afternoons when the smell of acetone made you heady and the thud of feet overhead was constant, Ray flew around like a trapped ferret. Today, he could barely move. A minute earlier, Jade had called down in some distress.

'What did she want?' Mickey adjusted his trousers.

'Nothing,' said Ray. 'Her clicker had jammed, that's all. Stupid cow. It's not as if there's a rush on. Two all day, and one of those was expecting a fucking fanny wax.'

'Maybe Jade just likes a bit of company,' said Mickey. 'It must be lonely for her all alone on that reception desk.'

'It's not a fucking holiday camp,' said Ray. 'And I wish she'd take her bloody coat off. She's about as welcoming as Myra Hindley.'

Mickey smiled, imagining the arrogant way Jade would have held her chin if Ray had said this to her, flitting a hand behind her head the way she did when she was annoyed, like she was swatting a fly.

'Anyway,' said Ray. 'You needn't worry about any of that any more.' He swayed into the room. 'I've just finished our latest money-spinner and, believe me, it's going to make *Big Sister* look like the *Antiques* fucking *Roadshow*.' He lit a cigarette, inhaling the first drag as he hauled himself on to the bench, flicking through an old TV listings. 'It's what this place is crying out for. Really put us on the fucking map.' He sent out a plume of smoke. 'And, of course, it'll be good publicity, for her.'

'I'm sorry?'

'Don't pretend you've forgotten.'

Mickey said, 'Oh yeah, right. Just remind me again why Madonna – one of the biggest celebrities on the planet – needs the publicity of a two-bit waxwork porno emporium?'

Ray jumped up. 'Shelf life, Michael, my son. Shelf life. We all have it. But for celebrities their time in the sun is very limited. Madonna has fallen overnight from a worldwide pop icon to housewife and mother of two. Her time in the sun is over. No, trust me on this. When she hears about this, she'll be thrilled. Besides that . . .' he sucked at the roll-up.

'What?'

'She's a Catholic bird herself. She'll be flattered. I mean, it's your modern-day miracle.'

Mickey turned to face him. 'You think, when the Pope hears about this she'll be canonised, do you?'

'How many waxworks,' Ray replied, 'have you heard of that actually lactate?'

'Er,' Mickey replied, 'actually none. The only miracle is how you've got a Teasmade to leak cartons of non-lactic soya milk out of her tits.'

'Michael Defoe, will you please keep your voice down?' Outside two car doors slammed in close succession. Ray sat down again. 'All I want is three lines in fucking *Time Out*, not a mention in the Vatican, for Christ's sake. That's all I'm saying. Make us a bit unique. Off the beaten tourist track.' He picked at a stray thread from his cuff, shifting his weight uneasily from one buttock to the other.

Mickey went back to his model. 'Besides that . . .' Ray hopped down and pushed past Mickey to the kitchenette and started filling a kettle. Mickey winced and tried to close his ears, 'they get up to much worse nonsense on the Internet. You can see Madonna doing a lot more than lactating, believe you me.'

'Yeah, well,' replied Mickey, standing up, his head cocked as if it expected to hit the ceiling. 'The thing about the Internet is you don't know who's doing it. If Waxy Ladies of 2a Brewer Street, London W1 2XB was to mount such a –' he paused – '*unique* exhibition, then I imagine Madonna's lawyers might just hazard a guess as to who's behind it.'

The kettle started to rattle. 'But,' argued Ray, 'that's not it. We're not mounting it. It just happened. That's what I'll tell reporters.'

'If I were you, I'd stick to your Erika Roe rolling programme. Tits that stick in your mind, but pose altogether less of a legal threat.' He rubbed his eyes as if smoke had got into them.

Ray absently jabbed the tea bag with a pencil. 'You mean your less litigious tit?'

'Pretty much,' said Mickey, hoping that would be an end of

it. 'Look, I've got to make a move. I've got to be somewhere at one.'

II

Sandy pulled at her cheeks in the hand-held mirror. Her hair, from sleeping on the pillowless futon, stuck up at the back like a badly done beehive. She pinched the open pores under her cheekbones. It seemed she was taking on the pallor of the city. Two grey gelatinous balls of sleep rested either side of her nose, leaking from her eyeballs, she thought – liquid leaving her body. She was in the bath, sitting on the ledge and squeezing tepid water from a sponge down her back. The dried bar of pink soap next to her was criss-crossed with deep dark cracks like a palm. She was wondering if she was safe to use it when her mobile rang.

'Hello?' She could only find a hand towel to dry herself, dripping on to hairy carpet tiles.

'It's Gaye. Are you OK?' She wasn't asking out of concern.

'Why wouldn't I be?' Sandy pulled her dressing gown round her.

'Your copy is late, that's all.' The background clatter was more pub-like than office, with the thickness of a sea of raised voices. 'We agreed you'd file by twelve at the latest. That's the way deadlines work, I'm afraid.'

Sandy said, 'The email's playing up. I can't send the attachment.'

'Oh,' said Gaye. 'Really?'

'Yeah, I'll give it one more shot,' said Sandy. 'I'm sorry if it's inconvenienced you. But you know how these things can be.'

'Yes, of course I do. Well, just make sure you do. This isn't a nail parlour, you know.' Gaye paused. 'What about pictures?'

'I got the guy at the restaurant to overnight them to the picture desk.'

'Oh, right,' said Gaye. 'Well, they haven't arrived yet.'

'Sorry.'

Gaye sighed. 'It's hardly your fault.'

'No, well—'

'I'll call you when your copy gets here,' Gaye said.

'Just one other thing,' Sandy intervened before she hung up. 'I was wondering if you might have any other invites for me to go to. Another restaurant, or much better would be some sort of celebrity do.' She tugged at a loose thread. 'Maybe I could speak to the diary editor?'

'The diary editor?' repeated Gaye.

'Yeah, whoever does your diary pieces.'

'I know what a diary editor does,' Gaye told her. 'The point is we happen to be between diary editors at the moment. This is the *Daily Pump* not the frigging *Tatler*—'

'What about features, then?'

Then the line went dead. At first Sandy thought her phone must have cut out, then she realised Gaye had hung up on her. She sighed. Anger, she'd learnt from afternoons watching a black-and-white portable, was such a wasted emotion. The dressing gown had dried her and it wasn't worth getting back in the bath. She pulled on a sweater over her head and pulled the scratchy woollen blanket from her unmade bed around her. She booted up the laptop and began to write.

> Imagine me, a dizzy girl from the country, sitting down to eat at the same table as Dustin Hoffman. Well, it's true. Last night, accompanied by one of the hunkiest . . .

She nibbled at an apple as she wrote, then she sat back, wondering if she'd done enough the night before. If *Big Sister* had taught her anything it was that you got nowhere without alliances. To Mickey she had to come across part innocent, part temptress. She remembered even spelling it out to him.

'Seduction,' she'd told him, just twelve hours ago, stretched out on the futon, 'has nothing to do with sex.'

'No?' said Mickey.

'No. It's fulfilling a psychological need,' propping herself up on her elbow, shaking her head forward, separating her hair at the back, and dragging two plaits to the front to cover herself modestly. 'Seduction is recognising what the need is and filling the gap. That's it.'

Then he'd asked her what his need had been. 'Or did I seduce you?' he'd actually asked.

She told him it was a secret, though it had been pretty obvious. Still, it was good to get an ally in her camp, and an ally with access to Honey Dew. She was edging closer to her all the time . . .

III

Mickey was the only patient out of the three waiting not to be engrossed in the pages of a magazine on his lap. He stretched his legs and exhaled deeply. His brain was trilling to 'The Look of Love' while his internal CCTV footage from the night before ran on an X-rated loop, freeze-framing the most lurid parts. He rested his head against the picture rail. 'Beep your horn if you had it last night.' A student banner he'd once driven past. True, he hadn't exactly had it, but he had come closer than at any time in the past two years.

He sank his head on to the wooden picture rail and thought of Sandy's limpet-shaped nipples. Even when she pinched at them with small badly varnished nails they didn't change their adolescent shape. They were the triangular peaks of the snow-capped mountains, drawn by a child. When he kissed them, rotating his tongue gently, she'd elbowed back the cover and arched her back. 'Don't knead them,' she told him. 'They're not a lump of bread.' She spoke softly and when she did he half caught her accent, though he still couldn't place it. She said, 'You should fondle them.' She shooed his hand away impatiently and showed him, flicking the backs of her palms over the top and then pushing them up. 'There, like this,' she said, 'it's a nice word that, fondle. You should remember it.' She said it slowly, reminding Mickey of 'fondant' and 'doll' rolled into one. 'Now suck them,' she said. 'Hard as you like. Bite them if you want to. I don't mind.' She pushed the duvet back and straddled his chest, pouring her breasts on to his face, behind the curtain of her hair, letting him suck so hard it must have hurt, as if he was punishing them. Her mouth was above his head and he heard the noises she made. Faint mewing noises, like a kitten.

But he didn't want to hurt her. He was worried about his weight on her, if he might squash the life out of her. It was the heat of her that had hit him first, the warmth of her skin, like dough left to rise in an airing cupboard. She had been the one to take charge. Not speaking, undressing in a functional way, holding his hand, he thought out of affection, then guiding it between her legs.

Lying next to her, he could get his arms round her more than once. It left his forearms unwanted and flapping over the edge of his futon. They kissed and the truth was he felt it had been he that hadn't wanted to do it.

Mickey said, trying to impress, 'Celebrity is the new religion.'

'No,' Sandy told him, 'that's bollocks. People say that. But all it is, people are interested in gossip. It's not new. I bet even in the olden days, even in the caveman days, people wanted to know stuff about other people.' She trailed a finger around the mound of his chest. 'I tell you what is the new religion, though.'

'What is?' The LCD radio on the floor next to him said 3.20 a.m.

'Parenting.'

'How do you mean?' asked Mickey.

'The fuss people make.' She yawned and stretched an arm over her head. The rest of her body was tanned; a pudgy joint of underarm streaked white in the soupy light looked, to Mickey, unbearably soft. 'The way they go on. The joy of it, the happiness and not just the women – these days men are even worse than women.'

Mickey didn't say anything. He listened to the hum of the fridge. The only light came from the dull green glow from his clock. Sandy went on, 'So you know what that makes us.'

Mickey said, 'Who?'

'People with no dads.'

'What?' Mickey asked, in spite of himself.

'Atheists.' She stroked strands of hair off his face and kissed him.

Remembering had made Mickey hard again.

'Mr Defoe,' the receptionist with a stud in her nostril was knocking appointment cards on the counter, 'the doctor will see you now.'

'I'm really grateful for the extra session,' said Mickey.

'Cancellation,' said the doctor. 'Actually she's moved.' He sat down. 'One of my patients. Four numbers came up on the lottery and they've moved to Adelaide, the whole family. Can't say I'd fancy it much myself.'

'Me neither,' said Mickey. 'Too far,' he said. 'Too much—'

'Sea?'

'Yeah,' agreed Mickey. 'Exactly.' There was a new picture above the doctor's head, a tribal scene of men dancing. They wore nothing but thongs around their middles, suspending cases for their penises.

'So how have you been?' asked the doctor.

'Not too bad,' said Mickey. He wanted to talk about Sandy but didn't know if it was appropriate. He felt disloyal to Sandy, and it might sound like bragging. But he also felt a communion with all males – the doctor, even the men dancing with penises in the picture. He asked, 'Are you married?'

'Yes, I am,' said the doctor. 'Two children, Horace and Queenie. Aged eight and four.'

Mickey said, 'Unusual names.'

'My wife's choice,' said the doctor, implying that would be the end of it.

'What is she,' Mickey snorted, 'a pearly queen?'

'No,' said the doctor, 'a QC.'

'No offence,' said Mickey.

'None taken,' said the doctor. 'So,' he exhaled, 'any more symptoms?'

Mickey asked him what he meant. The doctor looked at his notes and reeled off a list of possibilities – increased ritualistic behaviour, more superstitious behaviour, avoidance strategies.

'All right, all right,' said Mickey. 'Steady on . . .'

'What about your childhood?'

'What about it?' Mickey shifted his weight.

The doctor said, 'Well, I'm trying to establish some sort of link between the ritualised behaviour of prepubescent adolescents and its sexualised form in adulthood. Sex is merely the grown-up form of play, you know.'

Mickey didn't know that. He said, 'What's sex got to do with it?' He was wondering if the doctor had somehow picked up on last night's sexual encounter.

The doctor went on, 'Hence the childish names lovers have for each other: Bunny, Pumpkin, Hoochie Coochie.'

Mickey pictured the Adebayo bedroom and the doctor in a judge's wig while his wife tapped him all over with his gavel.

'The act of making love has its roots in childhood. Tweaking and sucking, for example.'

Mickey felt a hardening around his trousers. 'Look, I just asked what you meant, OK? There's no need to go on about it. Making me out to be some sort of pervert.' He rubbed his palms the length of his thighs. 'There are other new things I'm doing too.'

'Such as?'

'Well,' he nipped his chin with his forefinger and thumb, 'I'm making a wax model of myself.'

The doctor sat up. 'I'm sorry?'

'Me,' said Mickey. 'I'm making a full-scale replication of myself in wax. At home, this is, not at the studio. Ray would go mad. I'm making it, like as a sacrifice.'

There was something else new in the doctor's room – a clock. Mickey couldn't see it but he listened to its ticktock, only it was softer than that, more springy.

After nine beats the doctor said, 'Really?'

'Yeah,' said Mickey. 'Really. And it's really not such a big deal. I just figure if I can somehow donate it to,' he paused and looked around the room, 'some watery place – I dunno, the sea, a river, or something – then all this fear of water would leave me alone. I read somewhere that on some Scottish island the people believe if you saved someone from the sea then the sea would always reclaim you. That's why if they saw a drowning man they wouldn't . . .'

'Wouldn't what?'

'Save him.'

'That's what you think,' said the doctor.

Mickey exhaled. 'Yeah,' he said. 'That's what I think.' He smiled apologetically. 'Then I'd be able to do normal stuff. Walk across the bridge without going ape. Be in the bathroom when I'm running a bath. You know.'

'When did you start?'

'The sculpture? I dunno, a couple of weeks or so ago, I guess. It doesn't take long. Once you get going. When you start to get a feel for it.' Mickey sat up, suddenly animated. 'Only now I've got this sort of girlfriend, I don't want her to think,' he scratched the joint of his elbow, 'that I'm weird. I mean, what should I tell her? It's not that weird, is it?'

When the doctor didn't reply, Mickey prompted, 'Doctor?'

He looked up from what he was writing. Mickey noticed some

of his letters sloped backwards – the capitals – but mainly they sloped forwards.

He stared at Mickey and laid the pen down. 'Does it excite you?'

'What?'

'Working on the waxwork. Do you find it autoerotic?'

'No, I bloody don't.' Mickey was offended. 'Look, Doctor, I think you might be getting the wrong end of the stick here. It's only a waxwork. Like a self-portrait; all artists do them.'

'So why tell me about it?'

'I told you. I just want to know what to tell my girlfriend.' Mickey qualified it. 'My sort of girlfriend, that is.'

The doctor rested his pen on his chin. 'You seem to think it's a self-portrait.' The hair follicles round his jowls were raised, as though he was allergic to shaving.

'Yeah,' Mickey said. 'I sort of do, but—'

'But,' agreed the doctor, 'we both know it's something other than that, don't we?'

Mickey didn't speak.

After a thirty-second pause, the doctor looked at his watch. 'Time's up, I'm afraid.'

On his way out of the reception, Mickey enquired if he might mop up some more of the sessions vacated by the woman who had taken her family to Australia. The receptionist asked if the doctor had agreed. He had, confirmed Mickey. In fact, he'd suggested it. Stepping on to the pavement was a relief. The air was milky with a light, sepia-coloured fog, damp weather that sucked the moisture from your skin and made it itch.

It was after two but office workers still huddled in deli doorways, spilling out over the pavement, jostling each other good-naturedly out of the cold. Holiday was in the air. No one seemed to care if they were late back or not. 'Who's going to sack us now?' their backs said as they bundled into another pub on the way back to work. Normal rules had ceased to apply. Women had an easy way, allowing the men to propel them through doors and along pavements with flat palms in the small of their backs.

He hadn't been back at the studio for more than an hour when the phone rang. Jade called down the stairs, 'Mickey, love, there's a woman on the phone for you.'

He felt a twitter in his stomach and a light-headed lack of oxygen in his brain.

'For me?' he asked needlessly, because he was alone.

'*Yes,*' confirmed Jade. 'It sounds like your mum.'

'Oh, right,' replied Mickey. 'Great.' His chest collapsed while his voice overcompensated. 'Put her through down here, can you?'

He picked up on the third ring.

'Mum?'

'Hello, Michael?' Her voice was strained and questioning, as if he'd called her from some exotic faraway place.

He said, 'How are you?' Then before she could reply, he asked, '*Where* are you?'

'I'm fine,' she replied. 'In fact, never better. How are you?'

'All right,' said Mickey, 'as it goes.'

'Still working in that wax place? What is it called now, Waxy Women—'

'Ladies,' corrected Mickey. 'Clearly, as you rang me here. Yes I am, as it goes.'

'Please,' said his mother in a familiar register, 'will you stop saying that?'

'What?'

'"As it goes",' she said. 'It makes you sound like some East End barrow boy.'

Up until the age of ten, Mickey misbehaved to provoke a reaction from his mum. At ten he was caught shoplifting chocolate buttons from the corner shop. Because of Mr Willough's Parkinson's disease, it took him five minutes to arrive in the shop after the bell on the door had rung. Mickey didn't want the sweets. He wanted his mother to become agitated and red-faced, like other mums, picking at her cuffs, and demand, 'What would your father say?' But she didn't. She made him write a three-page apology to Mr Willough telling him he knew why it was wrong to steal and how the fabric of democratic society hinged on its social conscience. Then he had to help clearing stock boxes in the yard behind the shop every Saturday for three months.

Mickey said, 'Sorry.' There was a silence for five conversational beats. Something about the resonance of the line, its lack of echo, made him say, 'Exactly where are you, Mum?'

'Me?' she replied breezily. 'I'm just off the Bayswater Road, just popping in on your Uncle Nigel.'

'Oh, right,' Mickey replied. 'What are you doing there?'

'Popping in,' said his mother. 'Christmas and all that.'

'Christmas isn't for another three weeks,' Mickey told her.

'Isn't it, darling?' she replied. 'Oh well, you know Nigel. He likes to get organised.'

When Mickey didn't reply, his mother said, 'I was half hoping to pop in to see you, at some point.'

'Really?' said Mickey. 'When?'

'Well, actually,' her voice wheedled, 'we might have a couple of gigs up here.'

'In *London*?'

'That's right,' she said. 'Don't sound so surprised, dear, you know the Movers and Shakers are making quite a name for themselves in the Home Counties.'

'But I don't think,' said Mickey, 'they'll go down so well in London.'

'Don't you be so sure,' said his mother. 'If you must know, people have reacted to the anti-Muslim backlash in surprising ways. The girls and I think it's a liberal sort of thing. Urban types don't like being told what to think, you see.' She paused. 'Whereas in Hertfordshire it's very much gone the other way. The

Hemel Conservative Club went so far as to cancel our Christmas gig, you know.'

'So what are you trying to say?'

'No compensation, nothing. It's times like that, Pammy says, that we really ought to have an agent—'

'Mother—'

'We've got three nights in the Battersea Arts Centre,' she said. 'Not all night, of course – that would be ridiculous. It's a show to make us all remember at Christmas just how much Islam has done for us. I mean not just Islam, the whole kit and caboodle of Eastern life. We just do a couple of sets. And . . .'

'And?' Mickey had his forefinger and thumb pressed into a piece of wax.

'I thought I could stay with you just to the end of the run.'

'Sorry?'

'Stay, dear, with you.'

'What about Uncle Nigel?' As soon as it was out, he regretted it. The guilt most children diluted over two parents, he concentrated on one. Before she had him, his mother had been an historian tipped to head the university department by the age of thirty. Twenty years on, she was one of a trio of belly dancers.

'But he's miles away,' she whined. 'You're just round the corner.'

'Yes, I am,' said Mickey. 'And it would be great to have you stay. Only, you see, at the moment I've got this new—'

'A few nights are all I'm after.'

'A few?' Mickey looked at the wax in front of him. He had stabbed a circle of indents into it with the blunt end of his knife.

'A few,' she confirmed.

'When do you want to come over?'

'How about tonight?' she replied.

'Tonight would be fine,' said Mickey, and felt the muscles in the side of his neck seize up and the skin on his forehead tighten to breaking point.

IV

Sitting in the carriage, on her way into the centre, Sandy imagined what would happen if the Tube broke down and the carriage became an autonomous unit, waiting until they were rescued. She observed her fellow passengers. Her peripheral vision, after years of evenings in the caravan watching her mother's hand on her glass, was exceptional. Who would be the leader and who would crack up? She wouldn't lead. Leaders were bossy and resented. Nor would she be too beautiful, too clever, or too confident – especially not too confident. She'd learnt that from her mum's afternoon talk shows. How the audience would egg on the shy, even if they were fat or ugly. 'Go girl, you can do it,' they whooped. But when the shy, fat and ugly became too full of themselves, too confident as they strutted on to the stage, squeezing into chairs, preening their hair, they would be booed and jeered. 'Girl, who the *hell* do you think you are?'

No, the extremes were always the first to go. She would be the nothing person. She would reveal only enough to appear vulnerable, and that she could make up. She would form alliances with those weaker than herself. Nothing people were the ones to watch. They were the ones who made it. The bland leading the bland was how she saw it.

The launch was in a West End store with two surnames, like solicitors. Sandy had heard of it but didn't know where it was. She looked the road name up in the back of her borrowed A–Z which had 'news desk' marked in pencil on its inside cover. Then she looked for the round blob of the nearest Tube station. The invitation, to the unveiling of Tiger, next year's eye shadow, by a French fashion house, wasn't made out to anyone. The gilt edged right-hand corner edge was dog-eared, nibbled almost, as if Gaye had deliberated over giving it to her. The writing began halfway down in fancy scrawl with 'RSVP' at the bottom and 'Canapés' on the third line. It wasn't the sort of invitation she had received before. The letters were glossy and in black, raised like Braille so she could trace them with her fingertips. Without hunger or boredom, or had the portable in her room worked better, she would have stayed at the B&B.

'What's the big deal?' she'd told Gaye. 'I don't get it.'

'It's glamour. Try to capture the infinite possibilities women feel when they use make-up,' Gaye replied. 'You're a woman. You wear it.'

'Only because my skin's bad.'

'Use your imagination. Explore,' she went on. 'Make it up. Failing that, find out if Vanessa Feltz really is a size twelve.'

Make up the make-up, she thought. She remembered the smell of her mother's nicotine-stained fingers when, standing behind her, she cupped her chin in her hand, smearing cold cream on her face before a pageant. In those days Sandy hadn't associated make-up with fantasy or transformation. When her mother said 'make-up' she took it to mean for a deficiency. She loathed the feel of it, its itchiness. Even on the screen test for *Big Sister*, she'd refused the make-up department's demands, even after they'd told her she'd look as washed out as a rag doll.

She got out at Bond Street, flooding up to the road with other travellers. When she raised her head the first thing she saw was Honey's photograph on the side of a stationary bus. She was square on to the camera but with her hands over her breasts, her lips were apart as if she was responsible for the caption underneath which read, 'Eight days to go . . . only in your *Pump*.'

Sandy gritted her teeth and adjusted her clothes until her anger subsided. Underneath her camel coat she wore a one-piece shift dress taken from her mum's wardrobe. It had bat wings that hitched her elbows up her coat sleeves, exposing three inches of wrist where her gloves stopped. She set off walking. As her body heated up and as her arms moved, she inhaled wafts of too-sweet perfume and cigarettes.

The department store fizzed with static and chrome. Territorial bubbles of air clung to counters, fighting to keep their own space, perfume counters clashing with the smell of the coffee shop. Sandy had worked in the Co-op in town and recognised this time as the four o'clock lull, the half-hour or so before the arrival of the volley of shoppers on their way home from work. Cosmetics girls doodled on the insides of their wrists with lipsticks, oblivious to the tinkle of the Christmas music.

'I'm looking for the launch.' Sandy spoke to a pick-a-stick-thin girl with two triangles of cerise on her cheekbones the same colour as a line of colour under her eyes. 'The one for the new eye shadow.' Keeping it vague showed she didn't care one way or the other. It would make it easier if nobody chose to help her.

The girl turned to her colleague. 'Paulette, what floor's that do on?'

'Hospitality, I guess.' Paulette's hair was plaited in rows and twisted into bunches. When she spoke she put her hand to her face and Sandy saw each of her nails had a different design on it.

Both of them stared at Sandy. 'You're the one off the telly,' the cerise one accused.

'Yeah,' said Paulette. 'It's that breakfast programme, isn't it?'

'That's right,' said Sandy, replacing a nail varnish tester. 'What floor's hospitality?'

'Nine,' said Paulette. 'The lift's in the far corner. But then I expect you know that.' Sandy didn't know it. She thanked them with a generous smile, reinforcing her candour because really they should be thanking her. Celebrity was like ripples from a stone. They'd report to their friends that they'd seen that woman off *Big Sister*, but that's where it would stop. No friends of theirs would pass it on. Not like they would if she was, say, Joan Collins or Madonna. Then again, maybe the girls were too city swanky to mention it to anyone. In London they must see plenty of famous people. Maybe it was uncool here. Not like in the Co-op when Gary Tatlock sold a Magimix to the bloke from Slade. That story went to friends of friends of friends. But it had been King's Lynn.

'I'm Sandy West,' she told the uniformed man with grey hair leaning over a lectern like a headmaster in the corridor. 'I've got my invite here—'

'No need, Miss West,' he said. 'You will find the cloakroom to your left. Then proceed to the main room.'

She glanced back at him as she handed her coat to a middle-aged woman, who seemed thrilled to receive it, and arranged her batwing sleeves. Inside the vaulted room she recognised no one. She felt a flame of fear lick up her spine as she went in, leaving her face perspiring and her body cold. A group of female journalists was in one corner, some smart, others deliberately down at heel to protest that attending make-up launches wasn't why they had become journalists. Sandy skirted over to them. The room was in twilight, with rows of white fairy lights crisscrossing the windows. Trails of silver floated from the ceilings behind a line of which stalked two tigers made of cardboard painted in unnatural stripes of purple and gold. Waitresses, in all-in-one leotards striped horizontally in the same purple and gold, handed out small circles of food from oval platters. Waiters made deft figure of eights with flutes of champagne. In the background, an actor's buttery voice recited Blake's 'The Tiger' and an intermittent roar came from a speaker in the corner.

'Urban jungle, you know. Isn't it simply marvellous?' The man who'd spoken looked out of place wearing a tweed jacket with a mousy slug of moustache under a thick nose. His accent was posh Scottish; he rolled his Rs so much he split the words in two. As he spoke he glanced behind him like a minder to a group of half a dozen men and women from which Sandy recognised a lunchtime soap actress. Sandy got the impression that, for him, talking to her was killing time and marginally better than standing on his own.

'Personally, I think it's tacky,' said Sandy. 'People are only happy because it's Christmas.' She tried to get the attention of a waitress. 'Or pissed.' She picked four different shapes from the tray, one, with a caramelised onion on its top, going straight into her mouth.

'Still,' said the man. 'I like the tigers.' He smiled self-deprecatingly, giving him the authentic air of a dentist. 'Actually, I'm a bit of a tiger man myself.'

'Really?' said Sandy. Using him as a block allowed her to eat faster than was polite.

'I shoot them.' He laughed. 'I mean with film, naturally.'

'Naturally,' said Sandy.

'Just got back from Kazakhstan. What a wilderness, a splendid place. I tell you, one night it was so cold my shampoo froze over. I was after the Siberian tiger.'

'Naturally,' repeated Sandy. 'So what are you doing here, then?'

He nodded and chewed the corners of his mouth. 'Truth to tell, it's a tad embarrassing, really. You see I'm scoping a doc. Just got the brief. Nonsense, of course, but needs must, I'm afraid.'

'Sorry?' Sandy ate a canapé off her palm like a horse with a sugar lump. It was a chunk of white fish coated in prune and almonds.

'I do apologise. I must introduce myself. Kenny Russel, the documentary maker. No relation to Ken.' A whoop from the corner made him twist round so she spoke to his back.

'Sandy West. Journalist.'

'Pleased to meet you.' He turned back. 'Look, I must dash. Looks like the person I need to speak to may be on the move.'

He made her sound like exotic prey. 'No problem,' said Sandy. 'Feel free.' Then she remembered her column.

'Who is it?' she called after him.

'Some trollop,' said Kenny. 'But, alas, that's where the money is these days. Ever since *Survival* went under. Some independent company wants it. Real TV or some such thing. Named after a fruit, or something.'

Sandy carried on eating. 'What is?'

'No, not what is. Who is. It's a she. A female of the species. Womanly type, by all accounts.'

'Sorry?'

'You're right, of course.' He nodded his head. 'It's preposterous I should be reduced to doing a documentary on her. A modern phenomenon, the making of a latterday heroine, or some such utter nonsense,' he said. 'I can tell you, what's happened at the Beeb these days – nothing short of criminal. Docusoaps, all day long. Anyway, you might have heard of her. She's over there.'

Overheard snatches of conversation had been of phobias. One woman had finished a monologue on her fear of the tomato. Her voice was piercing, wailing in and out of focus like the noise made rubbing a finger on the rim of a wet glass. 'Ever since I discovered they had a placenta,' she said, 'my feelings for them changed. The thought of them makes me sick. I mean really, really ill.' Even without seeing her, even without hearing her, Sandy knew who she was. The crowd parted and Sandy saw a woman sitting in a floral high-backed armchair, her back arched and her head tipped up, like a cat in full stretch.

'Honey Dew,' said Sandy.

'That's the fella,' he said. 'Do you know her at all?'

'You could say that,' said Sandy, with her head down. 'Do you mind if I take your card?'

'Be my guest.' He fished in his inside pocket for a silver case and pulled out a beige card with more writing on it than Sandy had ever seen on a business card. As his jacket flapped open she smelt a mixture of body odour and leather. He wore a military leather belt with a foreign buckle that his stomach tumbled over.

Sandy smiled. 'I might have an idea for something,' she told him. 'You never know.'

'Well, quite right, young lady,' said Kenny. 'Ideas are my currency. Now,' he made a half-salute at her, 'wish me luck.'

He turned towards the chair under the window.

'Yes,' said Sandy. 'Good luck. Not that you'll need it, I'm sure.'

She was careful to avoid Honey's corner for the rest of the launch. She spoke to a PR girl called Lucy, who mistook her for a fashion journalist and praised her batwing sleeves, ate eight more canapés, drank two glasses of champagne, then took the Tube back to the B&B. In the carriage home she fingered Kenny's card, coming at it from different angles, wondering how she could make it all fit together.

V

'So how is Uncle Nigel?' Mickey dragged the suitcase that no longer possessed its wheels into the sitting room. For a woman unused to men, his mother adapted easily to chivalry.

He'd met her at six, waiting at the wrong entrance to Vauxhall Tube station. He was on foot and ten minutes late because Ray had wanted to discuss his Madonna project. Crossing the concourse to check the other side, he spotted his mother's familiar duffel coat trimmed below the knee with a flimsy length of cotton sundress, hippy-style, in swirls of orange and brown. Her body was tilted towards a man in drag wearing an Afghan coat, speaking in falsetto on a mobile phone.

'Darling,' she called to Mickey, 'thank heavens you're here. Poor Patrice has been locked out of her flat.'

The man in the Afghan snapped his phone shut. 'What a bitch.' He had a French accent and theatrical mannerisms. Against a platinum-blond wig his face was tanned, with blue and purple eye shadow the dominant colours. He wore fishnet tights and unlaced Doc Marten boots. 'I come all this way and the bitch won't see me.'

'You poor thing,' said Mickey's mother. 'And in this weather. People can be so cruel, can't they, Mickey?'

'Mother,' said Mickey. 'I really don't—'

'Imagine coming all this way, just to be shut out.'

His mother was oblivious to the rain, whereas Mickey edged back into the shelter of the station.

The Afghan man turned to him. 'You so lucky boy.' He put an arm around Mickey's mother. 'She a wonderful lady. She your mother, you must cherish her.' He tossed his head back. 'Always.'

'Look,' said Mickey, suddenly exhausted, 'it's been lovely to meet you but I'm afraid we really must be making a move. We really mustn't keep you.'

His mother and Patrice looked at him. Before she could object Mickey grabbed his mother under her arm and pulled her and her suitcase away, feeling like the riot police.

'Goodbye, Patrice,' his mother called over her shoulder.

'Ah, *oui*, farewell then, Madame Defoe,' replied Patrice, his left arm raised in a tragic salute. 'I am charmed.'

Not wanting to pause for a break in the traffic, Mickey pulled her along the pavement. Rush-hour traffic was bottle-necked, spluttering and stalling out of town.

'For Christ's sake, Mother, you gave that man your name?' Mickey was still hauling her by the arm.

'Of course,' his mother told him. 'Actually I did more than that, I gave him your address.' She smiled and tugged her arm away from his clenched fist. 'In case of emergencies.'

The flat was untidied from the night before. The smell of curry from the communal hall followed them up past two mountain bikes somehow stapled to the unpapered wall, and a slippery film of misdirected post. Music leaked from the corners of the door opposite and occasional spurts of young men's laughter. Mickey had three sets of neighbours. Two ground-floor flats were split between a single Irish girl with fragile ankles that almost buckled on her way to work under the weight of a leather briefcase, and a childless professional white couple. The man caught the bus towards the City in the morning while his dumpy blonde wife imported French baby clothes. They grew marijuana under cloches on their back window ledges. Opposite Mickey was a doe-eyed teenager called Claude, who worked in the deli opposite and specialised in chatting up middle-class white women. He gave Mickey the conspiratorial wink of the fellow hunter, which was one of the reasons Mickey preferred to shop at the Jack's Seven Eleven, even though it was less convenient. Mickey was embarrassed because when it came to entrapment, Claude, with his loose-limbed walk and slow smile, was Premiership and Mickey was not even Nationwide League. He corrected himself: *not until now*.

Mickey had to push the flimsy interior door on a spring to close it. 'How's Nigel?' The futon was not made up, a shirt and towel lay across it. Two unfinished pint glasses of water on the floor either side of it signified company that he knew his mother would ignore, if she saw them. More likely she wouldn't notice. To the right, up three steps, the arched door to his studio was shut.

'Oh, you know your uncle.' His mother sat on the edge of the futon. 'What these cement types are like.'

Mickey dumped the suitcase with an exaggerated puff. 'Not really,' he said.

Oblivious to the unmade bed, his mother plumped on the far end, causing a mechanical ruche in the middle, and started skimming the back page of an out-of-date Sunday supplement, 'You know, solid. One of your merchant classes.'

'How about,' he followed her in, kicking CDs out of her path, 'you put the kettle on and I make up the bed?'

'Righto.' She stood up and tossed the magazine behind her. They met shoulder to shoulder in the doorway. She smiled. 'What about a real drink, dear?' she said, coat still buttoned as she strode into the kitchen. 'Got any wine on the go?'

In her position, Mickey thought, he would be looking for clues, the way to Rubik's cube a child's life together in order to say, 'Ah, so that's my son.' His mother, on the other hand, seemed supremely disinterested.

The kitchen's bare bulb starkly showed a used ashtray, half a dozen empty beer bottles and four side plates dusted with toast crumbs. 'I thought not,' said his mother, 'so I brought some. Got a corkscrew?'

He listened to her wrench drawers open as he clunked the futon back together, pummelling the duvet and pillows into the space between it and the wall. He found two plain blue cushions thrown under a book shelf. When she returned he was waiting, straight-backed, one foot crossed over the other.

'Cheers.' She sat down next to him with phoney bonhomie. He was aware of her size and the acidic smell of cheap perfume, both of which seemed too large for the space. Rather than sitting down, his mother collapsed on to seats, as if her knees had given out.

'Poor Patrice.' She held the glass between her thumb and forefinger. 'What a rotten trick. Especially at this time of year.'

'Yeah, cheers,' he replied. He cupped the bulb of his glass, taking two gulps. In his other hand he clenched the remote control, a silent device to warn her what would happen if she continued. Her interest in Patrice irritated him. It was typical of her, this showy interest in the lives of strangers. Neither spoke. Mickey was aware of the chime of early-evening shoppers going in and out of the deli. His mother, lying back, using an empty wine box as a footstool, drifted into a reverie, her toes twitching.

When he could stand it no more, Mickey said, 'Why do you wear those dresses?'

'What dresses?'

'Those hippy Indian things that make you look like you worship the maha-bloody-rishi.'

'The who, dear?'

He didn't reply. She sighed. 'I suppose I must like them,' she said. Mickey was sitting exactly opposite the TV, which he flicked on to an American cartoon.

After two minutes he said, 'So at least tell me what's he up to, then?'

'Who, dear?' She frowned and looked at him. 'Patrice?'

'No, not bloody Patrice.' He leant forward to put his glass down. 'Nigel, of course.'

'I told you. He's very well. He sends his love.' She sat up and started unbuttoning her coat. From next door came shrieks followed by a man's low reprimand, deep, like gravel being dragged by the sea. 'He asked what you're doing for Christmas,' she said. 'I said I thought we would be having it alone.'

'Tell him he can come if he wants to.' Mickey didn't look up from the screen. His mother opened her mouth to speak, then paused.

'So, then, how about something to eat? I'm starved.' She set her glass down on an upturned wooden box with writing in Spanish on the side of it. 'Shall I cook?'

'No,' he said. 'I'll get a takeaway.'

Mickey skulked into the kitchen to phone the order, doubling the size of his usual request and adding a naan bread, without asking his mother.

He popped his head back into the sitting room. 'I won't be a tick,' he told her. 'They don't deliver.'

'Really?' she replied. 'That's unusual.' She'd switched the regional news programme on.

Even though he'd lied about the delivery, Mickey took it as some sort of criticism. 'Yeah,' his tone was flat, 'isn't it?'

He kept his coat unbuttoned. A thin sheen of water reflected by the streetlight turned the pavements a dull aubergine. The drizzle had stopped but still clung to the air in a damp, fetid smell. Mickey skulked, head down, shoulders rounded. On the far corner, the communal glow from the Tube station, with its silhouette of hawkers and drunks, beaconed like a staging post. Six till seven was his witching hour. Opened curtains and subdued coloured rooms, children in primary-coloured all-in-ones tumbling and tottering on the floor. Couples cupping their faces in their hands, elbows propped on scrubbed kitchen tables, pouring red wine into elegant stemmed glasses and comparing days. No telly. He stopped just before home at the deli to pick up four cans of beer.

'You entertaining?' Claude was wearing a green apron knotted at the front, emphasising his slim waist and the mound over his crotch. He raised a single eyebrow and ran his opened palm from his chin over his head to the back of his neck.

'Yeah,' said Mickey. Claude had the most perfect skull he'd ever seen, his hair shaved close to it. 'Give me half a bottle of that whisky.' He pointed to the shelf behind him. Claude whistled. Mickey looked at his change. 'No, hang on. I thought I had another fiver. Just the beer, then.'

Claude lowered the four-pack into a red and white carrier. 'I wish you well, my friend. I hope your,' he smiled as he handed him his change, 'lady friend enjoys lager.' Mickey pocketed the change without checking it. Claude went on. 'Remember what they say, man. Neighbours must look out for each other.'

'How do you mean?' asked Mickey.

'Let me know,' Claude replied, 'if the babe has a sister.' He winked.

Mickey thought of his Auntie Joan. 'Righto,' he said, 'will do.'

Back home, they ate the food decanted from metallic dishes on to mismatching unheated plates in front of the portable. His mother was halfway through her prawn tikka masala, shovelling, Mickey thought, like a Kosovan refugee, when she said, 'Someone called for you, dear, just now.'

'When?'

'When you were out, at the restaurant. Which reminds me, you must let me give some money towards this. I can't—'

Mickey interrupted. No one called him at home. 'Who was it?' he demanded. 'Man or a woman?'

His frenzied tone made his mother bend her head away from the TV to look at him. 'A woman,' she said still chewing. 'She said she'd call back.'

'When? Didn't you ask who it was?'

'I don't know, dear, sometime tonight. I didn't like to pry. Last time you told me not to ask who was calling.'

'Great.' Mickey slouched back on the futon, pushing his plate on the floor.

'If she likes you,' his mother told him, 'she'll call back.'

'What's that supposed to mean?'

'Nothing.'

Mickey told her he was going into his studio and she wasn't to disturb him unless there was another call. She agreed and tucked her feet under her like a teenager, and started watching a black-and-white film. Mickey tutted to himself. Neither of them made any effort to clean the dishes. On the way into his studio, he 1471ed the call and rolled his eyes when he learnt the number had been withheld.

His studio was more an enlarged closet space, a narrow room suspended into the garden atop a non-weight-sustaining roof terrace overlooking railway cuttings. His trestle table fitted into the cubbyhole left by the stairwell below it. His current project, stretched out in front of him, angles under a striped cotton sheet, was his self-portrait in wax. Due to the L-shaped confines of the room, the figure was supine – the legs languid, toes akimbo, with arms crossed over his chest, coffin-style. The pose didn't matter, it was the physicality of it that counted. The colour of the wax was a translucent icy blue, as flat as a sunless winter sky. Mickey smoothed his hands up from the ankle over the distortion of the knee to the swell of the stomach. When he heard his mother call him, Mickey was using a chef's blowtorch at a distance from the chest, moulding the pectorals, hot wax sealing his fingertips. 'Phone,' she called from the futon, 'for you.'

Mickey switched off the gas. 'Hello?' His mother hadn't moved after passing the receiver. Mickey wandered into the kitchen.

'Hiya,' she said. 'It's Sandy.'

'I know.'

'How ya doing?' He hadn't heard that voice before. It was too casual, considering.

'Good, thanks, very well.' He leant against the counter, accidentally putting an elbow on the brown takeaway bag. 'That was my mum,' he added. 'She doesn't live here. She's just staying. She's a dancer.' He paused, waiting for her to speak. When she didn't he said, 'Exotic.'

'Cool,' said Sandy.

'So, how are you?' Mickey asked. He had shut the door but his mother had turned the TV sound up.

'Good, thanks.' There was a pause when Mickey was aware of their breaths booming towards each other down the line. He wanted to ask her where she was but realised it was not, yet, any of his business. 'I thought about you today,' he said, sweaty palms gripping the phone, 'at work.'

Sandy snorted in derision. 'She wasn't in then?'

'Who?' said Mickey, confused.

'Miss Honey Dew, that's who.'

'No, why do you ask?'

'No reason,' said Sandy. 'I was wondering if you wanted to meet up again. I've got to go on this premiere. A film thing. Only I've missed the actual premiere so it'll just be going to the pictures.' She paused. 'I'll just have to make up the premiere stuff, get it from *Hello!* and that.'

'Yeah,' said Mickey. 'That'd be great. When?'

'Tomorrow night.' She stated it as a fact rather than a question. 'Meet me at Leicester Square station at seven.'

'Great,' said Mickey.

'See you, then.'

She hung up. Mickey was too excited to face his mother. He picked up his jacket draped over a kitchen stool and went out. Curtains were drawn now. A couple of suits strode from the Tube, shoulders bunched like they were allergic to air. The queue from the chippy spilt out into the road. Mickey swaggered into the deli.

'I'll put that whisky on this,' he told Claude, showing him a credit card. 'And a big bottle of Diet Coke, please.'

'Sure thing,' said Claude. As he was about to swipe the card, Mickey threw in a women's magazine for his mother. Claude read the headline out loud. '"Twelve secrets you must discover before you meet your lover tonight." Go for it, my son.'

'Sorry?'

'Going well, is it?'

'Oh,' said Mickey, straightening the cover towards him. He shrugged. 'You know how it is.'

'With the ladies,' the words rolled out of Claude's mouth.

'With the ladies,' repeated Mickey.

When he got back his mother had fallen asleep on the sofa. She had released her hair from a French plait, and a thick hank, dotted with grey, fell over her face. Mickey had stopped for a swig of whisky on the way home, taking a detour, leaning with his back to the cemetery wall, listening to the commuter trains groan as they stopped and started, feeling the vibration along his back; like ECT, plugging himself into the mains of London.

'Care for a nightcap, Mum?'

She sat up, one hand against her head like she was shoving a nightmare away while the other flexed into fists repeatedly to stave off pins and needles. 'Why not?' She stretched. 'Then I really must unpack.'

'You have the futon,' said Mickey, pouring the drinks in the kitchen so she couldn't see the nip he'd had. 'I'll sleep in the studio.'

'Well, it won't be for long,' his mother told him.

'Whatever.'

Mickey drank his whisky neat and poured Coke in his mother's. He wanted to tell her about Sandy. Had resolved to, if she'd asked. But she didn't. She told him about the gig, how it had come about. Where the other 'girls' were staying: Pammy with her sister in Hendon and Elaine at a guest house in Victoria.

'What's Nigel doing these days?' Mickey asked. 'You seem to be seeing a lot of him.' Mickey was on his third glass, the bottle an inch off empty.

'Not really, dear.'

'You've known him, how long?'

'You know perfectly well how long,' his mother told him. 'We were at university together.'

'That's right,' said Mickey, staring into his glass, pretending to mull it over. 'Just about twenty-eight years.'

His mother nodded.

'He never married,' said Mickey. 'Did he? Funny that, good-looking chap, good career. Didn't he stand for Parliament once? Quite a catch. He's not gay, is he?'

'No, of course not.' His mother frowned and brushed hair from her face. 'He just never found the right woman. It does happen.'

'Keen on you, though.'

'We're friends. Always have been. He liked looking out for you when you were little. Babysat sometimes, gave you little gifts.'

'Birthdays, Christmases—'

'That sort of thing. Please, Michael, don't start all this again.'

'All what?' Mickey finished his drink.

His mother said, 'You know what I mean.' She stood up. 'I'd like a bath now, please. Then I'm going to bed.'

'Suit yourself,' he said. Mickey stayed where he was, anxious not to be near the sound of running water. He tucked aside a sweatshirt drying on the radiator and poured the rest of the whisky into his glass. Cheap whisky made him morose. Where had he heard someone say that before? Ah, that was right. Nigel, the Christmas before last.

Chapter Four

I

The billboard in Wardour Street read, 'Day seven and the nation counts on . . .' Honey Dew was sitting on a back-to-front chair, this time her breasts obscured by two green velvet arms. The tone of the caption was authoritative, even sententious, as if it was trying to give a global feel to the event. That morning's *Pump* horoscope warned Mickey that a clash in Venus meant he must watch out for interlopers. He read Sandy's column and smiled an insider's smile.

'How's your mum?' Ray looked up with his eyebrows arched, crinkling his brown forehead into rivulets. 'Jade said she was stopping with yer.'

Mickey straightened up. 'You know parents.'

'Well,' said Ray, rubbing his nose and shrugging, 'you haven't got them for ever.' He picked up his mug. 'Which reminds me.'

Mickey wiped his hands under his armpits. 'What?'

'You'll need to call at Honey Dew's place. For the negligée – for what she was wearing when she bounced off the show. She called before you got here: she was planning to drop it off but she can't make it, got a telly thing. Wants one of us to pick it up. I told her you'd go.'

'Cheers,' protested Mickey. 'I've got the other one to do.' He thought saying Sandy's name might jinx it.

'Which other one?'

Mickey didn't reply.

'Oh, that Sandy bird. The skinny one. Look, no one cares about an also-ran. Getting Honey up and running is our main priority, especially before she gets her norks out. I told her you'd pop in tonight. If she's not in she said she'd leave it with the concierge. The address is by the phone. Chelsea Harbour or some such place.' He shook his head and pinched his chin. 'I tell you, Michael, the places no talent and a double E cup can get you these days.'

Mickey had jerked himself upright. 'I can't,' he protested, 'not tonight. I'm going out.'

'Where?' asked Ray, resting the small of his back in the bench behind Mickey.

'None of your business.'

'Look, Mickey, don't jerk me around.'

Mickey stood with his back to him.

'I need you to get that fucking negligée tonight. I need that model up this weekend.' Mickey heard the insistent tap of a pencil on a wooden surface. 'You know you're not the only out-of-work sculptor in the world.' Ray threw the pencil, rattling it into a corner, then stood up and made to leave.

'OK,' Mickey said, 'keep your hair on. I'll go.'

II

'How's work?' Dr Adebayo was lying back in his chair, legs crossed, with two all-leather burnished black brogues resting on his desk. Mickey's general demeanour was one of dampness, his hair made moist by the fine afternoon drizzle and his boots wet from puddles.

'Not bad,' Mickey said, replying to the doctor's casualness by arching his knees out and leaning back. 'Actually, do you want the truth?'

'I would expect so.'

Mickey laced his fingers together and cradled his fists in his lap. 'Then, I spent all morning trying to convert a second-hand Teasmade to lactate out of a waxwork statue of Madonna.'

'*The* Madonna?'

'If you mean by that,' said Mickey, 'the one married to Guy Ritchie then, yes, *the* Madonna.'

'I see,' said the doctor. He frowned, took a pencil from behind his ear and tapped it on the side of the A4 pad on his lap. Together they formed a companionable forum.

Mickey let his eyes roam the room. At ninety degrees to both of them he read the title of a SOAS pamphlet entitled 'Smashing the Eurocentric Model', in a bold triangular font.

After half a minute's silence, Mickey said, 'I'm sorry, I didn't mean to shock you. I just thought if I gave you some sort of idea about what I did, the sort of things my job entails, it might help you to understand that I'm not as mad as you might think I am.'

'Do you think you're mad?'

'Sorry?'

'Perhaps,' said the doctor, 'you could give me an example of your compulsions.'

'My nuttiness,' interjected Mickey.

'Your words,' the doctor told him.

'OK then,' said Mickey, shifting his gaze to the book shelf, 'I turn the handles of all my mugs to the same angle before I leave the house.'

'Mmm,' said the doctor.

'And,' Mickey went on, 'I put my clothes on in a certain order, or always enter a building with my right foot, or count the number of steps—'

'Precisely,' said the doctor, putting a pink palm, latticed with the lines of a treasure map, in the air. 'It's all for what end, exactly?'

Mickey pulled his hands apart and slid them under him. 'I

dunno, really.' Inside his head he heard, 'Step on a crack, you'll break your mother's back.' 'It stops stuff happening.'

'Have you got any evidence of that?'

'What, like my lucky gonk helped me pass my maths GCSE?'

The doctor sighed through a smile. 'Does it ward off fears of death?'

'Not really,' admitted Mickey. 'It's more all round than that.'

The doctor looked at his watch. 'It must be a childhood thing.'

'Oh great,' said Mickey. 'What's childhood got to do with it? My childhood was A1 hunkydory, thank you very much.' He flushed and was aware his right hand had left the warm space under his thigh and was drumming a forefinger on the doctor's desk. He inhaled and held the breath in his lungs. 'What it is, Doctor,' he told him, 'is like, don't you ever think that if you just changed a couple of things in your life, then everything would come out normal? If you just ate the right combination of food or read the right book? I think there's one giant secret out there that only a few people know about.'

'Only in your case the secret is putting your socks on before your underpants.'

'Pretty much.' Mickey sat back and relaced his fingers.

'Do *I* know the secret?' the doctor probed.

Mickey sized him up, how the seams on his shirt rested exactly on the swell of his shoulder; he thought of his wife the QC and little Horace and Queenie. 'Yeah, Doc, I think you might.'

'And what if I told you that I don't, that there is no secret and I think your superstitious behavioural patterns were likely formed in early adulthood?' His fingers played with a spiral notebook.

In the sudden silence Mickey said, 'Then I'd say it's just as well I've got my lucky stone with me.'

The doctor used the sharpened end of his pencil to scratch his head. His smile was taut. 'When can you set up your next appointment?'

'Soon as you like,' Mickey told him.

'Good,' said the doctor, 'see the receptionist on the way out.'

The cadence of the sentence fell in a final sort of way. Mickey stood up and reached out for the doctor's hand. 'Thanks, Doc,' he said, 'though I had wanted to touch on a couple of more personal issues.'

'Next time,' the doctor told him. 'Good luck,' he added, not looking up from his pad. Then he looked up and added, 'Sorry, force of habit, no offence.'

'None taken, mate,' Mickey told him, pulling the heavy door towards him and aligning his footwork so he stepped across the threshold with the right.

III

'Weird, that.' Inside the cinema, Mickey hadn't dared drape his arm round her, only just snaking his hand along the back of the padded seat. But outside it was Sandy who threaded herself round him, tucking her hand into his back pocket in the crowd of people frothing down the steps into Leicester Square. The film was a romantic comedy set in New York about a subway busker and a society heiress, aimed to capture teenagers on school holiday. It wasn't his sort of film. He spent the time counting the seats and the wall tiles surrounding the stage. Every time it came out with an odd number meant he would sleep with Sandy again.

'What?'

'Covering a premiere,' said Mickey, 'that's already showing.'

'Don't ask me,' she said. 'It's that paper. You know what they're like.'

'Not really,' admitted Mickey.

She screwed her nose up and buried her face in her scarf. '"Man's hat blows off, see inside pages for full-colour details", that sort of thing. Making news out of nothing.'

'Someone must like it,' Mickey told her.

'Tittle-tattle and gossip. Personally, I can't stand it. Like a load of old women. Worse, really.' She pulled her hand from his pocket and skipped in front of him. Without heels the crown of her head reached the crook of his armpit. Inside her coat he noticed a bare strip of toffee-coloured stomach that swelled as she moved. 'Nah,' she said, pushing him towards a wall of protein-rich American teenagers spread out in a swagger across the pavement, 'let's get some ice cream.'

His face fell.

'What's up with you, don't you like ice cream?'

'Actually,' he told her, 'it makes me sick.'

'How come?'

He shrugged and half smiled. 'Childhood thing.' He snagged down a feeling of panic. 'Don't let me stop you, though.'

They sat at the booth nearest the window, looking out into the square, where two men dressed as robots had attracted a crowd. Mickey elbowed the previous occupants' plastic plates away. When she lodged herself opposite him, unzipped her anorak and loosened her scarf, cradling her chin in her hands, he could see the curve of her breasts. He sipped a plastic beaker of cappuccino.

'So, how's it coming along?' Every time she took a spoonful she poked her tongue out to guide it in.

'What?'

'My waxwork, you doofers.' She put the plastic spoon down and stared straight at him. Her lower lashes were clogged with dark mascara in the corners and she had a smudge of black under her left eye.

'Actually, no offence,' he said, 'but it's a bit back burner at the moment. Ray's gone bonkers about getting me to finish Honey's.' He pulled his cuffs down. 'Celebrity doesn't last for ever, that's what Ray keeps telling us.' He put on an Irish accent. 'They're like buses: wait five minutes and another one's along. He wants to cash in on this whole publicity drive the *Pump*'s doing.'

As soon as it was out, he was aware he'd said the wrong thing. Sandy buttoned her coat up and wrapped her scarf another turn around her neck. She stared over his shoulder, her gaze too unfocused to be reading a poster on the origins of ice cream. Then she blinked. 'Still don't fancy one?' she asked.

Mickey glanced down. 'Er, no.'

'Well, I feel like some chocolate fudge sundae.'

'Go for it,' said Mickey, limply pushing his chair back from the table so she could get out. Her bottom jostled against a low dado rail at which the décor turned from light to dark blue. 'You know, I didn't mean you,' he said when she returned with two melting brown scoops. 'The celebrity thing. I mean, you're different.' He pushed his plate away and fingered a glass American-style sugar dispenser sticky with handprints.

'Like how?' Their knees clashed as she sat down.

'Well, you seem to me to be in it for the money, I guess. You're not star struck like the others. You're not in it for the fame.'

'Not like Honey,' said Sandy.

'I don't know about her.'

'She got the money, though, didn't she?'

Mickey didn't speak. He concentrated on a Japanese family behind them, all four of them eating in silence. Sandy licked the back of her spoon, the pink tongue stained brown. 'Maybe you're right.' She suddenly tossed the spoon down and sat back. 'A girl likes to be appreciated, though.'

'Sure,' agreed Mickey. 'Look,' checking his watch, 'talking of Honey, there's something I really have to do.'

'Oh yeah,' said Sandy, 'like what?'

'Pick something up.'

She frowned. 'What's that got to do with Honey?'

Mickey said, 'It's her negligée.' He felt her bridle. He went on, 'The pink one she was wearing when she won. I wasn't going to bring it up, because I know you still have some hostility issues with her.'

'Mmm,' said Sandy. 'Hostility issues.' She rolled the words around her mouth along with the fudge sundae. 'You could say that.'

'But as you mentioned her—'

'Pick up,' said Sandy, 'as in from her house?'

'Yeah, it's—'

'Take me with you.'

'I'm sorry?'

'Take me with you.' She said it urgently, like a demand. When she spoke he noticed that her lips barely moved. It was definite. So definite that Mickey believed if he was ever going to feel a live nipple again, he had better do as she said.

IV

Some nights Carlo Franchetti kept his salon open until as close to ten as he could justify from a heating and lighting point of view. The run-up to Christmas was a dead duck. He'd be busy the days just before the twenty-fifth with seasonal trims for young men returning to their mothers, and older men giving in to their wives' requests, but three weeks before it was all drinking and office parties. He was on the verge of telling Andy to haul in his 'Haircuts while you wait' sign from the pavement when the doorbell rang.

The man filled the doorway so entirely that when Carlo looked up from the local free sheet he was reading, the red and silver lanterns from the Chinese restaurant opposite were blocked out. The man, wearing a dark green double-breasted coat that seemed to be cut from a tarpaulin, paused, either waiting to be asked in, or just getting his bearings. When Carlo asked if he'd like him to take the coat, he refused as if Carlo had implied he was about to steal it.

'How you like it, sir?'

The man said, 'I don't know,' not as if he didn't care, more as if he was surprised to be asked. 'An inch off all over?'

Carlo was watching his face in the mirror. When he spoke it was unanimated apart from a pink slug of lower lip moving atop a ginger beard. His hair was bristly and lifeless but the scalp was warm, as if he'd just swiped off a hat.

'Certainly, sir.' Carlo swirled a green poncho over his head and slid a comb from a glass jar of disinfectant.

After twenty years of cutting hair, Carlo knew the customers who were happy to talk, something about the attitude of the chin. Usually confided more than they wanted to. He knew why. It was to do with the mirror. English were inhibited from childhood. No eye contact. They only ever let their guards down when they were drunk. But at the barber's, the mirror removed the need for eye contact. Beards usually signified silence, but here was a man who wanted to speak.

'What you think?' Carlo asked. 'It come on to rain again?'

The man raised his eyebrows, pulling the lines around his cheeks up too. 'No, not now. Clouds are too low. Pressure's wrong and, besides that, the wind from the south is too warm.'

'Blimey,' said Carlo. 'What are you? Weatherman? Celebrity status, maybe?'

The man shook his head and snorted a laugh of derision, making Carlo lose his grip on a tress of hair.

'So,' Carlo went on, 'you local?'

'Not to London,' he told Carlo. 'I mean not originally. I live here now. Have done for seven years. Got my own business. I run a pleasure cruiser. Moored just past Vauxhall Bridge.'

'Really?' said Carlo. 'That's what I like. Enterprise.' He jerked his back upwards to show the customer his smile in the mirror. 'Not so many people like you and me, these days. Most people they want to work for the big company, the big salon. No individual status, none whatsoever.'

The man looked at Carlo in the mirror and carried on looking as he spoke. 'It's in their natures. You can't blame them for that.'

Carlo could blame anyone who worked for Toni & Guy. 'I

guess not,' he said. Clumps of hair, light grey and ginger, fanned on to the linoleum. Carlo cut on in silence. The radio played an old Christmas hit, rasped by an old singer who disguised his voice with a fizz of bells.

'How is it then, business?' asked Carlo. 'Quiet now, no?'

'Winter always is.'

Neither spoke. Carlo held his breath as he trimmed around the ears. Long lobes, both of which had been pierced. The man cleared his throat, jogging Carlo, making him tut, then he said, 'I know one of your clients.'

'Really?' said Carlo.

'Yeah,' said the man. 'I've seen him coming here before.'

Carlo was guarded. 'Like who?'

'Tall chap. Young. Well, youngish. His name's Michael.'

'Nah,' said Carl, 'you're not ringing no bells.'

'Works near here. He works near here. Some gallery—'

'Ah Mickey!' said Carlo. 'Why you not say? Yeah, sure I know him. Mickey's a great kid. Kinda reminds me how I was when I was younger. Apart from he's not messing with the women like I was.'

'How do you mean?'

Carlo stood up and shifted his weight on to his left leg. 'You know, laid-back, like he doesn't care for nothing.' Neither of them spoke. Carlo went back to cutting hair. Then he said, 'Great kid, talented. He waste himself with the titties made of wax. How do you know him?'

The man said, 'Well, I don't, not really.' He had somehow shaken Carlo away from his hair so they were both looking at each other in the mirror, Carlo with his scissors still poised. 'I'm keen to find out more about him, though.'

Carlo frowned. 'What are you, the fuzz or some sort of pervert? You want to know about Mickey, you go and ask him yourself. Carlo is no snitch, no sir-ree.'

'Fair enough,' said the man. 'No big deal. He helped me once

– saved me, more like. I got in some difficulty on the water. He rescued me.'

'Mickey? Hero?' Carlo stood up. 'Well, I'll be buggered.'

'Don't say anything about it,' said the man. 'He might be embarrassed. You know what kids are like.'

'Well,' said Carlo, returning to the scalp, 'Mickey Defoe, the hero. Hah!'

V

They took the Tube to Earls Court, changed on to the District Line and got off at Fulham Broadway, all north of the river. Mickey considered getting a bus from the Underground because the longer the mission took, the more reluctant it might make Sandy to return home on her own. Then she stuck her hand out for a taxi.

'What a dump,' she said. 'It's worse than King's Lynn. What does she want to live in a place like this for?'

'Well, a lot of people consider it one of London's more fashionable addresses.'

He was going to reel off a few to make him sound connected, but he couldn't think of any. 'Jeffrey Archer, for one.'

'He's in the nick,' replied Sandy. 'Don't blame him either, if I had to look at this every morning.' She pressed her nose against the taxi window. 'It's like a lunar landscape gone wrong.'

The taxi's rear-side wheel caught the kerb of a mini roundabout, Sandy gave a short yelp and fell into Mickey. 'Sorry, mate,' the cabbie called.

'Whoops,' said Sandy, pulling away but not before Mickey had smelt her hair, the same smell of wool drying as two nights ago. Sandy said, 'Are we nearly there yet? Which one is it?' She was now wedged beside him, gripping the seat-belt fastener in one fist and overhead strap in the other.

'Look,' said Mickey. 'All things considered, I think it would be better if you didn't come in with me.'

'What do you mean,' Sandy looked at him, '*all things considered*?' She snorted and went back to looking out of the window. 'You make me sound like some sort of petty criminal.'

'No,' said Mickey slowly. 'It's just that less than forty-eight hours ago,' his voice strained not to be heard by the driver, 'you came up with the idea that you would like to kill this woman.'

'Oh, rubbish,' said Sandy, letting go of the strap and shifting her weight towards him. 'That was because you made me drink so much. Who do you think I am?' She shook her head. 'You forget that I spent two weeks with the woman. I'd like to see her again. Find out what she's been up to. How life is treating her, that sort of thing. Besides all that, it'd be good for my column.'

Three identical towers, each topped by a different coloured pyramid roof, rose out of riverside wasteland on their left. Every other apartment had a balcony staining the wall underneath with a wash of acidic rainfall. Rancid urban boxes, thought Mickey.

'Well, I still think it'd be better if you waited for me,' he said.

'What,' Sandy replied, 'if you're embarrassed about our relationship? Worried what she might think seeing us together—'

'No, of course not.' He turned to see her face in the streak of blurred lights as they drove past an arcade of antiques shops. In the pause that followed, he tried to rotate the word 'relationship' in his mind. But above the sound of blood trammelling suddenly through his brain, he couldn't grasp it.

'Where do you want, mate?' The cabbie switched his overhead light on and pulled into a bay past a bus stop. Other than a ragtag huddle of cleaners with shoulders bunched against the wind, not a soul stirred. The recently resurfaced road, lined with leafless tree stumps draped in white fairy lights, was free from traffic.

They were dropped next to a yellow dump truck open to the elements where someone had stuck a mangy fir tree into the driver's seat. An upturned sledgehammer frozen in the earth gave the impression that it was growing. The taxi left in a belch of cloudy carbon monoxide, leaving them surrounded by a quiet so deep, Mickey could hardly believe they were in London.

He gathered his coat and looked round, trying to get his bearings, instinctively turning away from the oily gloss of the Thames in front to the left. To calm himself, he totted up the number of lights shining from windows in the block before him. Eleven.

'Christ alive,' said Sandy, 'it's freezing. Do you think we should have kept hold of that taxi?' She had her back to him, watching it drive away. 'It's pretty dead around here.'

Mickey came up behind her and put his arm round her shoulders, pulling her towards him. 'Don't worry,' he told her, 'something will turn up.'

They started awkwardly towards the first tower block, her two strides to his one.

Gusts of damp wind, squalling off the water, funnelled between the buildings and hit their faces like frozen steel.

'What's that noise?' Sandy kept her neck bent towards the pavement. 'That jangling noise like sleigh bells?'

Mickey heard the tinkling sound two steps after Sandy, stopping to turn his head to the direction of the noise.

'It's the halyards clinking against the masts. There's a dock here, for private yachts.' The sound made Mickey's insides wring out in a contortion of memory, making him dizzy and leaden at the same time. He stood still while his head spun. At the same time he felt his bowels fall, making him grip his buttocks together.

'What's up?' she asked.

He didn't speak, just waited for a blast of cold wind to dry the perspiration from his face.

'Weird, it is,' said Sandy, who waited next to him, thinking he was just trying to place the noise. 'Eerie,' she said. 'Like ghosts rattling their chains.' She shook her head in an involuntary spasm, allowing Mickey to catch the smell of her saccharine breath. 'Are you sure there's nothing wrong?'

'No,' Mickey said, 'it's nothing,' trying to smile. 'That noise. It reminds me of when I was a kid. This place by the sea my mum used to take me to catch crabs.'

'Yuk.'

He pulled his arm off her shoulder and turned left up a flight of polished marble stairs. His voice was thin. 'Come on, this is it.'

'What do we do?' She followed him up the stairs.

'If she's not in she said she'd leave it with the concierge.'

'It's a lot of fuss for a bloody negligée, if you ask me.'

'I thought you wanted to come.'

'I do,' said Sandy. 'I'm just saying.'

The double doors opened automatically into a metre-long cavity, where heaters blasted warm air from either side. As they walked through, another glass entrance slid open, leading them into a wide, high-ceilinged reception. Both walls and floor were of limestone-coloured marble flecked with brown. The desk, which seemed to rise seamlessly from the same block, was in perfect opposition to a solid man-sized modern sculpture, with a series of varying holes gauged out of bronze. Its angles caught the sunken lights, making the inescapable impression that it would soon discolour to verdigris. Mickey felt the familiar gnaw of regret when he saw a well-proportioned bronze – the gnaw that he was wasting his time with celebrity waxworks. A rectangular black leather settee backed the window.

'Can I help you, sir?'

'Yeah, actually you can.' Mickey approached the man behind the desk. He was wearing a light tan uniform in flimsy cotton with dark brown lapels. He had the sunken cheeks and grooved face of a shiftworker. Mickey's heeled boots clicked officiously on the marble, whereas Sandy's trainers slid soundlessly. 'I'm here to see Miss Honey Dew. Number forty-six.'

The receptionist's slab of face fell. 'I'm afraid Miss Dew has already left for the evening.' He made her sound like a call girl. He was keeping an eye out for Sandy, who had joined Mickey, a few inches behind his elbow.

She said, 'When did she say she's going to be back, then?'

'On that point, miss,' said the receptionist, 'I'm afraid I have no idea. I'm not here to keep tabs on the residents.'

'No?' she replied. 'What are you here for then?'

'Sandy . . .' said Mickey.

'Well . . .' She exhaled and looked at her feet, kicking her toes against the reception desk. 'If you want my opinion, this place is hardly better than a caravan park, so there's no need to be so snooty.'

Mickey edged forward. 'Did Miss Dew leave anything for me in reception? My name is Michael Defoe. It's a bundle, a sort of parcel,' he prompted.

The receptionist righted himself, red-faced, keeping the Tesco bag at arm's length as if it housed a dangerous animal. 'Would this be it?'

Sandy spluttered a snort of laughter. 'Cheap cow,' she said, loud enough for Mickey to hear.

'Yeah,' he told him, 'that'll be it, cheers.' He turned to the door, bag under his arm, hands rooted in his coat pockets, bracing himself against the cold and the sounds from the marina.

Sandy said, 'Can't we at least go up there?'

'No,' he told her. 'Why are you so keen to see where she lives? Anyone would have thought you'd have seen enough of her in that house.'

'This is different,' said Sandy. 'I told you why.'

'Yeah,' Mickey was walking ahead, shoulders hunched, hoping not to hear the boats again. 'Your vendetta.'

'That's right,' Sandy replied, 'my vendetta.' Mickey kept walking. 'Anyway,' she went on, 'I've got what I wanted.'

'Oh, yeah, what's that?' He looked over both shoulders for transport away from the complex. When he checked on her,

Sandy's head was down, her hair scraped back by the wind as she pushed into it.

'The number,' she said, a cold trail of spittle leaking out of the side of her mouth. 'I now know where she lives. Thanks to you.'

Mickey wasn't sure if she meant genuinely to thank him or she was implying she'd caught him out. He stopped at a temporary bus stop without a shelter.

'So what form is it going to take?' he asked her. She went to the lee side of him, using him as a windbreak. 'This vendetta of yours?'

'Look.' She tried to catch his eye. 'How would you like it if someone cheated you out of a hundred thousand?' Before he could reply she cut him off. 'Honey Dew is a scheming bitch. Once I get my share of the money back, I'll forget about her.'

'And how do you plan on doing that?'

'Ah ha.' She tapped the side of her nose with her forefinger.

'In other words,' said Mickey, 'you don't know.'

'For your information I am currently pursuing two lines of enquiry.'

'Really?' said Mickey.

'Yeah, really.'

Mickey had the sinking feeling he was coming to the end of his usefulness. Neither spoke as a black Mercedes with darkened windows and an Arabic number plate drove past, its tyres shattering frozen puddles. After a minute's silence, which Mickey spent counting the stars, making a pact with himself that if he could see more than ten, Sandy would move in with him, a yellow Hopper bus trundled round the corner. Despite his raised arm, it didn't pull in to their stop. Mickey made a grab for Sandy's hand and came up with bare skin at the top of her wrists.

'Come on,' he said. They ran after it as far as the first junction. Reluctantly the driver pressed his door release button.

'Against the law, that,' he told them.

'Very much appreciated,' said Mickey.

'Still, it's no time for a youngster to be out, is it?' Sandy had already sat down in the seat reserved for disabled passengers.

'Exactly,' said Mickey. 'One and a half to Fulham Broadway, please.'

The patter of bus chat stood still until Mickey had buffeted his way to the seats. As the bus pulled away he collapsed next to Sandy.

'You see?' She sounded triumphant. Mickey saw little apart from a tar-black landscape and the fact that she now owed him fifty pence. She was craning her head towards the back of the bus. Most of their fellow passengers were Asian or black, wedged into seats, spiralling bursts of laughter, one or two of them with plastic bags hauled on to their laps.

'Cleaners,' said Sandy.

'Odd time to clean,' Mickey told her. His watch now read 10.51 p.m. It was the first chance he'd had to open the bag. He untwisted the neck and peered in, a scent so sweet and familiar, of powder puffs and make-up, oozed up his nostrils. The bag must have been kept by a radiator because, even now, it retained heat. The negligée was crumpled in the bottom. 'Smells like my mum's handbag used to,' he said, holding it under Sandy's nose.

'Yuk,' she said. 'Probably hasn't even washed it. The filthy cow.' She swatted it away from her with a tiny unravelled palm. 'You're not listening to me.'

'What?'

'It's not an odd time to clean,' she told him. 'I used to do it. This is a good time to do it, especially if you've got another job. It's quiet and . . .'

'And what?' Mickey relaxed his body so it leant lightly on her.

'And the person you're cleaning for isn't there.' The bus slowed between two sleeping policemen, speeded up and then braked again.

'Fascinating,' said Mickey. 'Listen, Sandy.' He turned his face to hers, pushing his coat collar down with his chin. 'It's late and it's not really safe for young girls to be roaming London at this time of year. I would ask you back to mine, but, as you know, my mother's staying.' He paused, inwardly urging her to turn her face from the window to look at him. 'What I mean is, I am prepared to escort you back to your hotel tonight.'

'Sorry?'

'I mean, I really don't mind at all. In fact—' The momentum of the slowing bus had flushed out three passengers, towards the exit, where '*bus stopping*' was lit up in green. One after the other, Mickey was bashed on the shoulder by three carrier bags.

'Our stop,' said Sandy, making to stand. 'Look, it's very kind of you and that. But I reckon I can get home OK.'

'Right,' said Mickey, letting her out first. 'Sure, I know that, it's just that—'

A sharp, hard angle caught him in the back of the knees. 'Is this your stop or isn't it?' The woman's hair was woven over her scalp in precise inch-apart furrows. The skin between looked so smooth and tender, Mickey wanted to stroke his finger along the groove.

'Yes, it is. I'm sorry.'

By the time he caught up with Sandy she was waiting outside the Tube, bouncing up and down on her heels. Her expression read as if she'd been standing there for three hours rather than three minutes.

'What kept you?' she said, not expecting nor wanting a reply. 'I've got to go.' She bounced up to peck him lightly on the cheek. He was expecting cold but her lips were warm and moist. She said, 'Thanks for everything. I'll be seeing you.' She turned towards the trains as a scuffle broke out at the ticket counter.

Mickey felt cut loose. He had no number for her and no address. 'I was thinking,' he said. 'If you're stuck for things to write about, I know a dance troupe that's about to debut.' Sandy turned at the ticket barriers. He went on, 'It'll be good.

I might even get you an interview with one of the principal dancers.'

Sandy shrugged. 'OK,' she said. 'I'll call you.'

'Great,' said Mickey, nodding as he watched her narrow back slide through the fenders into the station. 'Great,' he repeated to himself, feeling in his pocket as he made his way to get a ticket to Westminster from where he could walk. Never had the Movers and Shakers had so much to do.

VI

He caught Honey's picture on the way to work when he cut through on to the Mall and walked past the ICA. The pressure was on to finish the waxwork of Honey Dew and, anyway, he felt the need to ration his mother's company. Already the flat was feeling tinier with her presence, and the appeal of working on a Saturday was somehow increased. This morning's poster was a collage, jagged, but definitely her. The caption read 'Six days till the big ones.' It was difficult to see what she was wearing but the prominent colour of the photo was flesh. Mickey had a feeling it was getting your tits out but in a post-modern way. The other advert was for ninety-nine per cent fat-free dog food. Mickey couldn't decide if it was irony or not.

VII

Sandy had two calls to make, although the second was dependent on the results of the first. For exaggerated worries about security she didn't want to use her mobile. Luckily she was no stranger to the telephone box. She asked Mr Eghbal for as many twenty-pence pieces as he could spare for the Launderette.

'You got any space in the drum,' he told her, using both thumbs to yank his grey underpants over his waistband, 'you take these.' Then he started unzipping his flies to hoots of laughter from Mr O'Leary and Mr Sudulka, still lolling in the dining room though it had gone three.

'I seriously doubt if that problem will arise,' she replied, yanking her fist away from him when he went to clutch her hand.

The telephone box fluttered with hookers' fliers and smelt of old cigarette butts and urine that she found comforting in the same way she enjoyed the fuggy closeness of the B&B. She propped her back on the shelf, where the strap underlining the words 'Letitia loves Dean' was stabbed in the intricate pokerwork of a lit cigarette. The call was answered on the seventh ring – so late in fact she had been on the verge of hanging up and redialling.

'Riviera House, hello.'

'Hello, Geoff?' Sandy had caught his name from the security tag the night before.

'Yes.'

'Geoff, this is Honey Dew, from apartment forty-six. I was wondering if you couldn't do me the most ginormous favour?' She didn't wait for a reply. Sandy knew enough of Honey's Midlands accent to fool the receptionist. Especially, she'd gambled, since Honey was unlikely ever to have spoken to him. 'I'm at a gala reception and I've just remembered I have a new cleaner starting today. I can't get back so I was wondering if you'd be a poppet and use your security key to let her in.'

'There are procedures about this sort of thing.' He sounded put out.

'Right. And I know you'll check her credentials. Hang on a sec.' Sandy held the receiver next to her bag as she riffled through it. 'These are the details.' She pretended to read. 'The company name is We Keep Our Promises. She's supposed to be there at seven. But you know what these women are like.'

'Odd time for a cleaner, isn't it?'

'Oh, you know me. I hate to be disturbed during the day.'

'I've strict instructions not to use these keys for anything less than an emergency. Can't you call the agency?'

'This is an emergency. I have *Hello!* magazine coming to interview me tomorrow.'

'Oh, well,' said Geoff. 'Well, why didn't you say so in the first place? We can't let our friends in the media down, can we?' For a split second Sandy thought he was being sarcastic, then she sensed he was serious.

'Exactly, Geoff.' She smiled and added, 'Oh Geoff, that's my car. I must dash.' She made a *mwah* noise down the line.

Geoff chuckled. 'And don't worry about that cleaner. I'll see to it. Have a good night, madam, and,' his voice, Sandy noticed, had changed from supercilious to deferential, 'enjoy your gala.'

Sandy hung up and looked over both shoulders in case a queue had begun. Shop lights had started to flicker on and a brightly made-up woman, eyelids shiny as a chameleon, tottering outside in a pair of high-heeled mules made her think of home and the fact she had failed in her promise to call. She rummaged in her purse between screwed-up receipts and bulky coppers for the card. Then she propped it against her bag and took a deep breath. It was an outer London number.

'Hello, is that Kenny Russel?'

'Speaking.'

'The documentary maker?'

'The very same.'

'Hello, you might not remember meeting me. My name is Sandy West. We met at a launch the other day.'

'Correct,' said Kenny. 'I remember. That was the selfsame day that jumped-up trout turned me down.'

'Really?' said Sandy. 'Who, Honey Dew? What for?'

'Well, hardly a dinner dance at the Ritz. Of course the bloody documentary. Couldn't believe it. I've had bloody Baftas in my time. In fact I'm looking at three of them at the moment. Best wildlife sequence, best underwater cinematography and the best bloody use of camouflage. I ask you.'

Sandy sounded plaintive. 'I'm sorry she turned you down.'

'Her funeral,' said Kenny, and sniffed.

'That's what I was calling about,' said Sandy. 'Not her funeral as such – I don't mean that. I've got an idea for a doc.'

'Shoot,' said Kenny. Sandy heard him sink into an armchair.

VIII

'Nigel?' Jennifer Defoe jammed the receiver between her ear and shoulder using both hands to pull apart an old tissue. 'It's Jenny. I'm sorry to disturb you. It's Michael.'

'Hello, Jen. How are you?' He didn't wait for a reply. 'What about Michael?'

'He's got that idea again. That idea of you being his father.'

'What's brought all this on?'

'Oh, I don't know,' she sighed, exasperated. 'It's the red hair.'

'But I haven't got red hair.'

'I know that, darling,' said Jennifer. 'He says your sister has.'

'Enid?' She listened to a yawn turned away from the receiver. 'So what?'

'Red hair denotes a regressive gene.'

'A what?'

'That's what I said. It means it must be in both families. I, of course, have natural auburn hair. Enid is, apparently, a reddish brown, and so, of course, is Michael.'

Nigel groaned. 'What's brought all this on this time?'

'You know how he flares up. There doesn't have to be a reason. Half the time I swear he just uses it as an excuse to have a go at me. You know children. Think the world revolves around them. You know what he said the other day?'

'Surprise me.'

'That I only had him as part of some Bohemian gesture. Everything I did was to "buck the trend". His words, not mine.'

'But you gave up everything for that boy.'

Jennifer nodded. 'He even brought up the time I apparently talked him out of studying law and *made* him take art. I said it wasn't me that *made* him do art, it was two Es in his A levels. He said I called it "bourgeois and mediocre, the province of provincials". I mean, it doesn't even make sense . . .' She tailed off.

'Called what bourgeois?'

'Law. Oh, Nigel, do pay attention, this is serious. He even wanted to know if he had any brothers or sisters. Said it would affect the future of his children.'

'What children?'

'Precisely.'

For seven beats neither of them spoke. Then Nigel stifled another yawn – not boredom; Jennifer had seen him do it before. It was more a way of bringing extra oxygen to his brain. He said, 'I suppose you think it's time we told him the truth?'

'Could you bear to, darling?'

Nigel said, 'Doesn't look like we've got a great deal of choice, does it?'

IX

Mickey was too listless to work.

'What's up with you, handsome?' He hadn't noticed Jade come through with two empty mugs clenched in one hand. 'Your mum getting you down?'

'No, not really.'

'What is it then, babes?' She was wearing a tracksuit top unzipped to under her chest and a pair of grey combat trousers, too short, so that, even in the semilight of the studio, he could see a hairless brown ankle. She was a twin. Her sister, Amber, was prone to depression. Jade said she felt responsible for her mood swings, as if she'd sapped all the good nutrients from their mother's womb, which was why she was so tall, while her sister was a full head shorter.

He said, 'Just stuff.'

Jade said nothing but raised a mug, asking if he wanted tea. Mickey shook his head. When she was filling the kettle, humming, he called in, 'Everyone has something they don't like, don't they?'

'Sorry?' He heard her turn the tap off and imagined her stop humming and cock her head.

He said, 'Something that really grates with them.'

'How do you mean?'

'An irrational dislike of something.'

She appeared in the doorway, drying a mug. 'Sure,' she told him.

'So what's yours?'

He was waiting for her to think about it but straight off she said, 'Porridge.'

'I don't mean something you just don't like the taste of—'

'No,' she said, 'I know.'

'Porridge,' Mickey echoed, thinking.

She held the tea towel by her side, flapping from the waist. 'And eels.' She shuddered the length of her spine, shaking her head, making her Afro sway. 'Ever since I read porridge is the same as brains, I couldn't look at it.' She paused and looked at him. 'As for eels, they are just too slippery.'

'Exactly,' said Mickey, smiling. 'Look, I'm knocking off now. Can you tell Ray?'

'No problemo, babes,' Jade called. 'I don't think he'll be back now anyway. Something about his Madonna idea.'

Mickey raised his eyebrows and rolled his eyes back, as he

pulled a sheet over the waxwork, touching its feet and then its head. By the time Jade came through from the kitchen, he had already left.

Mickey had devised two routes home from the studio, both designed to spend as little time as possible exposed to the river. The Houses of Parliament added a useful barrier if he chose Lambeth Bridge, but most times he preferred the extra walk towards Victoria that presented him with a direct route on to the Vauxhall Bridge. Mickey regulated them to prevent dependency. Since he'd started work at Waxy Ladies he gave the money he would have spent on his Tube fare to a series of down-and-outs whose business it was to shamble along the Embankment. There were two of them: Bagman and Conspiracy Man, and he divided his money into two – one pile for the tramp on either bridge. The doctor would have called it ritual, a payment for his safe passage across the water. Mickey preferred to call it charity. Wasn't that what all donations were about? Paying the homeless to keep their bad luck to themselves. This evening it was Bagman that awaited him, his shoulder turned downstream, away from the wind.

'Evening,' said Mickey.

Strands of inch-long faded multicoloured polythene fluttered from the tramp's costume. Not that it was a costume. He wore layers of supermarket bags so that today he looked like an exotic scarecrow. Most early evenings he sat on the same bench, the City to the left of him condensed into squat grey shapes and to the right of him the haphazard sprawl of West London. His face was nut brown with charcoal lines of dirt. The fingernails were thick yellow hoofs, bending in on themselves. Mickey felt in his pocket for the money. It was the giving of it he disliked so much. He would prefer to avoid the exchange, just leave it in a heap at the foot of the bench.

The tramp looked at him with hard sultana pupils adrift in rheumy eyes. 'There you go, mate,' Mickey told him as he laid the money on the slats of the bench a foot from him. The tramp's feet were clumped in plastic bags as if his legs were sprouting from Gro-Bags. 'Don't spend it on anything I wouldn't.' He stood back and wobbled with fake bonhomie. A gust rattled the carriers, whipping him. Bagman grunted but Mickey couldn't see if it was through gratitude or contempt.

Claude was alone in the shop, Rat-a-tat-tatting prices on boxes of cocoa powder. He looked up when the bell went and held the ticket gun up in a form of salute.

'Met your lady,' he told him, giving Mickey a lazy smile as he passed him.

'Really?' Mickey replied.

'You're like me, son.' Claude went back to the box. 'Prefer the more mature model.'

'How do you mean?'

Claude ignored him, thinking his own thoughts. 'Nice,' he whispered, melodious and nodding approval.

Mickey stacked up forty pence on the counter. 'Who is?'

'Lady said she was staying with you. Tall.' Claude raised a box of cocoa to head height. 'Well-stacked hippy chick. The one you been buying the whisky for.'

'Oh right,' Mickey said, '*her*.'

'Will you listen to the white boy,' said Claude. 'Exactly how many you got in that harem of yours?'

'You know how it is,' Mickey told him, and shrugged and picked up his milk. 'See you.'

His mother had left a note, dappled with the blond discoloration of spilt herbal tea, propped between two unwashed plates. 'Gone to shiatsu, no hot water.' Unable to tell if one clause was dependent on the other, he crumpled it and lobbed it towards a stuffed bin with its jaws forced open. He sighed, sat on the unmade futon and ran a hand over his head like a wash mit. Mickey was aware that some mothers cleaned their children's living spaces, pretending to be appalled but inwardly rejoicing at their sons' dependence. But in his upbringing it had been the other way round. 'I would clean, darling,' his mother told him, 'but all the dirt comes back again so there just doesn't seem to be much point.' So it was Mickey who guiltily used his rolled-up wet sock to wipe away the bathroom crusts of white or his sleeve to push away the dust from under a row of plain wooden ornaments.

He lay back and pulled his knees towards his chest, hearing the flimsy springs collapse beneath him. For the last two nights, camped out along the length of his study, he had slept badly. He shut his eyes and fell asleep to Claude's sonorous shop bell and the calming whirr of early evening traffic. It was Sandy's call, sharp and persistent, that hauled him from sleep an hour later.

Chapter Five

I

Sandy was watching the winner of a reality TV show set on a Pacific island interviewing Honey Dew, wearing a diamanté-studded bikini and cowboy boots, on his afternoon talk show. Half the panel was against her national striptease, while three others, led by the ageing owner of a lap-dancing club off Hanger Lane, were all for it. The foyer of the television centre, according to the chat show host, was under siege from a picket of real actors, striking against the docusoap phenomenon. Meanwhile, in the studio, the banner at the back of the studio was in the same *Pump* red as Honey's bikini top and read 'Six Days to Glory'. Sandy thought, what glory? Then she flicked the TV off, but carried on thinking. For her scheme to have any impact she would have to act fast. She was listlessly tapping a comb on the side of her cheek when Gaye called; the clock on her mobile phone read just gone four. Gaye sounded put upon, but Sandy had noticed that Gaye, who opened the conversation with, 'Are you sure you went to this premiere?' liked to feel like she was being taken advantage of.

While she spoke, Sandy chewed on the cuticles of her left thumb. 'Of course I went to it,' replied Sandy stonily. 'What's the matter with you? Something not right with the copy?'

'No,' said Gaye, attempting some form of conciliation, 'the

copy's fine. I just don't remember anyone else saying John Travolta was there.'

Gaye put the comb down and snatched at the glossies open on her bed. She felt a bubble of anxiety shoot to her bowels. It was true. Somehow, she'd stuck two pages together and confused pictures of the Leicester Square premiere with *Celebrities Step Out* – central to which was a grainy snapshot of John Travolta walking his dog. Thinking back she had wondered what a bull terrier had been doing at the cinema, but had put it down to a publicity stunt.

'I'm telling you,' Sandy urged, 'Johnny was definitely there.' Neither woman spoke. Sandy counted to ten.

'Well,' said Gaye finally, 'I suppose I'm just going to have to take your word for it. At least you give a good rundown of the plot.'

Sandy didn't speak. With one finger she traced the spirals of her unopened reporter's notebook.

Then Gaye said, 'Are you sure you're all right?'

It was obvious to Sandy she wasn't asking out of concern. 'How do you mean?'

'I don't know,' said Gaye. 'Something about the way you're speaking. You sound different.'

'Different how?'

'I mean you sound posher. Like you're putting on some sort of act. You're not putting on some sort of act, are you?'

'I don't think so,' Sandy told her.

'Good,' said Gaye. 'Because if there's one thing our readers can't stand it's an act. They can see through a pose in a second.'

'Really?' said Sandy.

'Really,' Gaye replied. 'Bear that in mind, in the future. We're paying you for your genuine small-mind mentality.'

'I think you mean small-town mentality,' said Sandy.

'Whatever,' said Gaye. 'So,' she sighed with exaggerated boredom, 'where's the next big scoop coming from?'

'Actually,' said Sandy, 'it's a dance premiere.'

'Covent Garden?'

'Kind of.' Sandy twisted the telephone coil. 'Kind of Covent Garden. Actually a bit more contemporary than that.'

'Look,' said Gaye with a strained snarl in her voice, 'I do not want something too hoity-toity. Readers of the *Pump* are more *Starlight Express* than Ballet frigging Rambert. You'd do well to remember that. I've got another call coming in.'

She hung up. Sandy knew there had been no other call. She sighed. She'd been out earlier trying to buy a paper that might list openings she could cover but had been told by the man on the newsstand that he'd given up stocking the dailies. 'It's not news people want now.' He pulled a length of gum from his mouth. 'People have had it with news. It's too much hassle, wars and that. I only get the mags. Much easier.' He had sounded proud, as if he'd invented a marketing niche. With no alternatives, Sandy had no choice but to fall back on Mickey.

II

When he dragged himself up to answer the phone, Mickey felt drugged, shot through with some massive dose of tranquilliser, his leaden body refusing to meet the soupy demands of his brain. Sandy had wanted to know if, in any way, the dance premiere he had invited her to could be called an artistic *coup d'état.*

'I s'pose it could.' He yawned and nipped at his face, trying to revive it. 'In the loosest definition of *coups.*'

'Who will be there?'

'How do you mean?'

'Celebs. Kate Moss, Stella McCartney?'

On the table by his left-hand side, his mother had turned the paper to the arts section, doodling and starring passages at random. Mickey noticed an advert next to a lithe woman bending backwards. 'Pina Bausch,' he said.

'Who?' demanded Sandy.

'She redefines the European modern dance genre.'

'I don't suppose she's ever been in *Starlight Express*?' asked Sandy.

Mickey looked at the ragged cut of the flimsy outfit the dancer was wearing. He didn't like to disappoint. 'No doubt about it,' he said.

'Excellent,' she said. 'It's the day after tomorrow, isn't it? What time shall I meet you?'

Mickey told her seven. Then he rubbed his eyes and flicked the heating on. The flash floods of sweat that he always experienced talking to Sandy had left him cold. He was still marrow chilled from his sleep and a dream that had presented itself to him, demanding attention like a scab not ready to be picked at. He flopped back on the sofa bed, intending to put it away, but found himself sinking back into its foamy embrace. It smelt of his mother, a thick musky perfume that clung to the insides of his nose, weighing his head down and making it ache. Everyone else's mothers smelt flowery and light, like washing left on the line. Trust him to have one that made you think of a Far Eastern gambling den. Outside his window, children mooched in the street. The jagged loops of their cries, echoing like seagulls, took him back to his waking dream.

There had been four of them – Granddad Charlie, Uncle Nigel, his mum and little Mickey, each of them weighting a corner of Nigel's tartan rug that had been flung down haphazardly by his mother. The slope to the sea was too great so anything circular had to be lodged behind shoes (Nigel's white tennis shoes, stained brown inside and flapping an odour eater). His mother, play-acting the role in front of Charlie, said 'Pooey' as she jammed a Thermos flask into the pebbles. A hot airlock of excitement jammed in Mickey's throat because picnics were different and as exciting as his mother's new family mood.

It wasn't beach weather. The wind had dropped, though there

were enough gusts to make the halyards twitch, and the waves uncurled as if they could hardly be bothered under a blanket of grey sky. It had been billed to Mickey as a treat, but he knew from the outset he was the silent observer of a grown-up summit. For a start, his granddad was there. For the first ten years of Mickey's life, Granddad Charlie had only made himself known by cards on his birthday and at Christmas and his visits. Both the times he'd given Mickey a paper bag of penny chews, shrimps and pineapple chunks that left a thin layer of castor sugar at the bottom. Afterwards, his mother said it was a present that 'showed an interest but could never be confused with caring'. But before his granddad's visit they sat in expectation at the kitchen table among long rows of yellow candles, the colour of old piano keys, and joss sticks that even, aged eight, Mickey guessed would irritate a grown man. He must have been cross because when he arrived, from his bedroom, Mickey heard raised voices, and his granddad never said goodbye as he left.

'Why should I call him Granddad Charlie?' Mickey asked when he'd gone, back at his place at the table. 'It's not like there are any to mix him up with.' At the same time Mickey picked balls of molten wax from the candles, seeing how long he could bear the temperature until he peeled it off.

On the beach, his mother said, 'Why don't you go crabbing?' It was typical of his mother, something she'd read about but hadn't bothered enough with the details of what it involved. On the walkway over her head, gulls squawked and dive-bombed on to a fish-and-chip paper.

'What with?' he asked, opening the car-hot tupper and biting into a sandwich sour with vinegar and gritty with mashed up sardine skeletons. The picnic eggs weren't boiled enough, leaving the middles molten gold. All of them had a layer of green round the yolks that Mickey took to be mould. He felt pinpricks of embarrassment for his mother on the back of his neck.

'Nigel, why don't you take him?' Nigel was telling Granddad Charlie that the big house on the spur of land opposite was where radar had been invented during the war. So used to hearing his mother's trilling, to Mickey the men's voices boomed low out to the water's edge and then back again. They were the only people sitting on the beach. On the promenade above them a couple walked hand in hand followed by a boy on a tricycle crunching through pebbles.

'Come on then, young man.' Nigel stood up, dusting eggshells from his trousers. 'Let's see what we can find.' His teeth were coated in yolk and saliva.

'Must I go, Mum?'

'Yes, a walk will warm you up.' She was unscrewing a flask that billowed up spirals of steam, handing the cup to Granddad.

'I'd prefer to sit in the car,' Mickey said. 'Listening to the radio.'

'You run along with Nigel, lad,' Granddad Charlie told him. 'There's a good boy. I've got something to talk to your mother about.'

He rose reluctantly. 'And remember to keep your coat zipped up,' his mother told him but he knew this was aimed at his granddad because she'd never yet bothered with maternal homilies. In the same way, Nigel never normally took his hand, but on this occasion he reached for his wrist.

Mickey would never understand what got into him that day. Nearly twenty years later he could not fathom what caused him to jump. Not bravery; certainly not juvenile heroism and definitely not concern for the drowning man. If anything he was trying to shame the ragtag collection of people that surrounded him. Prove to the dog walkers and fathers heading the young families that he wasn't really part of the absurd group pitched out on a tartan rug in February.

Nigel had told him to wait on the quay, away from the edge, while he went to enquire at the wooden café if they sold crab lines or nets. Closer to the river, the wind blew off the land, pointing all the noses of the sleek moored yachts in the same direction. To the left of him, further downriver, statuesque houseboats wallowed in the mud. Mickey turned his back to the wind, away from the smell of the fish stall, and stubbed the toe of his Wellington on wooden slats matted over with green seaweed.

Either the man didn't see him, or took it that a skinny eleven-year-old boy dressed in an oversized cagoule made an unlikely saviour. Mickey thought, by the way the man was studying the drop, dressed in canary yellow oilskins, that he was a fisherman, tinkering with his line. When he heard the splash he believed it to be a rock, flat and heavy; the type that made a low plopping noise. Then he heard a scream from the shore and Mickey understood, rather than saw, that the man had fallen in.

In less than five seconds, without thinking, Mickey joined him – aware only of the cold, salty water up his nose and down his windpipe. The current had caught him and he grabbed the first thing his hand came in contact with. They were less than ten yards from the quay but the current was dragging them down like a centrifuge, immobilising Mickey's clothed limbs while his mouth dragged black salty water in and out. He used his body as a prop under the fisherman, kicking his feet, ice-cold fingers grappling to grip his collar. They maintained their odd, intimate embrace until they were fifty yards from the quay, Mickey's neck struggling to keep his head up, watching the shore flash by from an unusual angle, aware now that rather than saving the stranger, they were both clinging to each other. By that time Nigel had joined the group watching them while others ran to and away from cars.

The local paper later reported that three dinghies were launched from the shore, 'in a bid to recover the mystery man' whose name never came to light. But it was a tender called *Terence* that eventually picked them up. Peter Jackson on his way back from provisioning his yacht to sail on the tide to Dieppe. Mickey remembered most the way the rowlocks cut into his stomach as he was dragged on to its plastic belly, after the drowning man. And the wind that was so cold it felt like it was burning him.

By the time they got back to the shore his mother and granddad had joined Nigel on the quay. She was even too worried to let strangers know that this was her brave son in the water. He was wrapped in the picnic blanket, clutched to her chest, making the hollow under her chin wet with his hair, and fed tea from the Thermos laced with whisky from Uncle Nigel's hip flask. A woman in the crowd had suggested hospital and another that he should at least have a hot shower in the sailing club changing rooms. Someone was trying to get him to eat an ice cream because the sugar was good for shock. But his mother insisted she get him home. He didn't remember the cold as much as the aching itchiness of the pins and needles when he thawed out on the unabsorbent black leather seat of Nigel's car. He had been trussed in Nigel's tweed jacket with nothing under it and the picnic rug round his waist like a sarong. He was naked underneath the jacket's cold lining, making him crouch low, embarrassed, in case passengers in other cars saw him as Nigel drove steadily in the slow lane. His mother, who often misread his actions, saw it as a sign of exhaustion and hauled him over to her side of the seat where, to the hum of the car radiator and the sound of men's voices in the front, he fell asleep. Beside him his mother, unable to tolerate Nigel's slow driving, twitched and readjusted herself.

'Who was the bloke?' Mickey asked her that evening when he was clean and his hair smelt of shampoo. It occurred to him that no one had bothered to ask.

'I'm not sure, dear. Just a fisherman, I think.' She was washing up and as he spoke her thick hips stopped bouncing against the sink in tune to a song on the radio.

'Will I be in the paper?'

She turned out her arm, putting it over his shoulder and pulling him into her armpit. He smelt the odour of her nervous perspiration because his mother didn't believe in the tyranny of deodorants. 'I doubt it,' she said. 'However would they know?' She'd made up a packet of lemon meringue pie, thinking it his favourite, for tea.

He didn't sleep a full night for a month, waking in the early hours thinking his head was underwater and his eyes staring through the dark green murk, speckled with algae, the terrifying loss of gravity, and he felt the hollow kick of his legs on the bottom of the dinghy as he was hauled out of it.

A week after the incident, puzzling over his maths homework at the kitchen table, waiting for his mother to finish with his geometry kit, he picked a ball of gelatinous melted wax from the candle closest to her. He rolled the wax in his palm and then stroked the paraffin glaze. Best of all, reaching for his discarded ruler, spilling a glass of water on it, he discovered how resistant the wax was to water. The pearls of wax shrugged the liquid off them, as though they hadn't a care in the world.

III

Sandy picked up the laminated card at just after five from a DIY shop next to the library that specialised in keys and shoe repairs. Unable to print anything from her computer she'd written it out in her very best writing, deliberately cutting off the last word of her fictitious cleaning company with a passport-sized photograph of herself she'd got done in an Asian chemist's. At the same place she'd also bought a headscarf sort of rain hat to set the seal on her disguise. The booth was one of the new sort that allowed you to select the pose you liked best. Ironic, she thought, considering she wanted to look her very worst. She didn't have to try too hard at altering her appearance to look like a cleaner. It was more attitude than clothes, and she planned to use a shoulder-hunched pigeon-toed walk of resentment. Next she slid along to an anything-for-a-pound shop on the high street just as it was closing and picked up a green bucket and three multicoloured dusters. Other stuff, a pink cleaning overall, Brasso and the like, she reasoned, could be taken from the airing cupboard on the second floor landing where Hanna, the Maltese daily, kept her cleaning products. For some reason, Sandy anticipated a lot of brass, as if she were polishing a paddle steamer.

On the way back to the Malindi Sands Guest House she trailed the bucket in a puddle, trying to dirty it, and then lodged it against the low brick wall that divided the B&B from a Launderette. She was trying to scuff it with the toe of her boot to give it an air of authenticity when Mr Eghbal came out.

'Why you kick that bucket?' He frowned at her, slamming the door while winding a scarf round his neck.

'No reason,' said Sandy.

'Bloody odd behaviour for young English lady, if you ask me.'

'Yeah,' said Sandy picking it up, one hand on the bell, 'well, no one is asking you.' Then she relented and smiled at him, allowing him to think he'd just got the wrong end of the idiom stick. Because, after all, she never knew when he might be useful.

It was 6.14 when she finally caught the westbound Piccadilly Line. The carriage was packed and passengers sighed and rolled their eyes at her when their legs snagged on the hard rim of her bucket. She stood with her head an inch off leaning against the back of a man in a beat-up leather jacket with her lips close to his blond ponytail that smelt of chip fat.

She'd planned to walk from the Tube but the slow clatter round the District Line and the wait at Earls Court station made her late. She wanted to be there before Kenny Russel. So when she saw a yellow taxi light loom out of the blur of shop fronts she raised her hand, unsure, when it pulled in five metres ahead of her, whether to give the driver instructions outside on the pavement or issue them from the back seat. Once again the taxi driver's phrase, from her first night, repeated itself. 'You are on the border of the knowledge.'

'Chelsea Harbour,' she told him. 'But just drop me off a bit beforehand. I'll show you where.' She didn't want to raise any observers' suspicions by sweeping up in a cab. She watched the cabbie's bald patch reflect in the light above his head as he reached out to reset the metre. 'No problem, madam,' he said. It was a nice touch of inverted deference, she thought, when she was so clearly far from being a lady. From her own experience, she knew that old-fashioned subservience got you a long way. Not that she would tip him. Even when he presented her change in a jumble of pound coins, she scraped every one of them into her palm, jamming them into her purse.

She was dropped at the temporary bus shelter under a clear black sky. It was so cold that she felt the night's iciness sear the back of her windpipe. She bunched her shoulders up and started creeping with the small steps of a woman reluctant to arrive. Inside the reception, she barely acknowledged the concierge when she put her home-made cleaner's pass on the marble counter saying, 'Flat forty-six.'

'Ah, yes,' proclaimed Geoff. 'The cleaner,' as if there was any doubt, or he was reporting it in court. 'Miss Dew told me to expect you.'

He turned away to unlock a small metallic grey safe. 'I'll have to let you in. Miss Dew is at a function.' Sandy kept her head down, not sure if Geoff would recognise her.

He chuckled to himself. 'Oh yes. We're a pretty exclusive bunch here, you know.'

Sandy followed him to the lift. After being outside, she was already too hot and she could feel a moustache of sweat forming under the spotlighting.

'Yeah, I'll bet,' she said looking at the floor. 'Biggest one I've ever done is the tall one from Westlife. Blond, I think, long hair.

I can't remember his name, though. He was in Barnes. Big penthouse with music that came on in every room you were in. Lot of takeaways. Know who I mean? Mind you, I don't suppose he had time to cook.'

Geoff sniffed and straightened his back; the reflection of his gold epaulettes bounced off the chrome dado. 'I think you'll find we're a step up from the boy band phenomenon here. We cater for your more established types.'

The lift opened. 'Right,' said Sandy, swapping the hand she was holding her bucket in. 'Like who?' She followed him out.

'Davina McCall, Trevor McDonald, Alan Titchmarsh.'

'Not much of a garden,' said Sandy. 'I thought he was a gardener.'

'This would be his in-town apartment,' Geoff replied, bending at the knee to let her in to Honey's apartment. 'Even this one used to belong to someone in the Cabinet.' For a second Sandy didn't know what he was talking about. She thought of a famous small man locked in a sideboard.

'Oh,' she said, 'you mean the government Cabinet.'

'What else?' He pushed the door open.

She hesitated, looking across the room to the far wall of windows overlooking the Thames. 'What happened to him?'

The concierge flicked a light switch on a bank of lights, some little spotlights plugged into the ceiling, others nestling in glass shells three-quarters of the way up the wall. It even activated a few terracotta bulb-bottomed lamps dotted around the room.

'Never you mind,' he said, trying to pat her bottom as she skipped past him. 'How long are you going to be?'

'Oh . . .' Halfway across the carpet she turned to face him. 'That all depends on how clean Miss Dew is in her habits.'

Sandy knew from her fortnight in the *Big Sister* house that Honey was not tidy. She suspected her failure to clean up after herself was more than just laziness. It was calculated as one strand of her loose-living lifestyle, hinting that all her household skills went into the bedroom. Not that Sandy had minded. Their on-screen personas were all acts, Sandy having gone for obsequious blankness with the rare flash of spunky.

Demographic studies of callers to the programme revealed Honey's core fan base to be men in the Midlands and the North. Men who in real life would never have stood for her behaviour, but on screen found it sexy. And yet, the room stretched out now in front of Sandy hadn't a hair out of place. Not a hair scrunch in the fruit bowl, or a dribbling pot of moisturiser by the fridge. So Honey's *Big Sister* untidiness on the programme had been affected – quite a gamble, thought Sandy – or she was too overawed by her current living quarters to do anything more than inhabit the corners. Now it was Sandy who was gambling – that Honey would be out on a Friday night. She didn't have a watch but the clock on the DVD player in the corner, squatting underneath a fridge-sized wide screen TV, read 7.05.

She'd told Kenny to meet her at seven, explaining that he should tell the concierge he was setting up for a *Hello!* shoot the next day. She'd told him to flash any ID at him. 'Such as?' he'd asked. 'I don't know,' she'd told him. 'You must have some sort of documentary maker's pass.' He told her there wasn't much call for them in the Kalahari desert. 'I don't know. Show him your bloody bus pass,' she said. Then she'd kicked herself and followed up with the purr, 'Not that I expect you've got one.'

He turned up at nearly quarter-past, falling through the door when she opened it, hidden behind two bulky canvas shoulder bags full of video equipment. 'I normally have porters to do this sort of thing,' he said, running a spotted red and white handkerchief across his brow. He was wearing camouflage fatigues.

'Glad you could make it,' she said sarcastically. Then quickly, 'Look, why don't you sit down? Would you like a drink?'

'Sure.' He looked round. 'It's a nice place the wee lassie has. Don't tell me this is all from that quiz show?'

'It wasn't a quiz show,' said Sandy. 'What do you want to drink? Is whisky all right?'

'A wee dram wouldn't go amiss at driving out the chill night air.' One of the shelves in a mahogany tallboy was given over to a drinks cabinet. She poured an inch of whisky into a squat cut-glass tumbler and passed it to him absently, not asking if he took anything with it.

'Thanks.' He sat down on the edge of a green leather chair indented with buttons in a series of valleys. 'So what is the big idea? I like cloak-and-dagger as much as the next man. Actually, truth to tell, a bit more than the next man. But what's so hush-hush you couldn't tell me on the phone?'

Sandy paced in front of him. She'd kicked her trainers off to feel the carpet beneath her. 'What exactly did Honey Dew say to you the other day?' When Kenny didn't reply she prompted, 'At the make-up launch? When you asked her about making a documentary?'

He took a drink. 'She said it would cost, depending on the length of the finished documentary and how long the footage took to shoot. Then she demanded complete editorial control of the final package. I said to her, "Listen, my good woman, I wouldn't give the head hunters of Papua New Guinea editorial control of my work, never mind a jumped-up little tart—"'

'In other words, she said no.'

'That pretty much sums it up.' He had one corduroy leg resting on his knee and was slowly rotating the ankle. Every time it went through a 360-degree turn the bone clicked.

'What did you think of her?'

'Me?' He finished his drink. 'I thought she was a piece of absolute poison. Why?' All of a sudden he seemed to get his bearings. 'Look, what am I doing here in the first place? Took me bloody years to drag my kit here. Then I had to almost bludgeon some jumped-up little receptionist to death to get up here. I mean, what's the big idea? If you were thinking of using this place as some sort of backdrop for some glamour shots, then I'm afraid to tell you that's not my bag.' He leered at her, implying it wouldn't take much persuading to change his mind.

Sandy glanced at her clothes. 'No. It's nothing like that. Look, I was on the same programme as Honey when she won all that money. It wasn't a quiz show – well, I suppose it was half a quiz show. It was reality TV—'

'Och, that. Don't talk to me about reality TV. Unreality TV, I call it. Listen, I used to get some pretty decent docs commissioned before the whole bloody country took to spying on people.'

'Yeah, well, that's as maybe,' said Sandy. 'That's where you come in. I thought that with your help together we could expose the whole idea of them.'

He looked at her through narrow, slightly unfocused eyes. 'I thought you said you'd been on one.'

'I did,' said Sandy looking at the clock on the DVD. 'But let's just say I was badly used on it.'

'"Badly used"?'

'That's right,' said Sandy. She had thought the language of Victorian melodrama might appeal to him. 'All right then, misused.' He still looked blank. 'Taken for a ride,' she explained.

'And what exactly do you want me to do about it?'

'We make our own documentary. We beat them at their own game.'

Kenny was sucking his cheeks in, making thoughtful chirping noises. 'You mean start the revolution from within.'

'Something like that,' said Sandy. She waited for a millisecond longer than she needed to. 'Now why don't you set your camera up because we probably don't have that much time.'

'I'll need a brief.'

'Let's just see how we go at this stage,' said Sandy. 'It'll give it that fly-on-the-wall feel.' He went to speak. Before he opened his mouth Sandy said, 'Well, not so much fly-on-the-wall as reportage. Original footage.'

'But all it is, is an empty flat.'

Kenny used both hands to push himself out of the armchair, at the same time knocking his tumbler on to a carpet that was much too thick to shatter it. He helped himself to another drink.

'It's background,' called Sandy from the bedroom.

Kenny settled himself back into the armchair. 'You know,' he said, crossing one leg over the other, 'it rather puts me in mind of a sequence I shot in Samarkand on Islamic fundamentalists—'

But Sandy was already going through Honey's bedside drawers and couldn't hear him.

'What I'm failing to grasp at this point,' said Kenny, 'is the motivation behind this. What's the story?' Twenty years' experience as a maker of documentary, and occasional short-story maker, was making him sceptical. On the other hand, despite the proletarian get-up, she was a shapely wee thing who he wouldn't mind videoing without the housecoat.

'Who wants to see a lot of dolphins shagging?' She turned to him, brushing a strand of blonde hair off her face. 'I'm trying to get you out of the Discovery Channel and on to main scheduling.'

'Granted,' he told her. 'Only, at the moment,' he surveyed the flat through his camera lens, 'I can't see a hell of a lot to grip the nation.'

'Exactly,' said Sandy, 'the nation doesn't want to be gripped. It wants to be reassured. Why do you think there are all these quiz shows? People want to know other people are the same as them. Not cleverer, not stupider, the same. Chat shows, soap operas – they want to be sure they're doing it right. The BBC, educate? *Jet Set Lottery* and *Airport*, pur-leeze.'

'So, how does your little exposé fit in? What's that going to change?'

'Nothing. It's not,' said Sandy. 'I don't know.' She was confounded. 'That's the point.'

'The evil at the heart of reality TV,' he said, not listening to her, but warming to the task.

'Hang on, I don't know about that so much. I was thinking more the evil at the heart of Honey Dew,' said Sandy.

'And the evidence of that would be what, exactly? From where I'm standing she seems a model citizen.'

'Huh,' Sandy scoffed. 'That's what you think.'

'Listen, hen,' Kenny started to pack up, 'when you get something more concrete to go on, I suggest you give me a call. Until then I have a proposal to get in on the lost yetis of Kamchatka.' He tapped his nose.

'All right, then,' said Sandy, standing up and facing him, holding a zipped holdall in her hand, 'how's this for proof?' She held a see-through bag of white powder at waist height.

IV

It was Sunday, and Ray was alone in the Waxy Ladies studio. He was sitting with his full weight on a rotating stool, his knees akimbo, straddling a waxwork Madonna. The singer was modelled kneeling, not in a religious pose but with her arms at right angles, such as she used to pose, Mickey had claimed, in the eighties. Ray was timing the lactations, the spout of the Teasmade jammed neatly into the peak of the metallic bronze cone of her breast. He had a teatowel ready to mop up any teething problems. Not for the first time that evening, he praised the nonabsorbent material of her top.

While he was waiting for eight o'clock he returned to his press release. For sure, he knew the papers wouldn't take him seriously. The most he could hope for was a jokey couple of paragraphs in one of the low-quality tabloids. He wrote by hand – Jade could type it up on her word processor in the morning – leaning on the bench behind the singer's head as he wrote.

Stunned wax sculptors looked on in amazement yesterday when a life-sized model of the pop legend Madonna started to lactate.

Housed at London's premier erotic waxwork emporium, Waxy Ladies, of 2A Brewer Street, the effigy began leaking milk from one breast (left) at noon.

Proprietor Mr Raymond Mallone could hardly believe his luck. He said, 'I am quite sure nothing of this nature has ever happened before. It is nothing short of a modern-day miracle. Interested parties who wish to view the phenomenon are welcome at any time between 11 a.m. and 8 a.m. any day except Sunday.'

It has been made known that the Vatican has been contacted.

Ray finished by adding his contact details to the bottom, hesitantly – worried about the legal ramifications of implicating the Pope in his scheme. He sucked on the end of his pencil and decided it was unlikely that knowledge of his lactating Madonna would get that far. As he was halfway through rereading it, he felt a plop of water on the back of his hand. For a split second, lost in his writing, he took it to be a leaking pipe. Then he licked it and smiled. Not water, but non-lactic soya milk. 'That's my girl,' he told her, and in the semidarkness was almost sure she winked back at him.

V

Mickey didn't want to sit with his back to the door, not because he thought he might be missing out on anything but because that put him on a low bar stool and any movement would ruche his shirt up his back. Mickey liked to be hermetically sealed in his clothes. So he sat alongside his mother on a dark velvet banquette running around the tapas part of the restaurant. From the street it looked intimate but inside the restaurant, further in from the bar, a larger dining area fanned out, made bigger by walls made of mirrors.

Mickey ordered a Spanish bottled beer and his mother a glass of red wine.

'So,' Mickey hunched towards her, 'how did the rehearsal go today?' He looked at the patterns on the tiled floor as he spoke, shooting a glance at eye contact only after he'd finished speaking.

'Actually it was a total bloody disaster. Elaine's on this cabbage soup diet which, she says, has made her swell up to twice her normal size. Actually, that was true, I felt it. Her stomach did feel like a medicine ball. I've told the girls not to diet. The whole point of the authentic belly dance is your stomach. The flesh is the idea.' Mickey looked at the protrusion of her stomach under her dress on which she rested the flat of her palm. She took a swig of wine, swinging the glass too forcefully and spilling some down one side of her mouth. She dabbed herself with a green linen napkin. 'Then the rehearsal venue was totally unsuitable. It was below stairs in a Greek restaurant where Pammy claimed to know the proprietor. They have this empty space, waiting for an extension. Then of course the music packed up—'

'Mum?'

'Yes, dear?' She never minded getting cut off; Mickey sometimes thought she hoped for it.

'What time is Nigel getting here?'

'He said any time after eight, depending on traffic.' She passed a hand through her hair. She was the only woman Mickey knew who wore the brightly coloured plastic rings from Christmas crackers all the year round. When he was younger he thought she'd done it just to annoy him; bring attention to the absence of any rings on her left hand as if it was his fault. She said, 'Do you want to order?'

'I'll get another beer. Maybe some bread.' He held up a beer mat that he had been rotating on the table to get the waiter's eye. It was an audacious move, one that he wouldn't normally attempt, but he felt the need, in front of his mother, to act.

'You wanna order something to eat, sir?' the waiter asked, smoothing the beer bottle with a napkin.

'No, we're still waiting for someone,' Mickey told him. He slid the empty bottle to the edge of the table for collection and picked up the next. His brain felt as though it had been trussed in gaffer tape, cut off from its usual supplies of nutrients. Ever since his waking dream, he'd felt gluey, his hands unable to form fists. The beer seemed to be diluting the stickiness.

'So,' he rocked the base of the bottle on the table, 'whose idea was this?'

'Spanish? I thought you were the one that—'

'No,' said Mickey. 'Not the food. Coming out. The three of us.'

'Oh, Nigel's,' she told him. 'He wanted to give me a sort of good luck meal, to wish me well for tomorrow night.'

Mickey grunted. Then said, 'Nothing to do with me, then?'

'You? No, dear. Should it?' She paused; he refused to meet her look. 'Would you like it to be?' When she'd wiped her mouth, his mother had smudged her make-up. There had been a time he would have told her to save her from embarrassment in front of Nigel, but right now he couldn't see the point.

'It's nothing to do with me what you and Nigel get up to.'

The door pushed in on itself and a middle-aged man bundled a much younger woman into the restaurant ahead of him, using the angles of his leather briefcase to herd her in as if he was scared she might make a break for it. The woman's high heels clattered and slid on the ceramic floor.

'Actually,' his mother picked up a bread roll and bit into it, not the nibble of other women, but ripped at a corner, causing a cascade of sharp crumbs. She spoke without swallowing, 'Nigel might have something to speak to you about.'

'Really?'

'You see, he's just been to a solicitor to draw up his will—'

'His *will*?' echoed Mickey. 'Why, what's the matter with him?'

'Nothing's the matter with him,' his mother told him. 'Everyone ought to have a will. We all could die.' She said it as if in her case there was some doubt. 'Anyway, he went to see his solicitor and—'

The door pushed in again and they both turned to look. The headwaiter advanced on Nigel with his arms out. Nigel waited limply, getting his bearings and waiting for the condensation to clear from his glasses.

'Nigel.' When his mother stood up she dislodged the crumbs from her lap.

'Oh, hello, there.' He sounded surprised to see them as he let himself be cupped at the elbow by the waiter and guided to their table. 'Terrible traffic on that South Circular. It really would be quicker to walk. Actually, what I got around to thinking was what about horses? I should think that might be a tremendous way to get about in London these days. What do you think, eh, Jen?'

'Where would you leave them?' said Mickey's mother, kissing him on the cheek. 'It would be too cruel.'

Mickey felt his hand before he extended it. It was greasy with wax and pleasantly repellent; he'd been working on his self-portrait while his mother was rehearsing. 'How are you?' he asked, half standing.

'Bloody sight better after I've had a drink.' He signalled to the waiter. 'What's everyone on? Jenny, wine. Michael, is that beer?' He ordered the drinks. 'You could tie them up outside. I bet there's no law against it. Every Englishman,' he looked at Jenny, 'and woman's birthright, probably, to own a nag.'

'Well, I still think it would be cruel. People might steal them.'

No one spoke. Mickey stared at the couple opposite, suddenly filled with loathing for the dominating way the man arched his arms out over two chairs, as if he was being crucified, and spread his legs at a wide inappropriate angle.

Nigel picked up a bread roll. 'So, Michael, how are you? Still making waxworks? What do you think of your mother's debut on the London stage? Shall we order?'

'We were waiting for you,' Mickey told him, slouching back into his chair.

'Well, I know what I'm having,' said his mother.

'But you haven't even looked at the menu,' protested Mickey.

'The *pulpo*, right?' said Nigel. 'Your mother loves *pulpo.* Don't you, Jen?'

She nodded and smiled, some sort of inverted smile Mickey had not seen before, where her mouth actually went down.

'Actually,' said Mickey, 'I don't think they do *pulpo.*'

'Oh?' Nigel put his hand up and beckoned the waiter over. 'You have *pulpo*, don't you?'

'Sure,' said the waiter.

'Then we'll have one – no, make that two plates of *pulpo.* Michael, *pulpo*?'

'No, I don't want any frigging *pulpo*,' said Mickey. 'What sort of people eat bloody octopus anyway?'

'Darling, please.' His mother was worried he was insulting the waiter.

'I'll have the frittata,' Mickey said, 'and chips.'

'Sorry, sir, no chips.'

'Darling,' said his mother, 'this is a *Spanish* restaurant.'

'I know that,' Mickey told her. 'If you remember, I was the one that brought you here.'

He turned to the waiter. 'The nearest chip-like substitute, then.'

The waiter's pencil seemed to stall, unable to move on his pad, then flowed on.

Nigel said, 'And I'd love some of those delicious lamb's kidneys. What are they called, Jen?'

'*Arannos al Jerez*?' She put on a ludicrous accent. 'Oh, me too. Michael?'

'Lamb's kidneys? Not bloody likely.' He finished his beer. 'And another beer, please.'

'So,' said Nigel, plucking his glasses from his head and cleaning them on a napkin. The couple opposite, who had drunk a bottle of wine while they picked at their food, moved towards the door, this time the man reining the woman by strait-jacketing her into a coat.

'So, then,' echoed Mickey's mother, staring into the middle distance.

Nigel seemed to be monitoring the passage of waiters in and out of the kitchen, as if he was thinking of a way of streamlining it.

Mickey picked up his latest beer and said, 'Remember that day I saved a man from drowning? Brave, wasn't I?'

'Of course I remember it,' said his mother. 'How could I forget? Yes, you were brave. Wasn't he, Nigel?' She looked at Nigel, who was still concentrating on his glasses. 'Imagine, you were only twelve.'

'Eleven,' corrected Mickey.

She went on, 'It was a freezing cold day. Heaven knows why we decided to have a picnic.'

'Granddad was there,' Mickey reminded her.

'So he was.' She shook her head and traced her finger along the side of the tablecloth. 'To this day I can picture your skin when they dragged you out of that dinghy. Cold as ice, and blue. I kept blowing on it to warm it up. It was translucent—'

'Waxy,' said Mickey.

'Yes, I suppose it was.'

'Never bloody forget coming out of that shop and seeing you dive into the water,' Nigel chuckled. 'I felt my insides turn over. I thought: what is it now? You were always doing something to get some attention. Cutting your thumb half off with a tin opener, hanging from trees by your toes. I thought, Christ, what the hell's his mother going to say?'

Mickey looked at him. 'What, that was all? "What's his mother going to say?" You weren't worried, then?'

'Of course I was worried.' He stopped as if he'd forgotten the end of the sentence.

No one spoke until the food arrived. And then they all made an exaggerated fuss over the plates. His mother moved his beer bottles while Nigel put the empty wicker bread basket on the next table. She told Nigel to order some more, this time with butter if they had it. Only Mickey sat back, slouched against the velvet, swirling his beer around in the bottle.

'Mum says you went to see a solicitor the other day,' he said, not moving, watching the steam stick to Nigel's glasses. 'About a will?'

'Did she?' Nigel eyed his mother, who didn't meet his gaze but shifted her weight slightly. Nigel set his fork on the side of the dish. 'Everyone should have a will, you know, even you. If anything happened to you then all your possessions—'

'I don't have any possessions,' Mickey told him. Then he regretted it. His interruption gave Nigel time to think. Nigel picked up his fork, searching for the plumpest ring of *pulpo*. 'It's simply this, I have willed everything – terrible term that; the solicitor kept using it. I thought it sounded terribly American. Like gifted. They think they can turn anything into a verb. Take such liberties with the English language – anyway, I have willed my estate – such as it is – to your mother.'

'Er, *why*?' Mickey frowned.

'Because I suppose she's the nearest thing I've got to family.'

'But you're not even married,' said Mickey.

'Well,' said Nigel, leaning back, 'you know your mother's thoughts on the institution of marriage.' He looked at her.

'Tyranny,' she said through a mouthful of food.

'Quite,' said Nigel, his brow furrowed.

'And what, exactly, would you know about marriage?' Mickey said his mother.

'Well, that's as maybe,' Nigel said.

'What about Enid?' asked Mickey.

'Who?' said Nigel.

'Your sister.'

'Oh, Enid. Enid's already well into her sixties. There didn't seem much point. Actually, I can't really say it occurred to me—'

'Darling, we thought you'd be pleased.' His mother lowered her eyes. 'It will, in the end, all come to you, you know.'

Mickey put his bottle down sharply, sending a fizz of bubbles into the neck. His mother and Nigel looked at him. 'I wish you would just stop all this fucking about—'

'Darling—'

'Stop darlinging me. I'm not a kid. Why can't you just come out and say it? What's the big deal? Why can't you just admit that you are my dad?' He sucked on his beer again and sat back, his neck propped on the picture rail so he was staring at the ceiling.

'Well, you see,' said Nigel, removing his glasses, tapping a metal arm on the tablecloth, 'that's the thing.'

Mickey, hearing the change in his register, sat up and watched him shake his head.

Nigel said, 'You see, I'm not.'

VI

Nigel left at just gone ten thirty, keen, he told them, to miss the rush of traffic. Mickey couldn't imagine such a thing on the Chertsey Road, on a Sunday evening, but said nothing. Not even he could begrudge Nigel's excuse to leave. By that time the restaurant at the back was thinning out. Mickey watched couples, keen to grab their coats and scurry into the night, and families keen to linger. Three elderly Portuguese waited by the coatstand, arms by their sides, waiting like toddlers to be dressed by the maître d'. The tapas foyer was empty save for Mickey and his mum.

'Well, I for one ought to get an early night.' She staged a yawn.

Mickey sipped a milky glass of pastis. One of the younger kitchen staff was sweeping up.

Mickey said, 'Why couldn't you tell me about Nigel before?' When she didn't reply, he went on, 'You both must have known what I thought.'

'I suppose so,' she said. 'I think we both tried not to think about it. Then it just seemed to evolve.' She looked down and then raised her eyes to stare at him. 'Have you any idea how difficult it was to be a single parent in the sixties?'

'But I was born in the seventies.'

'Oh, for God's sake, why must you be so literal? What difference does it actually make?' Her face was flushed and she was trying to keep her voice down. 'If you really want to know, my own mother disowned me and I was forced to quit my job. Would you have preferred if I'd sent you to an orphanage or had you adopted?'

'I didn't ask to be born.'

'Oh, for goodness' sake.'

'Well, it's true.'

'Do you think,' she sighed, 'you might see things from someone else's point of view for once?'

Mickey didn't speak. He watched the waiter's long brush strokes combing out cocktail sticks and paper napkins from under tables.

'So, if it's not Nigel, then who is my father?'

She raised her eyes to the ceiling and exhaled. 'It was such a long time ago.'

'Jesus Christ, Mum, I'm not asking you to remember the Christmas number one, or the headline in *The Times.* It can't be that difficult. Unless, of course, there was more than one candidate.'

She raised her eyebrows and rolled her eyes back. 'You used to say you didn't want to know.'

'Well, I changed my mind.'

'OK, then. His name was Harold. He used to work on the ships.'

'You mean he was a sailor?'

'No, not that,' said his mother. 'He was what you could call a stevedore.'

'A what?'

'Paid to take things off ships, stack them up on the quayside.'

'Like Marlon Brandon in *On the Waterfront*?'

She reached behind him for her coat. 'Not in so many words, dear, no.'

Chapter Six

I

Mickey woke at just before seven, a nanosecond before the clock radio clicked on. The headline news was the actors' strike that had overnight factionalised into two – one dubbing itself 'Variety', led by a man who had made a name for himself with a dummy ostrich, and the other 'Real', headed by a black Shakespearean actor known for his redefinition of Iago at the Barbican. Both factions' aims were similar as they picketed the BBC HQ in White City: to ban fly-on-the-wall documentaries. Then the director general of the BBC came on, claiming to have fallen victim to 'tinpot censorship'. The female anchor announced an interview with Honey Dew at the quarter-past slot, drumming up enthusiasm by saying 'the nation was on tender hooks'.

The words 'tender' and 'hooks' reminded Mickey of something nautical. He reached over and slammed the snooze button. He had a dry feeling in the back of his throat and the sensation of small birds pecking at his insides. His joints ached as if they had spent the night expanding, absorbing information. When he tried to train his consciousness on the evening before, his body took over, pulsating hangover. The sky outside was murky but with the beginning of light shining from beyond the clouds. The red taillights of a plane arched its early morning course to Heathrow – a bubble full of people with none of his cares. Mickey reached for a glass of water stored at arm's length under his work bench in case he'd thrashed into it during the night. He nodded off to the dull stirrings of his mother next door, the twang of springs as she eased herself out of bed and her footfall on the way to the bathroom. He heard the lavatory flush and then pushed himself down into his sleeping bag in anticipation of the shower. Then he woke suddenly at eight thirty with a cold flush of lateness. The flat was quiet but still resonated with his mother. The sofa bed had been reassembled in haste, with the cushion put back upside down and the table not replaced in front of it. Burnt toast crumbs surrounded the kettle and an unwashed plate and mug had added to the pile in the sink. On the back of an unopened telephone bill, propped against the toaster she'd written, 'Appointment with costumier. See you tonight? Mum.'

It was careless girl's writing with uncontrollable loops and wide, expansively crossed Ts. He used to be proud of its floweriness that set him apart from the crabbed scrawl other mothers used. 'Please excuse Michael from swimming this week as he has a verruca,' he made her write every Tuesday evening, wailing in her ear over the sound of the kitchen radio until she had finished. Or an ear infection, or athlete's foot, he wasn't proud. The eleven-year-old Mickey made her write the letter excusing him from swimming so often that, in the end, she'd suspected Mr Jones, the scrubby, bearded PE teacher, was interfering with him. Mickey shook his head. Typical of her, he thought, too much knowledge and not enough understanding. The same way that when he stayed overnight with his new best friend Pete, and washed his hair with pungent medicated shampoo, she'd asked if they had been smoking drugs.

Mickey turned the mug handles on the draining board to the left, grabbed his coat, checked he had his door key, and headed downstairs. Outside, the layer of early morning clouds had lifted and the air was bright – distilled, sharpening his senses with rarefied oxygen. So much so that he knew that in the future these high-pressure mornings would remind him of the time when he first had the information.

Just a name, that was all it was. An inadequate, flimsy, easily duplicated male name. Harold. No surname. Not one that his mother said she could remember, in any case. And the name of an east coast port where she'd lodged when she was writing her final-year university thesis on the influence of the Normans in Glamorgan. How could she remember that, he'd asked, in such microscopic, *adenoidal* detail, when she could relate nothing of the man who was his father? She told him she still had the thesis, for which she'd gained an upper second.

'You still have me,' he'd wailed, loud enough to stop the waiter in his tracks.

'I remember,' she said. By that time the restaurant was empty, the plates had been cleared from in front of her, and Mickey was swigging at another beer. 'It was a Latvian ship and the cargo was cranes.' He put his head in his hands. 'We met in the swimming pool. Not an indoor one, it was outside. I used to take my books there so I could read and sunbathe at the same time. It was October but the weather was so hot. A lido, they called it. He said he went there on his afternoons off, if they finished the ship early. He said it was for his back, which used to spasm with the weight of the cargo. I remember he always wore the same outfit. Black sort of canvas trousers and a white three-button T-shirt.' Neither of them spoke. He had other questions but didn't want to disturb the sanctity of this moment when his mother was so precisely in the wrong.

She broke the silence. 'There. Do you feel any better knowing all this?'

He didn't reply, savouring the details. Suddenly, there was so much water: the sea, ships, a swimming pool. It had made his head spin.

His mother had been back at college a little less than a fortnight when she had discovered she was pregnant. She told her boyfriend, a philosophy undergraduate and jazz fan, who finished their relationship when she let him know the baby couldn't possibly be his. Then she wrote to the man, the stevedore, his *father*, on college headed paper, but having no address sent it via someone called Molly, a cleaner at the lido with a lisp, who had befriended her.

'So,' Mickey concluded. 'You can't say if he knew about me, or not?' He made his face deadpan. 'Did you ever hear anything from him?'

His mother shook her head. 'Nothing, not a word. That's why, you see,' she said. 'That's why I didn't want to say anything. Didn't want to upset you. For goodness' sake, we did all right on our own, didn't we?'

He didn't speak but moved his napkin from his lap to the table, making ready to leave.

'You know,' said his mother defensively, 'Nigel was the only one that stuck by me from college. The only one who didn't judge, or gossip, even when I sat my finals eight-and-a-half months pregnant. You know, before then, they'd asked me to stay on to do a doctorate. Of course I didn't. They didn't ask again. Besides, by then I was a mother and you could say my priorities had changed. I had this unit by then, you and me. That was what was important to me then.' A strand of hair fell across her eyes and she had moist patches under them – not tears so much as sweat. 'It still is, actually.'

Mickey's head squirmed with unanswered questions but all he felt was exhausted. 'Come on,' he said. 'Let's go.' He saw she thought he was cross, but it wasn't that. He just felt tired.

'What was his surname?' he asked her as he put his key in the door. He watched her clench her elbows close to her body, steeling herself.

'I'm afraid I never knew, darling.' She shrugged, trying to make light of it. A warm blast of the smell of garlic bread hit them.

'You never *knew* his surname?' He realised after he'd said it that he'd meant to say 'never *even* knew', but something had stopped him.

'You have to understand it was all a bit more ad hoc than that.' She stepped over the threshold ahead of him. 'Please don't go on about it. It was such a long time ago. Please don't *judge* me.'

'I'm not judging you,' said Mickey. 'I'm just curious. Surely even you can understand that.'

'I suppose.' She already sounded like she'd had enough.

Nine hours later, Mickey decided to test himself and make Westminster Bridge his crossing point. The water was low in the river and a squally wind tunnelled over it, disturbing the smell of wet mud beneath the green seaweed tidemark. With his head down, he passed his daily markers of commuters, the tired metronome to his life, pacing in the opposite direction. The copper-haired American whose head bobbed as she speed-walked in trainers, and the tousle-haired young man who lit a cigarette by the same lamppost every day and wore a permanent frown, despite the glint of a wedding ring. Big Ben chimed nine as Mickey bounded up the steps to the bridge past a tourist booth swamped in Japanese, mainly groups of young women in identical coats and Burberry hats, twittering as they took it in turns to click the camera. He took the Bakerloo Line to Regent's Park, crossed the road into Portland Place and cut through on to Harley Street. Traffic surged past him sluggishly, too late to make nine o'clock, and now acting as if it had the whole morning to play with. Two nurses scurried out of a Regency block ahead of him. He was the only one in the waiting room when he got there at nine twenty-two. The magazines hadn't lost their straightened formation and the crocheted cushions were at the same angle on each leather-back chair. The air smelt clean, not the breathed out, tired version you got with a five o'clock appointment.

'Mickey Defoe, here to see Dr Adebayo at half-past,' Mickey announced.

Carole, the receptionist, looked up from returning a radio from jaunty breakfast music to classical. 'You all right, love?' The dial settled into violins.

'How do you mean?'

'You look a bit different, that's all.'

Mickey twitched his shoulders, not definitely enough for a shrug, more as if he was batting the comment away. On the way here, he'd seen an advert for a Paul Klee exhibition that had reminded him of the wax drawings he had made at school. Pictures on which you would crayon a multicoloured background and then scribble over it completely in black, making it disappear. Then you scraped away at the sea of black, with the edge of a ruler or a fingernail, or coin, and the other colours would leap to life, like magic, as if they hadn't been blotted out at all. While the rest of his classmates scratched and chipped away until hardly a scrap of black was left, Mickey preferred to leave his picture a sheet of matt dark, delighting in its glossy heaviness that left a sheen on his fingertips. All except a triangle in the bottom corner the size of a toffee. It got so bad that a young work placement teacher sent him to see the student counsellor. It was the second time that he had to visit the draughty room that smelt of cold turf because it looked out on to the playing field and was rarely used and never heated. Mickey had no explanation why he preferred to keep his paintings black. It was a waste, he told the counsellor, that was all. If you wanted colours you shouldn't draw over it in black. At the time, Mickey remembered nothing of the interview, hearing it only from his mother later. He could only remember deliberately dropping his pen to avoid the counsellor's furrowed gaze, and under the table seeing her dark leg hair, squashed against thick calves, and trapped under light brown tights. When he followed her to the door, holding back to avoid her arm around him, he saw her legs were mottled at the back with mud.

'So, how are you, Mickey?' Adebayo was dressed casually in green cords and a light lilac shirt. He didn't stand up, didn't look up from a sheaf of notes.

'Good,' Mickey replied, sitting down without taking his coat off. 'In fact, I walked an extra half-mile by the river today, on purpose. And didn't leave the flat while my mum had her shower.'

'Excellent,' said the doctor. He raised his hand, making Mickey flinch, thinking he was going to high-five him, but he just smoothed his hand over his scalp. 'You've got your mother with you. How are you finding that?'

'OK, I guess.' He sounded sulkier than he would have wanted. 'I mean, how would you like it?'

'I have an excellent relationship with both my parents,' the doctor told him.

'Yeah, well, so do I, as it goes.'

'What about your father? Where's he? Are they together, your parents?' The doctor sat back so casual, it annoyed Mickey. He looked down at his notes and continued, 'You're an only child, aren't you?'

'Yes, I am an only child and my dad's fine. What's he got to do with anything? Shouldn't you be telling me how well I'm doing?' Mickey fell silent for a few seconds. He picked up an elastic band from the doctor's desk and twanged it between his thumb and forefinger.

'Do you play any musical instruments?' the doctor asked.

Mickey looked blank. 'Sorry?' Then without waiting for a reply he said, 'No, none. What sort of question is that?' He had expected praise but received none.

'You seem agitated, that's all.'

Mickey let his head fall back. When he listened to the doctor his voice was disembodied, flattened on purpose when he wanted to disguise the inflection, or make it soft and buttery. Only on some of the vowels and the R could Mickey sometimes detect an accent.

'Is there anything you want to talk to me about today?'

Mickey pulled his head up and shrugged.

The doctor went on, 'At our last meeting, you mentioned a waxwork model you were making of yourself. Is that process ongoing?'

'Kind of,' admitted Mickey. 'Only it's a bit difficult finding the time, with my mum staying and that.' He wound the elastic band around his finger.

'Does she know about your model,' the doctor asked, 'the effigy?'

Mickey took exception to the word 'effigy'. 'No, I doubt it. It's not like it's a secret, nothing like that, only my studio's out of bounds. Not just to my mum, to anyone. It's my space, if you like.'

'I see,' said the doctor. 'What do you think she'd say if she saw it?'

Mickey let out a blurt of laughter. 'She'd say, "*Darling*, a self-portrait, just like a real artist. How simply marvellous."'

The doctor didn't speak for a moment. Then: "A real artist", you said. Do you think your mum doesn't take your career seriously, then?'

Mickey jerked his head back, thinking. 'No, I'm pretty sure she does – as serious as she takes anything. Which isn't that serious.' He let a couple of seconds fall away and added, 'Apart from herself,' flicking the elastic band on to the floor. 'Look, Doc, I ought to make a move now. I've got a lot on at the studio right now. But I should let you know that I'm feeling much better. The whole water thing, I really think I might be over the worst. Turns out I'm from a sailing background. I do think it's going to be all right.'

The doctor smiled broad enough to show pink gums speckled with black. 'Glad to hear it, Mickey. What do you say to carrying on our little sessions, just for the time being?'

'Yeah, righto.' Mickey stood up and then swooped down to pick up the elastic band. 'If you say so. You've probably got a patient quota to meet, or something like that, eh, Doc?'

'Something like that,' the doctor replied. 'Just remind me again how old you are?'

'Me?' said Mickey, turning his mouth into a shrug. He plunged his hands in his trouser pockets. 'Twenty-eight. Why?'

'No reason.' The doctor smiled again.

When the door closed after his patient, Dr Adebayo recapped his fine-nibbed Mont Blanc fountain pen and turned to the second bookshelf from the top. He eased a leather-bound textbook from the shoulders of two identical editions, jamming it open against the shelf with his weight leaning into it. On page 349 he read, 'Classic symptoms of adult phobias, though present in a milder form throughout a lifetime, become compounded in the patient's late twenties. The actual age for this is oftentimes twenty-seven, the first year in which the adult has any real sense of his or her own mortality, when they are old enough to see that death exists in more than the abstract.' He sat back down and uncapped his pen, tapping it lightly on his chin before he started to write. Mickey Defoe was developing into a textbook case.

Mickey was on the street, batting the low winter sun out of his eyes, when it came to him: the first time he'd been sent to the child psychologist counsellor. When he was eight, sharing a low melamine desk with a diabetic with his own special lunch box, and pig-tailed Angela with too much saliva in her mouth and who smelt of stables. Two, three, four times Miss Paton would send him back to redo his newsbook. 'There's something wrong with the way you have drawn the people,' she told him, not unkindly, even patting his head.

'How?' he puzzled, returning to her after adding socks, then shoe laces and then even elaborate hats. And each time being sent away again.

'Can't you see?' the teacher asked him.

He shook his head.

'None of these people,' she said, 'has any arms.'

When she came to mention it, it was obvious. But he kept on doing it.

II

'I don't understand,' Kenny stirred a third teaspoon of sugar into his white coffee and looked up at Sandy confidentially, 'why we don't just call the police?' He was dressed in a beige safari suit, every pocket of which bulged with a piece of equipment, a torch in one, pliers in the other and the metallic clutter of spare batteries in the third.

'And where would that leave us?' hissed Sandy, hoping he would keep his voice down. A waiter on a break looked up from the classified section of the *Evening Standard*. 'I'm after more than a ruddy Community Action Trust reward, you know. I thought you were too.' She clattered her metal chair away from the table in a jiggle of annoyance.

'But I can't see how some video tape of a bag of cocaine at a flat that may or may not belong to Honey Dew is going to help us.'

'Please,' urged Sandy, 'will you keep your voice down?'

Kenny pushed his cup away, coffee dribbling down the side. Inside it a skin clung to the bottom over a cold beige pool. When the door opened with a newcomer to the bistro, a gust of mothballs from his safari suit hit the back of her throat.

'Suggestion, that's what we're after here,' she told him. 'That's why I needed to enlist the help of such a renowned filmmaker like yourself. This is ground-breaking stuff. Not everyone is good enough to do what I'm asking. That's why this morning's footage is so vital.' She looked at the clock above the counter. It was a huge-faced dome with Roman numerals, the type she associated more with an American diner than a French coffee shop. It was close to ten. She raised her eyebrows and nodded at the plates in front of them. Kenny reached for his wallet while she finished the last corner of a croissant and apricot jam. They scraped their chairs back. Instead of saying thank you, the bowl-faced East European waitress, pitted with acne scars, said 'Please' when Kenny left two twenty pences on a chrome dish as a tip.

Outside Sandy told him, 'And besides, this couldn't be any better.'

'How come?' asked Kenny, reaching for a pair of sunglasses.

'Because this charity do she's attending, it's a homeless charity and they're always banging on about their antidrugs stance.' She waited for him to catch her up. 'You see? It'll make her look like a hypocrite.' She put on the low accent of a voiceover: 'By day . . . celebrity icon, but we introduce you to the seedy demimonde of Honey Dew . . .'

'My dear little Nancy Drew, until I get a shot of the lady in question with her hooter up a bagful of charlie, I really don't think this whole thing is going to come together. Besides that, you haven't told me what you plan to do with this footage. Going to the police is one thing. But, I mean, if it's blackmail—'

'Look, pal, who said anything about blackmail? This is a serious journalistic endeavour. It's what I call Real Reality TV, the real truth behind the Honey Dew legend. Why else would I bring your expertise in on it?' She smiled weakly but enough to be convincing. 'Plus.' She spun round and pushed Kenny into the doorway of a new building. 'I've already told you what's in it for you.' She rubbed her thumb in circular movements over her forefinger, signifying money.

Kenny fell camera-first through a thick security door that must have been on the latch. Sandy followed him. Inside the corridor smelt of paint and cement dust, a fine layer of which had settled as a gritty carpet on the concrete floor. The air was damp with undried plaster. The noise of voices in an empty room bounced from one side of the corridor to the other. A reception desk at the far end made in blocks of primary colours reeked with the heartiness of charitable endeavour.

'Can I help you at all?' She was small with a grey-blonde bob, and trussed in a large brown throw that swaddled her arms to her body and trailed as low as her sharply angled knees. The cape meant she could only use her hands by flapping them.

'Sandy West, the *Daily Pump*, and Kenny Russel, Channel Eight News,' she said. 'We're kind of teaming up on this one.'

'Jocasta Wilson Right,' she smiled, nodding rather than putting a hand out.

'Right,' agreed Sandy, standing slightly to attention, moving her bag a little further up her shoulder.

'No, Right is my name,' said Jocasta. 'Wilson Right. It's double-barrelled, though heaven knows what will happen if I choose to marry someone with a double-barrelled name. Can you imagine?' Sandy could not, so she shook her head in disbelief and wonderment. Wonderment that a woman so well into her forties could still think marriage was an option.

Jocasta went on, 'The *Pump*, you say? Isn't that the outfit she's doing the strip for?' She screwed up her nose. 'Good of you to cover this as well. Still,' she said, 'two bites of the cherry can't be bad.'

'Just what we thought,' said Sandy.

'Ho hum, the more the merrier, I say.' Jocasta moved like a penguin. 'Do follow me. The rest of the gang's through here.'

Further into the hostel, the scent of junket – perfume and lightly fragrant food – overpowered the smell of just-finished construction. Jocasta hovered at the door. 'I'm afraid the hostel's not quite up and running yet but the PR lot told us we simply *had* to open now.'

'What with the temperatures falling,' said Kenny, nodding. 'You know it puts me in mind of a Brazilian story I covered in 'ninety-eight. Tried Channel Four with it, but they claimed it was too "newsy", if you please. In the end I did it for French TV. *Les enfants de rue du Sao Paolo*, or something. Terrible to see the little mites' suffering.'

Jocasta looked blank. 'No, good heavens, nothing like that. It's the Golden Globes. A couple of our meatiest patrons are actors. They tend to be needed out in LA at this time of year. If all we can attract is a couple of dead-beat hangers-on then we might as well give up.'

'Who, exactly, will be here?' asked Sandy. 'I've gone and left my details back at the office.' She patted the side of her shoulder bag. 'You're sure the winner of *Big Sister* will be making an appearance?'

'Oh, yes. We are hoping.' Jocasta's head made a sweep of the room. 'Quite a coup on our part, even if I do say so myself. That bloody lot of slime buckets at Destitute put in a bid for her. Meaning we at Homeless very nearly had to bankrupt ourselves to get her. Still, column inches, and all that. We'll come out of it best in the long run, I guess.' She swayed slightly, eyes down. 'I've got a sinking feeling that if she doesn't turn up we're reliant on the chap from *Supermarket Sweep* and one of the Crankies. Thank God for this actors' strike.' She hailed a passing tray of champagne. 'Do tuck in.' She caught the eye of a man in the crowd and, turning to leave, winked at both of them before slithering into the throng. Suddenly she twisted round, calling over her shoulder, 'The ceremony kicks off at eleven. Plenty of pictures, please.'

'Extraordinary woman,' said Kenny.

'Never mind that,' Sandy told him. 'Hurry up and set up so we get some pictures of Honey Dew coming in.' She turned to face the far wall where a twenty-foot poster of the celebrity was strung between two clusters of balloons. She was supine on a goatskin rug in front of a fire, her head propped up on one hand, and the dark crevice of her cleavage led into her like a forbidden fairytale pathway. The caption read, 'This Year, Don't Leave Them Out in the Cold.' 'Get a shot of that too,' Sandy urged.

Kenny tutted. The noise in the room, exaggerated by its emptiness, reached a critical pitch. The urgency was added to by the trill warbles of mobile phones clamouring for action. Jocasta and another identically dressed woman were using their hard middle-aged bodies to buttress stragglers into the centre of the room.

It was gone five to eleven by the time Honey Dew arrived. She was escorted at the elbow by a broad, squat man in shades, whose knees buckled as he walked. But it was Honey who wore an expression of fierceness. Her face crumpled in on itself with a sour pugdog look. She was wearing an ankle-length fake fur coat and a bright orange boa.

'Uh oh,' said Kenny. 'She doesn't look too pleased to be here.' His voice became muffled by his viewfinder. He looked up and smoothed the hair on his forehead before making a square using the thumb and forefinger of each hand. He exhaled heavily and squatted back down, one hand resting on his bent knee, his plain green tie dangled away from his chest.

'Stop poncing about,' said Sandy. 'She's not some frigging yeti. Just get her in shot.' A bank of photographers leapt up as if charged by the same electrical current, smothering Honey from sight. Cameras flashed and whirred as films rolled out. Kenny and another camera jostled for space at the front.

'Bloody snappers,' said Kenny. Then remembering what Sandy had said, added, 'And don't bloody tell me how to work.'

'Sorry.' In seconds the room had transformed from a cocktail lounge to a media bun fight. Even the smell seemed to alter from fragrant to the turf odour of unwashed Gore-Tex. Whether from the reflection of the lights, or by dint of the attention she was receiving, Honey's bronze-powdered cheeks did have the genuine glow of celebrity to them. Her puffy look of disdain had vanished in favour of a practised smile, glinting up through her lashes. The more the shutters snapped, the bigger the crowd seemed to become, inflating on a surge of relief that the photo call hadn't been in vain. 'Honey, love,' they called at her, hoping to get her full on. Background music of her TV theme tune distorted through two speakers.

'Holy schmollers,' said Kenny, coming up for air. 'I've not seen anything like this since the Peruvian currency collapsed in 'seventy-eight.'

'Is there any film in that camera?' asked Sandy.

Before he could answer Jocasta had bobbed on to a raised podium; she must have adjusted her wrap because her left arm had been freed to welcome Honey to the stage. 'Ladies and gentlemen,' she beamed, 'and members of our esteemed press corps.' She nodded her evident appreciation. 'I am delighted to welcome the star of *Big Sister* to open our latest West End Homeless shelter. I am sure you are all familiar with the not inconsiderable body of Miss Dew's work, devoted as she has been recently to countless charitable causes.'

Momentarily cut off from their prey, the photographers had fallen into a sullen silence, stirring only when Honey looked up, letting off a volley of shutter clashes.

Jocasta went on, 'As you know, the slogan for this year's campaign is "Please don't leave them out in the cold." Who better to spearhead it, then, than the woman whose generosity and common sense warmed all our hearts on that long-running television series.' Sandy wondered if she'd ever watched the show. 'I am delighted to present to you,' Jocasta beamed, 'Miss Honey Dew.'

Another spurt of the electronic TV theme accompanied the camera shutters' applause. The rest of the audience tapped their free hands on wrists taut under the weight of champagne glasses.

Sandy's eyes were lowered, supervising Kenny, when the commotion started. She felt it before she saw it – a collective inhalation of breath, sucking the air from the room, followed by its transformation into a cacophony of jeers and catcalls.

'Well, I'll be jiggered,' said Kenny. 'How absolutely extraordinary.' He was following the room's gaze towards the podium. 'And here was I, thinking this was a do to help the homeless.'

Sandy grabbed his arm at the elbow. 'Just shut up and tape it,' she said.

On stage Honey had shrugged her fur coat from her shoulders. It slid down over her bare neck and then she wriggled it down further over the mound of her breasts, naked but for a pair of long silver tassels. The snappers were incandescent as, after thirty seconds of mayhem, her stubby clenched fingers dropped the coat. She was wearing a silver G-string to match her tassels.

Beside her Jocasta looked on, not bothering to conceal her benign expression of triumph. 'Worth every penny,' she said aloud, although no one heard her.

Honey remained on stage for a minute until she sensed an imperceptible tailing off of the density of shutters, a microsecond before the photographers themselves realised they were starting to lose interest. Without turning round, she bobbed down and picked up the coat and scampered back out into the corridor. Only a lanky photographer from the *Guardian*, wearing a Breton jumper, noticed that no one had bothered to draw back the blue velvet curtain to unveil the plaque to commemorate the shelter opening.

'Good heavens,' said Kenny. 'I'll be blowed. Quite incredible. Tell me, is this always what happens at press dos, these days? I appear to be somewhat out of the loop.' He started to pack up, unscrewing lenses and cleaning them on a rag hauled from an inside pocket. The last of the snappers was leaving, mobile clasped to his ear, phoning the story through to the picture desk.

Out of a cluster of catering staff, Jocasta sidled up to them. 'So, then, get everything you wanted?'

'I guess so,' Sandy told her.

'It's so difficult, you know, getting something visually exciting together when one is dealing with the homeless. They are such a desperately unglamorous bunch.' Jocasta shifted her weight.

'Oh well,' said Kenny, 'you seem to have pulled something off here.'

'I know,' said Jocasta. 'Isn't it terrible what we have to do in the name of publicity these days? *Entre nous*, your rag the

Pump had something to do with it. Keeps her in the public eye.'

Kenny grunted and bit off a piece of chewing gum.

'Actually,' said Sandy, taking a step forward, 'I was wondering if you wouldn't mind doing a piece to camera for us. You know, an overview to bring the whole thing together.' She raised her eyebrows at Kenny.

'Well, you know,' demurred Jocasta, 'if I must. I always say it *is* in a good cause.'

'Quite right,' agreed Sandy. 'While Kenny's setting up I'll just run over the questions I'll be asking.'

Jocasta nodded, using the metallic circle of her wristwatch as a mirror.

'Firstly,' said Sandy, 'why you chose Honey for the campaign.'

Jocasta was using the corner of her wrap to wipe away black smudges from under her eyes.

'Then there'll be a bit about the hostel itself. And then I want to concentrate on drugs.'

'*Drugs?*' Jocasta looked up.

'It's just that I know your organisation is very antidrugs,' said Sandy.

'Well, yes, of course.' Jocasta nodded. 'They're an absolute scourge to the working classes.' She glanced anxiously at Sandy, who wasn't writing. 'By that, of course, I mean disadvantaged young people.' She went back to arranging her hair and feeling her earrings to check they were straight.

Sandy nodded, moving her head up and down to tease more information out. When no more appeared forthcoming she said, 'And that'll be about it.' She spoke with breezy efficiency and a comforting smile. Then she looked at Kenny: 'Ready to roll?'

III

'You mean you've already sent this out?' Mickey's eyes skimmed the final paragraph of the press release. He made himself take a deep breath and hold the air in his lungs. The air in the basement studio was dense with the smoke from Ray's new brand of cigarillos – a sign, Mickey thought, that he was going up in the world.

'Too right, I have,' said Ray, blowing hot air into his cupped hands. 'Jade emailed it first thing. Now it's just a case of sitting back and waiting for all the free publicity to wash all over us.' As he spoke he ran his hands over his body as if he was in the shower.

'And has it?' Mickey looked at Jade, who has leaning against the doorjamb biting her bottom lip.

'Not yet, exactly,' said Jade, not wanting to discourage. 'But I reckon it's pretty early days. By the time it ends up on the right desk . . .' She moved into the room. 'Really, when you think about it, it's a pretty difficult thing to quantify, in terms of *news.* Is it, like, the religious correspondent, or arts, or entertainment?' She nodded. 'I'd give it a week, babes.'

'No worries,' said Ray, flicking through a magazine as if he couldn't care less. 'That's exactly the time frame I was working to meself. I didn't want to create all this hype only to have all them punters disappointed because the exhibition's so goddamned behind the times.' He stopped flicking and looked accusingly at Mickey. 'You know, the freshest tits we've got on display are Judy Finnigan's. That is not the way to attract punters. That's where you come in, see?'

Mickey shook his head as if he couldn't hear. Ray said, 'We're way behind on those *Big Sister* girls. Did you even pick up that negligée, like I told you to?'

'Yes, I did,' Mickey told him, precisely measuring out the words.

Jade took three steps towards Ray. Her body arched forward, accentuating the curve of her buttocks, caving out her lower spine. 'You, babes,' she said, pointing at Ray, 'you leave him alone.' She rested her hand on her hip. 'He works harder than you'll ever know. He's got his mum staying and it's disrupted his routine. Hasn't it, babes?' Her pointing arm fell lifelessly to her side.

Mickey frowned at her when she turned to him expecting him to stage his own defence. But all he added, churlishly, was 'If you say so.'

Ray flicked his cigarillo butt fizzing into the unfinished remains of a can of lager. 'I don't care if he's got the fucking entire troupe of Dagenham Girl Pipers staying with him.' He dusted a frosting of cigarillo ash from the front of his V-neck. 'I want those waxworks up and running.' He reached on the back of a chair for his coat. 'I'm going to Carlo's. And, think about it,' he tapped the side of his head with his forefinger, 'I'm getting pretty tired of being the only ideas man around here. You might like to scoff, Defoe, but I don't hear you coming up with any great plans to save this place. We'll all be out on our arses unless we can think of something.' He turned to address Jade directly. 'Call me on the mobile if anyone rings up about the Madonna. But don't you go saying anything. This has got to be handled with some tact.'

'Charming,' Jade called up the stairs after him. 'Honestly,' she said to Mickey, 'I don't know why we bother. I'm telling you, that one is such an ungrateful jerk.'

'Oh, well.' Mickey straddled a rotating stool and removed the muslin shroud from the unfinished waxwork of Honey Dew, which still required some touching up. 'I guess we can all be a bit cranky some days.'

Jade slid on to the counter behind him. 'What the hell's got into you? You're usually the one having a go at him.'

'Yeah, well,' Mickey told her. 'I've got things on my mind today.'

She sounded as if she was drumming a pen on a magazine, disguising her interest, when she said, 'Such as?'

Mickey took three seconds to weigh up the consequences before he spoke. Then he said, 'I've got this sort of project underway to find out the name of a Latvian container ship.' He held the spatula still, a foot from Honey Dew's ribcage. 'One that docked about thirty years ago.'

Jade stopped drumming, 'Er, babes, like why?'

He ignored her. 'What about the Lloyd's List? Don't they have the names of all the ships? I wonder if their records go back that far.'

'You got me,' said Jade. 'Why would a bank list *ships*? I reckon you'd be better to look in the phone book.'

The radio in the kitchen played the number one, a cover version of a Four Tops song recorded by a four-piece band voted for by members of the public. When it finished the DJ reported that several 'real' bands were thinking of joining forces with the striking actors.

'Babes?'

Mickey stood up and stretched over Jade for a graffitied copy of the Yellow Pages lying open by the phone. Close to, she smelt flowery, and the hollow where her clavicle turned to shoulder was smooth and brown. 'When are you going to give all this up and start doing proper art? You know you aren't fooling no one with this rubbish. I know what it is that you want,' said Jade.

'Excuse me,' said Mickey, pushing past her, towards the phone. 'Look, budge up. I'm going to try to get hold of them. What would it be under? Insurers?'

Jade put her head back and rolled her eyes. 'I told you,' she said, 'it beats me.' By then Mickey was snatching at the pages with his thumb and forefinger, holding them to the light. Jade picked up a mug and pretended to examine the blond stains on the bottom of it, as if she didn't mind being ignored. When she spoke it was to the back of Mickey's head. 'I was just thinking,' her voice was quiet, 'not if you don't want to, only my brother, you know, the bass player? His band's got a gig coming up tomorrow and—'

Mickey turned on her with one palm held high and the receiver in the other. His eyes were narrow as he shook his head. When he spoke into the receiver he said, 'Hello, is that Lloyd's List? I wonder if you might be able to help at all . . .' His voice trailed off as Jade pushed herself off the counter. Even if she hadn't heard the bell rattle upstairs, it was time to leave.

When she was almost out of the door, Mickey put a hand over the receiver and called to her, 'Jade, there might be a girl calling for me today. Put her straight through if she does.' Jade kept on walking, not even acknowledging that she'd heard him. On the seventh step she said, 'Yeah, whatever.'

IV

Sandy marked the copy for the attention of Gaye Butterworth. She'd been trying to get her email to work since midday but when the connection clicked on, a sign flashed up that the remote server had hung up. With the printer not working either she had no option but to write the copy out in longhand, using as neat a set of black capitals as she could manage. Then she marched it to the Italian dry-cleaners on the high street that had a discolouring card in the window advertising a fax and photocopy service. It was an immigrant's business – determined to wring out every possible penny of profit. A booth at the far end of shop was devoted to a twenty-four-hour photo-developing service, discretion guaranteed. Best of all, Sandy liked the old ice-cream container of old black-and-white portraits under the caption 'instant family'. How efficient that would be, thought Sandy, if you could pick your ancestry from a plastic box.

Ahead of her in the queue a woman in a green waxed coat was threatening to take the proprietor to court in recompense for a torn sleeve. Sandy used the delay to reread her story, wary of the clock overhead now approaching her two o'clock deadline.

> And they say celebrities are selfish, *she began, setting the scene*. Dozens of household names took the time from their business schedules to attend one of the capital's most needy causes. I joined the privileged few, including my old pal Honey Dew there to cut the ribbon, at the opening of Homeless' latest shelter. Miss Dew is a headliner in her fight against drugs, which she believes are responsible for keeping teenagers in destitution. Over champagne and lobster canapies she told me, 'I fight drugs with every fibre of my body. There is nothing in today's society that—

'You want some help, miss?' the man behind the counter had a dog-eared look, with a flat expression turned blank by hostile customers.

'Could you fax this, please?' Sandy fanned the sheets out.

'Where to?' he sounded sceptical.

'Inner London,' Sandy said, 'it's a paper.'

'How you mean? A *news*paper?'

'Yes.'

The man stood back with one hand flat against his hip and the other in the air. 'Normal rate is fifty pence per sheet. Papers is one quid—'

'What the hell are you talking about?'

'Not my laws, missus. You want, or not?'

'Jesus Christ,' said Sandy, opening her purse. 'Looks like I don't have a great deal of choice in the matter.' She shook her head in a way she had seen her mother do. Had she not felt the net closing in so neatly on Honey she might have taken her indignation elsewhere. She had five hours to kill before the next phase of her plan. All in all, things were working out very well. She pressed a two-pound coin in the shopkeeper's palm. 'Keep the change,' she told him. It was, after all, she reminded herself, important to maintain the moral high ground.

V

It very nearly irked Mickey, the way Sandy began conversations halfway through, as if voices in her head were always putting their points of view across. Half an hour before the show was due to start, she said, 'Plus,' turning to face him. 'Who the hell is Pina Bausch anyway?' She was finishing a packet of Cheesy Wotsits, licking the chemical colouring off her fingers after every mouthful as if she still regarded bar snacks as some sort of treat. They were one of the last to be admitted to the foyer. Mickey balanced a plastic container of lager in one hand and flailed a one-sided programme in the other. He was skimming it, hunting out his mother's name in order to impress Sandy. He'd already smugly claimed their places by his inclusion on the guest list, nodding with assurance as a man with a ponytail ticked them off a list. Not that Sandy had noticed.

Mickey said, 'She's some sort of German dancer. Modern.'

'And is she here?'

'No, of course not.' Then Mickey thought she could well be there. In all likelihood he wouldn't recognise Pina Bausch if she tangoed over him. 'Then again, she might well be,' he added.

Sandy rolled her eyes. 'You did say there would be some celebrities here,' she sniffed as she rolled up her Wotsits packet. 'Otherwise it's just some crappy arts event.'

'It says here there's an Iranian stand-up who's been on the *Richard and Judy* show,' Mickey read. 'A comic *tour de force*, they say here.'

'Big wow,' said Sandy. 'I didn't mean who's in it. I meant who was going to be watching it.'

The audience was made up of arts students with loose-fitting clothes and facial piercings. There was none of the usual expectation before a theatrical performance. Newcomers floated in to join groups cross-legged on the floor, unaware that there was any other focus but themselves. Two of the girls were barefoot, wearing footless tights, stopping short of bare legs wafting underneath tiered floral skirts. Three other white couples in their thirties eyed each other across the room and tried to loosen their body language. One of the men, in combat trousers and a hooded sweatshirt, tried to beat the rhythm of the Moorish music that was playing, using a finger on the side of his wine glass.

'Look out for an old bloke on his own with clumpy hair and a tweed jacket,' Mickey told Sandy. 'That'll be my Uncle Nigel.'

'What's he do?' asked Sandy.

Mickey frowned. 'Runs a cement factory. Why?'

'Just wondered.' She had led them to a table nearest the door to the auditorium. Neither of them had bothered to check their coats in and, rather than drag them round, chose to keep them on, meaning they sat stiffly opposite each other. Mickey took a long swig of lager and, not stopping until it was halfway down, said, 'So, how have you been then?'

She smiled and gave him three shallow nods, as if replying in full would be a hardship she wasn't up to. When the music finished, she said, 'You know that waxwork you've got of Honey Dew?'

He frowned, 'Um, yes. I should do. I—'

'Well,' she pulled at a cuticle with her teeth, 'I was wondering—'

She spun her head as a man in a blue suit, carrying a raincoat over his arm like a shield, jolted into her left shoulder. 'Michael, I thought that was you.' He looked back. 'Oh, do forgive me. I am most terribly sorry. Did I give you a knock?

Sandy took her finger out of her mouth and examined it. There was a pinprick of blood on the nail. She held it up in evidence, though Nigel treated the action as a greeting.

'Pleased to meet you,' he said, draping the coat on the back of a spare chair and putting out a cluster of thick, weathered fingers.

'Hi, hello, yes,' said Mickey. Suddenly, he couldn't remember ever introducing two grown-ups to each other. 'This is Nigel,' he said. 'I mean, Nigel, this is Sandy; Sandy, this is Nigel.'

'Hello,' she said. 'I'm Sandy.'

'Very pleased to meet you, Sandy. Nigel Blain. How do you do?' He took her hand. 'Drinks anyone? I'm parched.' He had a film of sweat on his upper lip and forehead. 'I honestly think, all things considered, the average London commuter would be better to travel by boat. Think about it. Why not *sail* in up the river?'

'Good idea,' said Sandy, nodding. 'Like they did in olden days.'

Mickey had never seriously considered the possibility of introducing girlfriends to his slipshod family. Had he been made to imagine it, he would have anticipated the embarrassed sniffs and long glances of social disaster. But here they were. Everyone appearing to know the right moves to make. Even him, it seemed. The events of the night before at the restaurant seemed to have been forgotten, or overlooked.

'I'll have another pint, please, Nigel,' Mickey said. 'Stella, if they have it. Sandy, would you care for another?'

'Orange juice, please.'

'Righty ho,' said Nigel. 'Coming up.' As he left to go to the bar Mickey sat back, laying an arm out over the back of Sandy's chair. He said, 'Nice chap, Nigel. My mum's boyfriend, I suppose you'd call him.' In case she got the wrong idea, he added, 'He's not my dad, though.'

Sandy said, 'Yeah, I guessed that.' She stared beyond him to a group in the corner. 'Here's a clue. If he had have been your father you'd have said, "Sandy, meet my dad." Get it?'

'Yeah,' said Mickey, 'I get it.'

Sandy started fingering her top button as if she was deciding whether to take her coat off. She said, 'Look, about what I was saying . . .'

'What?' Mickey watched Nigel's back at the bar, hunched over, trying to make himself understood.

'The waxwork?'

'Of course,' said Mickey, 'you probably want to know when yours is going to be finished. Well, it's like this—'

'Mine?' She sounded as if her thoughts were elsewhere. 'No. Why should I care when that's finished?'

'Has Ray settled up with you yet?'

Sandy looked blank. Mickey went on, 'For posing. He needs to give you some money. Whatever price you agreed on. Only don't let him wriggle out of it, because he will, you know, if you let him.'

Sandy nodded and went back to her damaged cuticle. 'It's not me I'm interested in.' Nigel was elbowing his way back from the bar, excusing himself as he went. 'It's Honey Dew. Well, not her so much as her model.'

'Should be finished in a couple of days,' said Mickey. 'Why are you so interested in seeing it?' For a glorious split second he thought she might be jealous.

'No,' said Sandy. 'I don't want to look at it. I'm more interested in borrowing it.'

'*Borrowing* it?' Mickey put his glass on the table half off a beer mat. 'What the hell for?' The final slurps of beer sluiced on to the table, finding a groove in the top and making a rivulet that dripped on to Sandy's lap. He swore and felt his jeans pockets for a handkerchief. 'Have you got a tissue?' he asked her.

'No, look, don't worry.' Sandy used the beer mat as a dam, sweeping her knees away from the seepage.

'This'll do.' Mickey pressed a folded sheet of A4 paper on to the lake of beer. When he tried to flip the page to cover up a pattern of red ink doodles, Sandy grabbed it. The design, a series of connecting leaf shapes, was nothing short of vulval. The ink bled into the beer, mingling on the unabsorbent white.

'Ooops,' said Nigel. He was carrying all three drinks in the triangular hollow made by his thumb and forefinger. 'Accident?'

'What is that?' Sandy asked, ignoring Nigel and unfolding the paper.

'Nothing,' said Mickey. 'It's some stupid press release that Ray's sent out. You see he's—'

Sandy's eyes were three-quarters of the way down the page when Nigel said, 'You'll never guess what? There's a set-to at the door. Coach party from Hereford claiming they'd booked for the *Sing Along Sound of Music.* Woman went absolutely nuts when she found out it was an evening devoted to *Worshippers of the Crescent.*' He took a long drink and pressed the end of his fist over his mouth to suppress a belch. 'I didn't know whether to order a red wine for your mother for the interval or not.' He nodded at the programme. 'Does it say when she's on?'

Sandy looked at Mickey. 'You didn't say your mum was in this.' She put the press release in her pocket.

'No, well, it's a bit awkward,' said Mickey.

'Awkward,' said Nigel, drinking again, through a frown. 'Awkward be damned. She's a belly dancer. And a jolly good one at that.'

Sandy raised her eyebrows at Mickey. She said, 'I love the way they make their hips do that. I always say I wish I could do that.'

Mickey made to stand up. 'People are going in. Come on, hurry up. We'd better find our seats. Nigel, you need to be by the exit so you can get off quick. Avoid the traffic at the end.' He finished his pint in one long draught, wiping his sleeve across his mouth.

'Steady on,' said Nigel. Sandy sipped her juice. 'Plenty of time.'

Mickey couldn't back down. 'Well, I'm going in. Don't blame me if they don't let you in.'

'We won't,' said Sandy, not looking up. 'So,' she turned to Nigel, 'Mickey tells me you're in cement.'

'Not literally . . .' Nigel's familiar booming voice tailed off. Even

Sandy's artificial titter had become recognisable to Mickey, amid the crowd's white hum.

Inside the auditorium it was theatre in the round, a wooden plinth jutting into three sides of the stalls. The ambience was impro, rough wooden slats and scaffold. It looked more to Mickey like no one had the conviction to finish it off, something temporary so nobody could be too put out when the funding was cut. It was by far the biggest venue that the Movers and Shakers had played in, but it wasn't just the size of the place that was making his stomach bristle. It was the expressions in the foyer, lofty expressions too eager to condemn the performance. Criticism was so easy. The art students he could understand, but the rest? The others were just desperate to witness a focal point that met their universal disapproval. Group affirmation, Dr Adebayo would call it. Other generations had Hitler or Margaret Thatcher. These days it was more confusing. Mickey was aware that a lot of Islamic types needed to be condemned whereas others, such as the Iranian *tour de force* due on stage after the interval, demanded respect. Which was probably why it was easier to have universal hate objects like Geri Halliwell, who was too thin, or too needy in love.

He felt in his pocket for his lucky stone and began his mantra – 'Please don't let Mum make a tit of herself', recited in clutches of three with a deep breath in between, so that when Sandy and Nigel joined him, he had his head down, held in his hands.

'Don't be nervous, old boy,' Nigel told him. 'I used to feel the same way. So nervous for her that I simply couldn't bear it. But you know your mother. She never lets us down.'

As the lights dimmed, Mickey wondered if they were talking about the same person. 'She's on after the Uzbek National Ballet,' hissed Nigel. 'I saw it in the programme.' Mickey looked past him to Sandy, still hunched in her coat. Her torso was twisted away from Nigel as if she belonged to the teenagers who had slid in next to her. Next to Nigel's, her jeaned thighs were arm-thin and her profile showed off the perfect dimensions of her skull.

He marvelled at the way her fine nose was sculpted out of the slope of her forehead and the way her narrow jaw drew the curve of her mouth down.

He was watching her unwrap a stick of chewing gum when Nigel turned to him. 'Truth be known, I can't stand all this sort of caper.' His breath smelt like burnt woodland and his mouth was so close to Mickey's ear he heard his teeth grind at the end of a sentence. 'I mean Eastern music. I'm more your Burt Bacharach kind of guy. But whatever you do,' he added, 'for Christ's sake, don't tell your mother. I'd never hear the end of it.'

Mickey nodded. In the darkness he heard the first act scurry on stage in readiness for the lights going up. He felt a sudden surge of wellbeing wash over him, wrapping around his head like a warm towel.

Chapter Seven

I

Mickey wondered, ambling down Brewer Street, when the billboard men found the time. No sooner had one pair of breasts been assimilated by members of the public, than they appeared again, in a different pose – this time, stretched in the space between the entrance of the Art Deco NCP car park and its first floor. Honey was dressed as a foxy sheriff wearing a spangly pair of low-cut chaps split over her thighs. Her midriff was bare but she was wearing a small leather waistcoat with all four buttons undone. She was pointing a pistol into the camera at waist level. Her lips parted in a pout, giving her the appearance of a woman in a heightened state, either from sex, or having pulled off a bank job. The *Pump* caption read, 'On the count of four'.

Was it Mickey's imagination, or did each picture reveal a greater sense of eroticism, or was he just feeling hornier? Despite his best efforts, Sandy hadn't allowed him to take her home. She drank white wine in the theatre bar afterwards until an archipelago of red blotches led down from her white throat on to her breasts. There were times when he had managed to edge the conversation around to the intimate. At just after half-past ten he said, 'You know you don't really act like a beautiful woman.'

'What's that supposed to mean?' Sandy had ordered a bowl of polenta chips.

'No, don't get me wrong,' he told her. Then quickly added, 'I like the way you are, all sort of spiky, it's just women that look like you do tend to be more, I dunno . . .'

'What?'

'Serene.' He picked up his bottle of Czech beer, the only type left after the performance. 'Like they don't have to do anything other than just, look.'

She screwed her eyes up and made her head tremor. 'You want to fuck me, right?'

'Er,' said Mickey feeling the heat coming from his neck. 'Yes, I guess I do. I admit I find you very—'

'And you think you're in with a chance, right? Otherwise you wouldn't be here.'

Mickey nodded. 'But it's not just that, it's—'

'Do you want to fuck her, over there?' She pointed to a red-haired woman, heavily bangled, in denim dungarees. She was broad-hipped but androgynous, with the type of thin, translucent skin that terrified him.

'No!' said Mickey. 'Of course not.' He wanted to add, 'Because I'm with you,' but knew it wouldn't work in his favour.

'So,' said Sandy, dipping a polenta chip in ketchup, 'I rest my case. Ours is more your tit-for-tat kind of arrangement.'

'How do you mean?' Mickey was looking at the auburn woman, hoping she hadn't heard them.

'Well,' said Sandy, chewing, 'I've got the tit and you've got the—'

'Tat,' Mickey finished for her, so she didn't have to.

Jade was on the front desk when he went in, mouthing along to a Walkman. As she moved her head her brightly coloured hair slides bounced with her. Until he opened his mouth, Mickey hadn't been able to tell if he was in a good or bad mood.

'Hi, babes,' said Jade, wrenching her earpiece out. 'How did it go last night?'

'Crap,' said Mickey, not stopping. It turned out he was in a bad mood.

'Aw,' Jade said. 'I bet she wasn't that bad. It's difficult to be objective with members of your own family. It's like when I see Paul play in his band. That reminds me: don't forget about his gig.'

Mickey stopped by the staircase. It was the first time since the performance he'd thought of his mother. Sandy hadn't asked and they hadn't discussed it. It was only Nigel who had dived backstage, anxious to congratulate her and whisk her off for a post-show celebration.

He said, 'Yeah, you're right. I guess she wasn't that bad. In fact,' he turned to Jade who was smiling, 'she was actually pretty good.'

'That's the way,' she adjusted the CD player. 'The kettle's just boiled if you want a drink.' It was her way of dismissing him.

'Cheers,' said Mickey, feeling oddly put out, suddenly wanting to loiter. 'Where's Ray?'

'Gone to Carlo's. He says he wants to get some real hair in if the papers are going to be here.'

Mickey told her fair enough and then made sure that no calls, apart from Sandy's – at a thousand to one – be put through to him. 'I'm pretty busy this morning,' he called up to her halfway down the stairs. 'Business.'

The studio had its early morning vegetal smell of dankness. He lit the Calor Gas using a spill from the cooker in the kitchenette and flicked the radio on. He ignored the waxworks on the bench in the far corner, instead dragging the stool over to the makeshift desk. Honey's would be ready in time for the tsunami (Ray's word) of media interest but he was superstitious about starting work on Sandy's waxwork, as if he could possess one or other of them, but not both.

In the corner, sticking out from under the Yellow Pages, Ray had unearthed a copy of an old-fashioned advert, a page of black-and-white writing of modulating Victorian founts. Ray would have dug it out for reasons of gravitas, hoping to elevate the artistic integrity of Waxy Ladies for the pressmen. The advert was a flier for Madame Tussaud's and dated 1863. The headline was 'Look at the Queen and her family at play. Lifelike wax sculptures bring this intimate portrait to life.' The Queen was Victoria. It dawned on Mickey that waxworks had been little more than the *OK!* magazine of their day. Before the widespread use of cameras, how else could the public see what royalty and criminals looked like, understand that they weren't any different from anyone else. The knowledge, as he pulled a sheet of paper from Ray's pad, gave him comfort. He was following in a noble tradition, even if that noble tradition was prurient.

II

Without rereading it, Gaye Butterworth mentally rejected the *Worshippers of the Crescent* piece. 'Christ Al-frigging-mighty,' she told Sandy on her mobile. 'It sounds more like a residents' association meeting than a celebrity function. Whatever were you thinking of?'

'I thought our readers might appreciate something more avant-garde,' said Sandy, coat on and on her way out of the Malindi Sands.

'*Our* readers,' scoffed Gaye. 'Since when were they your readers?'

'Sorry,' said Sandy.

'No, I'm sorry, because it just will not do. You'll have to come up with something else and pronto.' In the corridor a Hoover banged its course along a skirting board.

'Like what?' Sandy spoke over the din.

'How the fuck should I know?' said Gaye. 'You're the roving celebrity columnist, not me.' She hung up after telling her to file by midday at the latest.

Sandy turned back and went to sit on the edge of her bed with her coat still buttoned. She looked at the magazines scattered in front of her. She had covered every function – albeit by proxy – that she thought she could get away with. She reached in her coat for a tissue. The paper she felt was shiny and folded into a neat rectangle. She pulled it out and unfolded it. It was a press release. The writing was blurred by spilt beer, but if she held it up to the light, there was enough text left to get the gist of it. Her appointment with Kenny was at two. She pulled her laptop towards her. She should just about have time.

III

Mickey was trying hard to concentrate on the letter but it kept coming back to him. What had she meant, exactly, 'tit for tat', and why had he told her no?

'I mean,' she'd told him, sipping her wine, 'these,' she then cupped her breasts in her hands, pushing them up, 'in return for the waxwork.'

'Which you think is tat.'

'It's just an expression,' she said, releasing her hands and smiling a bored, hooker's smile. 'Come on. What do you say?'

'Why?' Mickey felt the dull beginning of tomorrow's hangover.

'Why what?'

'Why do you want it?'

She rubbed her nose. 'It's a publicity-type thing.' She looked up; her lower eyelashes were clogged together. 'Kind of.' The lights in the bar had come up, turning her skin to a putty colour.

'No.' Mickey spoke with an authority he didn't feel. He didn't care if Sandy took the waxwork or not, but he had a feeling in his stomach that moved it like quicksand. If he allowed her to take the waxwork that would be the last he saw of her.

She said, 'Oh, great,' put her unfinished glass down flat on the table and picked up her scarf.

Mickey moved his chair back. 'Has that been what all this has been about?'

'I'm sorry?'

'You, me, this,' he narrowed his eyes. 'All you were after was a bloody waxwork?'

She stood up and, again, Mickey was amazed at her lack of height. 'Draw your own conclusions, pal. I'm off.' But she shuffled awhile, knocking the back of the wooden chair, scraping her change together, before she left.

'Terrific,' he said, as she went. He took out one of his lucky stones, a supply of which he kept in his jacket pocket, without even stopping to finger it, and tossed it in the soupy grey quagmire of the ashtray, snuggling under the blanket of Sandy's third empty Wotsits packet.

Now, he regretted telling her no. Upstairs he heard Jade's feet scrape on the wooden floor, and the soft edges of the sugary voice she used to greet customers. Mickey picked up his pen. He'd discovered the names of six of the ships that had docked at Harwich during the week in question. Two of them, the *Sophie Maersk* and *Woden*, were German; one was Korean; the *Baltic Trader* from Latvia; one, the *Alexandrian Star*, from Egypt, and one, the *Yun He*, was Chinese. A phone call to the harbour master provided him with the ship's agent, East West Shipping. The company had offices in Southampton, Dover and London. Mickey decided to try the Admiralty Arch branch first.

He began writing. 'Dear Sir, I wonder if you might be able to assist me in my quest . . . ?'

He was four paragraphs down when the call came through.

IV

It had been a slow news day at the office of the *Pump*. So much so that the news editor, Tom 'Greengrass' Jones had sent Karen Baxter and Frank Plowright out to get news in the old-fashioned way, on the street. 'And don't come back till you've got something,' he'd bellowed after them. By three thirty both had. Karen had made a dent in her Christmas shopping and Frank was a tenner up in the Centrepoint 24-hour snooker hall. Stories vying for the front page were the proposed use of a live donkey in a primary school nativity and a celebrity chef's indiscretions with a sous called Bob.

Managing editor Tony Miles said, 'It's not what you'd call exactly news, is it? What happened to politics?'

'Difficult to drum up much interest,' said Greengrass, 'when the politicians themselves seem to have given up.'

'Well, you know what I think.' Gaye Butterworth was standing in for the chief sub, Angus McCreash who was off for the fifth day with flu. She was tapping her diamond engagement ring as she spoke and crossing and uncrossing her legs to show she had more important places to be.

'But it's a diary piece,' said Tony. 'It's hardly a splash.'

'It's a solid festive story,' said Gaye.

'Greengrass, what do you think?' Tony fiddled with his cufflink.

'Well, boss, it'll take a bit of digging to stand it up.'

Gaye drew breath and sat up straighter. Tony said, 'You're right. Get on to it, can you? In the meantime, Gaye, see if you can get a line on the donkey. Toddler terror, you know the sort of thing.'

Gaye smiled through gritted teeth. Sandy West had, after all, been her invention. If anyone was going to rewrite her copy it should be her. Men, she thought, tapping her diamond. It might well be time to revisit her exposé on sexism in the workplace, this time naming names and damn the consequences.

V

'How's tricks?' Ray, sitting in the shop's front alcove with his back to the window, put his mug of instant coffee out to accept a shot of grappa.

'Bloody crap,' said Carlo. 'Not a bloody dickie bird so far this week.'

'What?' said Ray, his neck in an involuntarily spasm at the strength of the drink. 'No one in at all?'

Carlo sat down in the window seat alongside his friend. A shaft of light through a broken blind lit up a spiral plume of steam from his mug. 'No, I tell a lies. That chef caught hanky-pankying with his assistant, he been in.'

'Nice one,' said Ray. He offered Carlo a cigarillo and lit one himself. 'Trim?' he asked exhaling.

'Front, back, sides and beard.'

'I'll give you a fiver.'

'Done,' said Carlo, not looking up, examining the tobacco tip of his smoke. 'Andy's swept it in an envelope for you. Ask him on your way out.'

They drank in silence. Now Ray said, leaning back, 'You know what would be truly terrific?' He puffed out a trail of smoke rings.

'Yeah,' mumbled Carlo, 'Nicky Clarke gets hair caught in freak accident that close all his salons.'

'If once, just for once,' Ray watched his cigarillo tip, 'I could get the hair of one of me models; the whole package, if you like. Now wouldn't that be grand?'

'Oh, yeah, terrific,' said Carlo. 'Scusey me, but Madonna not come in here lately.'

'Oh well,' said Ray, stirring himself and scratching his balls.

Carlo was not enjoying his friend's new phlegmatic mood that bordered on mellow. 'I tell you who did come in here the other day, though.'

'Who's that?' Ray finished his coffee and wiped his upper lip with the back of his hand.

'Chap asking after Mickey. He was a big bruiser bloke.'

'*Mickey?*' Ray hoisted himself up. 'Why was he looking in here?'

'Said he'd seen him come in here—'

'He'd been following him?' Ray cupped his balls as he swung his legs together.

'That's right,' said Carlo.

'What did he want?'

Carlo shrugged. 'He looked pretty serious, as well. I reckon you got something bad coming your way.'

'Oh, terrific,' said Ray.

Carlo chuckled. He'd succeeded pretty well in rubbing the smile off Ray's face.

VI

'Call for you, babes,' Jade shouted down. 'Can you pick up?'

'Who is it?' Before she could answer, Jade had put the call through. Bearing in mind Mickey's instructions he was fifty-fifty confident that the next voice he would hear would be that of an apologetic Sandy.

'Mickey Defoe?' It was a man, Mickey's stomach did a lift-shaft lurch.

'Speaking.'

'My name is Tom . . .' Whether from the sound of the blood still thundering through his ears, or the fact the man's speech pattern was indistinct, Mickey missed the caller's introduction.

He went on, 'I believe you've got a miracle going on where you are. I'm on the *Pump*.'

'Sorry?' Mickey's mind buffeted between Sandy and the letter he had been writing.

'The Madonna?' the man prompted.

'Oh, right,' said Mickey, 'that.' He cursed Jade for putting the call through.

'Tell me, how did you feel when you first saw it?'

Mickey thought about the Teasmade. 'Oh, I think you can say I was pretty amazed. We all were, really.' He meant amazed at how Ray could stoop so low, but thought the reporter would pick up on the irony.

'I wonder,' said the reporter, 'what suddenly made her start up . . .' he paused, 'you know . . .'

'What?'

'Lactating.'

'Yeah,' said Mickey, still sarcastic, 'we thought it must be because she's just had a kid.'

'Who?'

'Madonna and Guy Ritchie.' There was a five-beat silence.

'You mean it's not the Mother of God we're talking about?'

'Jesus Christ Almighty,' said Mickey, 'it most certainly is not.'

The reporter was breathing harder. 'You mean it's a statue of the pop legend that's doing it?'

'The very same.'

'Then that,' said the reporter, now controlling his breathing, 'puts a very different spin on it. Is it OK if we send a snapper to you?'

Mickey had already decided to go home early. 'Absolutely no problem,' he said.

'Expect him in ten,' said the man.

'Righto.' Mickey hung up, addressed the envelope, checked his wallet for a stamp and went to catch the afternoon post.

Jade heard the back door slam on his way out. She ran from

her post, stooped at the top of the stairs and called down to him, 'Babes, don't forget about tonight . . .' She kicked herself when she thought she'd missed him.

VII

By the time Sandy made it out to Kenny's semidetached older-style property in Loughton it was gone four. Sitting-room lights had started to come on, or the net-curtained rooms were illuminated by the grey glow of televisions with children sprawled out in front of them. It wasn't the bare-boarded Manhattan loft space of Kenny's dreams. But Sandy knew him better than that, had him pegged as an off-the-rails divorcé used to having women making decisions for him. The houses to her left and right, squat 1950s, each with a bay window, were the functional type favoured by women.

Kenny was wearing his house clothes – green combat trousers and a sweatshirt with 'I survived the coup . . .' across the front. It didn't mention which coup and Sandy didn't ask.

'Glad you could find me,' he said, with no hint of irony at her lateness, ushering her in. 'Come on in, hen.' The hallway smelt of damp. There was a shallow bowl of pot pourri on the telephone table that must have dated back to his marriage.

'Wife not here?' Sandy asked.

'I'm afraid Margaret left some time ago,' said Kenny. 'She couldn't handle it.'

'Couldn't handle what?' Sandy passed him her coat.

'Och, you know, me being away all the time, the danger, never knowing when I'd be back . . .' He seemed to run out of steam, or conviction.

Sandy nodded. 'Through here?' She pointed to a panelled door glossed white. The carpets were thick and cream but stained with smudges of dirt.

'No, upstairs,' said Kenny, 'the edit suite is upstairs.'

He followed her up. A ledge halfway up was cluttered with batteries and a viewfinder, covered in dust. 'Straight on,' urged Kenny when she got to the top of the stairs. The room was the box room, one assigned to him by Margaret that he hadn't felt allowed to leave. The curtains to the window overlooking the back garden were pulled shut, leaving a pewter-coloured gloom. Inside, a jumble of videotapes and recorders flashed times or dates, though many seemed to glow with a series of zeroes. Sandy thought, oh boy.

'I've been splicing,' said Kenny.

'Great,' Sandy told him. 'What have we got?'

'Well, there's the footage from the flat, obviously, then the Homeless place.'

'And the stuff you got of her shopping,' added Sandy, 'in Bond Street.'

'And her leaving the LWT building,' said Kenny, 'and I've got pictures from billboards.' He stuck a video in the machine. It fizzed and then Honey Dew came into focus, tottering along a West End street with a fuck-you look on her face, her lips pouting with disdain; then more crackle and it segued into the charity hostel opening. Then more fizz and the camera started to pan around her flat, resting on the spines of leather-bound books and caressing the curves of vases. It was pretty clear, to both of them, that material was thin on the ground.

Sandy shook her head. A lot of the shelves in the room were given over to medical kits. There were a couple of trophies, but in the darkness she couldn't make out what they were for. One appeared to be holding a pool cue.

'Still,' said Kenny, 'there's nothing till we get her at it.'

Sandy sighed. 'Look, I've already explained about that. We shoot on Friday, at her flat. She'll be there.'

'You mean a hidden camera-type jobbie?'

'Something like that,' said Sandy.

'You know,' said Kenny, 'I've been thinking . . .' He edged closer to the chair Sandy was sitting in. 'If all this goes tits up . . .'

'Yeah?' Sandy smelt whisky on his breath.

'What's in it for me?' He pursed his lips together. 'What I'm wondering is, if a bird in the hand wouldn't be worth two in the bush.'

Sandy had been expecting this. 'How do you mean?'

'I wonder if you wouldn't mind taking part in a little private video. Just for me.' A fleck of spittle appeared in the crevice of his mouth. 'What do you say?'

Sandy sighed. 'You mean you won't carry on with this project unless I take all my clothes off and pose nude for you?'

'It would'na take so long.'

'The room had better be warm,' she said, stood up and took her coat off, all the time wondering what it was that Kenny's wife, Margaret, really couldn't handle.

VIII

Mickey chose Vauxhall Bridge on some days, like today. He preferred the broad sweep of the walkway with its four lanes of traffic to the narrower thoroughfare of Westminster, deferentially touching the coattails of Parliament. Vauxhall Bridge, cocky in its closeness to the austerely confident MI6 building, was brasher. Mickey instinctively felt fewer bad things would happen to him on the Vauxhall Bridge. He fell in behind a renegade group of workers bunking off early, smoking defiantly. He'd once read in a childhood annual of a torture where victims were strapped to a quayside post and slowly eaten by the incoming tide of rats, or piranhas, or sharks, depending on the story. Walking over the bridge made him feel the landborne equivalent. He felt pincer-toothed animals were biting at the edges of his internal organs, clouding his brain with actual fear and a nameless future dread. His childhood had been full of these fears. A trickle of sweat flowed down his back under his belt, joining the sweat from between his buttocks. He dug his fingernails into his palms to override the circuit using actual pain.

Once over it, he felt the flow of relief through his body. He kept to the left side of the bridge, doubling back on himself, taking the riverside path that looped around an office block. He fumbled in his trouser pocket for the Bagman's £1.80 toll. Out of the lee of the building, rounding on a grass-tufted verge that backed away from the water, he saw him, prone on one of two benches side by side. Mickey speeded up, walking quietly on his heels, confident he could present the money and slip off before he was noticed. The dusty scrub around the seat was littered with stubbed-out cigarette butts and a can of Kestrel that had been knocked over and leaked a rivulet of cider. The air around the bench smelt sour. As he approached, Mickey watched the Bagman's sleeping face, knotted with dirt. Three feet away, with Mickey's hand already extended, he woke up.

Phlegm bubbled up before he spoke. 'You scared me, creeping like that.'

'Here,' said Mickey backing away. 'Have this.'

'Charming,' said Bagman. He was using a new-looking John Lewis bag as a cape. 'You know some people actually buy us a cup of tea.' He hauled himself up with his hand cupped over his face and coughed up a ball of mucus, making his makeshift plastic wardrobe rustle and shake. Mickey had never been this close to the tramp before. The back of his hands were black and his nails hard as hoofs but, as he reached out to pick up money from Mickey's drop-off point by the bench leg, his plastic sleeve rode up his arm and Mickey caught sight, upside down on paler flesh, of the start of a greenish tattoo reading 'H' in an amateur style.

'Sorry,' said Mickey. Had it been a better day, Mickey told himself, had things gone more swimmingly for him, he would have stopped and chatted, even bought the tramp a cappuccino from the Italian deli opposite. But, as it was, Mickey just nodded at him, twitched his hand with a noncommittal wave, and scampered off past the Esso garage in the direction of home. At times like these, Mickey liked to remind himself he'd been a hero once in his lifetime. Maybe that was enough.

IX

Kenny told Sandy to keep her pants on but take her top off, including bra. He was forceful, making it the first time that Sandy was convinced he actually possessed any directorial skill.

'Now what?' Sandy had stripped before but she wasn't sure, in the context of the master bedroom of a suburban semi, what to do next. Kenny's room was empty but for the double bed under a grubby, unmade duvet with both pillows dragged to one side.

'Lie on the bed and writhe around a bit,' he said.

'Like what?'

'Christ alive,' Kenny looked up from the viewfinder, 'like you're thinking sexy thoughts.'

She sat on the bed and then fell back. The duvet smelt of hair wax.

'Spread your legs,' said Kenny.

'Charming.' Sandy hunched her way up the bed, catching her boot heels in the duvet. Then she started running her hands over her body. Kenny was right, it did help when she thought sexy thoughts. Thoughts about how she would spend the money when it came to her. How she would move to the south of Spain, buy her own run-down *finca* and grow almonds and olive trees.

'Now put one hand down your pants and pretend to play with your pussy,' said Kenny.

She concentrated on the contours of a damp patch above her

in the shape of the horn of Africa, and a cobweb dangling in the corner, riding invisible currents of air.

'And will you look as though you're enjoying yourself, for Christ's sake?' Sandy pulsed her middle finger and gave a low groan. Other than the hum from the video recorder and Kenny's laboured breathing, the room was quiet. When she thought she'd achieved enough below, Sandy pushed her hands under her breasts, kneading them. As far as she was concerned she'd made a deal with the Scotsman that he'd now reneged on.

'That's right, hen. Now play with your nipples.'

Not all women would have allowed themselves to be videoed for a stake in half a hundred thousand pounds, but she wasn't everyone and she'd done the beauty pageants for free.

'Now turn over on all fours and let us see that pretty little arse of yours.'

And as far was she was concerned it was pretty cheap.

X

When Mickey got home his mother had gone. She'd made an attempt to reconstruct the sofa bed, haphazardly chucking the cushions back, in an order that couldn't possibly make sense. Her note, scribbled on the back of a demand for council tax, rested on the kettle. 'Darling, thought I was cramping your style a bit. Especially when Nigel told me about your new girlfriend! So I've gone to stay with him till the end of the run. Did you enjoy it? Pammy thought she could see you in the audience but you know how blind I am. Mum.

'P.S. May have to join the actors' strike. I'm not keen but Pammy says we ought. Turns out her cousin used to be a fundraiser for the Bader Meinhof. How little we know. M.'

Mickey scrunched up the note and lobbed it in the bin. The sink was stacked with unwashed plates, the kitchen rug was ruched in the middle and none of the mug handles, as far as he could tell, were aligned to the left. He poured himself a whisky and resolved to get back to his self-portrait in wax as soon as he'd finished the drink. He had the idea that the sooner he could finish the sculpture and return his likeness to the river, the sooner his life would start making sense.

The sitting room had trapped the afternoon sunshine. He toured its crevices – the book shelf, then the table – slow and deliberate, using his body to disturb the air, deflecting any lingering traces of his mother's scent. Now, still standing, he flicked the TV on to a quiz show, sat down without adjusting the cushions and took a drink, before lying back.

It was the rasp of the doorbell that woke him. He rose up, dry-lipped and groggy, not sure if he'd dreamt the noise. He nipped the corners of his eyes and shook his head, waiting for his mind to return to him. In his dream he had been riding in a hot-air balloon with Sandy, who was dressed as a young Elvis. The hot-air balloon was sponsored by Calor Gas, whose logo was a picture of Honey Dew's breasts being inflated. Underneath the balloon his mother and Nigel struggled to keep hold of the guy ropes.

'Jade.' Mickey staggered to the door, pulling it open no more than a third. For Mickey, the best-case scenario had been Sandy, coming over to make up; the worst case, his mother having forgotten something. Jade was a halfway house. 'What are you doing here?'

'Nice to see you too, babes.' She was wearing a three-quarter-length fake fur coat, open at the front, revealing a short red skirt and blue jumper. Her legs were so dark he couldn't tell if she was wearing tights or not. He thought, probably.

She said, 'Why don't you answer your phone?' She pushed past him into the flat. 'Listen, babes, it's bad news. My brother's gig has been cancelled. He said it was a racist thing. I said it's no one's fault if the church hall gets flooded.'

Mickey followed her in. She spoke over her shoulder. 'I couldn't get hold of you, so I thought I'd better come round. Besides which, we can always go out for a drink round here.'

Mickey sat on the edge of his futon, put his elbows on his knees and yawned. He'd switched the overhead light on and Jade cast a long shadow up the wall. 'Jade, it's really great to see you and all that but it's really not the best time—'

'You forgot, didn't you? I said to Ray that you'd forget. He said, no way, he'd be mad to.' She was still standing, using her forearms to act out her dilemma like a puppet show.

'And he's right,' said Mickey, getting up, 'I didn't forget.' He walked into the kitchen. 'I'll just get my coat.' He swivelled the mug handles to the left and checked the taps weren't leaking. 'Where do you want to go?'

Jade was smiling with crack-toothed delight, highlighting a lick of silver sparkle on the top part of her cheek. 'It's your manor,' she said. 'You choose.'

XI

Dr Adebayo took refuge in his study at the top of the house. The view over the mansion-block skyline was undisturbed as far as the park. To the right of the window, the blue and red lights of the Telecom Tower shone like a benevolent UFO. Earlier that day, the doctor had interacted with, and then read to Horace to reinforce male socialisation for a full half-hour. Queenie was fed and bathed and watching an hour's BBC Choice with her mother until it was time for the grown-ups' supper. His wife was in the middle of a high-profile fraud appeal from an MP imprisoned for fiddling his tax returns, so her husband had offered to cook. Nothing elaborate, poached sea bass and a green salad. It gave him half an hour over a glass of Chablis to write up his case studies. He switched on his laptop and started to write.

Michael Defoe is typical of a growing number of young men in post-industrial Western society. His symptoms present themselves in a series of obsessive compulsive disorders, hydrophobia, and a primitive belief in the power of magic by which he believes he can control his environment. He is alienated from his family and falls under the general category, by profession and outlook, of an outsider.

In a phallocratic society, he uses his art as the structural prop with which to connect with the world. It is no accident that his current work – a self-portrait in wax – is intended as a sacrifice to the earth as a means to assuage his questions of what it is to be human, namely the fears of uncertain sexuality and death.

In line with cultural mores he takes part in the prevalent societal worship of the female breast (his profession is that of sculptor of the crude erotic female form). However, rather than a celebration of the female, in the Greco-Roman tradition of the Mother Goddess, embodied in Artemis and Cybele and Hecate, the female is viewed with unease and even distrust. And yet at advent of the third millennium, despite society's evident leaning towards machismo and sexual robustness, women are the more solid, the real power. By ridiculing them they are tamed . . .

Dr Adebayo resolved to discover more about Mickey's relationship with his mother. He was also keen to determine the shape of the genitals on his waxwork; could it be that they were both phallus and vagina? He looked up, his eyes skirting the leather-bound books in his bookcase. His wife was calling him. It was time to start the supper.

XII

The pub he'd chosen was The Eagle, his local, part of the Thatchmere Towers estate and in the same black-bricked community style as the health centre next door and the one-storey library, two blocks further off the main road. Drinkers too poor to make it inside collected on two metal benches around a low bald bush outside, drinking carry-out bottles of cider from the Kwik Save on the corner. The down-and-outs' mood modulated between red-faced hostility and open acts of affection. Mickey checked to see if Bagman was among them. He was not.

Mickey's walk, back from the bar, was one of exaggerated ease.

'So,' said Jade, when he reached her, 'you'll never guess what happened today after you left.' Jade was drinking a half of lager.

'Ray got the Nobel prize for artistic endeavour.' He stretched his knees to run the forty-five-degree angle of the cigarette-gouged table, enjoying the eyebrow-arched looks of disbelief coming from four old West Indians playing pool, all of whom Jade seemed oblivious to. She let out a peal of laughter and hit his arm. 'No,' running her tongue between the gap in her front teeth. 'This bloke from the paper turned up. Wanted to take a picture of Ray's waxwork.'

'Was Ray there?'

'Nah,' said Jade. 'It was down to me,' she patted her chest, 'to let him in, make him a cup of tea, show him round. Kept asking me all these ruddy questions.'

'Like what?' Mickey watched one of the pool players stoop to line up a shot. He was bald with a halo of grey hair running round his nut-brown scalp from ear to ear.

'How often the milking thing happened, who saw it first. Then he wanted to examine it. I said not on your nelly.' She finished her lager, setting it down with the childish expectation it would be refilled.

'Did he stay long?' Mickey hoped she hadn't travelled far to see him. He had an idea she lived in a flatshare in Clapham with her boyfriend, who Mickey thought drove an ice-cream van.

'About an hour.' It struck Mickey that he knew very little about the woman opposite him. Something came back to him, one of Ray's comments when they had a rush on in the studio.

'You went to art school, didn't you?' he asked.

'University of the South Bank,' Jade said, screwing her face up. 'Sculpture. Three years.'

'You're kidding,' said Mickey. 'What are you doing at Waxy Ladies?'

'I could ask you the same thing,' said Jade, picking up her empty glass and heading for the bar.

The counter in The Eagle was behind a metal grille, with only a hatch to the left to pass drinks through. A middle-aged white barman with tattoos on his forearm where the skin had started to slacken appeared and disappeared. Jade returned to the table with a pint and a half and a packet of crisps. Mickey drained the remainder of his pint and started on the other.

'Of course,' he said, quiet enough not to be overheard by the pool players, 'bronze is really my thing. I'm your Epstein sort of guy. And Giacometti, of course.' He thought something about Jade's elongation reminded him of a sculpture. 'That's what I really want to do, you know. This stuff is just filling in time.'

'Really?' said Jade. She arched her eyebrows like she didn't believe it. 'You ought to watch yourself that you don't get stuck in a rut. Art's one of those things you either do, or you don't. There is no in-between.'

'It's not me,' said Mickey, 'it's finding the money.'

'Yeah,' said Jade, 'whatever.'

'Well,' said Mickey, annoyed by her attitude, 'what about you?'

Jade took a drink and looked up at him; her lower eyelashes were long spider's legs fanned across her cheek. She said, 'You have no idea about me.' She ran her tongue over her top lip. Mickey shrugged and picked up his pint.

'So,' Jade said, after twenty seconds of silence. 'How's it going with that *Big Sister* bird?'

'How do you know about that?'

She raised her shoulders and touched the side of her nose to show she wasn't going to let on. 'What are you then, some sort of item?'

'Yeah,' said Mickey. 'You could say that.'

'She looks a bit dippy to me,' said Jade, sniffing. 'In a frontal lobotomy sort of way.'

'How do you mean?' asked Mickey, more curious than offended.

'Like she's a blank canvas, waiting to be painted.'

'Blank,' Mickey repeated, and thought, Jade can talk. From the other side of the bar came the dull metronomic thud of pool balls. 'Well,' said Mickey, 'blank she's not. Then again, the workplace isn't the best place, is it?'

'For what?' Jade leant into him.

'Getting to know people.'

'I guess not.' Jade sat back quickly, like she'd been slapped, making her hair slides quiver. She looked at her watch. 'You know what,' she said, 'I think I'm going to see if I can't catch my brother's second set, after all.'

'I thought you said it was cancelled.' Her drink was half full.

'Just the first half.'

'Oh right.' Mickey picked up his drink. Two pool players were high-fiving each other. 'Do you want me to come?'

'Nah.'

'Walk you to the Tube?'

'I think I can find my own way.' She stood and picked up her bag. The pool players had put down their cues and were sitting in a line with their backs to the flock-papered wall. When Jade stood up the angle of their heads rose accordingly.

'I think I'll just stay and finish my drink then.'

'Fine.' The sparkle from her cheeks had smudged down to under her chin. The bone of her clavicle formed a proud plateau above her breastbone, making shadows out of shadows.

'Jade—' Mickey called after her, loud enough for her to have heard, but she kept on walking.

Mickey put his glass down, shifted his weight and thought, oh well. He shrugged at the pool players, whose eyes followed her wake and then looked back to him. Rather than gloating that the white boy got what was coming to him, their attitude was nonplussed. Women, they all seemed to say, shaking their heads. Mickey stood up. The sooner he got in, the more time it gave him to wait for Sandy to call.

Chapter Eight

I

Jennifer Defoe was midway through her first full day at Nigel's. Her afternoon mood, waiting for the start of *Watercolour Challenge*, was one of subdued militancy. Pammy had just called to tell her an arts co-ordinator had phoned earlier, telling her the last performance of *Worshippers of the Crescent* had been cancelled due to the actors' strike. She spoke too quickly in a tight voice, unable to put the information in a logical sequence. Jennifer managed to glean that Stephanie, the assistant stage manager and Equity rep, had called on the backstage technicians and artists to amalgamate with the 'Real' faction. Central to their concerns was the influx of out-of-work TV actors, flooding live theatre. It was, agreed Jennifer, a blow to the future of the Movers and Shakers.

'Bloody typical,' she said later. 'Every man for himself.'

'Or herself,' said Nigel, point-scoring. In order to make her feel more at home, he'd taken time off from the cement factory, the stresses from which he was feeling more now than he had ever done in his twenty-five-year career. Bumper-to-bumper traffic on the M3, jostling for position with the sports cars heading out to Silicon Valley, was his biggest burden. More than once he'd told Sylvia, his secretary, that he would prefer to work from home until the advent of teleporting. He'd meant it tongue in cheek, but Sylvia was nineteen and had given it as a reason for his absence at a client meeting with a group of sand importers from Birmingham.

'I don't see why they can't do without me for another afternoon.' He slid into the Parker Knoll next to Jennifer's, pushed his weight back and waited to let the foot rest take up the strain. Jennifer was more erect as she considered anything more than a forty-five-degree angle during the day to be slovenly. The *Guardian* billowed on her lap with the jaw of its middle pages wide open. Jennifer made a great show of reading the paper, her bracelets jangling from behind the foreign pages. Really she was looking for a breakthrough mention of Movers and Shakers. 'They could at least mention us on the women's page,' she'd argued on more than one Wednesday. 'After all, Movers and Shakers is in ironic reference to the patriarchal power structure endured by all women of the world.' Then she added in parenthesis, with her trademark wink to convey the following information should be flagged high importance, 'And not just in Turkey.'

Nigel felt the burden of his masculinity and didn't reply.

'Dear Nigel,' she told him, 'Naturally, when I talk about the power of the phallus, I am not referring to you.'

'I should think not,' he replied.

All the furniture in his Bayswater detached house had been bought with Jennifer in mind, which meant it jarred with the Regency interior. *Fusion*, the watercolour over the fireplace in the front room, was too abstract for him and the red velvet chaise longue didn't fit into any part of his day, while the high-wicker-backed chairs in the conservatory hurt the back of his head. (The Parker Knolls, inherited from his uncle on the South Downs, came by default and were by far his favourite pieces of furniture.) Not that he truly believed Jennifer would ever move in permanently – she was far too much of a free spirit for that. But having at least the focus of a woman helped him choose.

'Nigel, really, I don't mind if you go in,' she told him, collapsing the paper. 'Don't worry about me. I've told you not to worry about me.'

Nigel didn't reply. He realised how frustrating she found it to be dependent on men for anything, especially stimulation.

He said, 'I thought we could play Scrabble.' Then added, 'Watch *Countdown*. Have tea.' He was trying to tame Jennifer by suggestion. If she was subjected to enough TV ads of men and women happy to be lowered in and out of baths, she might start to see it as the norm.

Jennifer grunted and went back to the paper. Nigel continued to suck on a toffee and stare at the ceiling. Most of his brain was given over to a concrete delivery to Budapest, due out the following week. Then he remembered he should be thinking about Jennifer. He put his head up. 'Come on, old girl. What's eating you?'

'I do wish you wouldn't speak like that. It makes you sound like a seventies throwback.' She folded the paper in two. 'Also, I am not old.'

'Quite,' said Nigel. 'Sorry.'

She put her paper down. 'No, dear Nigel, poor put-upon Nigel. I'm the one who should apologise.'

'OK then,' said Nigel. 'Though there's really no need.'

'It's just Michael. This quest to find his father. You know, he's contacted the local papers to check the archives to see which ships were in dock when I was in Harwich.'

'Rather enterprising,' said Nigel. 'I wouldn't have thought he had it in him.'

'That's hardly the point, though. Is it?'

'No.' He shook his head like a child that doesn't know why it's being told off.

'Then,' said Jennifer, 'he's planning to contact the Merchant Navy for lists of sailors on various ships.' She ran her hand through her hair.

'Good heavens,' Nigel said, 'that should keep him busy. Fancy a cuppa?'

Jennifer tutted, rolled her eyes and collapsed heavily back on the Parker Knoll, which Nigel interpreted as a sign he should put the kettle on.

Later, when he was halfway down his mug, wondering if he ought to get the Saturday boy to prune his cherry tree, the only significant piece of flora in his boxed concrete garden, he said, 'What would be the harm in the lad finding out the name of his father, anyway?'

'Oh, Nigel,' Jennifer snapped, rubbing her socked feet together on the velvet foot rest as if she was in pain, 'you simply wouldn't understand.'

Nigel nodded. He weighed up his chances of getting away with retuning his kitchen radio from Classic FM to Capital, in order to check for roadworks. But she always knew when he'd been tampering with it. Always told him in the same voice she used to chide that he never could find the exact spot.

II

At just gone three, when the first of the leavers were straggling to the door, Kenny asked, 'Have you ever been attacked by a wild boar?' He sounded as if he was accusing her of something. Sandy shook her head. 'Not that I can remember,' she answered, yawning into her cuff. Neither of them made any reference to the impromptu porn flick of the afternoon before. For her part, Sandy was glad to have got it out of the way and for his, Kenny found it easy to compartmentalise the sex function of his brain. Besides that, in the last few days, Sandy and Kenny had struck up a tired, easy alliance such as that of cricket commentators. She could pretend to be affronted, but it didn't suit her purpose.

Kenny touched the button on his safari suit and went on. 'Happened to me once. Chased for a mile in the jungle of a Pacific Island, the Marquises, if memory serves. I was shooting something for the Discovery Channel on swimming with porpoises, with some damned idiot soap star. Anyway, the blighter chased me for what must have been a good mile—'

'The soap star?'

'No,' Kenny frowned, 'the wild bloody pig. In the end I was jammed between the boar and a two-hundred-foot cliff, plunging into the Pacific.'

Sandy nodded, to avoid eye contact that he might take as encouragement; she focused on an egg stain on his tie.

He said, 'Do you know what I did?' Sandy kept quiet. 'I turned on the brute and started yelping like a dog. It must have been an urge. Something quite primeval because I hadna a clue that they hated dogs. The boar turned tail and legged it.'

'What makes you say that?' said Sandy. Now she'd seen the heart of his filmic empire she saw no reason to go along with his fantasy. The champagne trays were on their third tour of duty.

'I dunno.' He shrugged and put his arm out for a drink. 'There's something about that woman that puts me in mind of a pig.' Cured hams and lengths of salami hung from the ceiling, scenting the room with garlic. Garlands of rosemary were tied to the bare brick wall.

They were guests at the launch of a magazine called *Tramp*. Because of the friction between 'real' and 'unreal' celebrities exacerbated by the actors' strike, the mood at the bar was choppy, not least because several of the 'unreal' guests were claiming they had been invited under false pretences.

Everything, from the gilt-edged invite from one of the leading PR houses, to the venue of an up-market Soho cava bar, hinted that this was the launch of the latest celebrity glossy. Most partygoers were into their second, or even third, drink before they discovered they were celebrating the relaunch of a monthly magazine for the rambling community. The 'real' actors, anxious to prove their professionalism and fizzing with their new taste of the spotlight, stuck it out, whereas most of the others had fled.

After two minutes Kenny added, 'Not so much a pig as a wild boar. Something about the way her lower gums grip her teeth.'

Honey Dew was holding court with a sour group of tabloid hacks, all women. She was basking in the crescendo of her celebrity. Today's pose, her atop a kitchen table and shot from above so that her breasts were like distant hillocks, had been the biggest yet. And an early morning news bulletin had hinted that talks were underway to have her final 'Day Zero' projected via a system of lasers into the night sky.

Sandy, keen not to be spotted, kept low behind Kenny's beige cotton sleeve. They had almost come head to head once before, when Honey was leaving the Homeless shelter. Honey had waved in a genuine way that made Sandy think she might actually be viewing their history as a done deal.

'And there's something about the way she eats food.' She was aware that Kenny was still talking and that all but one of the cava waiters had packed up to go. Even the celebrity ramblers, including one member of a boy band and an eighties keyboard player, who had famously disappeared to the Isle of Lewis, had left. 'It's like she's rooting for truffles.'

'Sorry?'

'That woman.'

'Are you coming?' Sandy reached over his camera bag to retrieve her shoulder bag that she'd dumped when she'd seen plates, rather than just napkins, were available. Before the buffet, she hadn't eaten since yesterday.

'Look, lassie, I don't wish to be rude but I need to know when this is going to be wrapped up.'

'Kenny, I've told you, Friday. We shoot the final shots then.'

'At her flat?'

'Exactly.' A scuffle had broken out at the bar at the back of the gloomy room. A small man in a canvas jacket and two-tone shoes collided with a taller man, whom Sandy was used to watching in black and white. 'You'll need to tell the guy at reception you're from *Hello!* again. Say you forgot to put a tape in the camera or something last time.'

'Then that'll be us over.'

'Correct,' said Sandy. 'I think you've had all you can expect from me.' She'd expected him to look pleased. But he just nodded and blinked with heavy water-retentive lids.

They separated and Sandy made her way out on to the road. She wanted to catch up with him to confirm the time, but the altercation between the two men was being barrelled outside by two bouncers. Party people watched the bundle as though it was significant. Sandy pushed past them; everything looked significant when you'd been drinking all lunchtime. She walked until she was out of range of the tussle and out of hearing of the matinée queue for *Mama Mia*, then punched out a number on her mobile. She had to work fast if her plan was going to come together in time to capitalise on Honey's big moment. At this stage there was only one real sticking point. Sex hadn't worked with Mickey in the way she'd hoped it would. He still hadn't seemed willing to trade, as if he was holding out for something more. Just when Sandy was about to hang up, a woman picked up.

'Hello,' said Sandy. 'Can I speak to Mickey?'

The receptionist told her to hang on while she put the call through, then she added, with some pride, that it was bedlam where she was. Not that Sandy had enquired. She watched the matinée queue while she waited. The weather had turned mild, barely even cold enough for a jacket, although several tourists in the queue, determined to make the most of their packing, wore ankle-length cashmere coats.

'Hello?' She didn't recognise the man's voice, but something about the hiccup of expectation at the end made her say, 'Mickey?'

'Hello,' he repeated. 'Sandy, is that you?'

'It didn't sound like you, you sound all weird.'

'Well, I feel pretty weird. There's a lot kicked off here today.'

He paused. 'You know it's great to hear from you. I kinda thought that—'

'How do you mean?'

'You know the way we left it last time, I thought—'

'No,' said Sandy impatiently, 'how do you mean "a lot has kicked off" there?'

Relief blunted the edges of his words. 'It's the papers, TV and all that. The media.' He paused. 'Somehow this story has made it into the *Pump.* Isn't that your rag?' he asked. Then, not waiting for an answer, said, 'At least it's not you that's done it. This has been written by some bloke.'

'What has?'

'The story about Ray's bloody lactating Madonna.' The background noise gave way to something quieter as if Mickey had moved the receiver. 'Here, I'll read it . . .' Mickey went on, '"Wax sculptors are denying playing any role in what some are calling a modern-day miracle and others have dubbed a sham."'

'You what?'

'"Wax professional, Michael Defoe, told the *Daily Pump*—"'

'Who wrote this?'

'. . . er, hang on. Tom Jones – he's a singer, isn't he . . . ?' His voice trailed off. 'Er . . . "Michael Defoe told the *Daily Pump* that he knew no reason why a model of pop legend Madonna has started lactating. He said, 'We all believe it is nothing short of a miracle.'"' Mickey stopped, 'I mean, I'd like to point out that actually, I never did say that. Then it goes on to say how I think the milk has been sent by Christ over the festive period for goodwill on earth. Then the rag has got some bloody bishop to denounce it and call me a Satan worshipper. Of course, Ray's over the bloody moon.' He was in full flow but slowed enough to add, 'Serve him right if I sued.'

'How would they have got the story in the first place?'

'God knows. Ray sent a bunch of press releases out but he

reckons not to all the tabloids. Still, as he keeps telling us, it's all good publicity.'

'How do you mean?'

'Well, the *Daily Sport* and the *Star* have been, and a crew from Channel Five's here as I speak.'

'Really?' Sandy scratched the back of her neck. 'Any more expected?'

'I guess.' She knew he was waiting for her to speak so she said nothing. Now he added, 'You know I've been meaning to call you.'

'Really?' Sandy was thinking, along with Honey's waxwork, the contact details for a few national TV crews was just what she needed.

'But I didn't have your number.'

'No, well—'

'I was wondering if you'd come out with me one night. I mean not *out* out, just, you know, a drink or something.'

'Sure,' said Sandy. 'How about tonight?'

'Brilliant.' She could hear his mouth go into a smile. 'Yeah, that would be great. Where? I was thinking, there's this place—'

'How about I come over and collect you?'

'Sure,' said Mickey. 'I warn you, though. It's pretty chaotic here. What with papers and TV crews.'

'Oh well,' Sandy told him. 'I'll manage.' Then she thought she'd better add, 'Somehow.' As if it really would be quite a burden.

III

'Gentlemen, please don't crowd her.' Ray had spent most of the previous night constructing an MDF plinth out of some outcuts Carlo had left over from a colouring cupboard. 'Hair tints,' the Italian added when Ray looked bemused. Ray was not a natural artisan. He found it easy to visualise the end product and consequently was impatient to get there. He'd started off with nails but ended up with super glue (left over from the customisation of the Teasmade) and the roll of gaffer tape Mickey used as temporary binding, either to let out, or take in, the waxworks' clothes. The last thing Ray wanted was for an overenthusiastic newsman to knock her over. Now, the Madonna was slightly raised above Cher to her left and Marilyn Monroe to the right. Ray made a mental note to tell Mickey to get some sense of order in the gallery. It was a 'classic babes-through-the-ages' continuum he was after here, not a hodgepodge of disparate totty.

The next and only performance (because resetting the Teasmade required major surgery) was due at four. Ray hadn't let on that the lactations were predictable, based as they were on a clock. He tried to discourage anticipation, even telling one satellite new anchor that he felt it was unlikely they would see the miracle today. Ray was nothing if not a master in the art of delayed gratification.

'Does anyone know if the real Madonna is still breastfeeding?' asked one hack. 'It could be, you know, coming out in sympathy.'

Ray nodded. 'It's a distinct possibility,' he said. He was pretty sure that the assembled media circus realised the whole thing was a con. But they were as prepared as he was to play along with it for the sake of a good story.

'Does she know about it?' asked a woman reporter who, like the rest of them, hadn't taken her coat off. He recognised her as what was now called one of the new breed of gossip columnists, now known as 'rumour verifiers' from Channel Eleven, current thinking being that gossip was only admissible when it could be verified by one independent source. She was attractive in a big-boned way with a sharp, interfering face. As she spoke her mobile phone rang.

'I have not informed the real Madonna,' Ray told them. 'I mean, to be honest with yer, I haven't really had the time. It was as much a shock to me as it was to anyone.' He shifted his weight and turned his palms, low by his knees, outwards. 'As soon as I realised the import of what we had here, I got straight on to you boys.'

'What about the Pope? Have you got word through to the Vatican?' The reporter was in his forties and, among a group barely out of their twenties, felt he had something to prove by adding a real storyline.

'I am,' said Ray, 'trying to get word to his Holiness as we speak.'

'What about miracles?' replied the reporter, who was wearing a New York Yankees baseball cap pulled almost over his eyes.

'Come again?' Ray picked up a mug of cold coffee from the brochure table behind it. Because he complained she never stirred it enough, Jade had left the spoon in. Ray played with the teaspoon.

'Miracles, you know.' He pushed the cap up. 'Blind seeing, the wheelchair-bound turning cartwheels, that sort of thing.'

'Christ, will you give her a chance? The bloody woman has only been doing it these past couple of days—' He interrupted himself, pretending to let his eyes be drawn to the plinth. Now he put one hand to his cheek. 'For the love of God, I never thought we'd be so lucky again.' Somewhere from the studio beneath them the radio measured out the time signal for four o'clock. 'I do believe it is happening again.' Suddenly there was a surge of movement forwards. Photographers arched upwards, raising their light meters aloft, pushing in front of video cameras.

'Don't get too close, please, gentlemen. The heat from your machines might damage her.' Ray's voice could barely be heard above the scrum. He'd changed her out of her conical-breasted top into a cotton cap-sleeved T-shirt with 'Material Girl' printed across it, which he guessed would be more absorbent and, therefore, more difficult to take a sample from. He had also ditched the cowboy hat, which obscured visibility. A dark stain around the letters *eri*, the size of a tangerine was spreading downwards.

Ray was about to say, 'God be praised,' then he stopped himself. He might be a showman, but he didn't want to push his luck. Instead he started to hand round leaflets of opening times.

Sandy had let herself in. Rather than opening the door to visitors, Jade had left the front door on the latch. It meant some members of the public got in for free, but Ray couldn't have cared less. This, he had told her, was a once-in-a-lifetime opportunity – a make or breaker – and the more people who saw it the better. It took Sandy a matter of minutes to make the rounds of the TV crews. At this stage all she needed was a card and a contact number. She hardly needed to introduce herself, just told them that she worked for Waxy Ladies. That way she was able to give them a card, 'All your erotic wax requirements catered for', in return. Altogether she had five, which she stashed in the middle compartment of her purse. She buffeted her eyes around the semidarkness, looking for Mickey, and then remembered the studio was downstairs.

When he heard Sandy's boots on the bare wooden stairs he looked up with a blank nonexpression with a hint of resentment that he should be missing all the fun. The look was intended for someone else. He had been cradling his head in his hands over a newspaper, as if what he was reading was important but impossible to assimilate, like a treasure map. When it registered that it was Sandy, he blushed, blood flooding through his cheeks and draining down his neck.

'Sandy. How did you get in? I told Jade to tell me when you got here.'

'The door was open. I just came in. It's quite a party up there.'

'Yeah,' said Mickey, looking down. 'I told Ray I'd rather stay out of it.'

'How come?'

He nudged the paper towards her. He repeated, 'I told Ray I didn't want anything to do with it. They've still quoted me, though. It's a load of bollocks. Embarrassing, really.'

Sandy picked it up. Gaye hadn't told her that her diary piece – taken from Mickey's press release – had been elaborated and used on the front of the *Pump*.

'Still,' she said, 'no harm done.'

'That's easy for you to say.'

Sandy couldn't tell if he was genuinely upset or had read the situation as an opportunity to elicit sympathy. 'Come on,' she said, smiling. 'I'll take you for a drink.' Mickey noticed a change in her. While she looked undernourished – she'd lost all the pudginess around her cheeks – she seemed to have gained substance. She looked more scooped out, more chiselled. Her hair was plaited in a new way, Red Indian style with two lengths resting on her coat collar. She seemed so changed he wondered if he would have to adjust the waxwork, which he'd styled with a deliberate teenage sexuality. She turned her narrow back away from him, assuming he would follow.

He said, 'I really ought to tidy up a few things here first. I can't just drop everything.'

'OK then.' She jumped backwards on to the counter without looking to see what was in her way. Nothing was. She was chewing gum, pretending to be oblivious to his display of tidying up, checking the answer phone and writing numbers in his diary.

'Actually,' she said after about three minutes when neither of them spoke, listening instead to the clatter of the press gang leaving above them, 'while I'm here.' In the background he could hear Jade's voice though it was too indistinct to make out what she was saying. 'I might as well check out the model. You know, of me. Well, the models of me and Honey Dew. Are they on display yet?'

'Not yet.' Mickey was aware of this as a source of potential friction. Now he stopped organising paper into sheaves. 'Well,

Honey's is. Ray was waiting for all this Madonna hullabaloo to die down first, before he does the *Big Sister* display.'

'He's not making the most of her getting them out then?' Sandy pulled a strand of gum between her teeth. 'I would have thought he would have done.'

Mickey shrugged. To show there were no hard feelings he pointed to the store cupboard in the cavity under the stairs. 'They're through there, if you want to see them.'

The waxworks were laid out in shelves like a family mausoleum. 'Don't touch them, though. They're easily scratched.'

He steeled himself for a whoop, silently rehearsing what he told people when they saw themselves in wax for the first time. Reassuring things, because so few people had any idea of how they looked in 3D, or how other people viewed them. But no noise came from the store cupboard. When she did emerge, two minutes later, her eyes stung by the brightness of the Anglepoise, she said, 'In real life, Honey Dew's not that big. People just think she is because she acts big. Actually, she's pretty small.'

'Oh well,' said Mickey, still waiting. When she added nothing he said, 'What about your one? I was kind of worried about the angle of the head. You have this way of looking up at things that—'

'Yeah, it was fine. I mean, it doesn't really matter, does it? What people look like.'

'Er, no,' said Mickey. 'I guess not.'

'Come on then. Hurry up,' she said. 'This basement is doing my head in.'

He gathered together the drafts of letters he'd written to shipping firms, instinctively not wanting Ray or Jade to know what he was doing, rolled them into a tube and rammed them into his inside jacket pocket. He told her to use the back door so they wouldn't bump into Ray. She walked like a dressage horse, picking her feet up high above a dustpan and bucket. Halfway to the door, she asked if it was all right his knocking off so early. He shrugged. He could make up the time later, he told her. When he said it, he felt the weight of his limbs flood with exhaustion at the thought. So when she asked him, with her hand on the doorknob, 'How much do they weigh?' he assumed she was talking about his arms.

'Sorry?'

'The waxworks. I mean, wax is pretty light, right?'

'It depends,' he told her warily, thinking he should have gone first. 'Compared to what?'

'Well, for example, people. It would be easier to lift my waxwork than it would me.'

'They're pretty unwieldy,' said Mickey. 'And easy to damage.' He reached round her to push the door open. Outside smelt of wet cardboard and damp soil, but after the cloying chemical smell of the studio it seemed close to fresh. Mickey spoke from behind her. 'Why do you want to know, anyway?'

'No reason,' she said, without turning her head. But they both knew she was lying.

The earlier sun had clouded over and the fading lack of natural light gave the shop fronts a flat, washed-out look but Mickey took heart with every step. Every metre they put between themselves and the studio determined this as no longer work but a social occasion. Sandy walked ahead of him to the left so that she wasn't aware of him studying her profile. Now, he thought the waxwork definitely had to be redefined. Or maybe he was just viewing her differently?

When they got as far as the road he felt able to ask her, 'How's work? Still writing? Still at that hotel? You know you really ought to think about getting a flat. They're not that expensive, depending on where you look . . .'

It was a batch of saved-up questions blurted too quickly. She stood by the gutter, looking down as if on the edge of some great precipice. He took up a position at an angle to her, staring at one of her plaits that had worked itself to the front of her coat and traced the curve of her breast. Wanting to linger, he dragged his eyeballs away.

'I'm still writing a diary piece, if that's what you mean,' she said. She waited for a motorcycle courier to snake his way through the line of stationary traffic in front of her, and then crossed. Mickey was aware of male drivers clutching their steering wheels as ballast while they craned their necks to watch her. Mickey hadn't forgotten how attractive she was, but he didn't always keep the information in an easily accessible part of his brain. Now he wanted to stash her somewhere, get her off the streets, somewhere dark, maybe even underground, where he could study her. He stopped himself from reaching out to her plaits and using them like reins to hold on to her.

'You seem to know your way around here pretty well now,' he said. She was leading him down an alleyway lined with caved-in wet cardboard boxes. 'Where are you taking me?' He had the impression she was biding time, filling in the assigned hour like it was something to get through.

'Nowhere much,' she said. 'It's some sort of Italian place. I thought we'd have a coffee.' Mickey's expectations sank into his boots. The passageway seemed to be getting narrower, the far end was blocked with two overflowing wheelie bins with the space between them and the wall barely enough to squeeze through. He felt that she was deliberately disorientating him, making him lose his senses like a man dropping off a ransom. He was still following her when her phone rang. She stopped with her back to him. Standing still, Mickey smelt the ammonia odour of urine. He dented a Coke can by standing on it, trying to occupy himself while he strained to hear the conversation. After a minute, he kicked the can against the wall, shifted his weight for a few seconds, hunched up his coat collar and made to move off, overtake her and lead the way. He had dawdled as far as the end of the alley by the bins when she looked up. The distance between them was now a full ten metres though she didn't appear to notice when she spoke.

'That was my brother,' she said. Something about the acoustic of the walkway made her voice travel. 'It's my mum. She's at the hospital.' For a split second he thought she meant that she worked there as a cleaner, or a receptionist. She went on, 'Some sort of accident. Jase wants me to get up there.'

Mickey thought, shit. He explored the idea that this was nothing more than an elaborate hoax to cheat him out of even the hour she was granting him. But, even in the dark, with his eyes slanted shut against the light drizzle, he could make out that her face had flattened, and by straining her neck she had made her voice tight.

'Look, this might sound weird,' she said, 'but I don't suppose you'd come with me, would you?'

Her hands had fallen by her sides. Trapped between the dark walls she looked like a Victorian urchin. She said, 'I hate all this family shit. But he says it's pretty bad. He wouldn't phone up otherwise. It would really help.'

'Where is it?' Mickey asked pointlessly.

'Near King's Lynn.'

'But you know I don't drive.'

'That's all right,' she replied. 'I'd go on the train anyway.'

He moved two paces closer to her. A clump of posters were turning to mulch by his feet; he thought he recognised the swell of Honey Dew's breast on one fragment. Now Mickey told her yes, of course he'd go with her. He even mentioned his appointment with Dr Adebayo, not in so many words, but hinted he would cancel it. He reached for his phone and started dialling the surgery. As his fingers felt for the buttons, he felt his bones tingle and fizz. The surge dissipated as quickly as it had come over him. This was life and death, and very probably the first grown-up thing he'd ever had to do.

Sandy had joined him, taking tentative, pixie steps. Her head was bowed and he noticed how jagged her parting was.

He asked, 'This place we're going to—'

'Near King's Lynn.'

'OK,' he said placidly. 'Is it near the sea?'

'Yeah, it is. It's on the sea. It's near a big port.'

He took in the information without reacting. Later, when they had started walking back the way they had come, he said, 'Don't worry.' He wanted to put his arm around her to be friendly and feel heroic. 'I'll find out the times of the trains.' All the time in his head he was repeating the mantra, 'If I never ask for anything else again, please let something happen to her mother.' If nothing else, she would always remember who she was with the day her mother died.

IV

The captain watched the couple across the bridge. The drizzle had turned to rain. There was close to a full moon out somewhere beyond the City, that flipped in and out of gunmetal-grey clouds. Neither of the pair wore a hood nor carried an umbrella. The man walked first, slower than his usual pace, his shoulders not quite square with the bank, giving her an opening if she chose to catch up. The captain watched. He sat with his knees up, and his back leaning against the bulkhead.

With its aerial propped by a cleat, the radio was tuned to a World Service programme on social work, women's voices strident and oppressed. He had a seaman's natural dislike of women. He wasn't superstitious – superstitions were for the peasant Estepona fishermen who took statues of the Virgin Mary down to the sea to wash them for luck – but he disliked having females aboard. Disliked even mentioning them, or indeed even thinking about them. It only brought an unquenchable feeling that went beyond longing. He pushed himself on to all fours and reached over to switch it off, fearful even the sound might somehow contaminate.

He went below, clutching the chipped varnished handrail, and straight to the cooker to fire up the gas cylinder. He peeled three potatoes and threw them into an aluminium pot kept on the front gas burner, lining up three sausages under the grill. While they were cooking he opened up a new paperback about an Arctic explorer that he'd swapped with the Australian who ran a second-hand bookstall outside the South Bank. Within a minute, condensation had clouded the portholes, blocking out the world. Underneath the sink a row of pans rattled with the shifting ebb of a passing boat. But it was no good, just the discordant sound of the woman's voice had unsettled him and he found it impossible to concentrate.

V

They made the seven o'clock by ignoring the queue and using the automated ticket machine. Mickey used a credit card to pay for two open returns without comment.

'I'm pretty sure she'll be all right,' Sandy said when he handed one to her. 'It's not the first time this has happened. Plus, my brothers are there. Still,' she conceded, 'you might enjoy it.'

She didn't take her coat off, but sat hunched, with her chin resting in her hands, staring into the matt blackness beyond the window, oblivious to her own distorted reflection. He faced her with his back to the front of the carriage. The train was full of angry commuters resenting the influx of Christmas shoppers on cheap day returns filling up their peak price seats. Worse still, families unaware of their trespass, filling the air with the nervous excitement of having spent too much. A charge that, at Ilford, gave way to gloom. Mickey and Sandy shared a table with two overdressed women who were feverishly pulling the pages of cookery books as if they were porn.

He'd nudged an *Evening Standard* crossword into her line of vision and a pen. Sandy ignored them. Mickey sensed that, after the shock, she was more annoyed by the inconvenience than concerned.

'Come what may,' she'd told him, 'I have to be back in London on Friday.'

They changed trains at Norwich, taking a one-carriage shuttle out towards the coast. Minute by minute Mickey felt the air thinning, molecules of carbon monoxide giving way to oxygen and then, when the train pulled into a station and doors slid open, the oxygen was overtaken by a cold blast of some terrible brackish chemical.

'How are you?' he asked when they had been travelling for ten minutes.

'Me?' she said, distracted, as if there was a tickertape running through her head. 'Yeah, I'm fine. I wish those bloody kids would shut up, though.' A gang of teenagers was kicking a bottle under the seats, cheering when it passed through some sort of makeshift goal. Mickey shuffled on his seat, wondering if she was asking him to intervene. When the conductor, who wasn't much older than the gang, ambled down the aisle Mickey asked if he could tell them to keep the noise down. Thirty seconds later a cheer went up and Mickey suspected the conductor had colluded. If anything his intervention made it worse, but at least as far as Sandy was concerned, he'd tried. To disguise the raised noise level he said, 'Do you want to go straight to the hospital?'

'I guess so,' she said. 'Still, it is pretty late. What time does visiting close?'

'If it's an emergency . . .'

'Yeah, but is it?' She was weighing up. Out of the window, the night sky was punctured by a crane's L-shaped lights. His watch said 10.17. He hadn't eaten since lunchtime.

'Well, I know what I would do if it was my mum,' he said.

'Oh yeah, what?'

'Wait till morning.'

They took a taxi from the station and Sandy let herself into the caravan using a key smaller than a Yale, the type that might unlock a piggy bank. Waiting for her to find her key, which she seemed to put off to the last possible minute, Mickey was aware of the slap and grind of waves in the distance. He kept his head down, chattering his teeth, to block out the noise, not daring to look up. From his shallow vantage point, Mickey took most of the caravans to be empty; he glimpsed a string of coloured bulbs draped around the entrance to a snooker hall in the far corner, but other than that the place was deserted. Whereas other caravans had nested themselves into the plot, with pairs of stumpy bay trees by the door, or a fenced-off patio area, Sandy's was more a functional living box. It had *Wild Rover* painted on the side, which Mickey thought an odd name for a static caravan. The landscape was bleak – the type of place where toddlers got washed out to sea and French exchange students went missing. The air smelt of yeast.

When she let herself in she became clockwork, automatically checking the gas cylinder before she sparked the fire using a lighter kept behind a jar in the shape of a teddy bear. They were insulated from the mechanical scrape of the waves.

'Soon have it warm,' she said, rubbing her hands with her coat still on. Mickey heard the echoes of someone else, probably her mother. Mickey loitered at the door. Poised over the gasfire, Sandy suddenly made sense. She was neither teenage vamp, nor sexual icon, she was an ordinary woman whose chest had developed too far, too quickly.

He tried to imagine her mother. Nigel had once told him, in a moment of unasked-for intimacy after half a bottle of sloe gin one Christmas that one (and by that he meant men) should never get involved with a woman until he knew her pedigree. Not a class thing, he'd added, in case his mother had overheard – her background. Had her mother been a bolter? Nigel believed adultery was a gene. Mickey felt uncomfortable seeing this side of Sandy. He couldn't understand why she'd deliberately kicked the pedestal from under her, leaving her dangling like a condemned man.

'Where is your brother?' he asked.

'Brothers.' She shrugged. 'On the amusements, probably.'

Mickey held his breath. 'What time will they be back?'

'Who knows? Maybe later. Maybe never.'

Mickey eased his way further into the kitchen. 'They didn't say exactly what she had, then, your mum?'

'Some sort of fall,' Sandy replied. 'She'd have been drunk,' she added without feeling. 'She usually is.' She sat on the edge of a plain caramel-coloured sofa that curved around the bay window at the front of the caravan. Mickey wanted to put his arm around her, but something stopped him. Three photographs were propped on the glazed wooden mantelpiece above the fire where the varnish had chipped in the heat. Two of boys uncomfortably trussed in school uniform and one of a young girl in a tiara, her hair almost platinum blonde, wearing a green dress shaped for an adult, cut low for a cleavage waiting to happen.

'Look,' said Mickey. 'I'm hungry and you should eat something. Why don't I go and get a takeaway? Somewhere must still be open?' He angled the sentence as a question.

'Bloody woman,' said Sandy. For a half-beat Mickey thought she was recommending a restaurant. 'She always does this. Any time she thinks I'm on the verge of doing something – anything really – she pulls a stunt like this. It pisses me off that I still fall for it. But there are the boys. I can't leave them with her.' She looked up at him. All of a sudden, her lids were damp as if she'd been struggling with eye drops. 'You see, that's the reason I need the money. That's the reason . . .'

Mickey shifted his weight, raised his eyebrows and nodded. 'I see that. I really do. It must be miserable for you. I mean parents. I mean your mum.' He rolled his eyes upwards, taking in the plastic ceiling, and ran a hand over his chin. 'So,' he told her. 'If I find a chip shop,' he adjusted the rucksack on his shoulder, 'would you prefer cod or plaice?'

* * *

MILKING IT

Monica West was contemplating her epitaph. She poured herself another ouzo which, in her opinion, always made for a special evening. Plus, it gave her dreams an almost hallucinogenic quality and kept her in a mellow mood most of the next day. It came in a small carafe with another one of water. Two phials of see-through liquid, innocently standing side by side before the alchemy of cloudiness that heralded the countdown to drunkenness. As a concession to local sensibilities, she also ordered a thick sweet thimble of coffee, which meant twice now men had approached her, taking her to be Greek. Almost too hot to smoke, she picked up a beer mat to fan herself. Whenever the waiter, who was younger than her by twenty years, looked over at her he jerked his head back in a series of rapid movements. She resisted the urge to smile. She looked at her thighs on the white plastic chair. Never had any complaints, she said to herself.

She didn't know where Reggie had got to and she didn't care. Most likely he was skulking by the lobster pots, hoping one of the fishermen would talk to him and he could say, slowly, in his idiot's voice, 'Yes. I. Am. A. Fisherman too. In Great Britain. Yes. Lobster also.'

Lobster, also, she thought. With his apple-red face and red V at his neck. Or, he might have gone for a beer on his own on the stretch of bars closer to the apartment that he preferred because he said they were more authentic and the à la carte was cheaper. In any case, the good news was that by the time they next met, he, or she, or both would be drunk.

She watched another glass turn milky. Opposite her, shaded under an umbrella advertising lager, a man with his shirt open to the waist was smiling at her from under his sunglasses. She smiled back and raised her glass. Cheers, Monica said to herself, nodding her head to one side, enigmatic but confident, because in twenty-seven years of men, she'd never had any complaints. And they could put that on her gravestone.

VI

As Mickey had suspected, the sofa in the bay windows, with the addition of a board, converted into a bed. There had been no hint that he would share hers when she dismally offered up a thin sleeping bag and a duvet for him to choose. When she was washing, and changing into a pair of teddy bear pyjamas, he'd sneaked into her closet room where the air was draughty and fresh. There was a single divan swathed in a pink polyester quilt, and a line of seashells on the plastic dressing table in descending size.

'If the boys turn up, they'll go into Mum's room,' she said, flinging the cushions on to the carpet-tiled floor. She said, 'Sorry about this, but you can see how it is.' The plates from the fish and chips were stacked in the sink, he couldn't find a bin so he'd let the chips, batter and ketchup, squash together. The room smelt of grease now, which was better than the residual gas fumes which, along with the sea air, were cheating him of oxygen.

'It's pretty cosy in here,' he said, watching her make up the bed. 'Nice and warm.'

'I hate it,' said Sandy. 'It does my head in.'

'Why don't you move, then?'

She turned to him – she had unplaited her hair, which fell limply round her face – and rubbed her thumb round her palm. 'Money,' she said. 'And then, there's my mum.'

'What about her?'

She shrugged. 'You wouldn't understand. If I could get my money back, everything would be different. I might even be able to move to London. In one of those flats you were saying about. That would be just so cool.' Then she asked if he wanted any drinking chocolate, trying the taps, and adding that the water was off in any case. He told her he was fine.

'Good night, then.'

'Yeah, night.' Not that he really wished her good night; he

wished she would wander out of her room and slip into bed with him. He wished it with every semi-spell left in his body. He was still wishing it when he fell asleep. To save himself from the noise of the sea he put a pillow over his head, grinding his teeth to shut out the waves' sighs.

VII

The same flexible-jawed woman, with thick, problem hair started her routine at the same time every evening. Always the same song, which she sang in the same way, her feet rooted to the concrete forecourt, rotating her trunk from side to side, she sang, 'Do me, do me one more time, once is never enough from a man like you.' No one corrected her English, and by tonight, her fourth night, Monica was used to it. She didn't mind the singer. They were of a similar age. Monica liked to think that, unlike her, the singer was a woman who had had a few complaints. She would be too passive in bed and sweat excessively in inappropriate places.

'Mind if I join you?'

'Not at all,' said Monica, kicking the chair opposite her away from her, out towards the stranger's midriff. 'I don't know what's happened to my friend.'

He approached her with the low evening sun glaring behind him. She recognised it as a tactician's move, putting prey at a disadvantage. Making them screw their eyes together and bat the rays away with their hand.

His name was Emile and he was an Egyptian shipping agent from Cairo. He had learnt his English as an MA student in ocean trade in Portsmouth.

'Fancy that,' said Monica as he signalled for another carafe of ouzo.

'Let us drink to getting further acquainted,' he said, raising a glass. Odd, thought Monica, the amount of foreigners who came out with that line. It just wasn't right. She felt it needed another layer of translation. Her head was reassuringly fuzzy.

'Cheers,' she said. 'To us.'

VIII

Because of the pillow over his head, Sandy was properly in bed, lying full length behind him, before he woke up. Mickey was in the middle of a dream. A man, whom he took to be his Uncle Nigel but who looked nothing like him, as if he'd been miscast, was blowing up pink balloons and urging him to join him. Every third balloon contained water, and burst in a marble bath, drenching both him and Nigel. Nigel's mood was gung ho, but Mickey was circumspect, only pretending to enjoy himself.

He moved when Sandy slipped a hand around his waist; warm fingers massaging his flesh. Not sensually, more the way a cat would. She was breathing evenly and, had it not been for the fact that the walk from her room to his bed had turned her body – or the points at which it touched his own – icy cold, he would have thought she had been there for hours. He held his breath, waiting for her to say something, but nothing came. The air under the duvet heated up; she smelt of citrus or maybe a peach, a fruit-bowl smell that reminded him of his mother. He felt the stumps of her breasts in his back and a tension go through his body and then focus on his prick. He punched his body back into hers with an unconscious sleep-filled sigh, followed by the twitch of a man deep in REM sleep. He didn't know if this was a sign she wanted him to hold her, or was just after a warmer bed. Until she made her mind up, he was prepared to lie back and see what developed.

Chapter Nine

I

Mickey had been awake since first light, but it was the knock at the caravan door at just gone eight that roused Sandy. The type of knock that doesn't expect to get answered, a cough to herald arrival, seconds before you push yourself in. Only this time the door had been locked from the inside. For three seconds Sandy didn't move, keeping her breathing measured and even deep inhalations and short puffs of exhalation. Thin light seeped into the caravan under curtains and through the skylight; a wind had picked up in the night buffeting the outside; in the distance the unequal thud of a rail that had got loose.

The visitor spoke first as he thudded against the door. 'Mon?'

'That'll be Jim,' said Sandy, her voice matter-of-fact, making no reference to the fact she wasn't in the bed she had started out in. It was calm in a way that made Mickey think this wasn't the day's first rational thought. The absence of her body when she swept out of bed left a funnel of cold air. Mickey kept his head under the covers as he listened to Sandy sashay across the lino back into the bedroom. The crown of his scalp was so cold he wondered if he'd been rained on in the night. Ten seconds later, he heard the rattle of keys and felt the shift of air.

'Oh, Sand,' said the man, making it sound like a pleasant surprise. 'It's you. I thought it must be one of the lads. What are you doing back?' He sounded like a man who didn't regard women as a credible source of information. So he didn't wait for a reply, using the time to let his eyes roam, in order to draw his own conclusions. 'She got off all right, then? Where are the boys?' He spoke in fits and starts like he was smoking. 'Only the curtain's drawn and I thought something must have happened. Terrible thing last week at the Spar shop on the far prom. Gang of teenagers no more than thirteen years old torched a car in broad daylight. Mr Levine told me they couldn't have been more than twelve or thirteen. He had the CC tape but it got cleaned accidentally, something to do with a power surge, he reckons.'

Mickey listened to Sandy agreeing, not speaking, buffeting around the kitchen, picking up cups and then the hollow noise of a running tap in an empty metal sink which he avoided by jamming his head further down under the duvet. He recited a mantra for nondiscovery, though neither seemed to have noticed him. He tucked his head further on to his chest, acrid breath filling the bed.

Then Sandy said, 'No, everything's fine. Just thought I'd come back for a visit. Check up on Mum.' A mug chinked. 'You know how it is.'

He said something Mickey missed, that Sandy's louder voice drowned out. Then he heard a laugh.

He said, 'We've been reading your stuff in the paper. Well, I have, any road. Of course Mon gets the *Star*, doesn't she?' There was a pause while he flicked a Zippo. Mickey imagined the visitor's face was ruddy and placid. Sandy's would be a gloss of enthusiasm licked over blank-faced disinterest. 'Who'd have thought it?' the man went on. 'Sandy West, friend to the stars.'

'Well, I wouldn't go that far. The thing about it is . . .'

Mickey sensed the voices getting louder as the visitor settled in. The kettle started to whistle. Mickey suddenly foresaw the embarrassment of the visitor sitting on the bed, causing him to reveal himself. So he poked his head out from under the duvet, yawning to signal he was in the middle of waking up. The gas cooker and the breath of the stranger had taken the edge of cold out of the air. Jim was smarter than Mickey had imagined, in grey workman's trousers but with a pullover, shirt and tie. He was well over six foot and broad as a farmer.

'Hello,' Jim said, addressing Sandy suspiciously, but not looking at her, tilting his face to Mickey. 'Who's this, then?'

'His name's Mickey.' Making him sound like he was a deaf mute, or a pet. 'He's a friend of mine. He came down with me when we heard about Mum.' When his head was raised from his pillow, Mickey discovered there was no place to lean it to sit up.

'How do you do?' he said, rubbing his eyes.

The man ignored him. 'I only popped in because your mother asked me to keep an eye on the place. She told me she couldn't rely on the boys and that a fortnight was a long time to keep the place unattended.' There was a hiss of cigarette ash being knocked into the sink.

'How is she?' Sandy broke in. 'Have you heard anything?'

'Well, you know your mother.' He sighed. 'You hear when you hear, don't you? I doubt if I'll get a phone call. She might send a postcard, though—'

'Tea, Jim?' interrupted Sandy.

'No, love. Thanks all the same. I've got the dentist's at ten. Root canal trouble's been giving me gyp all week. I'm trying that place in the precinct. The other dentist left a while back, wasn't it? Now it's some sort of Thai woman, so there's no queue. I can wait if you want me to drop you anywhere?'

'No thanks,' said Sandy. 'I guess I'll make my own way there.'

Jim shifted his weight and jangled the loose change in his trouser pocket. 'Where?'

'The hospital.'

'You're not feeling too good?'

'Anyway,' said Sandy, suddenly pouring water into a stainless-steel pot. 'How's Maggie doing now? Baby OK?'

'Right as ninepence.'

Mickey eased himself upright, flipping the curtain back to use as a barrier to the steel-cold caravan wall. Sandy looked over at Mickey and said, 'Jim's daughter Maggie had a premature baby. Three pounds and two ounces was all it weighed. Isn't that right, Jim?'

'Well, the midwife gives you it in kilos but I can't be doing with that. Means nothing to me. Bag of sugar was what I said. Wasn't it, Sand? Baby Maureen was in an incubator for four months, though. Tubes, the lot.'

Mickey nodded. No one spoke.

After ten seconds had dragged on, Sandy said, 'OK then, Jim, thanks for looking in, I'll tell Mum you were asking after her, but you mustn't let us keep you.'

Jim looked surprised. 'Don't tell me you're going there too? Mind you, you'll be earning some with that column of yours. That's what I told Maggie. And she agreed.'

'Most definitely,' Sandy replied.

'And remember, you won't need a lot of stuff this time of year. I told your mother she'd packed too much. Though what a woman like your mother is doing with Reggie Withers, I cannot imagine. Whatever they say about her, your mother's got that touch of class. Only woman I know will not touch the coronation chicken at a buffet.' He looked at Mickey. 'Never smokes in the street, either.' He looked back at Sandy, rubbing the inside of his shirt collar. 'Besides which, it'll be hot, I told her.'

Sandy had pushed the door open and was shepherding Jim outside, saying something softly that Mickey couldn't hear. He put a hand up, flashing it out of the duvet, by way of farewell and yawned in the smell of gas and cigarettes. During the night, he'd shifted closer to the wall to accommodate Sandy so that now it looked obvious the bed had been shared. By the time Sandy turned from the door, he'd moved his weight back to the centre, in case she didn't want to be reminded.

Looking for neutral territory, he said, scratching his head, 'What did he mean, that she'd packed too much because it would be hot?'

Sandy reached up into a cupboard, dragging the synthetic material of her dressing gown over her buttocks.

'You know what hospitals are like these days,' she said, not turning round. 'They have the heating on full all day. They have to keep everyone ambient, that's the thing. Better to keep them too hot than too cold.' She squished the teabags around the pot with a dessertspoon. 'Is a Wagon Wheel OK for breakfast?' She turned to look at him. 'Or there might be some Harvest Crunch. Mum stocked up on biscuits, though.'

'Well, it can't have been all that serious if she had time to pack,' Mickey told her.

'True,' said Sandy, pouring the tea. 'Is this all right? Only the coffee's run out. Which is odd because she normally likes to stock up.'

'Tea is fine,' said Mickey, understanding there would be no reference to the night before. 'But I'm saying it must be a good thing,' he persisted, 'because if it was an emergency, like you said, then she wouldn't have had time to pack.'

Seeing Sandy in the caravan reminded him of the way he used to toast crisp packets on the fire when he was a kid, watching them shrink to a perfect miniature. The smaller he got them without melting the letters on to the coal the happier he was. Now it was as if the substance had gone out of her. That she had condensed to fit the space available.

'You know what hospitals are like,' said Sandy, smelling the top of a carton of milk. 'They encourage you to bring all your own stuff. When Maggie went in they told her she'd have to bring the lot. Blankets, nappies, sanitary thingies, all that sort of thing. Jim said he reckoned they'd have told her to bring her own forceps if she had them. That's the way of it now, I'm afraid,' she said.

She passed him a mug of tea that was chipped around the edges, as if someone had gnawed on it. She leant against the kitchen cupboard with a forearm across her stomach and a 'World's best mum' mug at her lips. He was expecting small talk. Instead Sandy said, 'You can't imagine how bad it is.'

'What,' said Mickey, 'the Health Service?'

'No, you dough-brain. My life, all of this.' She let her head roll round and he saw the underside of her chin was damp with the steam from her tea. 'My life circumstances. Look at it.'

'Sure,' said Mickey, hunching the duvet round his shoulders, 'but this is your mother's place. You could easily move out. Live some place else.'

She carried on, her small hands fluttering over the surfaces as she paced. 'If anything happened to my mother this would be my responsibility. Who would look after the boys?'

'It doesn't have to be,' he argued, moving to accommodate his swollen bladder.

She put her mug down to make a point. 'What about the boys? Who would look after them? If you look at it, on many levels it's nothing short of tragic.'

Her robe had fallen away at the front. She adjusted the belt but didn't cover the brown dunes of her breasts. Mickey tried not to look.

'It's a pain, I admit,' he told her. 'If you ever needed anywhere to stay, you know you are always very welcome at my place. It's not so big, but my mum and me managed—'

'What I want to know is, why should I have to live like this when other people have got huge places? Mansions even.' Her eyes reached out to him as if it were his fault. Oddly enough, he did feel culpable.

He waited for as long as he dared for her to change the conversation before he said gravely, 'No one ever said it was going to be easy.'

For a second he saw the colour drain from her face and her eyes narrow. 'What are you talking about? I had money and I lost it. Or rather that woman stole it from me. I have a plan, a good one to get it back and all I need –' she lifted her head – 'all I require from you is for you to lend me that waxwork for one lousy morning. Forgive me, but I would have thought, under the circumstances, namely my mum being at death's door, that wasn't such a big deal.' Her voice had started to quiver. 'Plus. What with my brothers about to be orphaned, I don't think it really would be too much to ask.' Then she started crying into the sleeve of her dressing gown.

Mickey knew he should comfort her but his bladder was full and he could feel the tingle of the start of an erection. Instead he stayed where he was. As a token gesture he put his mug on the floor and said, 'Look, don't cry. Please. I promise everything will turn out OK. Just please don't cry. We'll get the money, somehow.'

'Yeah, how?' The pink sleeve was damp and he could sense the mucus in her nose.

'You can have the waxwork,' he said. 'As long as Ray doesn't find out about it. You can borrow it.'

She frowned, still not ready to give up on the tears. 'Tomorrow morning?'

'If you like.' He picked up his mug to hint that normal behaviour should now be restored.

'OK, then,' said Sandy, biting at her sleeve. 'Thanks.'

'So then,' said Mickey, leaning back. 'What about that trip to the hospital? Visiting hours start pretty early, usually.' He knew this from Nigel's hiatus hernia in the Royal Free.

'No rush,' said Sandy cheerfully. 'Fancy another cup? Then there's a towel you can use in my bedroom, if you like. There's a sort of shower thing in the bathroom though the hot water gets jammed, so you have to watch it. And wait till there's some steam before you get in because it looks right out on to the bingo hall.' She paused. 'Not that anyone's playing bingo at this time.'

Mickey nodded as if he did know. Mickey felt as if he had been corralled into a pen just as the shepherd gated the only available exit. He finished off his tea. 'Go on then,' he said, putting out the mug to be collected. 'I'll have another cup.' Being hemmed in wasn't so bad. This was his thought while Sandy filled up the kettle so he didn't even notice the sound of water echo around the kettle's chamber.

Mickey dressed right down to his shoes in the bathroom. The inside of the shower curtain was slimy with mildew and the soap dish filled with a reservoir of cloudy water. He ran the shower while not actually getting in. The cosmetic applications in the bathroom were sucked out and dusty. An empty Chanel No. 5 bottle took the best position on the shelf, muscling in front of dehydrated L'Oreal bottles and a squeezed out Body Shop shower gel.

He wiped the condensation from the claw mirror that could be spun over to double the magnification. While he was washing he heard the sound of male voices above cupboard doors opening and closing. Then he heard the caravan door being slammed shut. He took the visitors to be Sandy's brothers. In his mind's eye they were both feral and knowledgeable about taking and driving away, and he was glad to have missed them.

Other than his mother, Mickey didn't have any family – certainly no young relatives to go on bike rides and discuss sweets with. At the age of eight, worried about his interpersonal skills, his mother had dredged up the daughter of a woman she had been at university with. The child's name was Kim and one day in November they set up home under a sheet draped over the dining-room table. Kim laid out a ward of dolls in beds made of pillowcases and told him he was the daddy. Mickey wasn't sure what to do and, when he asked her, Kim encouraged him to leave the silken confines of their house and look after things outside. Still unsure, he played with his train set by the electric fire until Kim told him his tea was on the table and he was allowed back in. It was an odd but enjoyable ritual so that when Kim and her mother left the next day, he missed her and for a week kept his

Action Man, a Christmas present from Uncle Nigel, stuffed in a pillowcase in homage to their time together.

Now, twenty years on, he really was playing mummies and daddies. Having her mother's illness so close at hand added another frisson, so that when Sandy called through to tell him she was going to the hospital, he felt an electrical charge of responsibility.

'Do you need me to come too?' he called out, his shirted back cold while he leant against a partition door to pull a sock on.

'No thanks,' she replied. 'It'll be easier if it's just me.'

'OK then,' he said. 'What do you want me to do?'

'*Do?*'

'You know, tidy up, cook?'

'Nothing,' said Sandy. 'Don't do anything. Just wait for me to get back. If anyone comes to the door ignore them. The boys are at the arcade. Watch the telly, or something.'

'Fine.' Mickey was both stung and relieved. When he heard the door pull shut and the noise of her locking it behind her, he realised he was more relieved than stung. Had she left the door unlocked he would have felt obliged to explore the area. Report back to her how he'd walked along the seafront watching the boats, or toured the slot machines on the pier, even won her some sort of cuddly toy. With the enforced captivity, his choices were limited. He aimlessly bounced from one side of the caravan to the other, touching the plastic surfaces. Now the smell of Sandy's perfume had started to wear off, he was left with a dusty, vegetable odour that came from sprouting potatoes.

She'd pulled back the curtains on a shallow terrace of badly paved concrete leading to a tarmac through-road with a half-dozen caravans facing him. Some trailers were clearly lived in; one, to the left, had a string of fairy lights in the window in the shape of a Christmas tree and another beamed with the grey glow of a switched-on television. Others were locked up. One had a printed sign in the window telling would-be burglars that the owners were away but that there was nothing to steal in any case. Something about it reminded him of Sandy in its functional straightforwardness. It looked worth plundering but all the signs, even from those who knew best, were that it wasn't.

The TV was tuned to an early morning talk show and Mickey was halfway through an overweight teenager's explanation of why she continued to date her crack addict boyfriend, when his phone went off. It was a muffled trill, deep in the bottom of his bag, and the wind was still beating a noisy path through the gullies of the trailer park, so by the time he caught sight of the number, it had switched over to voice mail. He had been expecting Ray, or work, which came up as words rather than numbers, but the digits he'd caught sight of (inner London) were none that he recognised. He watched while the teenager's putty-faced mother produced the girl's first boyfriend, who claimed to still love her, waiting for the message to beep. The signal was scratchy when he played it back, bending in and out of focus. It was a woman's voice. She sounded Eastern European but spoke English in a sliding way, not defining the ends of words and making only a stab at the consonants in the middle, making her accent more American than English. She said, 'This is a message for Mr Michael Defoe.' As if heading up a letter it went on, 'Mr Defoe, this is East West Shipping. You have written to our manager, Mr Prost, recently asking if we maintained a list of personnel for merchant ships up to thirty years ago. Mr Prost has asked me to give you a call. This I am doing.' Then she took a sharp intake of breath, weighing up whether or not to carry on. 'I wonder if you would be so kind as to call.' She recited a number and then repeated it, with the emphasis in different places as though she took pleasure in her own efficiency. Then she added as an afterthought that her name was Helga, she had a surname but none that Mickey would be able to reproduce.

On the chat show, the vacillating girl had decided to give her first boyfriend another shot, making Mickey think she was only after the attention. Then her uncle revealed the crack addict had been seeing the girl's best friend. The mother sat back, crossing and recrossing her legs, as if to say, 'See what I have to put up with?' Mickey stabbed the off button.

He drained his head. It was more information to add to his file. Back in London he'd also written to the Merchant Navy for a list of sailors who might have been commissioned in any of the ships, records permitting. Mickey was prepared to hunker down for the long game. For Mickey, this represented a flurry of activity, a whirlwind prodding of the bureaucratic process that he would hardly have thought he was capable of. How much he really wanted to discover the identity of his father and how much he was doing it to annoy his mother, he couldn't say. If anyone made him comment he would have said fifty-fifty. Perhaps, he reflected, picking aimlessly at foam stuffing oozing out of the tartan banquette, more seventy-thirty in favour of pissing off his mother. Typical of her to sleep with a man without knowing his name, never mind his full genetic make-up. But it wasn't lost DNA that had initiated this flurry of activity. It was more the way his mother's voice had dropped when he'd mentioned it. The reality of actually confronting his father was a different thing. Which was why he pressed the save message button, making a note to call Helga when he got back to London.

He mooched his way to the sink and ran the mugs under the cold tap, ignoring an ashtray where the grey dust had turned to paste. He rammed the discarded biscuit wrappers in a bucket under the sink already jammed with empty plastic tonic bottles, and was wondering about the logistics of dismantling the bed, when the phone on the wall rang to an odd one-beat ring before clicking on to the answerphone. The receiver was attached to a long cord that would give you access to most of the caravan while you spoke. In Mickey's first flash of panic he rooted himself to the carpet tiles. If it was Sandy, he'd pick up. When it spoke, nicotine bubbled out of the woman's voice and she sounded weary, as if she had far better things to be doing.

'Jason, if you are there, pick up,' a gravelly voice broadcasted into the room, tight with an echo on the line. 'Come on, love, pick up the phone,' she wheedled. There was a two-second pause when the tone dropped from pleading to irate. She went on, 'OK, then, be like that. I just called to say that I forgot to tell you we're overdue with the ground rent but Neville knows about that so don't worry if anyone comes round. Also, you need to tell doughnut Beryl to cancel my shifts. Her number is on the pad.' She waited, weighing out how much she should temper instructions with chat. 'Anyway, hope you're both well. Jason, keep out of those bloody arcades. The place is great. Hot. Reggie sends his love.'

Then she hung up. The last sentence was said with less conviction than the first two. Mickey sat down and tapped a pen on the side of his left temple. There had been a noise on the line like a hair dryer. Since when did people in hospital refer to the place as 'great'? At that moment he heard a key in the door.

'Only me,' said Sandy. 'Everything OK?' She bustled her way in with two brown paper bags and a plastic carrier.

II

The queue was at its fullest a day after Waxy Ladies was called a 'phenomenon' on Capital Radio's midday bulletin. It stretched from the gallery entrance as far as the Danish video store on the corner opposite the S&M emporium that hadn't changed its window display in all the years Ray had known it. Not that fashions in that department changed necessarily, he conceded, but it was a question of marketing. The scope of the gallery's new punters moved with the hour hand. Lunchtime saw a clutch of office workers, but mid-morning and afternoon the queue wasn't so very different from those outside *The Lion King*, or waiting for their spin on the Millennium Eye. In other words, family units, Ray told Jade. Perhaps it was fathers who saw the miracle as an excuse to steer their families from Oxford Street to Soho. Once inside, the mothers shielded their children from the Hot Wax gallery, but all in all the spirit was one of festival.

'An honest bit of voyeurism is nothing to be ashamed of,' Ray told them at the entrance in a reassuring voice designed to edge them towards purchasing the new £12.60 family ticket. 'Isn't that what your man Madame Tussaud is all about? We all want to take part in the extraordinary.'

By four, when the queue had dwindled to a family of Japanese, thinking this was the entrance to Handel's home, he said to Jade, 'I can't believe Mickey would have missed this. Where do you think he's got to?'

'Search me.' Jade was downstairs alone with Ray in the studio, leaning with her back to the cupboard, at the start of her twenty-minute break. Since the day before yesterday, Ray had taken on Anthony, one of Carlo's Saturday boys, to help on the door. He was a giant of a youth who shuffled on his heels with a round-shouldered stoop as if he still leant over a broom.

'Besides everything else, I need someone to go and fetch another load of T-shirts from across the road.'

'I don't mind,' Jade told him.

'Would you?' said Ray, breaking into a smile. 'Only you can see how I'm fixed.'

'What do these ones have on them?' Jade pulled her mobile from her bag checking for messages. '"I saw Madonna's tits"?'

'Less of your cheek, madam,' said Ray. 'If you really want to know, it says "The Miracle on Brewer Street". And while we're on the subject, I should remind you that this little caper means the door is up five hundred quid a day. Plus, you need to know there's a TV crew coming round from some French news programme. I told them after six. If I'm not here, let them in, can't you?'

'No problemo,' said Jade. 'I don't mind hanging around a bit later tonight. I'll wait to see if Mickey'll show.'

Ray inhaled on the butt of a roll-up, holding it between finger and thumb like a joint. He picked a strand of tobacco from the tip of his tongue. 'That bum. Trust him to miss all the hard work.'

'That's not fair,' Jade protested. 'Anything could have happened to him. If you want my opinion, he's been acting weird recently. You'd do better to be worried.'

'Bollocks,' Ray said, grinding the cigarette out. 'I'm off to Carlo's. Get upstairs and send that Anthony on a break.' He stared at the wall like he was figuring something out. 'The boy is a shite. In fact I've half a mind not to pay him.'

'Ray!'

'He moves about the place like something from the Hammer House of Horror. It puts people off.'

'Yes, but we can't all have your charm,' Jade told him.

'True enough,' said Ray, shrugging his coat hanger shoulders into his anorak.

III

'You were going to tell me why you needed it,' Mickey looked at his watch, licked his finger and wiped a stain off its face. Sandy sat opposite him, reading a magazine. The train had been at a standstill for more than half an hour. A man introducing himself over the PA as the chief steward told them, with a thick country accent, it was due to a 'faulty receptor' at Kelvedon. Sandy and Mickey's relationship had developed so that anything of note, broadly under his tag of 'future', was discussed while they travelled. Domestically, in the caravan, they talked about other stuff. He'd even maintained the pretence of believing her mother was in hospital when she got in, asking her how long the doctors planned to keep her. More than a week, but less than two she'd told him, staring straight at him unblinking. By all accounts, they'd never seen a thrombosis like it. Right up her leg, it went.

No kidding, Mickey told her, because part of him, most of him, was reluctant to give up on the idea that Sandy's mother was close to death.

'Why I need what?' She didn't look up. While other people skimmed through magazines, snatching at pages and ignoring whole sections, she studied every word, even moving her lips slightly as she read.

'The waxwork.' They had caught the 11.13, too late for shoppers and commuters but too early for theatregoers. A woman whose uncombed hair fell at odd angles and looked like she hadn't seen her own reflection for months, tried to pacify three toddlers with a colouring book. Mickey didn't like to be overheard in public. When it had been just his mother and him, taking the train to visit Uncle Nigel, they travelled in silence.

Sandy, on the other hand, couldn't seem to care less. 'I've got a plan to make a lot of money,' she said. 'Or, should I say, get it back?' A scream went up opposite them when the colouring book ripped in half, spilling two cartons of squash.

'Such as?' Mickey dropped his voice to a whisper to encourage her to do the same. Against the odds she responded, with her face angled towards the table.

'Well, it's like this—'

The electric door chugged open. 'Tickets from Hatfield Peverel.' The conductor was dressed head to toe in shades of burgundy, like a bellboy. It was a startling uniform, designed to show the company's commitment to improved rail travel.

'Any idea when we'll be moving again?' Mickey asked as he handed over his ticket.

'Couldn't tell you, mate,' replied the conductor, as if he'd asked him something utterly beyond his remit.

'Typical,' Mickey said when he'd moved on. 'It's incredible. Like he's proud of the fact he knows nothing.'

Sandy looked at him incredulously and said, 'Relax. What can you do? We'll get there sooner or later.'

Mickey raised his eyebrows and sat back, leaning his head against the seat. 'It's all right for you, I've got to be back in London for two thirty.'

'Why?' She looked up from her magazine.

'An appointment,' said Mickey, keeping it vague.

'Yeah,' Sandy went back to reading. 'You said. The doctor's?'

'Kind of . . .'

She was pawing the photographs as she read. It struck Mickey she might think he had something unspeakable or untreatable. 'It's nothing medical,' he assured her, 'good God, nothing like that. It's more like a counsellor.'

'You mean,' she spoke in a flat voice, 'a shrink.' Mickey couldn't tell if she was being nonjudgemental or she couldn't care less.

'Ish,' Mickey told her. 'A shrink-ish.'

Sandy twisted her torso down into the aisle to reach into her bag and pulled out an A4 pad and pen. A frown chiselled its way into Mickey's forehead. He misread his sudden energy and thought: is she starting to take notes?

'Relax,' she said, uncapping her pen and looking straight at him. 'A shrink's cool. I knew someone who went to one once. He had this thing about managing his anger. Well, that's what the doctor said. He referred him to some sort of anger counsellor. I thought he was just a headcase.' She bent down to start writing.

'So?' urged Mickey.

'So, what?'

'What happened?'

'Oh,' she said. 'We lost touch.' She nodded as if that was the end of it.

'No,' said Mickey, 'I mean what happened at the anger counsellor?'

'I dunno.'

'He didn't go?' Mickey sat forward.

'No,' she said, 'he went, but the clinic thing was late opening, so he hit the doctor.'

'Terrific.' Mickey moved his weight from one buttock to the other.

'Yeah, well, it happens.' Sandy looked at him. 'The way I see it is that you get the hand you're dealt and then the real test is how you deal with it.' She had opened the pad and was sucking the end of the pen as though on the verge of a great thought. 'I mean, take you, for example. It so happens you don't have a father—'

'I do have a father,' said Mickey. 'Actually—'

'OK.' Sandy put her hand up. 'So, big deal, you have a father. But,' she looked like the next bit was weighted in significance, 'not one that you know about.'

'So?'

At the table opposite two of the toddlers had started making a noise like a car alarm. A businesswoman stood up theatrically, as if everyone was looking at her and swayed past them, heading for another carriage.

'So,' Sandy went on, 'rather than letting it ruin your life—'

'Who says I let it ruin my life?'

'No one, I'm making a model here.' She shook her head. 'You want my advice? Just get on with it. To my mind, I've been dealt the worst hand since cards were invented, but I don't let that stop me.'

'It's tricky,' said Mickey. 'I don't want to hurt my mum.'

'Bullshit,' said Sandy.

'How do you know it's bullshit?'

'An educated guess. She hurt you, didn't she?'

'What do you mean?'

'Making you half an orphan. Listen,' she cocked her head on one side, 'the natural tendency of the child is to blame the parent,' she said. 'I read that. Plus.' She stopped as if she'd lost her train of thought.

'Plus?'

'That guy in the anger counselling?'

Sandy nodded. 'He told me something interesting, once.'

'Such as?'

'Well, his dad was a boozer. Used to be plastered every night of the week. Came home and was mean to everyone. Didn't hit anyone, though, but he reckoned he came quite close to walloping his mother. Well, he used to say the best thing you can do, like ever, is to forgive your parents.' She nodded in a way that irritated Mickey – he didn't know whether from her fortune cookie profundity or the fact it sounded as if she'd slept with the guy.

'You don't say?'

'Yeah.' She went back to her pad, her pen painfully slow on the paper.

'Yeah, but . . .' argued Mickey. The train churned and groaned into motion, lurched forward a metre and then fell back as if a rope had broken. Mickey fell back into silence. The sun was shining but the leafless scrub either side of the track had a glint of frost still clinging to it. A couple of red berries shone out from the underneath of a bush.

'I mean,' said Sandy, 'my mother was a shiftless sort of bitch who gained credibility by putting me through beauty pageants. But then, so what?' Sandy shrugged. A stain of red had appeared in the shadow to the right of her throat. 'You know how I did so well on that *Big Sister* shit? I have no delusions about myself. I am what people want me to be. You want to manipulate people? You act dumb and work on their vulnerabilities.' Mickey found himself unable to look at her. 'Why did that woman in a suit just move carriage? Because she was pissed off by the noise of those kids.' She hushed her voice when she spoke. 'How come that affected her? Because she thinks it's not fair she hasn't got some of her own.' She smiled. 'And that's the Achilles heel that you'd work on.' She shrugged. 'Simple.'

Mickey continued to look out of the window. Sandy didn't speak, though he could hear her breathing, which was irregular.

'So,' Mickey said, needing to lighten her mood and let her know he didn't take her comments seriously, 'how have you assessed me?'

She shrugged and went back to her pad. 'Stuck in the past. You look back rather than forward.' She nodded at the respective seating arrangement. Mickey had his back to the front of the carriage. 'See what I mean?'

Mickey snorted back a snigger. He said, 'Come on, Confucius, you can't hold that against me. I only sat like this to keep the sun out of your eyes.'

Sandy put both hands up. 'Whatever.'

She went on writing. Mickey suddenly said: 'What are you doing? I hope that's not about me.'

'It's my column, you freak,' she said frowning. 'I might as well use the time.'

'You're writing about a rail delay in Kelvedon?'

'No, headcase.' She smoothed down the centrefold pages of the magazine in front of her and took a slurp of coffee from a plastic cup. 'Right now I'm at the opening of the,' her finger traced the line she was on, and she read from the magazine, '"latest funkiest artists' hang-out to hit the scene this year. The Blue Oval in ever-so-chic Hoxton."' She shrugged and went back to writing. 'Up to my armpits in caviar, if you must know.'

'Imagine,' said Mickey. Again, he felt the strain of the cogs wrestling into life as the chassis edged forward another inch. He didn't like to say anything, but the caviar picture was not an entirely attractive one.

Mickey was thinking about Sandy's pop psychology. He thought, is it time to get my life on track and, if so, how?

Sandy looked up; her eyes were fired, and the white flecked with tiny chips of orange. She said, 'Do you spell whiz, with one Z or two?'

'One,' he told her, looking at his watch. It was gone one thirty and there was no sign any movement was imminent.

IV

The captain was one of the few people queuing to have brought a book, other than a guidebook, with him. In the end, by the time he arrived at gone four, the lack of people meant he only spent a page with Shackleton's account of his voyage to the Antarctic on the *Endurance*. It was a pity, he thought, because he looked forward to dipping into the near tragedy, marvelling at the crew's wonderful (womanless) adventure. To pass the time, as they bedded down for their second Christmas locked in the ice, they tortured themselves by describing their favourite puddings. Some wanted steamed, another – the first mate – favoured an egg tart. How much better for them, how greatly increased their chances of survival, the captain imagined, if the crew had never heard of spotted dick or tasted custard? How much easier life would be if you had no knowledge and therefore no expectation.

'Are you alone?' The black woman behind the till had a nametag: Jade.

'Yes,' he said. 'I suppose so.'

'Then that'll be eight pounds sixty.' She nodded at a price list stapled to the wall.

'*How* much?'

'That includes access to all galleries,' she told him, flicking open a pink fist and ringing the amount up on the till, meaning he was now obligated.

'Does that mean the one with the contestants from *Big Sister*?' He undid the Velcro on his canvas wallet.

Jade frowned. 'You're not here for Madonna, then?'

'Her as well. I just thought I would have a look at the rest.'

'Suit yourself,' she said. 'But not all the *Big Sister* lot are up, yet.'

'What about that Sandy West?'

Jade frowned and her head shot back in bafflement. 'Nah, not yet.' He handed her a ten-pound note, whistling at it to make sure it wasn't stuck to any others. 'But the others are pretty lifelike.' She listed them, 'Erika Roe, Pamela Lee, Lady Godiva, Jordan – prepregnancy, of course.' She dropped his change in a pitcher's mitt of a hand.

'Of course.' He was past the umbrella stand on his way into the gallery, Jade having moved on to serve a family of Swedes, when he called back to her, 'Mickey been in, at all?' as casual as a bar regular. And before she could remember who she was speaking to, Jade replied. 'Not been here all day. Will be tomorrow, though. Got to be.'

Only when she'd finally explained the family ticket to the Swedes, refused their offer of euros, and scalped a twenty-pound note from the holiday purse, did Jade wonder who the man with the fuzz of short peppery hair and gardener's hands was.

V

They parted at Liverpool Street Station in the stagnant pool of people waiting under the departure board, resisting the tidal ebb into the cavern entrance of the underground. Mickey told her he was going to walk to Moorgate and get the Northern Line home. He'd rehearsed it on the train. He didn't want their farewell (a kiss?) to be in a Tube carriage under the hot eyes of other passengers straining from their magazines. This route took him under the Thames, and he would feel the pressure in his head build until he made it from Bank to Elephant and Castle, but today his need to get home outstripped the alternative walk. He'd had to postpone his appointment with Dr Adebayo until tomorrow.

'You'll be OK?' he asked her.

'Sure thing.' She hitched her shoulder bag up, businesslike, feeling none of his reticence to leave.

'So . . .' He smelt a buttery waft of croissant or waffle.

'So,' Sandy said. 'We're still on for tomorrow?' She was chewing gum with ferocious little chomps.

Mickey wondered if he'd missed something. 'Sure,' he said, 'what do you fancy?'

'No, you dork,' she said. A flutter of numbers flitting on the board above them meant another train had left. Workers going home, couples coming in. 'Tomorrow,' she spelt it out. 'We do the waxwork.'

'Yeah, course I remember,' Mickey told her, as if he knew he'd been goofing around. Then added fast, 'Only what do you plan putting it in, a wheel barrow?'

'Der . . .' said Sandy. 'My friend's got a van.'

'Your friend?'

'Relax,' she said. 'Not that sort of friend.'

'So it'll be the three of us, then,' said Mickey. 'You, me and the friend.'

'And the waxwork.'

'Remind me again what all this is about.' He put his hand out to steady her as a woman in a long camel coat buffeted past them.

'I'll let you know tomorrow.' She reached up and kissed him on the cheek. Her lips smelt of raspberries and when he touched his skin she'd left a snail's trail of gloss. 'Trust me,' she added, still chewing. 'Oh,' she turned to join the whirlpool, 'thanks for coming with me to see Mum.'

Mickey was nodding at her narrow back, her shoulder blades jutting through the thin material, long after she'd disappeared into the Tube.

VI

Mickey exited the Tube and set off on foot towards the Oval. Red buses overtook him, sucking him in and out of their slipstream like an artificial lung. Kennington Lane was for him a good route, on the rare occasions he was coming from the City. The labyrinth of sixties office blocks and out-of-the-way terraces shielded him a good half-mile from the river. The air was dimming and thickening with the sense of abandonment, a desolate hour that heralded the end of the day before the evening waded in. Bulbs were being flicked on. The pavement, greasy with puddles Mickey hadn't seen form, was empty and shone from headlights. Even the bus stops, save for a couple of drunks, were deserted in the slow hour before offices emptied. Mickey hunched his coat around him, put his head down against the west wind and tried to make himself walk, and think, in even, logical steps. But it wasn't easy. After a quarter of a century of luck-seeking, lop-sided gait, Mickey automatically avoided the cracks. Which brought him to his first point.

With luck, he could finish his self-portrait in wax and then return it, in lieu of himself, to the water, preferably the sea, though any water would do. Hopefully this would mean the start of a new phase of his life. His demons would be appeased and he would be free. Free to be normal. He would be able to unlock the secrets others took for granted. Secrets that prevented him from sitting on interest-free sofas watching water-cooler programmes, and knowing the best type of naturally carbonated mineral water on the market. That's how it would start. But before he knew it he would be talking about mortgage rates and house prices, bar facilities in Düsseldorf airport and the comparative merits of Courchevel 1600 and 1800. No more lucky stones, no more talismans. He just needed a kick-start. And the kick-start was the effigy.

Somewhere deep to the left of him he heard a car horn. Mickey looked up. Closer to, the insistent beep of the green man told him it was safe to cross the road. Ahead of him, the gulley down to the Thames between a coffee shop and a Launderette was the most exposed this route got to the river. He rounded his shoulder against the view and kept his eyes slit shut, as a precaution against the wind as much as anything. So that when he saw the tramp, back-lit by the string of white bulbs, running along the embankment, for a split second Mickey took the streamers of red hair and long strips of fluttering coloured polythene to be some sort of fire.

Bagman was waving at him. Mickey felt a current of alarm that sent a trickle of sweat down his spine. But, still twenty metres away, Mickey felt in no immediate danger as he tagged off to the left. He estimated he had three metres until he was out of the tramp's line of vision.

'Hey, man.' The tramp was calling to him, shuffling towards him with both pigeon-toed feet swaddled in carrier bags. 'Wait up.'

For a down-and-out, Mickey later reflected, he moved fast. Mickey speeded up to his maximum speed without breaking into a run as Bagman rounded the corner. Now they were under the lee of the concrete extension of an office block that reached over the pavement, hobbling from pillar to pillar. Bagman called something again that Mickey missed because of the depth and splutter of his breathing. Mickey was reluctant to look behind him. Instead he read the alarm on the faces of people walking in the opposite direction. A young mother pushed a pram in a wide arc to avoid the whole scenario, and the delivery man dropping off office stationery retreated quickly into his van. Only when the faces of passers-by returned to blank normality did Mickey slow up, which was when the tramp, who had detoured around an uninterrupted concrete column to Mickey's right, caught him. He grabbed him with a hand on his shoulder, firm but not hostile, and the smell of burnt rubber and tin.

'Hey, man,' he said. 'I knew it was you. What's been up with you?' Straight on, the pores on his face were clogged, giving his mottled red skin a dappled look. His nose looked like a month-old strawberry while his eyes were the colour of bluebells.

Mickey turned to face him, aware that the game was up. 'Mate,' he said, 'I didn't recognise you. How are you?' He went through his pockets and came out with a two-pound coin.

Bagman grunted. Mickey wondered if it was possible to snub a tramp.

He said, 'Look, why don't you take this?' He searched for a strip of plastic that might have been an arm.

'It wasne the money so much as the company,' said Bagman. 'Knowing someone cares. You know?'

'Course,' said Mickey. 'Look, I'd love to stand and chat but I'd better not keep you.' Mickey curled the coin back into his palm.

The tramp said, incredulous, 'Keep me from what?'

'Oh,' said Mickey. 'You know.' He turned on his way, wishing somehow that he'd managed to offload the coin. On the other side of the street a group of schoolchildren started to jeer, led on by a girl in lumpy platform shoes.

'I'll see you then,' said Bagman, almost as if he'd picked up on Mickey's discomfort.

'Most probably tomorrow,' Mickey told him, walking backwards, air whistling down his collar, anxious to be home. Suddenly, from nowhere, Mickey shouted, 'Sorry, I forgot to ask your name?'

'What, my name?' repeated Bagman. 'My name is Harold.' He spoke firmly but after a pause, as if irregularity of use, as happened with a credit card, had called it in to question.

VII

Helga Kristiakova would, at the date of the Russian Orthodox Christmas, have been at East West Shipping's London branch for seven and a half months. She knew it exactly because she was looking forward to moving back to Tallinn in the New Year. Lack of professionalism and citywide graffiti were the reasons she planned to give on her exit interview. The real reason was that the affair she'd hoped would blossom to maturity with the head of the Pacific Rim had withered on the vine – in fact had got no further than a fevered kiss in a hospitality tent at Ascot. What was the point, she asked herself, of her unerring efficiency if she had no one to share it with?

Working beyond her remit was so standard these days, she'd all but given up on commenting on it. Take for instance the request of Michael Defoe. A man who thought it was nothing for her to dig out the archive from nearly thirty years ago – a time when the Tallinn office wasn't even open – to come up with a list of crew for the *Baltic Star*, berthed at Harwich from 17 August 1973 to 19 August 1973. Did he think she had nothing better to do?

Lucky for the little so-and-so, she thought, that Helga Kristiakova took personal pride in her work. She'd come up with the list all right: eight Yugoslavians, twelve East Germans, three Lithuanians and one Scot. If he'd only return her call, if that one small courtesy wasn't too much trouble, then she'd give him the name.

Chapter Ten

I

Honey Dew woke early for two reasons. She was thirsty and her head was thick from last night's launch party of what she was dubbing the debut of her screen career. An Internet search engine called Boob were paying her a one-off five-figure sum to appear as an interactive URL on the Website, click on either nipple. It wasn't the screen she dreamt of, but it was a start. The other reason was because she wanted to see the penultimate shot of her countdown. She picked up the remote control, switching the television news on, as she stumbled across the bedroom. The dual billboard on the opposite side of the river had been following the *Pump* series, alternating it with a garden centre advert. In order to keep watch on it, Honey kept a pair of small binoculars, which she'd found in a kitchen drawer, on the windowsill. The photographer hadn't told her which shot would be for which day. By Honey's calculation they were a farmhand shot down. Sure enough, her eyes met a projection of herself dressed as a rustic milkmaid. The caption read, 'Prepare to get pumped up for the big one.' As her eyes traced the contours of her body falling into shape, she heard the news anchor report a twenty-four-hour light entertainment blackout due to the strike. Honey did a quick totting-up of how this news would affect her. It would not. She replaced the binoculars, picked up her mail, and sat at the dining table.

As the countdown to Day Zero had gone on, Honey Dew had felt the pressure of exposure in a literal and figurative sense. Her thought, as she went through her stack of mail, was what if everyone saw her bare-breasted, and understood her nipples for what they were, two circles of dark flesh? That, she said to herself as she sipped a glass of orange juice, she did not deserve. What scared her to the bottom of her acidic stomach was that offers were drying up. True, she was still owed twenty-five grand from the *Pump* for the final shot, but would that cover the remainder of a life should it have to survive outside the media spotlight? Last week, other than the Boob offer, she'd received an invitation for a celebrities and their bras show on cable, and to be a topless weather girl from a Spanish station aimed at ex-pats that broadcast out of Marbella. She'd anticipated an increase in interest in her in the run-up to the last day, but interviews had waned. Yesterday, a producer from a mid-morning chat show had cancelled her interview, fearing a feminist backlash. 'And women do,' she told Honey, 'make up our core audience.' Honey has responded by slamming the phone down. She sensed the beginning of the media back-off and Honey was a girl who deserved more.

The invitation stood out from the rest of Honey's post: junk mail from credit card companies, loan firms and computer-generated Christmas cards from make-up counters. As usual, the letters had been noiselessly rested on the wool twist carpet outside her door. It had been a struggle getting the janitor to agree to bring the post up to her, but Honey found the interruption of getting dressed, or throwing at least a few clothes over her nightie, in order to take the lift to the ground floor to check her pigeon hole, completely ruined the equilibrium of her early morning routine. This way, by having them left in a special box outside her door, she could assimilate the function seamlessly into her day. That was what she'd told the bursar, that exact phrase.

Since then her mail had been delivered straight to her door.

Meaning she opened it over breakfast while drumming the heel of her Agent Provocateur mules against the table leg. The invitation wasn't one Honey Dew was used to. Usually there was a gimmick on the envelope, a stylised logo, or her name in some funky seventies font. This came in a plain white envelope, straight to her home address, and was handwritten in gold pen with heart shapes instead of dots. Handwritten she could understand; PR companies used immigrants to copy out addresses to separate their mail from the rest of the junk, give it a fair chance of being opened, make you think it had come from a friend. Honey couldn't remember the last time a friend had invited her to anything.

She used a paper knife to slice it open, scarlet nails, like eager drops of blood, ferreting out the information. There was no address in the top right-hand corner and no date. It wasn't a greetings card, more of a thank you notelet written in an intriguing scrawl.

> Festive greetings, Honeykins.
>
> Didn't get much of a chance for a yarn last Friday. What a bash!! Me and the girls are having a catch-up tomorrow morning and wondered if you could make it. It'll be at Greens first for the HTV Awards, natch, and then we're off to Morphia for lunch. Sorry it's late notice but you know how it is. Can't wait to see ya!!

It was signed in a series of concentric circles. Honey had no idea who it was from. Neither had she heard of the HTV Awards. Were they a hybrid of MTV and Hampshire television, or ITV and HIV? In either case she hadn't received an invite. She sifted through the remaining pile to see if she'd received a late one. Nothing. And who was this woman whom she hadn't caught up with last Friday, who sounded friendly to the point of being needy? That, combined with the HTV Award snub, made her think she deserved a trip out. She finished her juice, licked the orange bits from the inside of the glass, sat back and started to think about outfits.

Mickey woke at 7.35 to the noise of workmen on the railway, bricks clattering hollowly on pipes. He rolled over with the sense that he was floating, that the extension that jutted fifteen feet into the downstairs neighbour's garden was a capsule in free fall. Jade had been in his dream, which was one of impermanence. They were camping on a strip of park in front of Hammersmith town hall, where Uncle Nigel had taken up a job as transport minister. The river was less than ten metres away and, sensing his disquiet, Jade had let him sleep on the springy tufts of her hair. He knew he should have felt comfortable but instead his sleep was ruined by her hair slide, which kept jabbing him.

At 7.45 Mickey twisted over again and pulled a plastic spatula, melted at the edges, from under him. Now his thought was of Sandy and their meeting that morning. Rather than one of undiluted joy, the idea of seeing her made his brain clog, as if the image of her barred the course of his electrical pulses. He rolled over. Although his mother had moved out, Mickey continued to sleep on the strip of space in his studio, lying alongside his waxwork. The sheet that he used as a throw to cover the statue had doubled as an undersheet not thick enough to remove the imprint of ridged carpet tiles from the pressure points of his buttocks and shoulders. He scratched the part of his forearm that had fallen away out of the sheet. When he opened his eyes and looked up, he saw the wax joint of his elbow mirroring his own, poking over the edge of the bench like an ice floe. Most of his duvet was hunched over him, up to his chin, protecting him from the day. A greasy light seeped in through the curtainless window, along with a draught that smelt of tarmac. Next door the jingle of a radio station danced above the sound of voices.

On the count of three, Mickey tossed back the duvet. Cooped up, thirty feet up off the ground, alongside his corpselike twin and alone in the room, Mickey decided that day it was time either to amalgamate or give up.

Jennifer blamed her sleepless night on the crumbs. But then, crumbs were standard. Jennifer took a slice of carrot or seed-ridden banana cake to bed with her most nights, to gnaw at alongside her Virago novel and gin and tonic. Because she disliked having to get up to wash her teeth, she kept a toothbrush and paste in a beaker next to her bed. When she forgot a bedside tissue, she occasionally wiped her mouth on the underside of her sheet, until she realised the milky stain made her look like a willing sexual partner. No, last night's thrashing certainly had nothing to do with either sex or the rivulet of cake crumbs nestling in the central spine of her bed. She reached out to the radio. For reasons not made clear, her usual radio station was not broadcasting. She returned to the World Service. As far as she could make out, a war appeared to be starting in the Middle East. All the interviewees seemed to understand how serious it was but none of them was able to make it relevant. One man banged on about the effect on the oil price, but the feeling was one of general lethargy. The item segued to a ban in the UK on fox hunting, which everyone felt quite militant about. Jenny agreed absolutely, so that 'poor foxes' became her first conscious thought. Then the Prime Minister came on reading a poem he'd written on the death of a rock star from AIDS. Jennifer harrumphed and turned her back on the radio, drowning it out with the sound of her grinding teeth. Her second thought was of her son and whether he was suffering from a mild form of autism. The medical profession claimed autism was a new phenomenon but, on the contrary, most people she knew seemed to suffer from it. Other than an unrecognised qualification in aromatherapy, Jennifer had no formal medical qualification, but her dictionary described the condition as 'abnormal self-absorption, characterised by lack of response to people and limited ability to communicate'. She'd memorised the definition. But when she'd brought it up with

Pammy and Elaine after a rehearsal they'd agreed the symptoms were common to all one's children; more than that, the whole younger generation.

In fact, they'd reflected dismally, by then on their third pints of organic micro bitter, ninety-nine per cent of the population. Pammy had made that last point, looking at Jennifer as she'd done so.

Mickey's lack of ambition was one thing. Lack of drive, she didn't mind. After all, rabid pursuit of one's career was so 1980s, so *male*. One day he'd stop creating those exploitative waxworks and become a real artist, one she could be really proud of. She groped for a pumpkin seed husk from the groove under her shoulder. Downstairs she heard Nigel filling the kettle. Had she been wrong to keep her son's father's identity a secret from him? Fathers, sons, grandfathers, uncles – so many men. If only she'd kept her power dry, not had a baby, but stayed an academic, chivvying her way through documents, reading and rereading in order to find the truth. When Mickey discovered the truth, would he blame her? (Almost certainly.) It wasn't as if she'd done the thing on purpose. It had simply happened. Did she deserve no credit for the sacrifices she had made bringing him up? Never expect thanks from a child. She'd read that somewhere. The only time you can change a man is when he's in nappies. She'd read that too. The voices coming from the radio were softer now. She heard Nigel depress the plunger on the Dualit and the bubbles of the percolator. She started to doze while the anxiety in her stomach crystallised. She and Nigel would have to visit Mickey today. She was even glad Pammy's militantism had made them join the actors' strike. After some debate in a Barnes teashop they had decided to throw themselves into the 'real' faction. 'Variety' sounded so Wayne Sleep. She turned over. She'd talk to the boy, one to one, reason with him. Sort the whole bloody mess out before it was too late . . .

* * *

Sandy propelled herself out of bed, tingling in that way when you heat up too quickly coming in from the cold. That was the way it felt, like the ice was breaking. Less than forty-eight hours and it would all be over. She had the waxwork, she had the evidence and she had the contacts. She groped her way to the bathroom, away from the window where the air was warmer, still groggy, having woken a nanosecond before the alarm went off, requiring a few seconds to piece together her surroundings. She peed and returned to the bedroom, switching the TV on. Two presenters, a man and a woman she'd never seen before, wearing the same red fur-trimmed hat, had the same irritating 'school's out' way of acting. Sandy tutted and, unable to find the remote, pushed the buttons until she found the news. Why the forced end-of-term mentality? She hated that – the way some people acted to others' agendas; too stupid to have their own.

Someone, a terrorist, had blown up the place where the baby Jesus had been born. But, rather than serious men in suits sitting in judgement, a six-year-old girl with bunches, dressed as the Virgin Mary, was telling a journalist what Jesus meant to her. When the camera returned to the sternly dressed anchor, she was in tears. Sandy thought: good for her. If they were going to broadcast that level of bullshit, why not make the most of it? She kept the news on while she filled the kettle and let it boil while she showered. She took her time and washed her hair, leaving it to dry as she made a cup of tea. She opened a packet of bourbons from a stash she'd stolen from the chambermaid's trolley. The meeting with Mickey was in three hours; until then she had a column to write, hopefully her last. As she completed each task she felt the picture clearing as if she was making her way along a dot-to-dot picture that formed a pot of gold when completed.

She frowned. After yesterday's Hoxton opening, she really had exhausted every function in her current shelf of celebrity magazines. She had no idea what the topic could be. There was simply no story left, so much so in fact, she wondered if she couldn't get away with commenting on the Middle East bombing. Then again, why should she care? Her obligations to the *Daily Pump* were close to being over – other than their settling up with the Malindi Sands – signalling the end of her bogus journalistic career. She had only one final ambition. Still in her pyjamas, with her wet hair curled on her shoulders, she booted up the laptop with one hand, holding a biscuit in the other and started to write.

> From where I sit high up in my penthouse suite it is easy to forget the meaning of Christmas. Unless, of course, we take time from our busy schedules to think of what Jesus did for us. Christmas, even for celebrities, is a time for giving. Kings and queens across the world will be doing just that at this special time of year.

The *Pump*'s editorial style was to highlight the first letter of each sentence. Another couple of paragraphs and, reading left to right, she'd have 'FUCK OFF GAYE BUTTERWORTH' imprinted on every edition. She knew that the act of rebellion served no useful purpose and was therefore an indulgence.

Sandy sat back and rubbed the tips of her fingers, trying to ease the blood flow. Now her head flashed to the lyrics of a song from a sixties album her mother had been given by a boyfriend. She must have been keen on him, because she played it the length of one drought-filled Cinzano-fuelled summer. After the boyfriend left, Sandy didn't see the record again. Had he taken it with him, or did her mother smash it, sell it, or leave it for the bin men? Sandy found herself singing it and, only on the fourth run through, discovered somehow the lyrics had got changed. Instead of 'Daydream Believer', she sang 'Daydream Schemer'. Singing it in her head, she had to hold the second syllable of dream for a beat longer, but all in all it worked pretty well. She smiled. Scheming for daydreams was what she did.

* * *

When the Beaufort scale was adjusted to count forces greater than twelve, Ray felt the need to update his hangover gauge. If anyone asked him, this morning's rated a straight eighteen. His neurons were acting as a chain gang, activated when he raised his head, each of them sinners who had been tried and convicted and were serving out their sentence. It was usual for Ray to feel remorse after a drinking binge. He'd grown up in a household where the adults drank to oblivion most nights. Until one of them, usually his father, thought to sidestep the others by opening another bottle. Like they were on a loop, or had no short-term memory – one everlasting, fearful Groundhog Day that Ray now recognised as Catholicism. His head was lodged between a bookcase containing his vinyl collection of northern soul, much of it imported from Detroit, and the end of his sofa. In front of him both shoes had been kicked off at spastic angles on the ash-smudged cotton rug where his last, forgotten cigarette of the evening had burnt itself out.

By the side of the sofa, a half-pint glass of clear liquid was so brim-filled he took it to be water and, dragging his hand out from under his hip, reached out for it, raising his head by no more than the angle required to swallow. The drink was vodka. After making such an effort, he felt cheated, then relieved. Part of him would have known that the drink wasn't water but carried on anyway. Who else but a man on the verge of an alcoholic breakdown (or a married man) could experience expectation, disappointment and relief in the first five minutes of waking? As he sunk back on to the sofa, waiting for the flow of alcohol to calm the chain gang and ease the hurricane, Ray discovered he wasn't alone. His armchair was out of his line of vision, but the rasp of Carlo's early morning cough was familiar. Carlo muttered a sentence or two in Italian. Ray grunted.

Then there was silence for, Ray imagined, thirty or so seconds. But when he next spoke he felt so revived there may have been a much longer gap, up to an hour, maybe more.

Ray sat up, knowing it was necessary to maintain the pretence about the water at least once more. 'Ah water,' he said, though there was no one to hear him, before raising the vodka to his lips for the second – and last he told himself – time.

'Christ, what a night,' Ray said, too low to be heard as he scratched his balls. Now he could see Carlo was asleep, his hair flattened on one side, a bubble of saliva inflating and deflating in the corner of his mouth. Ray began at the end of the evening and played back the sequence of events in reverse. The after-hours drinking club underneath the Chinese restaurant off Carnaby Street where they only sold cans of lager and the grease on the tables was so thick that Carlo stuck a ring of matches in it like a fortress. Before that a pub from which he had a memory of the barman refusing to serve them, after being chucked out of a casino on Great Douglas Street that had barred them a month past, where Carlo had claimed, as he always did, to know the owner. They had started off in the Draymen's Arms, innocuous enough, with a couple of pints of Guinness.

Talking, talking, jaw jaw, heads together, he remembered, stooped over a document of some description. A letter that, now, filled him with some unspecified dread. Ray looked around him. Carlo, still mewing, had shifted his weight under a crocheted throw so that it only stretched as far as his knees, like a peasant girl, almost comical enough to make Ray laugh. On another morning, with less vodka, or more, it might have done.

The letter was on the floor, one brown envelope with a hand-written address and hand-delivered. Like a bailiff's calling card. Why was the most deadly correspondence always the tamest-looking? Ray reached down for the tumbler, no longer bothering to pretend, even to himself, it was water. Hadn't he heard a man on the radio the other day, some American, describing his father as 'suffering from alcoholic dependency'? Didn't that sound grand, the *suffering* part, as if it was being inflicted on him against his will. Ray put the glass to his lips and drank. Boy, was he suffering.

* * *

The captain knew it was bad luck to set sail on a Friday and, everything else being equal, he wouldn't have done so. But the other portents were good. A pale winter sun gave the light a diluted feel, the tide was slack and the choppy easterly wind had dropped. More than that, this evening's booking was the first party the *Lady J* had had since October. A firm of turf accountants had hired her for their Christmas party. The voyage would be as far as the *Cutty Sark* at Greenwich and then back again. Twenty bookies arriving on the County Hall jetty at seven at a tenner a head, catered for by a Spanish deli in The Cut. More than enough time to take the old girl out for a run. He straightened his hat, inhaled a lungful of river air deep enough to taste the sea in, put her into gear and turned the engine on. The tide was against him going up to Greenwich, but a run-out was all he was after. So at 10.19 a.m., he decided to steer her down the river. With the wind behind them, they might make it as far as The Swan in Chiswick for lunch.

II

'The doctor will see you now.' Mickey didn't like the look in the receptionist's eyes. There was concern, and then there was prior knowledge. Was Carole informed about Mickey's degenerative mental state? Was that what caused her eyes to cave in as she gave him that half-smile when her lips didn't move?

He stood up and returned his golfing magazine to the table. 'Surely,' he told her, and swaggered towards the doctor's room with bravado. Then it occurred to him it might be a style of walking common to nutters. So he scampered on; relieved when he looked back that no one was watching. But it meant that when

Dr Adebayo greeted him, Mickey had his head twisted out of the surgery as if checking for pursuers.

'Mickey,' he said on his feet, 'please take a seat.' He waited for Mickey to face him adding, 'How are we today? Everything OK?'

'Sure, Doctor,' Mickey said. 'Absolutely tickety-boo.' Mickey didn't feel great so had the need to overcompensate, or cover his tracks.

'Glad to hear it.' Neither of them spoke for five beats. Then the doctor eased himself forward and said, 'So how can I help you today?'

'*Help?*' He rolled the word around his mouth. It hadn't occurred to Mickey that the doctor's role had been one of aiding.

'Yes, what can I do for you?' he asked slowly, the question going down like a gauntlet. 'You sound pretty jaunty today,' he went on. 'How are things? Work OK? What about that effigy of yours? Are you still working on it?'

The doctor was wearing a Donald Duck tie, which Mickey didn't associate with the plight of the Anglo-African. A hardback version of *Sexual Politics* was upside down to Mickey's viewpoint, but he recognised it by its grey-black cover. His mother called it a 'seminal classic' or she did until she realised the root of seminal was semen. Then she referred to it simply as classic. The other pamphlet spread-eagled on his desk was titled 'Yams and their Influence on the Indigenous Tribes of South America'. How much influence could a root vegetable have? It occurred to Mickey that the doctor might be undergoing his own personal crisis. He decided to fight fire with fire.

'So how are Horace and Queenie?' he asked.

'Skiing with their mother,' the doctor said, his forehead creasing into four perfect grooves. 'Just left this morning. I plan to join them when I can get away. How's the waxwork coming along?'

'It's funny,' said Mickey. 'I mention your children and you reply by asking about my effigy,' he paused. 'What do you think that tells us?'

The doctor ignored him. 'The last time we met, you spoke of an improvement *vis-à-vis* your thoughts *re* water. Tell me, how is that going?' He said the word 'improvement' in three questioning syllables, insinuating, Mickey thought, he'd been making it up.

'Pretty well, as it goes,' said Mickey, lightly but wanting to wound him. 'In fact, I'm thinking of applying to join the Merchant Navy.' He nodded. 'Follow in the footsteps of my dear departed father.' It was an odd way of introducing his father; Mickey hadn't considered the possibility that his father might, in fact, be dead. But he couldn't help blurting it out, and killing him off made it so much easier, so much neater, that he wondered he hadn't thought of it before. Also, he wanted to smash the doctor's beam of smugness, which was like the sidelights on a German car: too full of themselves to switch off.

'Your father?' The doctor seemed to peg it as a new development. 'It's the first time you've made reference to a father. I rather thought you didn't have one—'

Mickey gave a lofty laugh. 'I hardly think so, Doctor. Everybody has a father.'

'Quite,' agreed the doctor. 'Was he a sea-faring man, this father of yours?' Mickey didn't reply, just carried on nodding. The doctor sounded as if he didn't believe in the existence of his father. Mickey watched him pick up his pen and uncap it with a laboured deliberateness.

'It's odd,' the doctor said. 'I wonder if you were familiar with water as a child? Maybe encouraged by your father?' He looked up. 'I mean holidays, boating, that sort of thing?'

He painted a picture of childhood that made Mickey want to swoon. The doctor and his wife the QC, guarding Horace and Queenie, their hairless, podgy arms dappled in suntan lotion.

'Crabbing,' Mickey told him, catching his breath. 'We used to go to this place crabbing.'

'And?'

'It wasn't like that, not the way you describe. It was cold. There were too many grown-ups . . . too much water . . . the noise of the halyards . . .'

Mickey felt his bowels loosen and his head go light, too light for his body. He tried to speak and knew he was going to faint, aware of oxygen leaving his body but none replacing it. His hands were wet and he knew he was massaging his fingers in and out of his palms to some internal rhythm. 'Look, Doc,' he heard himself say, 'no offence, but I think I need some air.' He stood up to go and saw that the doctor's movements were mirroring his own, a hand out across the desk to steady him. 'Air,' Mickey repeated, and turned to the door. The panels of books swam into each other but, even while his head was floating like a helium balloon, he had the sense that this would be the last time he would be here. He stumbled out of the surgery. His last thought – the one that took him all the way down the stairs and as far as a bench under a silver birch tree outside – was whether the doctor would have enough material for his seminar on psychosis and the post-modern male.

'Seminar,' he repeated to himself. 'The root of which is semen,' he said out loud before his head fell back against the flaking wooden slats.

III

After the car had been stationary for seven minutes, Jennifer said, 'I'm just worried he might do something to himself.'

'*Do?*' repeated Nigel. The old-style shark-grey BMW snaked along the Euston Road. As he spoke Nigel craned his head as far to the right as the window would let him, searching for the reason for the hold-up. They were jammed between a window cleaner's Transit van and a white four-by-four Jeep with silhouettes of divers swimming round it. 'Do as in do?' Nigel repeated.

Jennifer continued to look straight ahead. She said, 'All this probing around, digging up the past, is so out of character for Mickey.' She was going through the bangles on her left wrist like worry beads. 'I thought he was happy as he was. I thought we all were.' The rattle of the bracelets and the hum of the heater were the only sounds inside the car. Outside they were aware of a pneumatic drill pounding a pavement, but the noise only emphasised their own hermetic seal. To their left, staring down at them from an out-of-date billboard stretched between a disused church and an office block was a twenty-metre-wide photograph of Honey Dew, her naked body wrapped in Cellophane. Where her nipples should have been were two red bows, the type you stuck on Christmas gifts. Her lips were in the shape of a kiss and she was using her hands under her breasts, pushing them up like a primitive set of scales.

'My, my,' said Jennifer, looking up. The caption under Honey Dew read, '*Six days to go and the nation waits on . . .*' She continued, 'Has the women's movement achieved so little?'

Nigel stopped drumming his fingers on the steering wheel. He looked up. 'Oh, I don't know,' he said. 'She's not so bad. I rather like it. Gives you a sense of community.'

'Sense of community?' Jennifer echoed. 'One derives a sense of community from village fêtes and neighbourhood-watch schemes, not the countdown to a woman taking her top off day by day, to the ultimate denouement of her revealing her breasts.' She'd stopped adjusting her bangles. The car was close, with the smell of air inhaled and exhaled too often.

Nigel said, 'You do it.'

'Do what?' A beam of sunlight lit up a ray of dust motes.

'Jiggle your bits in public.'

'I do not "jiggle my bits",' said Jennifer. 'The Movers and Shakers are a professional dance troupe. I, myself, am a professional dancer. I express myself. I honestly have no idea what gets into young girls' heads these days. What's that woman expressing?'

Nigel thought for a while. 'Still,' he said. 'I bet she's making a lot of money out of it. Expression or no expression.'

'That, Nigel,' Jennifer told him, 'is a very long way from the point.' When he didn't reply she added, 'Isn't it?'

Nigel slipped into first gear and edged forward a car's length. 'Yes,' he said. 'I guess so.' Behind him a car beeped. Nigel muttered, 'Bloody traffic.' He was wondering, as he often did, if he was simply a task to Jennifer, some sort of reconstruction project. He glanced across at her knees, wrapped in an African print skirt, extending out roundly as far as the dashboard. He thought of a barmaid he'd bedded at an overnight concreting conference in Worthing, a tiny, micro sort of girl with sandy hair, bitten nails and hands that smelt of onions. He'd written to her twice care of the pub on childish paper so as not to alarm her but heard nothing back. 'I really think,' he said, 'they ought to think about a total traffic ban in the centre of London, like Venice.'

'And how the hell would that work?' Jennifer's voice was brittle. 'We'd all get about in bloody gondolas?'

'Perhaps,' said Nigel. 'Utilising the canal system may, indeed, be one way to go. Or bicycles. Having said that, of course, I have had the experience of cycling in Beijing. At that world of concrete symposium, 1996, you remember.' Jennifer shook her head, exasperated. 'Bloody terrifying, all those chinks on bikes. Made a left turn absolutely impossible.'

It was just after 10.30 when, viewed from above, the car drew level with Mickey's park bench only two blocks to the south of them. It was unfortunate that neither party had knowledge of the other.

IV

Friday's first edition of the *Evening Standard* reached newsagents at eleven a.m. As far as media discrepancies went, it was a small one. On this day, Ray need not call on Mr Rajinder because the billboard outside said it all. He called in anyway, nonchalantly buying a copy along with twenty full-tar cigarettes. The headline read 'Soho Waxworks Accused of Milking It', in bold type. Underneath, smaller print said, 'Lactating Madonna Exposed as Fake'. Ray read as he walked, as he lit up a cigarette. 'The waxworks at the centre of a "miracle" row has been closed after trading standards officers swooped.' To Ray's mind the three uniformed officers with the words 'Westminster Council', where their epaulettes should have been, had shuffled uncomfortably, rather than 'swooped'. He read on. 'The midnight raid followed a complaint from a Catholic cab driver that the wax statue of Madonna, said to lactate, was a sham.' He'd got as far as the door of the gallery.

'Catholic cab driver be buggered,' said Ray to himself as he unlocked the door. He hadn't heard Jade come up behind him.

'You what?'

Ray said, 'Have you seen this?'

Jade nodded. 'Load of bollocks,' she scoffed, 'saying the Pope is going to sue us.'

'I *am* a Catholic,' Ray protested. 'The bloody cheek of it.'

'How's your head?' Jade sat behind the cash register, dumping her bag behind the counter. 'Where did you end up?'

'Buggered if I know.' Ray leant against the counter, not remembering Jade being with them. He had his back to her and exhaled. 'Some dive in Chinatown that Carlo got us thrown out of.'

'Normal sort of night, then?'

'You could say that.'

He shook his head and looked straight at her. The wind along Brewer Street had induced tears that collected on the outer edge of his lids. 'Jade, what are we going to do?' The inside of the rims were liver red.

'Well, how long can they shut us down for? If it's just the Madonna—'

'According to this "a host of celebrities are up in arms".' He hit the middle of the paper, winding it.

Jade screwed her face up like a schoolgirl. 'Er, like, why?'

'For putting them in the waxworks. I mean, I swear to God they ought to be grateful. Bloody bunch of litigious has-beens. What in the name of sweet Jesus has Erika Roe got to complain about?'

'Search me.' Jade shrugged. Neither of them spoke. Already the gallery smelt shut up, of plaster and stale air. 'What do you want me to—' The phone near her elbow rang. She picked up.

'Waxy Ladies, good morning.' Ray turned to face her and light another cigarette, contemplatively knocking it on the wooden counter before putting it to his lips. Jade jabbed the receiver towards him. She said, 'It's the *Mail*, they want to do a piece on us.'

'Tell them I'll call them back.' He struck a match. While Ray instinctively disliked the sound of such a piece, he was reluctant to turn down free publicity.

Jade hung up. Neither of them seemed eager to go downstairs. It was as if the more they got on with the day the more they accepted the end of the gallery. Ray kept his head down, making small circles with his feet in front of the reception desk, inhaling deep on his cigarette. Jade remained stock-still, unflustered and awaiting orders. That was their stance when they heard the noise.

He jerked his head up. 'What the hell's that?'

Jade shrugged. 'Sounded like someone clattering about downstairs. You don't think they can repossess them, do you?'

'I should bloody say not.' Ray trod on his half-smoked cigarette as he ran to the stairs. 'Where's Defoe when you need him? If those fucking people think they can just march in here . . .'

Jade didn't leave her post so she missed the end of the sentence as Ray disappeared into the basement. She was still unmoved when he returned. She raised her eyebrows. 'So?'

'Well, if that's not the oddest thing I've ever seen,' said Ray, 'And I mean, ever.'

'Oh yeah,' said Jade. 'What is?'

'I could have sworn I just seen Mickey and some woman disappearing out the back carrying one of the waxworks over his shoulder.'

'Er, why would he be doing that?'

'I can honestly say I have no idea.'

'Were any of them missing?' Jade scratched her nose.

'Yeah, that *Big Sister* one,' Ray told her, shifting his weight. 'But I can't remember if she wasn't in the lot that they took away yesterday.' He rested his hand on the counter. 'For forensics, like.'

Jade waited a couple of seconds before she said, '*Would* it be illegal, then? Making out it's real milk coming out of a waxwork's tittie. I'm trying to think of the exact charge.'

Ray smiled and frowned at the same time. 'The truth is, I'm buggered if I know.' He put both his hands out. 'Come on then, the pubs are open. What about a drink?'

Jade weighed it up and then hopped off her stool, slipping her bag back on her shoulder. 'OK, then,' she said and followed him out.

V

Honey had been waiting twenty-five minutes before she smelt a rat. She signalled a waiter to ask him where the HTV Awards were being held.

'Sorry?' She could tell he recognised her but couldn't yet place her. How could he not? Her breasts bore down from every other billboard in the capital. In most cases, lack of immediate recognition tended to make young men think they'd seen her in a porn flick. The waiter blushed.

'The HTV Awards,' she repeated. 'I'm supposed to be meeting someone.'

'Could you just hold on a minute, please, ma'am?'

Honey Dew was wise to him. One of the lap dancers she used to hang out with at a club called Poles Apart off Hanger Lane started a career as an air hostess. Rules said that if she was asked for something, *even if she knew it didn't exist anywhere on the plane*, she had to be seen to go and check. Honey picked at her cuticles as she waited for the waiter to return from his charade. Was it any wonder women turned to exotic dancing when the career alternatives were so ludicrous?

'I'm so sorry, madam.' He held a silver tray perpendicular to his side. 'There are no award ceremonies being held today.'

Honey felt a belch of hot indignation bellow up from her stomach as she yanked her fur from the back of the green velvet chair. She said nothing as she stormed out, heading for home. She simply did not deserve to be treated in this way.

Chapter Eleven

I

Sandy looked past him, out of the van, at a shop front twinkling with flashing lights. She said, 'You know you didn't have to come.' Three of them were jammed together in the front of the Transit, Sandy in the middle, a man Mickey didn't know driving. She went on, 'You don't even look that great. What's the matter with you? Are you sick?'

Mickey thought, yeah, I must be. Very. He said 'Cheers.' He'd planned to compliment her on her hair or outfit. She would turn to him, touch her thigh absently and say, 'What – this old thing?' but smile. Now he said, 'What did you think – that I was going to let you take her on your own?'

He turned, gestured with his head to the back of the van, to the waxwork wrapped in a blue blanket scorched by an iron with 'Property of Malindi Sands Guest House' running along one edge. Then he turned away from her, concentrating on the traffic.

When he spoke his breath caused condensation on the window. He said, 'They cost money, you know, waxworks.' It was an hour since his meeting with Dr Adebayo, sixty minutes of trying to loosen his brain and stop feeling as if there was a thin gauze separating him from the people in front of him. 'Michael Defoe believes there is a cloth between him and his classmates, through which he cannot be reached. He appears to prefer it that way.'

That had been the verdict of the educational counsellor with the trapped leg hair on the eight-year-old Mickey.

After a wait of a minute he added, 'Why are you dressed like that?'

Sandy was wearing dirty black leggings and a pink overall over a blue polo-necked jumper. Her hair was scraped back off her head.

'Because tonight, Mickey, I am a cleaner.' Then she laughed as if she found it genuinely funny. Mickey said nothing.

The van burst through a snag of traffic on the Ritz side of Piccadilly, then pulled up behind an Audi. Mickey, still looking out, said, 'Tell him he can use the bus lane, at this time of day.'

Sandy said, 'Tell him yourself.'

'Who is he, anyway?'

The driver turned to Mickey. He had rough, calloused hands and a Glasgow accent. 'Kenny Russel, film-maker. No relation to Ken. Pleased to meet you.' Mickey wanted to tell him to keep his eyes on the road. They shook hands over Sandy. Mickey found himself using the downward beat of their clench to graze against her thighs.

'Mickey Defoe, wax sculptor.'

'Is that right?' said Kenny, impressed. 'You're the fellow who made the lassie in the back.'

'Yeah, that'd be right,' said Mickey.

'I bet you never thought you'd be using her for this caper.' Without looking in either mirror he pulled into the fast lane. Between them Sandy was examining her nails, picking the cuticles and biting the ends.

Mickey didn't want to let on that he had no idea what purpose the lassie in the back was being put to. He said, 'You could say that . . .'

'Oh, and for the record,' said the Scotsman, 'I've driven a Jeep down sniper's alley in Sarajevo, an APC through the streets of Grozny under fire and was in the front line in Desert Storm.

I think I can manage driving a Transit van through central London.'

He braked behind a taxi, both hands clutched at midnight on the wheel, slumped over his elbows.

'I was only trying to be helpful,' Mickey said.

A courier on a bike swerved past them from the outside lane to the inside. At Green Park the traffic flow eased as far as Hyde Park Corner, when they jolted bumper to bumper with a Green Line coach. Kenny watched the line of traffic fit and start to his left as he tried to accelerate on to the roundabout. The radio was tuned to a talk show discussing the rights and wrongs of the exposure of Honey Dew's breasts. A feminist called it pernicious exploitation. The radio host seemed to support the editor of a man's magazine, who considered it a bit of a laugh.

'Ironic, eh,' Sandy said, 'if you think what we've got in the back of the van?' When neither man replied she went on, 'No, seriously, it makes you think.'

The radio host introduced a man called Professor Roger Clarkson, a psychologist from Birkbeck College whose area of expertise was female breasts through the ages.

Kenny Russel snorted out a laugh, 'What other sort of breasts are there?'

'Male breasts,' said Sandy, dragging a fingernail out of her mouth. 'If a male breast is stimulated enough, it will produce milk.'

'Bollocks,' said Kenny, his elbows fully extended, locked on to the driving wheel.

Mickey felt unwell. 'Bollocks,' he added, a split second later.

The sudden force of the van shuddering around the roundabout threw Mickey against the van door. He wondered where, or who, Sandy might hold on to. In the end she just sort of steeled herself against the motion.

He felt her body relax, then she said, 'Well, I'm glad you two seem to be getting on so well.' She jerked her head from side to side embracing them with a glance. 'As you'll both be working together.'

'What exactly do you mean,' said Mickey, '"working"? I thought you needed the waxwork for some sort of promotional work.'

'Who told you that?' Sandy asked.

'I thought you did.'

'No fear,' Sandy told him. 'We're framing her,' she went on proudly.

For a half-second Mickey thought she meant frame as in portrait. 'Like what?'

'Oh, you'll see,' she replied.

Mickey said, 'I really would prefer it if you told me now.'

'Honestly, will you stop being such a fusspot?' Sandy said. Kenny Russel started to laugh, making the buttons on his safari jacket strain. Behind them a taxi beeped, urging him to fill the recently vacated ten yards of tarmac in front of them.

Mickey said, 'If you don't tell me, I'm going to—'

'And we also thought,' Sandy told him, 'you'd qualify for part of the takings. What with your involvement and all.'

'What involvement?'

'We decided it's only because of you that we've come this far.' Kenny was drumming his fingers on the steering wheel, happy to be moving.

Mickey scratched his head, swerving in and out of reality. He said, 'So exactly how far have we come?'

'Oh miles,' Sandy replied, airily. She nudged Kenny. 'That's the turn-off for Chelsea. Don't miss it.'

Mickey concentrated on his breathing, trying to alleviate the tightness in his chest. He watched the window mist and demist with the condensation from his breath. The radio programme had turned to a swaying salsa tune. It seemed like a good time to mention it. He piped up as casually as he could muster, 'Everything else being equal, I wondered if we might not drive along the Embankment.' Kenny frowned and shrugged.

Sandy biting her nails said, 'Whatever.'

On the radio the chatterers returned. The professor said, 'Never before has a society so worshipped at the altar of the breast. Women in twenty-first-century Western cultures have been effectively reduced to a mammary gland.'

'Blimey,' said Sandy, and giggled.

II

'What should we do now?' Nigel stood back while Jennifer knocked on the wooden surround of the door of Waxy Ladies until her knuckles were red. He looked at his watch. 'I thought the gallery opened at eleven. It's gone that.'

'I have a terrible feeling,' Jennifer said, touching her neck. 'A mother's sense of impending disaster.'

'Oh, don't be so bloody melodramatic,' Nigel told her. 'Have you tried his mobile?'

'Yes,' she hooted. 'Of course I've tried his bloody mobile.'

'Not at home, either?'

'No,' she said, as if repeating it for the millionth time.

'Then the lad's probably just out somewhere.'

'That's very easy for you to say.'

A municipal street cleaner slugged its way along the street, rotating two giant brushes as it went. A few tourists dawdled in shop doorways but the only noise came from bins being emptied, the only movement from shopkeepers running to open up on time. Waxy Ladies was in shadow, the other side of the street washed in weak sunlight.

Nigel rubbed his hands together. 'Well, I suppose as we've made it this far into town we might as well start thinking about a spot of lunch somewhere. What do you say? Somewhere nice, cheer you up a bit.'

'Food,' Jennifer looked at him pityingly, 'at a time like this? Are you mad?'

'Everyone has to eat,' Nigel told her.

She made a noise at the back of her throat that he recognised as bad-tempered acquiescence. He set off to the Brewer Street car park with her following four paces behind, then said, 'I guess we might as well leave the car parked. You can manage the walk, can't you? It's still a fraction early for lunch. You want a turn round any of the shops while you're here?'

'No.'

In fact, Jennifer wanted both a turn round the shops and lunch but considered indulgence in the face of personal tragedy to be bad form. Then she thought, what personal tragedy? Chances were Mickey was just out. She said, 'Maybe a quick dash around Lillywhites.'

'Right you are.'

Half an hour later, after a fruitless trip to the ski department, her mood had changed. Nigel and his hedonism were once again the enemy. Now, when they waited for the lights to change by the Eros statue, Jennifer's studied disinterest caused her to stare into the middle distance.

'Oh my God,' said Jennifer. She was watching her son staring out from the passenger seat of a dirty grey Transit van. 'I told you. I told you something was wrong. Look.' She pointed after them. 'He's being kidnapped.'

'Oh, for heaven's sake.' Nigel put his hand out to stop her as she started dodging traffic, trying to cross the road, as the van pulled away.

'Quickly.' She turned to Nigel and her hair blew across her face. 'We must follow them.'

Nigel assessed the line of traffic, closed his eyes and sighed. Just when he'd allowed himself to think of a lunchtime stiffener followed by the Dover sole, he was being hauled back to the car and an interminable line of traffic.

III

Gaye Butterworth held the wire report in one hand. 'Well, fuck me.' No one on news or features, or even the hornier outposts of the subs desk would, so no one looked up. In fact, they stared at their keyboards with greater intensity, as if any acknowledgement of the statement signified a subconscious desire to fuck the deputy features editor.

Gaye went on, undaunted, 'They've closed the waxworks place.'

Greengrass Jones resented the features department going anywhere near the news wires. He made a mental note to bring it up at conference. Gaye and her ilk made a mockery of PA, the way they turned global conflicts into style issues. The recent thousand-worder, 'Toro Boro Phrwoah. Why Osama Bin Laden is hot' was a case in point.

He looked up and called out, 'Bob, get on to it. Five hundred words on it, please, page seven. Don't go mad. It's a follow-up only. No need to push the boat out.'

Gaye eased herself on to the clippings desk, reluctant to give up her place in the newsroom spotlight. She said, 'Still, I guess it's kind of fitting. I mean, that was Sandy's story and today is the final Sandy West column.'

'Oh yeah?' Tim Prescott would do anything for a distraction.

'Yep. As of tomorrow, yours truly will be back on that page. The much-demanded return of the "The Gaye Divorcee" column. Two thousand words of sideways comment on the hilarious world of the second marriage.'

'Can't wait,' said Tim.

'Yes,' agreed Gaye. 'I do believe it's going to be rather special.'

'Actually, Gaye,' Greengrass called over, 'that Sandy West has been on the phone this morning. I heard her speak to Tony. She wants to come in for a meeting.'

'Really?' Gaye stood up. 'Well, the little trollop can't think she's keeping that column—'

'No,' said Greengrass. 'Nothing like that. Said she might have got a scoop on her hands.'

'Bugger me,' said Gaye. Around the newsroom, eyes returned to their keyboards as Gaye flounced towards the editor's office.

IV

Sandy hopped down from the van, inhaling the underground car park mixture of petrol and exhaust fumes that caught in the back of the throat. The van straddled two spaces but, at midday, washed in a sulphurous fluorescent strip light, bay H was close to deserted: a tan Nissan Prairie and a long white Mercedes that looked like long-stayers were all. Kenny yanked the sliding door at the back of the van. The way she'd mapped it, there would only have been her and Kenny, but something about Mickey's wan insistence had made her relent. Times like this he was puppy-like, with an irritating need for attention. Offering him part of the money was regrettable but also bought his complicity.

She looked at her watch. She gave them an hour before Honey realised the invite was fake and returned home. That was the worst-case scenario; ideally she would take the time to shop or, with less than twenty-four hours to the revelation of her breasts, she would be on a PR junket or at a beauty treatment.

Kenny was hauling the waxwork from the van, Mickey urging him to be careful, telling him wax wasn't bloody concrete. Kenny told him, breathing hard, that he knew that. Sandy walked round and stood between them. She said to Kenny, 'You're telling the doorman we're from Hello TV. Kenny, you've been here before, so he might recognise you. Mickey, just say that you're some sort of gofer.'

'Right enough, hen,' said Kenny. 'But what are we telling your man that this is?'

'I don't know,' said Sandy. 'A prop?' She scratched her head. 'You're the one that's been shot on seven continents. Make something up.'

'There aren't seven continents,' said Mickey.

'And if you don't shut up you can wait in the car.' Sandy thought, do I have to think of everything? She grabbed her bucket of cleaning products from the back. 'Kenny, you know which number it is. I'm going in first. Give me ten minutes and then follow me up.'

'Are we going to rob the place?' asked Mickey.

'Don't be so bloody stupid,' said Sandy. 'Do we look like masked raiders? Plus, what the hell would Honey Dew have that we would want?' She checked a dry J-cloth; a canister of Mr Sheen cosseted the bag of white powder at the bottom of the bucket.

Mickey leant against the side of the van and ran a hand through his hair. Through his brushed cotton jacket, the metal side cooled his perspiration. 'Of course,' he said. 'This is where Honey Dew lives.'

'Correctomondo,' said Kenny. 'Well, not here, obviously. This is a car park. She's got a luxury riverside condo-type affair, upstairs.'

'Riverside,' repeated Mickey, weakly. 'As in, by the side of a river.'

Sandy turned to them and shushed. For the first time Mickey noticed a determined glint of hardness, her pupils were wild and black. He tried to fix the warmth of her maggot-naked body in his mind, but found it impossible. She was stooped slightly when she spoke. 'Remember, we haven't got much time, so please don't fluff it.'

Of all the rallying cries she could have used, fluff was the worst, the most ridiculous. It used to be the word, the code, he and his mother used for fart. 'Don't fluff,' he told himself. He wanted to laugh but tiny tears wrung themselves from his water-logged brain, like the distillation of his fear.

V

Nigel was drumming his fingers on his hide-bound steering wheel, trying to quantify how hungry he was when he saw the tramp flutter by. He said, 'How utterly extraordinary.'

Jennifer said nothing. The road had dipped on to the river by Cheyne Walk. She was tersely navigating, punctuating directions with hypotheses. 'If he hasn't been kidnapped, then he's on his way to somewhere.'

'Ye – es,' said Nigel, 'I think we can accept that much.'

'Drugs,' she said. 'Picking them up or dropping them off. That's why he's been so odd. Parents are always the last to know.' The car crawled on another ten metres past a row of homely houseboats painted muted pastel colours. Now she said, 'But in a *Transit* van. It's so criminal. Mickey simply doesn't know anyone in a Transit van.'

Ahead of them the van slowed at lights. Jennifer shifted her weight to look at him.

'What's extraordinary?'

'That chap over there.' He pointed with a nod of his chin towards the river.

'Covered in plastic. He really does look most extraordinary. Like some sort of human scarecrow.'

Jennifer looked and then looked away. 'For heaven's sake, Nigel, can't this car go any faster?' She wriggled in her seat, keeping both hands in her lap; a tic pulsated her right forefinger. To steady it she wrapped her left hand around it. Nigel considered he'd been underestimating the situation. Jennifer was more nervous than she'd been letting on.

Chapter Twelve

I

Mickey slouched against the smooth corridor wall, his back to the apartment. 'Lookout,' Sandy told him, slapping a can of Mr Sheen and a duster in his hand.

'What for?'

'No, duffers, you *are* the lookout,' she said. 'Anyone sees you, pretend you're a cleaner.'

'Cleaning what?' The pale lemon corridor was empty. Two doors down on the opposite wall was a painting of a seaside selected for its décor-matching pastels and there was a red-boxed fire alarm next to Honey's door.

'Skirting boards,' she told him, pointing down. 'Just remember to let us know if she comes back.'

'And you'll do what, exactly?' Sandy estimated the lift was twenty metres from the flat which, given the nature of Honey's top-heavy totter, would give enough time for . . . ? Enough time for, she didn't know, but lookouts were what they had in the films and they always managed to sort something out. Plus, Kenny had agreed that they needed a doorman.

In the bedroom, Sandy set about dressing the model, unwrapping her from the towelling blanket and easing clothes over her limbs – clothes with no zips or buttons: a pair of dark brown cotton palazzo pants and a white T-shirt selected from a large carpeted walk-in wardrobe. The effect was good, the materials hung loose enough to reveal the unnatural contours of her trademark body. Her wax expression, framed in a curtain of red hair, was still one of expectant lasciviousness but that might well suit the purpose. The biggest hang-up was the pose. Honey Dew's model was standing – one hand cupped under a breast and the other extended in a come-hither pose.

'Oy, Kenny. Give me a hand,' Sandy called from the bedroom. Kenny put his camera to one side and joined her.

'Not bad,' he said, sizing up the model. 'Put it this way, I'd give her one.'

'Don't be so disgusting and help me get her out to the kitchen.' Sandy was out of breath. 'I'm going to lean her against the breakfast bar and put the drugs in lines. I think with all the toast and that still out, it'll give the impression of more desperation.' Kenny took the legs.

She said, 'What about the camera, where will that be? We're after a sort of secret filming look, don't forget.'

'You know what I'm thinking?' said Kenny, after he'd shot the breakfast bar sequence. 'We really need a bit of movement here.'

'Like what?'

'Like her walking across the room.'

'Kenny . . .' Sandy looked at her watch. They didn't have all day. They had been in the apartment for close on half an hour. 'I don't know if you've noticed, but she's pretty inflexible in the walking department.'

'Aye,' Kenny replied, sizing up the possibilities. 'I see that sure enough. But what about just seeing her top half above the sofa moving. It'd only have to be for a couple of seconds.' The apartment door was wedged open with an old-fashioned foot scraper. The metallic ping of the lift opening, and the grunts of their heavy breathing, formed the soundtrack to their work.

'And how would we do that?' asked Sandy.

Kenny rested a hand on the back of an armchair. 'You could always crawl along holding her legs.'

'*You what?*'

'She's not that heavy,' said Kenny, 'and you could lean her against the back of the sofa. Sort of shimmy her along.'

'What about the top half?' Sandy righted the model. It was true she wasn't that heavy, just stiff. 'Wouldn't it look a bit odd her sauntering along with one hand out and one under her tit?'

'Obviously,' laboured Kenny, 'I'd keep the camera away from the tit side. It'd only be literally five seconds of shooting.'

Sandy weighed it up; movement would be good. 'OK then.' She grabbed the model by the waist. 'But make it quick.'

They propped the waxwork against the sofa. Sandy took up a position on all fours by the waxwork's ankles, too uncomfortable and too absorbed to listen out for pings from the corridor, and started to shuffle the waxwork along, edging her by a slight twist to the left and then to the right. The carpet prickled through her leggings, making her knees hot and itchy. It smelt of dogs and it was all she could do to hold back a sneeze. After ten seconds she did sneeze, which was why she was the second one to hear Mickey.

II

Riding the lift, Honey Dew thought, odd. Odd, that the invitation had been bogus and odd that the concierge had claimed to have let a TV crew into her apartment. She hadn't lingered. 'Only a day to go, now, Miss Dew,' he'd slavered. 'Then we'll all see what you've got. What's so hot under your blouse.'

Pervert, thought Honey, as the lift opened. Is that what people thought? That she was so vain as to think the sight of her knockers was worth fifty grand? It was the paper, not her, that had come up with the idea. She looked down at the channel of her cleavage. There they were – just an average pair of outsize knockers. How much easier, she thought, to be laughing from the safety of the crowd than be the naked foolish emperor. She bet some desperate PR girl had been behind that stunt, urging the King to make a fool of himself for her twenty per cent.

So deep was she in thought that she was inside the flat before she noticed she wasn't alone. She let one arm fall on to the back of the sofa while the other shot to her open mouth. 'Jesus Christ Almighty, what the fuck . . . ?' Her shoulder bag snaked on to the floor. Two men were in her sitting room, one with a video camera, the other with a can of Mr Sheen.

'Holy shit,' gasped Sandy, returning from the balcony. 'What the hell are you doing here?'

'Jesus Christ, Sandy West,' said Honey. She stayed at the door, unable to move. 'What have you just put on my balcony? And why are you dressed like that?'

'Like what?'

'Like a bum.'

The two men kept quiet, huddled and low down in the corner. Sandy looked exasperated and put out. 'Me, like a bum?' she said. 'You were the one supposed to stay out for longer. You weren't supposed to see all this.'

'Oh, excuse me.' Honey moved into the room, heading to the kitchen. She picked up a leftover glass of orange juice, drinking slowly, even chewing the bits, insinuating it would take more than intruders armed with a video recorder to faze her. 'Sandy, what the fuck are you doing? Are you robbing me?'

She'd put the shutters of control down over anger, making Sandy think: typical.

Honey pointed her chin towards the far side of the room. 'Why is my breakfast bar covered in crap? And what are those two jokers doing?'

'Filming,' said Sandy, all matter-of-fact.

Kenny stood up and smoothed the creases from his trousers.

'Kenny Russel, film-maker. Pleased to meet you. No relation to Ken, in case you were wondering.'

Sandy said, 'The other one's Mickey, the bloke who did your wax sculpture.' She pointed at the figure leaning against the wall. 'We kind of brought him along for technical support.' She nodded at the balcony. 'It's out there if you are interested.'

No one spoke for thirty seconds. Honey finished her juice, mopping her mouth with a linen napkin. Mickey sank down the wall and sat on the floor with his knees raised at right angles and his head in his hands. Kenny started to hum a tuneless Scottish ditty while he fiddled with his camera. Sandy plucked at loose threads from the back of the sofa with deft airy movements.

Honey set the glass down on the table, deliberately, pushing an unwashed plate holding four bitten-off crusts away from her. She had pulled her mobile from her bag and held it in her right hand, hinting she could activate it at any time. She said, 'OK, then, Sandy. Do you think you could let me know what you're doing?'

'The truth?'

Honey shrugged. 'Why not?' Her mood had gone from shock then calmness to a suppressed anger.

Sandy bit her tongue; as far as she was concerned this hadn't gone according to plan. She said, 'OK then, here's the deal.' She inhaled and sat on the arm of the sofa, Kenny in her line of vision to her far right, Honey facing her to the left.

'We thought we'd make a kind of surprise documentary for you. A tribute. Like a *This is Your Life*-type deal to give you when—'

'Bullshit,' said Honey. She jiggled her phone in the nest of her palm.

Sandy looked down. 'OK,' she said. 'It is a documentary.' She looked at Kenny. 'Sort of.'

Honey picked at a toast crumb, letting Sandy know she knew she was lying but was prepared to wait.

Sandy put her hands out. 'OK,' she said. 'After you cheated me out of my money from *Big*—'

'Excuse me?' Honey looked up from the counter. 'After I did what?'

'Oh, come on. You and I both knew the deal was that we would split that money fifty-fifty.'

'Since when?'

'Since we made that pact. In case you don't remember, in the airing cupboard. If I got that question right, you'd give me half the money.' Outside they heard a police siren. The light was disappearing fast. Pretty soon someone would need to switch a lamp on. 'I was up in the polls, it was only because of me you won that show.'

'Whatever,' said Honey, letting it pass. 'That was the game. We all made pacts. Only the suckers got caught out.'

Sandy waited enough time to let Honey know she couldn't be bothered to react. Then she said, 'What I'm up to –' she cast her eyes around the room – 'what we're up to, is getting back what is rightfully mine.'

'Right,' said Honey. 'Like some sort of holy fucking crusade.' She looked at the men. 'How the hell did you two get roped into this?'

In the corner Mickey grunted while Kenny, who seemed to be enjoying the dogfight, looked away.

Sandy said, 'I'm only after what's really mine.'

'So you keep saying,' Honey replied, straightening her back. 'You know what it sounds like to me? Hard fucking cheese. If the roles were different you'd have done exactly the same. You just can't stand being beaten at your own game, missy.'

Sandy carried on as if she was unaware of the interruption. 'And the way I was going to do that, and still might,' she looked across at Kenny, 'was to blackmail you.'

'Gee, thanks,' said Honey.

'I thought, how could I portray a sleaze in a sleazy situation? I knew it couldn't be a compromising situation with men because, at the end of the day, who gives a stuff?'

'Max Clifford,' said Honey sarcastically, 'had better beware.'

'So then I thought, what about drugs? How about framing her taking drugs?'

'Terrific,' said Honey. 'Apart from the fact I've never touched drugs.'

'Says you.' Kenny looked up from cleaning his lens. 'We broke in and found enough drugs to sink a wee ship. Eh, lassie?'

'Yeah,' said Sandy, twisting a loose strand of hair away from her face. 'Not in so many words. Not exactly. That was me, more than anything. Me and a jar of Ajax.'

'Oh, for heaven's sake,' said Kenny, putting his camera down. 'You told me you found it here—'

'—in my bag,' said Sandy.

Kenny tutted out loud. 'I swear to God this is the last time I work with a woman.'

Honey ignored him. 'You broke in?' she said, hands on hips. She still had her coat on. 'If you're so bloody great, let's see you get out of this one.'

Sandy leapt up. 'What are you doing?'

'Calling the police.'

Kenny flinched and Mickey said, 'Oh no.'

Sandy strode towards her. 'Now, hang on. That's not going to get us anywhere.'

'It's going to get three total headcases out of my flat.'

'But it's not going to get us *anything*.' Sandy smiled crookedly. 'If you see what I mean.'

Honey, phone in hand, said, 'No.'

'Look, before you do anything rash, just hear me out.' Sandy stood up and walked to the front of the sofa. She said, 'I've got a plan B.'

Out of her pink overalls she took a bundle of business cards and arranged them on the glass-covered coffee table like a game of patience. Kenny stood up. 'Have you got any beer?'

'This is not a frigging house party,' said Honey.

'You could let him have one,' said Sandy, 'under the circumstances.'

'In the fridge,' said Honey, nodding behind her. She looked at Mickey. 'I don't know how you got caught up in all this. You always seemed . . .' Sandy turned to hear the noise of jeans studs scraping against plaster as Mickey elbowed himself to his feet as if he had no strength in his legs. Now, before he had straightened all the way up, he lurched forward, his heavy footfalls scudding on the carpet.

'Mickey . . . ?' Sandy moved out of his lumbering path, his unzipped jacket flapping loosely at the side.

'What is that boy *on*?' Kenny said, watching from the kitchen, at ease enough to lever off the ring pull on a can of Heineken and lick the froth.

'I told you he didn't look well,' said Sandy, moving her bucket towards the window. 'He just needs some air.' The sun had gone in and a bank of clouds was replacing it, mopping up the light. She pulled at the balcony's sliding door watching as Mickey passed her, keeping his head down against the wind squalling off the river, then pulled it shut.

'All right then, Sandy,' said Honey. 'Shoot.' She'd lit a cigarette and was turning the ash at the tip into cones on the side of a heavy blue glass ashtray. 'What's Plan B?'

'How much are you being paid to get your norks out?'

'Excuse me?' Honey asked. Kenny retreated to the corner where he'd left his camera.

'How much?'

Honey squirmed and sucked on her cigarette. 'Fifty grand.'

'Is that all?'

'Yeah, well, the *Big Sister* money wasn't all that much and besides, I need that for my operation.'

'What operation?' Sandy scoffed.

'Never you mind.'

Sandy frowned. Kenny knocked back half a can of lager.

'So you've got fifty grand to come,' Sandy said, thinking, thank God I haven't gone ahead with the blackmail.

Honey stood up straight. She said, 'When the paper coughs up, yes, I will have. If it's got anything to do with—'

'You mean to say,' said Sandy, standing, 'the paper hasn't paid you yet? How are you paying for this place?'

'I'm not. Not as of next month. I won't be able to afford it. I used to work in a video shop, you know. I'm not a millionaire.'

Kenny muttered something about exploitation. Sandy looked at the cards on the table. 'This is perfect,' she said. She looked at Honey. 'Why don't you stop them showing the final tits-out picture, if you haven't been paid yet?'

'Like how exactly?' She inhaled on her cigarette. 'Get a government injunction? It's a pair of bloody nipples, not a state secret.'

'What about,' said Sandy, sitting upright, not listening to her. She rubbed her nose. 'What about this . . . ?'

Mickey looked over his shoulder without turning into the flat. A fug of condensation and cigarette smoke was building up. Someone had switched a table lamp on; three cans of beer were on the coffee table and a Sting CD was playing. It was a family scene, people linked, no matter how randomly. A scene that he had shut himself out of, suspended in space, alongside a waxwork. The river below him was full, high above any tidemark. The wind carried the terrifying chirrup of halyards to him. Stubby waves rocked in short squat peaks. In the lee of a thick office block on the South Bank with 'To Let' stamped in five empty rooms, a billboard of Honey Dew and another advert rotated and rotated, swirling flesh, forming and re-forming.

A flat empty cargo ship chugged seaward, overpowering the snapping waves. Closer too, puttering towards him from downriver, was a smaller vessel. As he watched the boat a gust caught the waxwork's clothes. Mickey knew what he had to do. More than that, what he wanted to do. Fate, or luck, had thrown an opportunity his way and he wasn't going to miss it. He pulled his last lucky stone from his pocket, gave it a final polish and sank it deep in Honey's side pocket. The halyards kept chirruping. Then he lifted the waxwork up by the waist and swung back as far as he could without hitting the window. Now he lobbed the model away from him, as hard as he could, into the water. When it slipped rather than flew from his hands, he was left with a film of grease on his palms from either sweat or paraffin. Inside the flat, none of the conspirators had noticed.

Mickey saw the waxwork arch through the air, then fall heavily, gravity pulling it down, wind buffeting at its clothes, and felt the release when it started to drop. A pair of weather-torn seagulls to the right, not overly put out, adjusted their course. It hit the blue grey water not head-on, diving, but with a tremendous belly flop, but by then Mickey had ceased to care. He leant against the railings, breathing heavily, feeling the air enter his lungs, soothing him, then expelling the misery. He focused on near objects: the red crease of his knuckles and the cracked black gloss of the balcony. He had no interest in the voyeurism of the water gobbling her up. And he would have turned into the steamy den of the apartment were it not for the scream.

He dragged his stare over the drop, looking down beyond the freezing knuckles clutching the barrier. He recognised the colour of the car, then its familiar shape, before its passengers. The same car that had been there the day he went crabbing. Then he remembered the same scarf fluttering at a woman's neck and knew that the scream, not truly unreserved enough to be real, was his mother's.

He made himself look at the water. The waxwork was rigid and afloat but next to it was the head of a swimmer, bobbing in the water, afloat like a watermelon. On the balcony, Mickey held his head in his hands as if the warmth might defrost his brain, spur it into making sense of the scene. Then he understood. His knees buckled. Nigel had followed the waxwork into the water.

III

Mickey fumbled a path across the sitting room, cartoon legs unable to keep up with his body. He was aware of heat and sound, too much of both. His left leg flailed into the coffee table, upturning the empties and making the full tins froth.

'And then,' Sandy was saying, 'do you see, we'll have to take them to court. Sue them . . .' Then her voice fell away. 'Mickey, where the hell—'

He heard Kenny laugh. A blast of cold air followed him in, cutting though the smoke.

'Free free, set me free,' Sting rasped. Honey told him to keep the bloody draught out. Mickey felt his bowels loosen and his mouth go dry as he catapulted himself down the corridor, screaming, 'Hold the lift,' as a couple walked towards him. She had white hair layered up in a bun while the man was shorter. 'Please,' shouted Mickey, 'this is an emergency.'

By the time the lift doors opened in reception he was thinking clearer. He paused for a split second to orientate towards the river, at the same time calling to the concierge to call an ambulance. His voice bounced off the marble walls, sounding unfamiliar in loudness and pitch. The concreted walkway between the glass double doors and the low river wall was less than a metre wide. The chill, fear and the sight of his mother clicked into recognition.

'Mickey,' she gasped, the wind taking her voice. 'I thought that was you in there.'

'Oh shit,' Mickey said. 'Where's Nigel?'

'He went after you,' his mother told him, making clutching movements at her throat. Her hair threaded around her head. 'He went in there to save you.'

Rather than think of discarding clothes, Mickey cast around for extra layers. Seeing none, he put his left leg in a metal groove halfway down the water barrier and levered himself over. No time for his lucky stone, which had gone anyway. No time for a lucky mantra or to remember not to touch the cracks. He tried to find Nigel as he jumped, but he wasn't even convinced Nigel was the point any more. After he hit the water he felt the current pull at his feet as if it was clawing his body. He couldn't see Nigel but he felt the taste of the water up his nose and at the back of his throat, sluicing in and out of his open mouth. He tried to find Nigel one more time but his head was getting heavy; too heavy to lift out of the water.

And then an odd thing happened: the greyness of panorama shrank from a hundred and eighty degrees. It kept shrinking. From out of nowhere he thought of David Hollingworth, his sixth-form friend, a tall, graceless boy and reluctant pallbearer at his father's funeral. How he described how the weight of the dead man had been like a force, unbearable on their shoulders, gravity and mass dragging the body into the earth. Now Mickey's legs were too heavy as the current clawed. When he next remembered looking up, the shrunken vista had re-formed into the shape of a tunnel. He had lasted thirty-eight seconds.

Chapter Thirteen

I

Fourth on Helga Kristiakova's list of tasks to be completed by the end of the week was to call the Defoe man. The fact that he hadn't returned her call didn't bother her. She was a professional and aimed at getting jobs done. Besides that, the manila folder she'd designated to his case was still in her in-tray. And Helga could not abide a cluttered in-tray, especially returning to it on a Monday morning. As ever, she had made a note of his contact details on the inside cover of the folder. After one glance she'd memorised the sequence and used an upturned Biro to punch out the digits. On the fourth ring it went on to voice mail. After the beep she spoke clearly, prepared to spell any difficult words.

'This is a message for Michael Defoe, at twelve forty-seven on Friday lunchtime. Mr Defoe, this is Helga at East West Shipping again. Should you recall, you asked me to check some information on your behalf, namely on the subject of a crew member.' She checked the seconds on her phone; often the messages cut out after a minute. 'I wish to confirm the name that you required. The name of the crew member on the *Baltic Star* was a Mr Harry Palmer.' She smiled, 'I do hope that is of service to you.'

She hung up at one minute precisely, closed the file and pulled her coat from the stand. The new boy in accounts had promised to buy her a drink at the end of the week, if she got to the Cricket and Glove early enough.

II

Mickey dozed on and off all weekend, dipping in and out of consciousness, finally coming to in the early hours of Monday morning, feeling oddly dehydrated, like someone had sucked out his innards and left him ten stone lighter. He had been oblivious for the last forty-eight hours of his life but had the feeling a lot had been going on while he languished in a hospital bed. He had been pulled out of the Thames on the thirty-ninth second of his being there. Dr Hamarda told him he was lucky. Had he been there a second longer that would have been it. The doctor's lower lip flopped out when he spoke and his teeth were stained turmeric colour. Mickey agreed he had been very lucky. The doctor nodded waspishly, as if getting his money's worth out of the emergency services had been Mickey's prime motivation for jumping. Mickey hadn't remembered having to ask about Nigel; someone – his mother? – had let him know early on that seconds after Nigel's ridiculous plunge, he had kicked his way back to a ladder against the river wall.

It was his third day in hospital; the youngest man on a diagnostic ward at University College Hospital. The doctors called it bilge water in the alveoli. Mickey liked the sound of it, Shakespearean-sounding, noble.

If he hoisted himself up high enough, using some sort of infirm person's rail, he could make out the tops of a row of silver birch that shivered in the wind. Beyond them was an Edwardian terrace and, as the daylight faded and lights switched on, he was able to watch a couple noiselessly make their way from room to room, both of them thinking they were too high up to be overlooked or that the hospital didn't have eyes. He no longer viewed them with envy, in fact their silhouette came up in angry relief – she pointing a finger with one hand on her head; he with his back to her.

It had been a passing trawlerman, according to the paramedics, who wrapped him in a wet oilskin before rowing him to the same ladder Nigel had clung to. Out of everything, he remembered the bony skeleton of the rowboat against his spine, water between the planks flowing in and out, and the grinding noise of the oars gyrating in the rowlocks. Then the smell of his mother's heavy perfume as she half lugged him to safety.

'How are you feeling?' Mickey tried to read the nurse's nametag but it was double-barrelled and too long.

'Bit woozy,' he told her, trying to look blurry. His knuckles were grazed and where his smock ended was an anchor-shaped bruise on his forearm.

'Well, you're bound to,' she said. 'For now.'

At just gone four, his mother appeared at the entrance of the ward. It was her third visit, the second when he'd been conscious. Mickey was on his side listening to Five Live, something about a poster campaign that had been overshadowed by the actors' strike being called off on the understanding the BBC broadcast no more than two hours of docusoaps a day. His mother was wearing a long dark coat with a multi-coloured Doctor Who scarf down to the linoleum floor. Mickey recognised it as a semi-mourning look.

From the door, she called, 'Darling.' Mickey smiled weakly. The West Indian family visiting the pulmonary embolism in the bed next to him had taken all the seats, leaving Mickey's bed as the only place she could collapse.

'Excuse me, mate,' he said to the taller of the teenage grandsons. 'All right to borrow a chair, for my mum?'

'Sure.'

She took the chair without acknowledgement and dropped heavily into it, making it skid on plastic floor tiles. 'Darling, my love, you're awake. Look, I can't stay long. You'll never guess what?' She narrowed her eyes and winked. 'The Movers and Shakers have got a part in a pantomime in Richmond. I can hardly believe it. Seems that we're more famous than we thought. Anyway, the producer wanted a whole Islamic slant to Cinderella—'

'Where will you be staying?'

'Darling, it's so sweet of you to be concerned. But, really, I might as well continue to stay at Nigel's.'

'How is he?'

'Who, dear?'

'Nigel, of course.' Mickey sighed and levered himself up. A collective whoop went up from the bed next to him. Even the old man at the centre was laughing at a family joke, trying to quieten his extended family.

'Oh, you know Nigel, one of the old school. Hates to be ill.' She bit into a grape and then peeled it with stabbing movements. 'Actually since the,' she paused, 'accident, we've been getting on tremendously well. He really did think that was you, you know, coming out of that window. I've never seen Nigel in that hero sort of mould before.'

'It was really good of him,' Mickey picked at the bobbles on his blanket. 'Fatherly, some would say.' Thinking: all that feminists really hold out for is a hero.

His mother looked at him. 'Please,' she said, letting her head fall to one side, 'not now . . .'

Mickey put his hands up and shook his head. For two minutes neither of them spoke. 'So hot in here,' she said vaguely, not taking her coat off. She peeled another grape. Mickey twisted the cord to his radio, picking at the waxy crust around the earpiece. His mother said, 'You know that thing that fell out of the window, that Nigel – ludicrously – thought was you?'

'Mm.'

'Turns out it was some sort of dummy. Police saw it but didn't manage to catch it. Can you imagine?'

'Not really,' said Mickey. He turned his head towards the

window. 'Look, I hope you don't mind, but I get a bit tired at this time . . .'

'Michael, say if you find this uncomfortable,' his mother kept her focus on the bed cover, 'but none of this *stuff*,' she made the word sound foreign, 'has anything to do with you trying to find your father, has it?'

Mickey suddenly did feel tired. 'No,' he said, 'it hasn't.'

She sat stock-still for three beats, twirling the tassels on her scarf. Then said, 'Good heavens.' She leapt up. 'Is that the time? I've got a costume fitting at five.' She twisted her scarf around her neck. 'Do you want me to leave yesterday's paper? There's an interesting thing about sculpture in the arts section.' On her first visit she'd let him know Waxy Ladies had been closed until further notice.

'If you like.' It was a left-leaning Sunday that he never read.

The family next door was filing out, clipping each other round the head, laughing, kissing the old man. As a unit they smelt of home cooking and coconut milk. His mother showed no signs of even having seen them as she loitered at the end of Mickey's bed, buttoning a coat that had never been undone.

'Mickey,' she said, finally, her face taut. 'I mean, we are all right, aren't we?'

'Yeah,' said Mickey, looking at her. 'I guess so,' he said, and smiled. 'You know you could always have stayed at my place. If you'd wanted to.'

'I know,' she said with a smile that let her eyes uncrease. 'Oh, by the way, I stopped off at your flat earlier, just to check up on things. There were a couple of letters I thought you might like.' She left the post on the chair she'd vacated, slightly out of reach. A couple of bills and a childishly written white envelope, with a West London postmark that caused an airlock to lodge in the pit of his stomach.

His second visitor came at eight, when the smell of gravy still hung heavy but the atmosphere was one of relief because now people everywhere were starting to act like they were hospitalised, putting on pyjamas and dozing by the television. Because of the warmth, the visitor's outdoor presence was keener still. The captain skulked uncomfortably, keeping to the sides of the corridors, maintaining a hand on something solid as he walked: a nurse's desk, the steel foot of a bed, a tea trolley.

'Do you have a Michael Defoe in this ward?' he asked the duty nurse. 'They told me at reception to come here.'

'It's no longer visiting time, I'm afraid.' Nurse Grahams flicked up her watch, sounding professionally harassed. 'Unless you're a relative?'

The man shifted his weight. He was wearing a black donkey jacket with reflective strips down both arms. 'I'm the man who saved him. Pulled him out, if you like.'

The nurse smiled. 'Bed three.' She went to stand up to escort him; she didn't do that with every visitor.

The man said, 'Please don't bother. I'm pretty sure I can find him.' She walked with him anyway, a half-step in front, talking over her shoulder. 'Lucky you happened to be passing. Another couple of minutes and that would have been it. We've got him on an antibiotics drip. Don't be alarmed, he's just got a touch of infection on his chest.'

Mickey's bed was at the far end of the ward at right angles to the outside wall. They passed a man with a white beard, sitting upright in front of the television, coughing into a steel dish. In between splutters he shouted out the answers to a quiz programme. Mickey was skipping through an Indian cookery book that he'd found in his bedside cabinet. He was waiting for Mr Morgan to finish with his tabloids.

'I'll leave you two to it, then,' was the way Nurse Grahams presented the visitor, before smartly turning round, beaming like a go-between or a chat show host.

'Mickey?' His face was weather red. It seemed more vivid under his dense layer of hair, which reminded Mickey of the gills of an upturned mushroom although it was grey flecked with red.

'Hi,' said Mickey, his expansiveness aimed to hide the fact he wasn't sure if they'd met or not.

'I'm the chap that rescued you.' His hand touched the bedding at the foot of his cot. 'I hope you don't mind . . .'

'Good heavens, of course not, I mean thanks. Thank you so much. If it hadn't been for you, they said, well, they reckoned I'd have been dead within a couple of minutes.' Mickey hitched himself up.

'Oh, I'm not so sure, you know.' The man stood still. 'They say that. I've a feeling that old river's kinder than we think.' His accent was hard to place. It rolled on the Rs; Mickey put it down as West Country.

Not knowing what to say next, he laughed, nervously hoping the visitor would continue. After a minute of silence he went on, 'It was a bloody good job you were there. All things considered.' Mickey slid out of the glare of an overhead lamp so he could look at the man better. 'I mean, thanks sounds so inadequate and all that.'

'Anyone would have done the same.'

Mickey thought of his mother swaying on the quayside, scarf flapping. 'I don't know about that,' he said. 'What are you?' he asked. 'Some sort of boatman?'

'Pleasure cruises. I was just taking her out for a spin down to Richmond.' He unfastened the top of his coat; the buttons were jet black and embossed with anchors. 'That other chap, did he get out all right? Who was he?'

'Nigel? Oh yeah, Nigel's right as rain, as he'd say.'

The man still looked expectant, while the frayed edges of his face seemed to be concealing some private mirth.

'What was he, then, your mum's boyfriend? What was it all about then? Was he trying to kill himself?'

It occurred to Mickey that the story wasn't his exclusively, that others had a right to know what had gone on. Something about the man was jarring. 'No, good God, nothing like that,' Mickey said. 'He sort of fell in and then I went in after him. Pretty bloody stupid, really.'

'You were lucky that it was slack water. Otherwise the countercurrent would have got you.'

'Yes, I was.' Mickey played with the edges of the book. The man said, 'Nowhere to smoke in here, I don't suppose?'

'I don't think they encourage it.' The man shrugged and looked away for the first time since he sat down. 'So what are you up to these days?' he asked.

'Me?' said Mickey. 'I work as a wax sculptor. Or I did. They've closed the place down.'

'Really? Not the one at the back of Brewer Street?'

'You know it?'

'Kind of,' said the man. 'Dirty models, aren't they? Naked women.'

'Tasteful reproductions of the female form in an underused medium, we prefer to say. But yeah, you could call them smutty.' He waited a couple of beats, flushed by the fact they had something in common. 'Look, when I get out, we must meet up. Let me buy you a beer, or a rum, or whatever you drink. A way of thanking you.'

'You don't have to do that, son,' he said touched. 'It would be nice to keep in contact, though. See how you get on. But as for thanking me, I prefer to see it as repaying the favour.'

'I'm sorry?' Mickey was starting to feel tired. He felt his lungs getting heavier. The theme tune to end the TV quiz thumped out and was switched off.

'It so happens I was rescued from drowning once.'

'Really?' Mickey's head slumped on the pillow, soothed by the sonorous stranger's voice.

'It was an odd thing. I was meeting my son for the first time, as it happens, mooring up, and I slipped. He was the one who saved me.'

'Blimey,' said Mickey, 'that must have made him proud.'

'How do you mean?'

The light was making his eyes hurt. 'The son,' Mickey yawned, 'saving his father like that.'

'I suppose. Only he didn't know at the time. I was only there, keeping an eye on him.'

'Really?' Mickey yawned again. 'I'm really sorry but I'm pretty whacked out—'

'Of course you are.' The man stood up, dislodging the hot air, sending up a plume of diesel fumes. 'Please, though, keep in touch. I'll leave my card with one of the nurses, on the front desk.'

'Righto,' said Mickey trying to put out his hand, but his eyes were already closed.

He woke at just after one, the stranger long gone, thirsty, and with the gnawing start of a headache. Dr Adebayo had been the protagonist of his dream. Using Mickey as a guinea pig in front of a lecture theatre of African students, threatening to slice his head open without an anaesthetic. The ward was stifling; Mickey kicked back his outer cover and balanced a leg on the cold steel of the bed frame. Lights were dotted about, beaming shallow rays into a restricted circle, like a landing aeroplane. He was too disturbed and too hot to sleep. He could hear the low babble of three nurses in a sectioned-off office at the head of the ward. He cast around for something to read. Mr Morgan's pile of tabloids, just within reach on the green vinyl armchair, was the nearest thing. He used his left hand to drag it up on to the bed. The headline of the *Daily Pump* read, 'Drugs Shame of *Big Sister* Star'. Mickey felt his stomach flutter in a mechanical way. The story went on.

> Community-minded *Daily Pump* bosses have decided to pull posters of the long-awaited final shot of Honey Dew, after it was revealed the *Big Sister* star was a cocaine addict.
>
> A shaming video tape showing the twenty-nine-year-old involved in taking the class-A drug at her luxury Chelsea

Harbour penthouse was sent to the offices of the *Daily Pump*, hours before the final shot was due to be exposed.

Editor Tony Miles said, 'It would be wrong of us to continue to promote the interests of Honey Dew in the light of recent evidence – especially as many young girls look to the busty star as a role model,' he added.

The homeless charity Homeless has also dropped Miss Dew from their campaign. Outgoing *Pump* columnist Gaye Butterworth said, 'Women have a right to be protected from these images.'

The story was continued on page seven, but unable to manoeuvre it under his drip, Mickey read no more. Instead he used his left hand to reach over for the letters that had been moved to the top of his bedside cabinet. He ignored the bill and single-handedly ripped into the letter. The handwriting was in a loopy backward, juvenile style that he recognised immediately.

Mickey,

Sorry if this is a bit short but we're at the airport waiting for the Malaga flight to be called. You see, it looks like I got my way in the end. Anyway, as promised here's your part of the money. We sold the video in an auction for almost a hundred grand. You should have seen them. In the end it went to the *Pump*. Irony or what? They said it would be better if they came clean rather than got exposed by another rag. Anyway, I guess you'll read all about it.

Then we've got Honey's solicitor to slap a libel writ on the paper. Honey claims the whole thing is a set-up and staged by people, using a dummy! Imagine that. She even reckons if you look hard enough you can see someone's hands moving it along. Not that they did look all that hard, mind you. He, the solicitor that is, reckons what with her loss of earnings and all the rest of it she could be looking at a half million.

I've learnt my lesson and got it in writing that this time it's a fifty-fifty split. Not bad. Actually, against all the odds, Honey and I have ended up pretty good mates. Turns out we share the same world view, as they say in magazines, only I never saw it. Hence we're off to Spain together.

Hope things work out for you, as you are a great guy. I'll be in Malaga if you ever fancy a manicure. Free, of course.

Yours, Sandy West.

PS. Be nice to your mum. Chances are she's not that bad.

The enclosed cheque in a name he didn't recognise and in a different handwriting was for twenty grand. Mickey's head felt as if it was being trodden underfoot. He sank back without switching off the light.

III

Jade was his first visitor of the next day, silently making her way towards him as he watched, without a fuss, her light steps eaten up into the floor. She was wearing a pale lemon smock dress and her dark bunches were tied in a ribbon of the same colour.

'So, how are you?'

'Fine,' he said, 'now.'

'You gave us all a scare, you know. Not at the time, mind,' she frowned at him, 'because we didn't know about it. Afterwards. What the hell were you up to?'

Mickey smiled. 'It doesn't really matter,' he said. 'Not any more.'

She ignored the chair, beamed across at Mr Morgan and sat on his bed, her weight hardly denting the covers. He said, 'So what's the news from the studio?'

'Not much. Ray and Carlo have gone on a bender. Last

thing I heard was they were going down the whole celebrity hair route.'

'Is that a route?'

Jade shrugged. 'They seem to think so. Can I have some squash?'

'Help yourself.' When she drank, her throat buckled. It looked smooth. He said, 'What about you?'

'Oh, you know. I'll try and find something.'

She sat back down again and wiped her mouth with the back of her hand, unselfconsciously, not disturbing the sheen of gloss. She asked if he wanted a glass. He told her no thanks, though it was nice of her to ask. Now he said, 'Maybe you and I should start something up on our own.'

'Like what?' She frowned, staring past him out of the window.

'I dunno, a gallery,' he shrugged, but found himself still smiling. 'Proper sculpture though, this time. Bronze.'

'Yeah, right,' said Jade. 'What with?'

'Bronze,' said Mickey.

'No,' said Jade. 'What money?'

'Leave that to me,' Mickey told her.

'Oooh,' she said. 'My white knight.' She smiled. 'Who would have thought it?'

'Something like that,' Mickey replied, and smiled back.

'What happened to that girl you were seeing?' she asked, frowning, but in a voice that aimed to imply she didn't care one way or the other.

'Her?' Mickey was enjoying the attention. Somewhere in the ward a trolley clattered past. 'She's long gone.'

Neither spoke. Now Jade said, 'Oh, yeah. One of the nurses on the desk asked me to give you this.' She presented the card she'd been flicking the corner of.

'What is it?' Mickey put his hand out.

'Some sort of card.'

Mickey took it. It was a business card with the name 'Harry

Palmer' on it. Underneath in tiny letters it said, 'Pleasure Cruises'. 'It's the chap that rescued me,' said Mickey.

'You owe him a lot then.' She picked up an apple and bit into it, staring up at him under long lashes.

'Yeah,' said Mickey. 'I reckon I do.' He lay back. 'Actually, Jade, you couldn't pour me a glass of water after all, could you?'

Jade's eyebrows creased, 'Water, babes, *you*?' Mickey nodded and then she smiled. 'Sure babes, no problem.'

'You know,' said Mickey, twitching his hand so it touched Jade's, 'I really am feeling a lot better.'

Afterword

The following story appeared on page three of the popular ex-pats newspaper *Malaga Today* on 5 January.

Spanish police are investigating the disappearance of a British nail technician alleged to have defrauded her business partner out of thousands.

Miss Honey Dew, from Dudley in England, contacted police after she discovered her business partner had sold their joint venture beauty parlour and three-bedroom beach-front apartment without her knowledge.

Police believe that Sandy West, 26, may be on her way to Morocco, travelling under a false name.

Honey Dew, 29, who faces an uncertain future in the country, said: 'What a total bitch. I cannot believe she did this. She told me she was my friend.'

Roberto Almeriro of Malaga Police warned the public not to approach the woman. 'She is dangerous. I advise men and ladies equally to avoid her at all costs,' he said.

Slaphead

Georgina Wroe

Terry Small wants a woman. And he's seen a catalogue full of them. They're in Moscow, employed by REDS IN YOUR BEDS marriage agency. Armed with his best Calvin Klein underpants and his new abdominiser, Terry, the most dynamic conservatory salesman in Basingstoke, is on his way.

Awaiting him in Moscow is Katya, the agency's Russian representative. The only mate Katya cares about is her delinquent six-year-old, Sasha – and Terry, probably her most unprepossessing customer ever, isn't going to pose a problem for a woman who's already despatched a redundant husband to Siberia.

But Katya hasn't bargained for the intervention of Fate. Not to mention Moscow's latest entrepreneur, Professor Modin, formerly Lenin's embalmer, now specialising in providing a mounting pile of dead Mafia bosses with the flashy, unforgettable funeral they so richly deserve . . .

Fast, confident and fantastically funny, *Slaphead* introduces a writer of anarchic brilliance to the fiction-writing scene.

'A female Carl Hiassen' *The Times*

0 7472 6203 9

headline

Fleeced

Georgina Wroe

Dominic Peach isn't your usual sort of environmental campaigner. The only environment he cares about is one that doesn't include his girlfriend. Thus far the job at Save Our Species has suited him quite nicely, especially since he rigged the database to make sheep (surely the planet's least endangered mammal?) his only responsibility. So when he's ordered to the former Soviet Republic of Belugastan on a high-profile mission to protect the *Beluga argali argali*, a rare wild sheep, it's a bit of a shock.

Particularly as it turns out that Belugastan's head of state, ex-gangster Tim the First, has invented the *Beluga argali argali* as a lure to cash-rich game hunters, props courtesy of his friend Erik's motorbike and his mum's sheepskin coat. And when the hunters include a mad Texan millionairess and her gun-crazy sons Hubba and Bubba, Dominic discovers chasing wild sheep can be an extremely hairy business . . .

Praise for Georgina Wroe's previous novel, SLAPHEAD

'If Kathy Lette had been born in Omsk, this is the book she'd write' *Mirror*

'Compulsive . . . crammed with action and wise-cracks and eminently readable' *Big Issue*

0 7472 7551 3

headline